Mer'edrynn Book 3:

SeamRipper

by
Stephy Dewar

This is a work of fiction
All names, characters, places and events created by the author are used purely fictitiously.

Text copyright © 2018 Stephy *Dewar*
All rights reserved

No part of this book may be reproduced, stored or transmitted in any form or by any means, electronic, mechanical, photocopying, recording or otherwise without express permission from the author.

ISBN: 9781728992075

Stephy Dewar lives in Lancashire UK, close to the beautiful countryside of the Ribble Valley and a few miles from the notorious Pendle Hill of the witches' fame. She is married and works with her husband as a partner in their accountancy company. She has two wonderful daughters, loves cooking, gardening, photography and is an avid gamer of pc games, preferably rpg, action and adventure.

Other titles by Stephy Dewar:

Mer'edrynn Book 1: Warping the Weave
Mer'edrynn Book 2: A Crash of Symbols

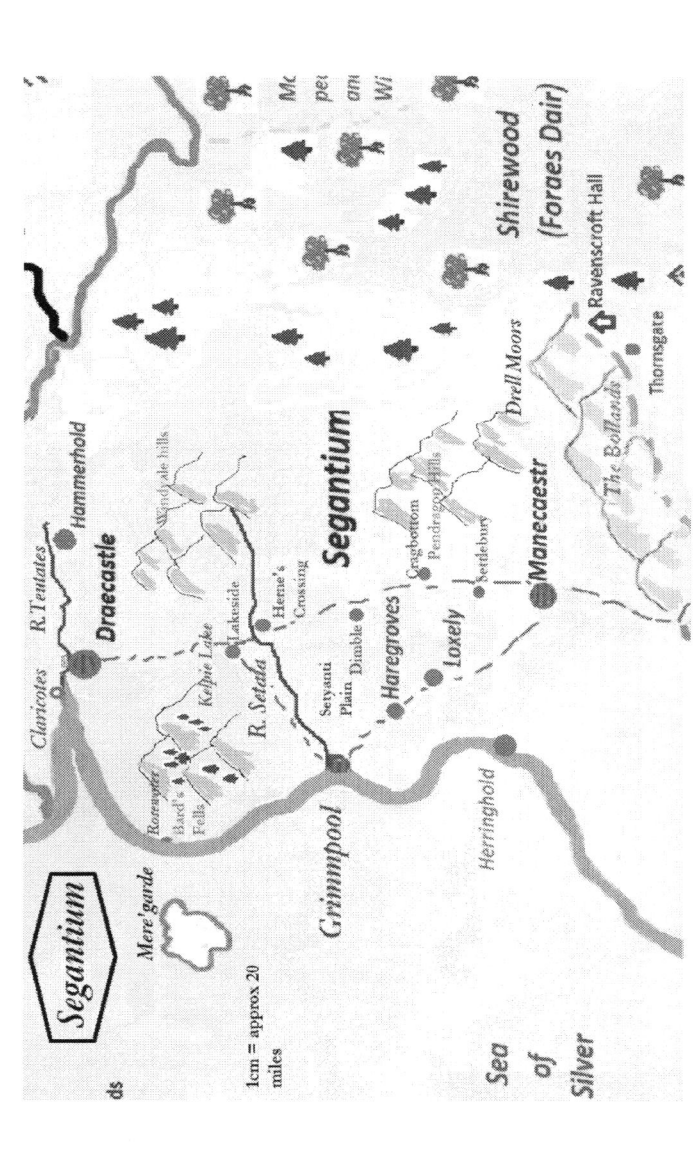

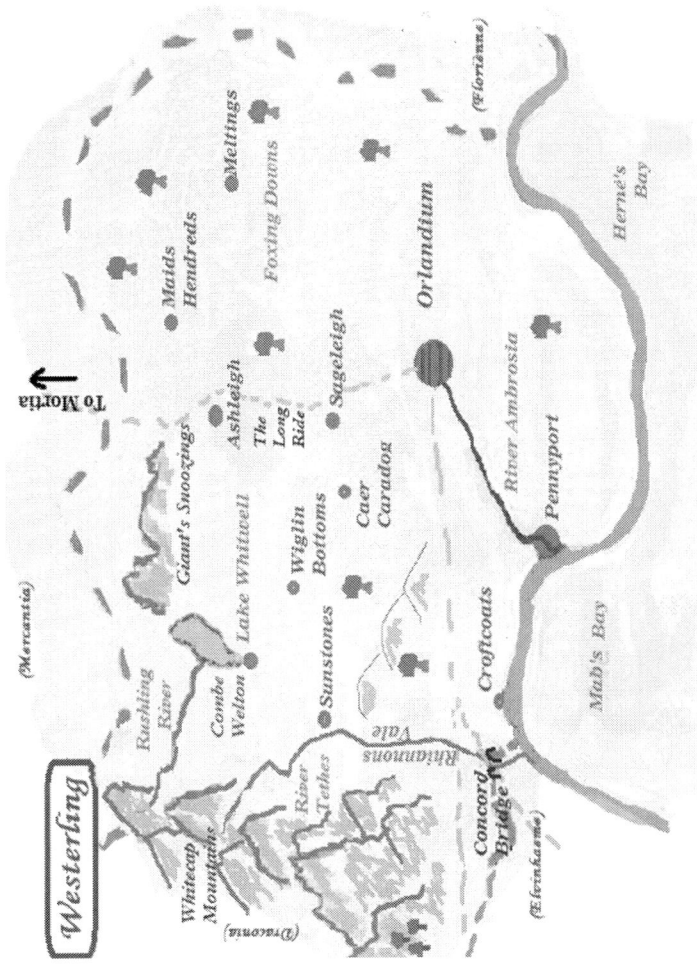

SeamRipper

Part 1: *Tapestry of Time*

Chapter 1

His power was the art of death taken to clinical perfection, the antithesis of life. Destruction came as easy as snapping two fingers, yet that alone brought no satisfaction; souls were not corrupted by simple murder. A *slow* death through suffering, pain and despair was desirable, calculable to the merest fraction. His preference however, was for an insidious moral degeneration; it dirtied a soul and weakened the spirit.

Who knows where such a being originated, nor why he stalks this world? His steps destroy life, and misery and sorrow walk with him.

Yet he is neither omniscient nor omnipresent; the world flows separately to his being and he cannot be everywhere, not now that he exists in time. His physicality was a means to the end, a mis-correction of the balance. For this purpose he wore a shell of masculinity.

No! ...that is wrong, not *masculinity*, for that holds truths and strength and wholesomeness. This wore none of those things, yet the shell looked male. *He/she/it:* some things are beyond sex, if he had worn a feminine aspect, *she* would have been just as cruel, just as evil, for *it* was the antipathy of life, *it* was death, yet not peace.

He was not of the cycle.

There were few beings with a soul warped enough to accommodate his essence, yet the hearts of many held a fraction of him, even though it was no more than a grain of sand.

At this particular moment *he*, for want of a better word, rode a frothing beast northwards, comprehending the danger to his protégé, time shortening rapidly. He had caught wind of this earlier in the day, its clandestine essence drifted on the ether.

He should, of course, have understood it before, but the Wielder of Light was an unknown quantity, always avoiding the obvious. He perceived him taking an erratic path to his goals whatever they were, a creature of chaos.

But then, this whole damn world was chaos.

He turned his mind instead to the steed he rode, willed it onwards, sending unreal but nevertheless acutely painful daggers into the poor beast's head. It struggled and galloped accordingly, could do no more than that. Its nature had been browbeaten into submission; regardless of itself, it obeyed. Rearing from the permanent pain and unseating the rider was unthinkable, not even as a reflex action. It ran as fast as four legs could move.

He was merely annoyed that for certain purposes, he had to make use of the physical beast.

He hurried onwards, disturbed at the looming threat to his General, he supposed that was probably the correct name for him? His son, he had called him, his first born, the name deliberately chosen to bind the boy to the master emotionally. He was a useful servant, a tool, a deceptive mouthpiece to sway men's minds while he worked silently behind the scenes to darken men's hearts. He had performed as planned.

Von Adamm had been one of the few humans who did not shy from him, most ran terrified from his presence. Whether that was strength, stubbornness or merely stupidity, he neither knew nor cared. He had no heart to feel sympathy, or empathy, or love. Nevertheless, his death would be a setback.

He therefore rushed northwards to put fear and pain and despair into good men's hearts, his natural path.

But his own path to Draecastle was baulked continually. Firstly, an angry pack of baying wolves came at him, frightening the horse even more. He ran through them, scattering them, but the horse stumbled. He lifted a hand and the wolves backed away, senseless now, minds turned to mush. It had been a temporary hold up, but still, it took minutes off his ride.

A little further on and a large flock of birds, rooks and jackdaws shot across his path, then veered round and came at him again. With a flick of his fingers he tossed them away, they drifted on the wind. But they weren't done and they didn't intend to attack *him*. No, their goal was the unfortunate horse; stop the horse, the weak point. Down they flew again, into the horse's eyes, through its legs, disrupting and interrupting the flow. It carried on regardless, stamping on the birds, black feathers flying everywhere.

The birds sacrificed themselves to give Estrién and the others a few more moments.

He came next to the main bridge over the rolling river Setaia, only to find the river had burst its banks, the bridge down, flooding everywhere. Herne's Crossing was no longer so. It was too deep and the river too fast for the horse to wade through. He had to go north east towards its source, until the river was weaker and there was a bridge he could pass over. That added more hours to the ride, for the river would not obey his demands. Rivers are a source of life, but *he* was not, the river spirits would not listen.

He was still, he understood, a long way from Draecastle. Twenty miles further on, close to the Windvale hills, he spotted a few glossy looking horses in a field. He slipped off the horse he was riding, took its bit and bridle, grabbed a beast from the field, leapt on. It was held by his mind, no choice but to submit. It was fresh and sound and he willed it to speed. The horse left behind fell to the ground and without a sigh, passed away.

There were eighty miles still to go, along the Long Ride to Draecastle. Beasts of field and air baulked his every step, many died attempting to disrupt that ride. Many tried and were defeated, terrified by his nature, ran or flew away, hearts overcome. But they tried nevertheless, they tried their best, as Merrie would wish.

They did indeed disrupt it - long enough for the tide to turn and for Estrién and the others to spend the day sneaking and shifting their way across the bridge and into the castle. Long enough for the mages to create their diversion later that night, to turn men's eyes south, while the real danger came from the north. And finally, long enough for the Adammites to be defeated later that night at the great fortress of Draecastle.

But for eighty full miles, he pushed the horse – or horses, he picked them up as he chose - onwards regardless. The final one, a handsome jet black stallion, was sleek and fast, seemed to have more spirit than most; he would enjoy breaking it.

As he neared the castle drawbridge he saw dawn appearing, a fine dawn too, or so the beings of this world would say.

He held an arm high, flicked his fingers. Storm clouds gathered, blotting out the sun.

He arrived just a few moments too late, watched von Adamm thrown over the balcony as he approached, a fall of three high storeys on to hard stone. It was frustrating; he looked down with distaste as he trampled the broken figure, the horse stumbling over the body, crushing it even more.

Damn the fool! Still, no matter, it had begun and would not easily be stopped.

He turned the horse, left swiftly through the castle gates and across the drawbridge. Few in the fortress saw him leave; eyes were closed in fear, faces hidden in caps or behind arms, none wished to see him.

One watched however, and he observed his exit with satisfaction.

The great stag saw him leave, a mad gallop into the thunderstorm. He raised his noble head proudly, the stag's stately antlers held high with satisfaction at the events of this day. If he'd had hands at that moment he would have applauded, but for now he was in full beast form. Estrién and the others ... they had done well, given so much, possibly too much, he was proud of them. His protégé had proved his belief in him. It was a start...

... but only a start.

Von Adamm was dead, thrown from the balcony of the Wall Walk next to the King's own chambers, crushed by the fall and splintered underfoot by the very being who had presumed to be his Master. The Master had no care for the servant and now the servant was gone.

No one knew, at least none of the articulate races understood, but the stag had played his part, keeping that

One at bay until it was over. His friends had helped, even the river helped as he'd had to ride around the river Setaia earlier, adding miles to his journey. It had flowed fast and wild, brimming over and flooding the land near Herne's Crossing. The stag threw back his antlered head and gave thanks, Setaia was his own river and that One had no title to it. Several packs of wolves - his own that is, there were some that had gone over - blocked the path, scaring the horse. He pitied the horse, as with the last steed, all his steeds, it would be ridden until death, then simply abandoned, nothing he could do about it. But of the free beasts and birds ... even the rooks came down and played their part, disturbing *him*, not for long though, but enough to shake him a little. Some ravens too, although many belonged to him. The stag was relieved that relatively few of the wild beasts were yet under the dark One's sway, because every day he gained power as his own waned. But the ones that *were* ... they were fierce and wild, beyond help. Only death could free them, and that would be *his* victory still.

The doe by his side nuzzled him, reminding him there were many with him, he wasn't alone. Their kind weren't finished yet.

If that One had arrived earlier ... the stag shuddered to think what could have been. But his ride had been interrupted, had been slowed so he came too late to save his disciple. Yes, the Great Stag too had played his part in von Adamm's downfall, though none should know it.

And that was how it should be.

*

Draecastle, the Haegudsael, month of Endurance.

Longshanks stumbled out of the King's chambers and stomped heavily down the steps towards the Great Hall, the Haegudsael. He shook his head and long red beard as if to rid himself of a horde of buzzing wasps, occasionally closed his eyes to shut out the scene. He made for one of the long tables at the side of the Hall, an oaken sideboard laden with meats and drinks. Grabbing a goblet, he filled it with usquebae, his throat almost scorched as he knocked it back in one gulp. When he finished he snatched up a large pewter tankard, went to a barrel, filled it with dark ale. He swiftly emptied the tankard.

Then he ran outside to be sick.

Whoever that was - *whatever* that was - he had seen, he never wished to see him again.

Estrién entered the Hall slowly, his movement automatic, his heart bereft.

Time had stopped for him, he hadn't stayed to examine the blood-splattered body on the ground below, nor had he seen the approach and disappearance of Von Adamm's master. His mind was in turmoil as he approached Dane bending over Amber's body. He could feel the blood thrumming through his veins, blocking his hearing, a heart-sickening lump in his throat.

'Victory?' he thought, 'what is victory? I've lost Amber ...' he looked across the hall, '... and my good friend Tamlyn,' as Salli chanted and touched Tamlyn with his wand. 'The death should be mine, not theirs.' He saw the pool of blood around her spreading slowly, her life force staining the cold stone floor scarlet. 'I only hope their sacrifice was worth it.'

The blood-soaked stone mesmerised him, all that life... just seeping away.

Bitter, wet tears fell softly down Estrién's high elven cheekbones. He looked out at the storm-darkening sky, a macro-cosmic symbol of his pain, the world around him sepia coloured now, no primary hues or rich shades. Everything dull, out of focus and his bright emerald eyes were dimmed. He crossed the floor to his wife, knelt by Amber's body, saw her white face, took her soft hand in his, it was still warm, for how long he knew not.

His love, his one love...

She was his future, the future for which he fought, the light in the darkness.

Laughter, joy, love; a smile radiating warmth on a cold day, generosity in a world turning selfish, passion when the world had become frigid. His friend, his lover, his mate. *Gone.*

He saw an ashen faced Dane stem the flow as he removed the dagger from her heart. Dane looked briefly at him. 'They say the touch of a true king is healing ...'

Estrién stared, 'I'll get Duggan then ...'

'Not necessary, Estrién, but I didn't mean him, I meant you.' His mage hands were busy over the wound, the reddened dagger now on the floor beside her.

Estrién shook his head. 'I'm no king, Dane, you know that.'

'You sure about that?'

Estrién shrugged and kept hold of her hand, kissed it softly. King or beggar, it made no difference, he couldn't face life without her. She had become the bedrock of his existence. 'She should die of old age, safely in her bed with her family around her mourning her loss, yet celebrating her life,' he told Dane.

'She might yet do that. Let's see how good a healer I am, huh?'

'*What*, she's not dead?' Hope kindled in soft elven eyes.

Dane shook his head, 'Not yet, her hold on life is tenuous however, and she's lost a great deal of blood. But see,' he showed the slice just to the side of her heart, 'she must have been moving at speed - you know what she's like - he missed it by a fraction. Leave me be, Estrién, let me work, I love her too much to let her go, and there are others needing help here. Go and find out about Tamlyn, I can't leave her.'

Estrién nodded, a smile forming sweetly on his face as the world began to appear normal again. One last lingering kiss of her hand and a squeeze of his friend's shoulder and he moved across to where Salli bent down by Tamlyn's side.

He watched incredulously as Tamlyn sat up, clutching his chest. 'Ah, *sentaé y maliatus!*' He exclaimed, then looked up and saw Estrién, he changed to Plaintongue. 'What in Merrie's name just happened?' Tamlyn asked, clutching his chest. 'I'm in bloody agony, feels like my heart and chest are bruised through.' He peered down at the blood on his breast.

Salli gently touched him with his willow wand again and stood to go, 'A little ease for that bruising. Others to see to now, take care.'

'Tamlyn, what's going on? Arne threw a dagger at your heart, I saw you drop.'

Tamlyn looked ruefully down at the crushed metal insignia of the White Shield crest he wore over his heart. It had dug through his leather armour, was sticking into his chest, bruising him and scraping the skin. He began to laugh and picked up the dagger a few feet away. '*White Shield*, and it bloody did, my friend, it shielded me from that.' He raised his hand, clasped Estrién's, pulled himself up. 'Didn't know it would be so useful ...' He stopped as he saw Dane bending over Amber, light shooting from Dane's hands, ran across the floor to her.

'*Amber!*' he cried.

'Shhh ... leave me be, let me concentrate.' Dane briefly looked up. 'Er, you recovered quickly,' smiling, as Tamlyn explained. Estrién passed him the usquebae from his hip pocket.

'Drink it and welcome, my brother.'

Tamlyn took it, drank heavily then sat down by Amber's side. 'Feel a bit dizzy, think I knocked my head on the floor, you go and see what's happening Estrién. Did you get him?' meaning von Adamm.

Estrién nodded, 'we tracked him up to that balcony, the Wall Walk, everyone was after him, he was running like the bloody coward he is ... *was,* I mean. Longshanks and me, we threw him over the balcony, not a pretty sight down below. I thought you were both dead ... don't do that to me again ...' He bent down, kissed Tamlyn's brow, 'just don't do that to me again, you hear?'

Tamlyn clasped his hand. 'Never fear, my brother, never fear.'

Another of the mage healers joined Salli, there were two with the group, Silva stayed with the King's troops, his powers would be needed more and more as they reached the port, but Mariel came back to help. They wandered the Hall attempting healing and repair ... or gently closed the eyes of those past help. They followed the cries of pain and administered healing when they could. A mage is a good healer, if a person can live, then he will live. But many were already dead, short though the battle had been. Other guards came to take out the dead, there would be a decent funeral pyre and a service for the passing of Kyneweth's troops, and a mass grave to be burnt ignominiously for the Adammites. ... *preferably started by a mage, magic fire to finish off the Adammites.*

Estrién moved on to find the new young King, Duggan. He was surrounded by his four brothers, disturbed from sleep by the mayhem, yet with enough sense to stay locked in their rooms until the noise quieted down. When they heard their brother shout at everyone to stop in the name of the king - King Duggan - they knew it was over.

Even the youngest realised that if the Adammites were beaten, their father would go too. They stood by their older brother, eyes dark and damp with sorrow. Yet each one went to Duggan, kissed him, vowed allegiance that cold morning. The storm raged on outside, but in here, peace fell quietly over the family. Briefly Duggan asked a question of Salli, but Salli shook his head.

'Go to him, he wants you,' was his reply, 'there is no pain, I've seen to that.'

Duggan walked solemnly to the base of the stairs where Gourien had fallen, bent on one knee before him. 'We got him, Gourien, we got the bastard.'

He gave a slight nod of the head, 'well done, young Duggan. Thank you, and thank those people for me - they are true to Mer'edrynn,' but the death rattle could be heard in his throat. 'Rule as your father once did, my boy ... when your mother lived.' Duggan cradled his old tutor's head in his arm, until Gourien slept an eternal sleep.

Yes, rule as his father once had, final good advice from his mentor.

He arranged for the funeral two days later, after the storm had eased and the fighting in Claricotes was over. An overcast day, but one of those where the sun suddenly dips below the clouds as it settles to sleep and brightens the world.

There was no commitment service or prayers to Lady Merrie, for Kyneweth had forgotten her, but he was a king and so deserved a king's ending. King Kyneweth was laid in a great burning barge to send out to sea, they followed the old ways up here, filling it with kindle, then as it began to sail, the king's own archers shot flaming arrows at it until it was ablaze. A great drum beat slowly and they all sang a last hymn to the fallen. Finally Salli played a soulful tune upon his flute, a strange sound, mournful, yet uplifting to the soul; the watchers believed they were following the spirits of the dead, a last goodbye as the funeral barge sailed solemnly downriver towards the open sea and the setting sun. The Sea of Silver shone golden as the final hours of daylight faded away, the sun scarlet on the horizon. The flaming barge would meet the fire on the water, and eventually King Kyneweth would rest in a watery grave, as he would have wanted and as his ancestors had gone before him.

He wasn't alone; in smaller barges surrounding his lay the bodies of his elite guard, they had stood by him to the death. They too would go the way of the warrior. An old custom, but a true one.

The bodies of Adammites were thrown in a pit and burned. Wolves came down in the night, dragged off limbs and enjoyed a hearty meal. No one mourned their loss.

Gourien was given a grave by the castle walls near the South East tower. This was his home, his bones should rest here, and occasionally Duggan could visit his old teacher, tend the grave, reminisce or meditate or simply mourn. His funeral was attended only by the family, some servants, and the Companions of the White Shield, Salli leading the service.

> *'To Her we send, who faithful was, his tomb the frosted ground,*
> *The castle walls his headstone, his grave a grassy mound.*
> *The science of his youth he taught, his wisdom given free,*
> *A lifetime's knowledge taken out by one who could not see.*
> *Yet he saw true, that once-keen wit, his psyche now in sleep.*
> *The night has come, the day cut short, in blackened hours we weep.*
> *Perception stilled; no will, nor words, no further truths to tell,*
> *The halls of restless mind at peace, we bid our friend farewell.'*

'Go in peace, my brother,' Salli's last words to a fine scientist and philosopher, before he placed his flute to his lips and played one last tune.

Strangely, Longshanks too was affected by his death. 'I got to like the silly old sod,' he explained.

Dane took no part in King Kyneweth's funeral; when he wasn't tending Amber, he was busy with other wounded soldiers. He and the other mages on constant watch, day and night, as brave souls struggled to live. But he came to say goodbye to Gourien, he had found a willing ear on the journey, and was glad to listen to his kind words of wisdom.

And Amber? Amber lay close to death also, too close. Several times Salli came to her, shaking his head, his willow magic at her disposal should she need it. He saw how restless she was, how weak and in pain, he would help her go over, *it would be gentle*, he told Dane.

Dane merely refused point blank. 'She lost much blood, but my magic holds true. If I have to stay with her every moment until she heals, I will do so. I am a good healer, Salli, and I know her body well. If I have to pour my own life force into her to help her live, she shall have it.'

Amber *was* weak, the dagger hit an artery, her blood gushed from her, her own life force fading as Dane saw what was happening across the Hall and ran to her aid, watching with further distaste as Adammites targeted her during their bid for freedom. None escaped.

He stemmed the flow, healed the wounds, yet she slept on. His own mother and father had died at the hands of these Adammites; he would not let his blessed love go that way too. He worked until he had mana no more, and Tamlyn brought him hot drinks, bade him rest, Dane worked through the night, the morning dawned cold, a bleak sun. Tamlyn would watch, he said, if there was change, he would wake him.

Estrién carried her to the infirmary, a bed was found, Dane slept in a chair by her side.

They took it in turns, Tamlyn and Estrién, watching and waiting until Dane woke a few hours later, took over his charge. The day waxed and waned, closed in, he worried now, no change in her, worse if anything.

It seemed he fought, not merely against her physical problems, but something deeper, a threat to her spirit, her psyche or soul or whatever it is that you call your inner being, your essence. *The inner 'you' which is possibly eternal.*

Amber lay pale and restless, her mind disturbed and confused as her body weakened. Inside, she travelled beyond to places only the dying and the near dead discover.

In the beginning she saw only blackness, a deep darkness to sink into, to forget. That was as it should be, a calming relief. But slowly twists of colour appeared, shaped themselves into abstract patterns, wandered off into the distance. More darkness, then acute flashes as pain hit her, sheer agony; a link, however harsh, with life. A gap came, a time of nothingness, she wandered aimlessly for eternal hours before she saw the river, pale and spectral, it looped lazily across a silver-grey landscape. She followed it, for nothing else existed and she wondered where it led? As she came close to the bank she peered into the deep water. It held depths she couldn't fathom, and she knew it waited patiently for her to enter and disappear forever, taking her on a journey to which there was no return.

This day? Tomorrow? Whenever... she wasn't sure, but the option was there.

And Amber wondered if that time was now?

Yet here, for Amber, time stood still, time hung eternally, forever and never. Amber watched the river, it flowed, therefore time passed, but it was not *her time*. She knew she stood separate to the river.

She coiled in agony as more acute flashes hit her, electric lightning, bodily pain, *life* pain. She heard thunder from afar, nearing or receding she did not know, she existed in two worlds and heard one as she saw the other. The river lit silver or gold as the sky flashed, each flash brought searing pain. She wanted to scream but nothing came out. She tried to think of her past, yet there were only clouds. She knew who she was, she was Amber, *Essence of Amber* ... who said that?

'Who am I?' she thought. 'What am I?' More to the point, '*why* am I?'

And she began to be afraid, she had thought she was alone in this almost empty world, grey haze at the edges running into nothingness. It wasn't the loneliness, or even death that bothered her, but she realised somewhere on that far horizon stood a dark shape. *It was a shape you walked away from, but never towards.*

Yet the shape was familiar.

Amber was in the pain of crisis, her consciousness weak, her body torn, for she had other wounds too. Trampled underfoot by sturdy Adammite boots as they fled, pierced by another sword thrust given on the off chance as one rushed by her hoping to reach some kind of safety, she lay battered and beaten. But the hopeful antagonist was down and dead long before he reached the Outer Bailey. Nevertheless, Amber lay in an agony of infinite time until Dane dashed across to help her.

As she saw the unnatural shadow across from her, she also felt the comfort of an ally.

His mage will entered her soul and she was glad, for her soul tumbled in time. Someone was sharing this with her, someone close and kind, she just couldn't remember who. But she knew the essence of him, felt his love for her, his life-giving power sustaining her. It was a good feeling, a fine feeling, he offered pleasure and passion and loving warmth to offset the cold and the pain.

Her senses began to awake.

Dane shared more than the agony of her physical pain, his mage senses felt the emotions running through her. Most of all, he knew her wish to die, for during that first long night, *He* had hold of her, although she was unaware. Amber travelled by the river, wandered close, often looked down, and wondered...? *He* pushed her on to fall in its depths, for she offered too much life to the world.

She had never truly perceived him before, she did not know he existed, yet he had dogged her most of her life. She may not yet be dead, but she was in greater danger now than ever, the very fact he was on her horizon, meant he was close by ... too close. Distance meant nothing to him in his true state; time and space were merely one.

Few ever perceived him, he rarely took corporeal form, unlike the stag who revelled in it. But those who did ... their lives changed forever. As his physical manifestation rode swiftly away from the castle that early morn, he took pleasure in the many deaths. *Nay*, not the deaths, for death was the end, but the act of dying, the pain of their passing. The loss of his 'first born' was an annoyance; his time had come sooner than he desired, but not unexpected. He had been a mere pawn. With a flick of indifference, von Adamm was dismissed forever.

At this moment it was important to destroy the woman, this mass of seething life force, she pulsated with emotion even now as she lay dying. Besides, she was too close to the Time Weaver and that blasted Wielder of Light.

Amber, her soul, or perhaps her spirit awakening, felt him on the edges of her consciousness. *Unnatural*, she decided pragmatically, something that should not be here in Mer'edrynn, an antithesis to her world. *A world she knew to be fertile with love and blood and emotion. A world where valour and courage meant something, and integrity, honesty and truth were still important.*

And little things, like kindness or consideration, made big by intent and deed...

... a world where none of this mattered to that which was abhorred by nature.

'I think, therefore I am,' the shadow informed her with frigid precision.

'I feel, therefore I live,' she retorted with heated passion.

He watched with distaste. *'Damn you, woman!'* ice-cold eyes told her. Amber steeled herself for whatever he was about to do, knowing it may be her final battle. She had faced adversity many times, often alone, although now she thought about it, she had not been alone the last year, the good year. Those three ... yes, it had been good. Three good souls supporting hers, and one of them with a heart kind enough to share this ... this realm.

She had to be ready for whatever came next. His will would destroy her, snuff her out of existence. She stood, ready for the onslaught.

Then she heard it, at first a whimper, then a sob, a poor soul in terrible torment. Amber's heart went out to help, the threatening shadow in the distance temporarily forgotten. Another needed her aid and so her own fears meant nothing. Compassion was the essence of Amber.

Who ..? She knew that cry, that sob, she knew that soul ... and she knew the soul was linked - nay, manacled - to that being on the horizon.

'Sister?' she cried into the darkness. It *was* her, it *was* her sister. She lived! ... She could feel her ... but this was not life, this was torment. She knew the shadow on the edge to be her sister's sufferance, her life-long pain. She had worked - and paid - to free Anaïs from the Alderfolk, only to send her to ... *that*? Her parents had told her to look after her, Amber was the strong one, Anaïs, well ... Anaïs was what she was. But they never told her just *what* she was.

For the first time Amber understood the depths of her sister. ...And perceived her pain. She knew her nights were tormented by him, every dream insufferable, her days long and weary from trying to stay awake. She knew there were times when he was there in physical form, times of pure torture. He was sadistic in ways unmentionable, the Weaver of Time must be punished into obedience. She wept for her, helpless as she was here in this strange world, flashes of her own pain still, her body so weak.

'I will come for you, Anaïs ...' she shouted across that dark land. 'I will help you.'

The shadow heard her, for one moment he grew, blackened the sky, *this could not be*. He filled the landscape, he would crush Amber now, while she was ill and weak. Now was the time...

He moved in.

But Dane was with her, felt his presence and he would not let it harm her. He was a warm hand caressing hers on a bitter cold day. He could not see him, but his mage senses knew a shadow existed. She was not alone. Nor were they merely two against *him*.

Estrién and Tamlyn too, both understood this was a crisis point, they were anxious and angry by turns while Dane worked within. The feeling of helplessness was worse than anything, they could do nothing now, the healing was left to Dane. But the three held true, as Salli had said, they were her shield.

They stood firm and strong, a triad of deep emotion and they stood together. *He* could not break through this protective triangle of masculine love. It held concepts he loathed - integrity and duty, honour and compassion. It discomforted him and annoyed him. Besides, there were many others that day weak enough to fall, he had little time to waste.

They held together, three minds in one accord ... *save Amber.*

He would leave ... for now, until he found a way to break all of them. Everyone had a breaking point, and he understood she was the key, he had learned that much. Knowledge is valuable.

Amber felt her loved ones around her, knew how loved she was, desired and desirable, caring and cared for. This dark one knew not that and never would. Not father nor mother nor husband, wife or child would ever care for *him*. And strangely, Amber began to feel compassion for the dark shadow. Her loving soul went out to him.

...*Essence of Amber.*

'May Merrie's Blessings be upon you,' she called to the disappearing figure.

It mattered not whether he heard her, for he would not have listened.

The warmth of the sun burst around her, as a new day dawned.

*

She woke fully a couple of days later, her mind refreshed, if her body was still a little weak, to see three concerned faces smiling at her.

'Hello, my loves,' she said, holding out her hand.

Three people solemnly kissed her, welcoming her back to the world. Three people dashed to find nourishing soup and stews for her to eat when she declared she was 'starving', three people anxious to lend a hand or a shoulder to lean on as she took weak, tentative steps. Dane, tired from helping others, continued offering her his own magic to strengthen her. She refused it, instinctively understanding he was exhausted.

'Time for you to rest, Dane, how many have you healed these past days?' taking his hand. 'And Dane, thank you, not just for how you healed me, but thank you for your support. I felt it, I knew you were there, I felt all of you.' She looked him in the eye, wondering how to broach the subject? 'Did you see it, that ... that shadow?'

He nodded. 'I'm a mage remember ... I see these things. I've probably always seen it, but, my blood, my youth, the magical life force that runs through me ... maybe I just dismiss it. It held von Adamm, didn't it?'

She nodded, it must have done. 'It runs through our world, destroying. Dane ... it has my sister, I know that now. I have to help her. She's alone, so alone, yet she ... she has something we need. If we can pull her free somehow...' She wasn't sure, she only knew she had failed her.

Dane nodded, 'I'm glad she lives, you told me about her, I'd like to help. I'll talk to the other mages, see what they say. This land needs mages, it needs the magical races, I've always said that. Without them, Mer'edrynn no longer exists.' He went off to talk to his own kind.

All the mages understood, it was something that dogged them too in the backs of their minds, never willingly brought to light. They felt it as they passed through the Bard's hills and the forest on their way to Rosewater, something that held the essence of *him,* a misbirth of a bygone era. None wished to feel it again. But they would help, there was a world to heal, they said. Von Adamm may be dead, but his followers still existed and there were towns held by them. They would do as they originally intended, help Lord Black and King Alexis, they both needed mages in their armies.

Dane wanted to go to Manecaestr; he couldn't stand what he'd seen there. Salli agreed, it shouldn't be left to fester; they both went to talk to the new king. Duggan hadn't even yet been crowned, but he knew his duty.

'I've sent riders to the mines, to Hammerhold, stave off the invasion. I intend to talk to the dwarves there, make reparations for my father. We owe them a great deal, most of our weapons come from them and father took them by force. I hope they'll listen to me, my father treated them badly, he took on the mantle of this cult.' Duggan worried about the extent of the damage, the hatred stirred up. He paused, considering all the work necessary. 'I have troops down at the harbour too, no Adammite ships allowed at Claricotes anymore. Once I've sorted these immediate problems, I'll turn to the south, I promise. But Manecaestr is a long way down, and every town is Adammite held before that - they won't give up so easily.' He sat on the large stone throne in the Haegudsael, he was trying his best, Merrie alone knew that, but it was hard. So much to do, he barely knew where to start. He was very young, he longed for his old mentor, some good advice.

To his surprise, Longshanks offered help. 'Let me talk to the miners, I know these people. In fact, young Duggan, I can help in a lot of ways - I know *people*, do you see? I'm no philosopher, I don't know stars or syndromes or what to do with an alembic, but I've held audiences in the palm of my hand for years, I throw out scraps and they lap them up. I've no circus any longer, and I miss it, but believe me, I can tell you what makes people tick,' holding out his arms expansively as he talked. 'I can make them jump too, whatever it takes. Don't worry about Hammerhold; I'll sort that in no time. Then, if you want an advisor, and you've got to admit - your people are currently in big trouble for allying with the Adammites - you're welcome to my years of experience. I helped get rid of von Adamm, remember?' He bowed gracefully, sweeping his hat almost to the floor in a long arch. He looked up, a chuckle in his voice, 'I know a few good jokes too, sonny, I'll put a smile on your face when you need one ... Hey, did you hear the one about the wild boar, the virgin and the woodcutter... ? She didn't half scream when she saw the size of his chopper ...'

Dane heard the young king laughing as they went off together to walk around the castle to discuss matters. He knew it was what he needed, but ... Longshanks? Still, it took all sorts to make a world, and as Longshanks often said, 'you can't keep a good dwarf down ...'

You certainly couldn't keep Longshanks down.

So ... he considered ... Manecaestr ... he knew he could wait no longer, even at the expense of Amber's sister. Where was she, he wondered? And was it already too late to help her? He went to gather whoever he could, perhaps get word to Lord Black. They would seek her out, discover her whereabouts if they could.

But Manecaestr was paramount. Duggan's forces might be tied up at the moment, so he went to see his own people, his family, they at least, had to help.

Chapter 2

Evil, like matter, is neither created nor destroyed.

It does not die, it merely changes character, the hue and the pattern alter according to the time and place. Names are meaningless; structure and form continue. The spokesman had gone, the mass movement still existed, for that grain of sand had entered other heads and many were happy to vie for leadership. Von Adamm was, after all, merely a figurehead.

As he fell to his death, the Adammites fled Draecastle to regroup around the port of Claricotes, followed swiftly by the new king's troops. Kyneweth was the only king within the realms of Mer'edrynn to keep a full army. There were far more of them than the Adammites, for it was their home base and they were all well experienced; every member of the King's brigades had spent their early days up at the borders, defending the realm from northern invaders. They were as well equipped as the Adammites and as disciplined; there could only be one outcome.

It was a nasty, bloody battle, as battles are, the clash of steel upon steel and the crunch of broken bones as screams rent the air. It is hard to say who was the most angry or desperate, as both sides had lost their leader, there could be no true victory that day.

And, when *he* rode through the battle lines, *he* did not truly care who lived or died, only that it was prolonged and painful and their misery fed *him* well.

He throve that day, despite the loss of von Adamm.

Von Adamm's Chief of Staff at Draecastle, Colonel Mackenzie, stood his ground for as long as possible at Claricotes, before calculating the odds and deciding a swift retreat was necessary. The loss of this particular port was bad, but the loss of more of his best troops would be worse. He sensibly sounded the retreat.

The Adammites ran to the ships, raised anchor and fled, first to their quarters on Mere'garde, and thenceforth to their home base of the Isle of Glasse. Colonel Mackenzie sent boats to Hollyporth to inform the Adammite colonies of Elvinhaeme, and runners throughout the land, by foot or horseback, to pass on the bad news and to convene a council to elect a new leader. They went swiftly, the Long Ride between Draecastle and Manecaestr still under the control of Adammite troops. They were nothing if not efficient, the essence of a good dictatorship.

As Mackenzie stepped on to the soil of Mere'garde, he learned of the death of Colonel Filby, another blow to the movement, for he believed he had been a good speaker. Mackenzie knew he was no contender for leader, he was a soldier - a good one - but still, only a soldier. He had command, he had respect, but not the ability to sway men's hearts as von Adamm had. Whether they had loved him or not was irrelevant, they certainly loved what he offered them, and they believed in his words. If they wanted their well-oiled machine to continue - and there was no reason it shouldn't - a new figurehead was essential. Mackenzie, as senior Commanding Officer, would have to convene a council, choose a new spokesman. Everything had to be done by the book, according to von Adamm's words and orders

Von Adamm is dead ... long live von Adamm.

The defeat of the Adammites at Pennyport by King Alexis and the elves of Floriénne back in the autumn had been a blow to the southern militia in Elvinhaeme. Colonel Grey, Commander in Chief at Hollyporth, had planned taking Belcast'el soon after he took Westlea, maybe a few weeks, certainly by Harvesthaeme, but orders arrived from von Adamm to go for the main port of Westerling, Pennyport, take it and begin the infiltration and invasion of Westerling instead.

Colonel Grey considered this was stretching his troops too far, much better to consolidate his position in Elvinhaeme, but orders are orders, he therefore sent several carracks to the port and waited for results. The news was dire, the loss of both Adammite soldiers and ships set back his Elvinhaeme campaign. He was a good soldier, a good officer and a good strategist, and until then, von Adamm had listened to his advice, at least militarily. He bitterly wished that von Adamm *had* listened to him, taken note of his knowledge and experience - he had been in several mercenary campaigns overseas spanning years, was a natural warrior, had learned much. Von Adamm on the other hand was no warrior - a speaker and politician, yes, but no soldier.

He lost soldiers he needed, thanks to von Adamm, wasn't best pleased at the fact von Adamm was holed up in Draecastle, tucked carefully away from any combat, happily sending out orders to all and sundry without true knowledge of the local conditions. Colonel Grey's own ambitions were thwarted, he wanted Elvinhaeme for himself and he had to waste precious time until more Adammite soldiers were trained up and sent over from the Isle of Glasse, or perhaps Mere'garde. Even so, they would all be greenhorns.

And all the while, the Dûc de Luxonne would be training his own troops.

Blast and damn both Luxonne and von Adamm!

Colonel Grey spent the intervening months turning the ports into fortresses and consolidating his positions along the west and south coasts of Elvinhaeme. He used elves as the workforce, they cost nothing and he didn't care a jot if they dropped down dead from exhaustion. He had them build more ships too; there was plenty of local wood, although Oakleigh forest would be better in his hands than the elves.

A brief foray into Oakleigh had resulted in nothing, there were skilled archers in the trees, archers he later learned were actually Freowulven ... the elves had the nerve to use Outlaws for defence! He couldn't believe it, it was against all convention, organised, it seems by that Estrién elf, the one with the sword he had heard about, the one on the Wanted posters. Part of this new group too, some filthy Merrievian sect, probably spent their days having sex and getting drunk, drugged to the eyeballs. Dirty swine!

The Colonel was frustrated by inaction.

When the boat-load of Adammite soldiers arrived at Westlea, all escaping from Draecastle far north, with the news of von Adamm's death, he took it pretty dry eyed. Colonel Mackenzie had allowed the troops a few days stay on Mere'garde to recover and recoup, then sent them straight down the coast to his fellow officer, with the note, *'Draecastle gone, von Adamm and Kyneweth dead, killed by White Shield. Keep Elvinhaeme at all costs - you may need these. Will arrange a Council for new leader - you interested? Glory to the Adammites!'*

Colonel Grey merely smiled to himself, looked out at the miserable late *Endurance* weather and decided now was a good time to go for Belcast'el while the poor little elves were all tucked up, hiding against the winter cold. He quickly sent scouts to the city who reported back that, yes, it all seemed quiet, there was some training going on in the palace grounds and a military headquarters complete with barracks had been hastily built - but it looked pretty jimcrack.

The Colonel took his troops and marched in their eight square formation through the countryside, villages and minor towns of Elvinhaeme to the gates of Belcast'el. He also took the massive battering rams he had prepared during the autumn months for the very purpose of destroying those large and ornate gates. He also included trebuchets and ballistae to be used against the elves.

He left devastation behind him.

Both the gates of the city and the gates of the palace stood no chance against his war engines, nor did the young and inexperienced soldiers of the city against his well disciplined troops. They did their best, they held out for almost a day as massive boulders hit the city and huge flaming spears shot through their lines. They stood on the ramparts of the city walls, shooting arrows and pouring boiling oil on the Adammite troops, only to find that the individual Adammite troops were also using a small version of a huge ballista - crossbows with metal bolts, fast and utterly lethal.

They even had a name for themselves, the Hellboys, everyone trained in the use of the crossbow. The eight square formations would march down the street, the front line and outer swordsmen holding up large protective shields. Then they would drop and a volley of steel bolts was shot out. The first row of crossbowmen then dropped and were covered by the shields as they prepared their next round. Behind them, the next line shot a volley of bolts into the enemy, to be protected by more shields. Then a third line continued the hail of deadly bolts.

There were several groups of these and they marched with precision into all areas of the city, killing archers, soldiers and citizens indiscriminately. People fled to their homes, hid behind hastily barred doors. Other groups of Hellboys took themselves up onto the ramparts of the city walls, once the archers were taken out, and proceeded to hail down bolts from their elevated position into the city itself.

It is safe to say that the blood which ran through the streets of Hollyporth back in the spring was nothing compared to the rivers of blood in the streets of fair Belcast'el.

The battering rams moved with the tightly knit squads, any gates or barriers were taken with ease. The beautiful gates of the palace went effortlessly as did the palace doors. The huge battering rams, along with ballistae and several trebuchets were pulled onto the once perfect lawns of the palace grounds. In the wet and cold month of Endurance, these became a quagmire of mud, great ruts ran through the perfectly scythed grass.

The Dûc de Luxonne, this time wearing an admittedly chic battle armour rather than his foppish silver slippers, held out as long as he could. His combat knowledge was nil, although he had some sword skills. An epee isn't exactly the greatest of battle weapons.

Colonel Grey laughed as he knocked it out of his hand with his own sabre, before slicing off the Dûc's head.

'Stick that on the pyre just outside the palace gates will you?' he said to one of his Captains, observing the number of dead in the marble Grand Hall. 'Pile all these bodies on and cleanse this place of filth. I want no reminders of elven so-called nobility, nor do I intend to have them strung up as martyrs to rally the elves. Burn the fucking lot and get rid of them. Take over those barracks and get barriers up around the palace grounds, keep the ballistae and trebuchets pointing outwards and double the number of Hellboys up on the city's ramparts.

Take random groups of elves and the lower races, leave pyres in every square as warning to the rest, and issue orders as we do in every town. All elves/dwarves etc. are now under servitude to ourselves. All mages to be put to death, whether elf or human.' He stopped and thought for a moment ' ... and you know what to do with the Temples of Merrie, don't you ...?' he chuckled. 'Bring a few of those damn priestesses to me, they can make themselves useful.'

Colonel Grey sat down on the plush purple velvet cover over the marble throne and sighed satisfactorily. He could get to like this - and there was no von Adamm to take it from him.

Chapter 3

Most of the mages agreed to travel with them, two stayed with King Duggan, there was more healing needed, and not merely physical healing. But six of the mages Dane had collected in Grimmpool were going, plus Salli, Trevaine and Robson, ten altogether and everyone willing to use elemental magic. *Quite a formidable team.* They would split afterwards, some going to Lord Black and some to King Alexis' Court. Naturally, Reave and Garrett were also with them, their skills were necessary.

Estrién changed the cart for a better carriage, donated by King Duggan. Amber wasn't yet well enough for a horse, one of the mages would ride it, and Amber could rest for a day or two. The carriage was large and roomy and the castle carpenters added a few special compartments, hidden hidey-holes where mages could secrete their staffs when they reached Manecaestr.

They travelled the Long Ride to get there, the quickest route. Estrién and Tamlyn rode their own horses, they needed to skirt the towns, they still couldn't be seen until King Duggan had retaken them. Everyone else dressed as merchants, they would stick to the main road and if anyone asked, they were fleeing the town of Draecastle, saddened by the loss of von Adamm.

The Rover clan said they would travel down also. Hammerhold had been retaken by them and they had defended the town as King Kyneweth's Adammite troops attacked. But it was soon over for the young king quickly sent word and Longshanks did as he had said, he smoothed over the cracks and got everyone talking again. Cash helped, as it always does, monetary reparation for goods forcibly taken from their mines and metal works. The Rovers said they had some scores to settle, especially along the towns on the Long Ride, and they would meet them outside Manecaestr.

Garrett and Reave sent word by hawk to Lord Black and King Alexis, who was still at Lord Black's castle. Alexis decided to move south, gather troops towards Elvinhaeme ready for any kind of push there. Lord Black sent troops up to the Segantium border, partly to stop Adammites escaping via Mercantia, partly to offer help to the new King Duggan.

'Will move in when young King Duggan gives word,' he explained in Gracie's note. 'otherwise it appears I'm invading Segantium. Best left to Violet.' Lord Black understood, brute force alone was not the answer, especially in such a city as Manecaestr.

Manecaestr is a large mercantile city full of independent and often wealthy people, now held by Adammite sympathisers. It is the biggest city in Segantium, owned and influenced by a large merchant's quarter, strong in political inclination. There is no castle or Hold as a focal point for Duggan to overpower, but there are various City Halls and buildings all used for the various needs of a large population, run by a democratically created Council of Elders. Many were 'Elder' in name only, the term being a courtesy title for someone of both knowledge and experience, wise in their years.

Part of Segantium, Manecaestr always paid dues and fealty to the King at Draecastle, yet kept a guard of its own and laid down its own rules, the people of Segantium being a proud and independently-minded set. At least, that is what had happened in the past. Now Manecaestr was run by an Adammite elite, although to be truthful, many of this elite had also been Elders.

Lady Violet understood that to destroy the Council of Elders and their various sub councils would be to undermine the free thinking system that had created the city. She believed the only way would be to take it from 'within', to change those hearts and minds, to root out the ringleaders, use forces somewhat more subtle than swords or axes.

In the event, it was irrelevant. Force or tact, neither mattered as far as the people of Manecaestr were concerned.

The members of the White Shield met up with Lady Violet and her entourage a couple of weeks later. The horses had ridden well, but the roads were poor at this time of year, there had been a lot of rain. A cold and miserable *Endurance* had given way to an equally cold and rainy *Icefall* month, much of the rain turned into sleet. The group turned into the yard of a wayside inn, glad to be off the road, happy to see the bright torches flaring in the night, candle lamps lit cosily in windows. Wet, bedraggled horses, equally wet and bedraggled riders and a dirty carriage that had to be pulled out of muddy ruts more than once, all tumbled into the welcoming sight. The horses were given room in the stables and were rubbed down, warmed and fed, the two-legged animals went into the inn likewise.

It was hot inside, fires burning merrily, steam rose from the moist cloaks and hats. It was one of those places with horse brasses hung on the walls, the laird's shield over the fireplace and a large shelf where locals kept their own ale mugs when they weren't playing dominoes in the tap room. Hot pies and pasties along with goodly ales were ordered all round.

'Tha' can't have that one,' the barkeeper explained when Dane pointed out a particularly good example of a pewter tankard for his beer. 'That be Bert's.'

The landlord believed in keeping the locals happy and the travellers satisfied, and he didn't care what cult, 'ism or 'ology anyone adhered to, there were to be no hostilities in his inn. A large and unwieldy looking mace was kept on a chain by the bar, and he wasn't afraid to use it if customers turned rowdy. His concern was for decent ale and food, warm beds and hot baths, and good stabling. He made a packet.

Estrién had just worked his way through a thick soup of beef and vegetables served inside an equally thick hunk of bread holed out in the centre, a platter of boar meat, beans and huge potato pasties, apple pie and custard and was just eyeing a cheeseboard covered in local cheeses, chutneys, more hunks of bread and a few apples thrown on 'for refreshment', when Lady Violet arrived. She declined the rest of the food, but helped herself to bread and cheese.

Estrién (and the rest) felt replete and were in good temper. They weren't ready for her news.

'We can't get into Manecaestr.'

*

In a tower near the strange Greyluming mountains.

His claw-like fingers dug into her neck as she stitched, drawing blood. It dropped onto the tapestry, oozed and dribbled over the fine threads. He drew more blood from his own wrist, let it drip into hers. There was a brief sizzle and steam arose.

The tapestry was beginning to smell now, the stench of those dark threads, the nasty ones made of nettle and blood and henbane and a host of life disturbing plants, now invaded the whole stitchwork. It could not be cleansed, the odour permeated all. The tapestry was no ordinary work, it reflected life.

Time had changed, life had changed, the happy familiarity between humans, elves and the rest of the magickal races of Mer'edrynn was no more. Discontent had been sown, a strange slant on that which was natural made to appear unnatural, words misused and given another context, made to seem insulting when none was meant. People were offered impossible dreams and immature wants. A time of take, but no payment...

... a sinking of souls.

She didn't cry out as the claws dug, as her skin was pierced and nerve endings registered the pain. Yet a single tear dripped and washed some of the blood off the tapestry, a tiny cleansing element, a small circle of purity in an unclean whole.

He pointed out the city, knowing it was now on the list of those to be liberated from Adammite rule. That damn Nim'randuel group led by the Wielder of Light, and that blasted mage - Dane was his name? He was more than that, what was he? There was something in his blood, he could smell it, something old and strong, he had risen from the earth itself, or perhaps the trees? He heard of how he used the staff at Sunstones that day, the electric storm, and how he controlled it. Of course, *he* hadn't been at Sunstones, how could he?

The Ringing of the Stones did more than just welcome the change of seasons ... much more.

He thought of the female he had almost destroyed, sister of this one. She had escaped, but only briefly and he would enjoy the torment of her when she was taken ... *as she would surely be*. As for now, the other sister was here and the city with all those souls, must be made secure.

A talon reached down to the walled city on her tapestry, scratched a line through the threads, opened up the weave. Anaïs looked up startled, no, that was wrong, not possible, it would play havoc.

It was a mere disturbance of the tapestry, a single broken thread, but it cut off Manecaestr as surely as a wide moat cuts off a castle. Unfortunately, unlike the castle, the city had no drawbridge.

*

They stood on the edge of a circle of nothingness.

'Told you,' stated Lady Violet, studying the phenomenon, 'can't enter. It's there - blink your eyes a few times and try not to think - there's a hazy outline inside the, well, whatever that is. You have to trick your mind, kind of think sideways.' She smiled, it was easy for her, thinking sideways was her natural way, new ideas popped in and added up the verticals.

They all did as she suggested, some saw, some didn't.

Garrett let Gracie soar towards the phenomenon, she rose, rose, and rose again, pushed backwards as if a great wind blew against her. She gave up and returned to Garrett. 'Can't get in from above either,' he declared.

'Anyone have an idea of what it is?' Estrién asked. The mages shook their heads and looked puzzled.

'No idea what, but I know *who* ...' replied Amber, she looked worried. 'I can feel *him*, the shadow I saw when I was unconscious. There's something wrong, unclean about it. Dane - you saw it too.' She turned to Dane, took his hand, 'what is it Dane, what is that thing?'

Dane took a deep sigh, cocked his head a little sideways as he tried to understand. 'I don't feel him as you do Amber, but I feel your pain - so yes, this is of him.' He lifted his staff, blasted a bolt of amberic lightning from the end, it frizzled horizontally across to the barrier, hit it, then changed course, a vertical line of blue and white flashing skywards against a non-existent wall.

'Never seen lightning shoot upwards before,' said Garrett pragmatically. 'Usually starts up there and comes downwards.'

The group of mages all moved gingerly towards the *not thing*, one or two elementalists like Dane tried out a few experiments with their staffs. Everything disappeared as it hit the barrier or shot upwards towards the heavens. Ten mages all shook their heads, they were at a loss with this one.

'It's quite interesting though, isn't it?' Robson, the youngest mage had never seen anything like it. Jaxon conjured up a few rocks, threw them towards where Manecaestr should be. They just hovered and disappeared. 'Wonder if they hit anyone inside?' he asked.

'Probably disintegrated,' replied Dane. 'But it seems physical things, like Gracie and my lightning can't get past the barrier. We elementalists take things like fire or water out of the air, use it via our bodies or staffs - it's real, it exists. Once it leaves us it is physical, an entity of its own. Your rocks,' turning to Jaxon, 'are only physical until you dismiss them from your mind; you conjured them from your inner consciousness. So - did they go through the barrier, or did you stop thinking of them?' It was a viable question.

Jaxon understood, 'didn't stop them, they just disappeared.' He looked towards the vagueness and concentrated. Three rocks suddenly shot out towards him. He quickly dismissed them, he and Richelda had often performed similarly on stage. She would throw rocks at him, he would detonate them in mid air, throw some back. The audience loved it, yet in the end it was only illusion, albeit a physical one.

'They were inside, most definitely,' he declared. He tried lifting a real rock, mage wise of course, with his mind, then threw it at the barrier, it merely disintegrated.

Garrett suddenly gave a gasp, he was examining Gracie in case she had been hurt by the barrier. 'Her feathers have turned white where she touched whatever it is ...'

Everyone turned to look at Gracie. Salli reached out his wand and touched her gently, then asked Sylva to examine her with his apple-wood wand. All healer mages crowded round while Garrett held her firmly. Finally there was a collective 'Aaah,' as they agreed on a diagnosis.

'She's aged,' Dane stated flatly. 'That thing is something to do with time - how or why I have no idea.' He looked sadly at Salli, 'Gourien would have loved to have seen this,' Salli nodded sympathetically, yes, just up Gourien's street.

Amber closed her eyes, lifted a hand to her forehead as pain crossed her features. It was all very well for the mages to view this as an interesting alchemical entity, people were trapped inside. She now knew what it was, she understood and she silently wept at the thought of what *he* must have done to her sister to create this. 'I's not just *him*, he can't turn time. But I know someone who can.'

Everyone looked expectantly at her, eyes queried, it wasn't a statement you made every day.

Her voice trembled a little as she spoke, 'you remember, Dane, you were with me when I ... journeyed ... . *He* was there, but so was someone else ... my sister, Anaïs. I felt her, oh dear Goddess, I felt her pain and it was terrible. She ... she's not like any of us.' She turned to them all trying to explain. 'I felt her and it blotted out the ... the Shadow. I didn't understand when she was small, none of us did, or perhaps my mother understood. It was only part there, she was always so quiet. I was the tomboy of the family you see, always into mischief, played ball games and cock-a-hoop with the lads of the village as a child, somersaulted my way across the village green once.' Smiles spread across the faces of Dane, Tamlyn and Estrién - yes, typical Amber. Reave too understood. 'Mother got annoyed because I didn't wear dresses and sit quietly embroidering or arranging flowers. Kept trying to teach me the 'creative arts', as she put it. Anaïs was quite the opposite, she knitted me a lovely scarf when she was six, embroidered my hankies and helped mother make my clothes. She was good at cooking too, much better than me, and helped Dad with potions and the poisons he made for the archers of the village, for their arrows. She often had her nose in a book, she was interested in everything, healing and herbalism and how the stars twinkled in the sky. She spent most of her early life being taught by my parents, both of them mages.'

She paused to try to explain what she now knew about her sister. 'When the Alderfolk took our village, she was very young, just fourteen. Her magic still hadn't formed, my parents had said this just before and that I was to look after her until it did, if ever. I think they both knew what was to happen, I think Anaïs did too, but she was in shock. She rarely spoke during our captivity, when she did, it was mostly incomprehensible. But she said one last thing to me when I helped her escape that night.

'There are tears in the fabric, time hangs on broken threads. I must set it right.'

I didn't know what she meant, I thought she was babbling. I only knew that she had to escape, she was gentle and kind and it was all too much for her with the Alderfolk. She ran off into the night and I haven't seen her since. But ...' she took Dane's hand, clutched it tightly, 'when I was ill, I saw something, Dane saw it too. It was a shadow, a being, not of the pattern, not of the weave. It wanted to destroy me, destroy all of us, and *it was connected to my sister*. That night, I knew my sister was still alive and I realised the deep heart of her.

She is part of the Thread of the world, she lays down the Tapestry of Time and records existence. I'm not sure, but she might even be able to change time, and I think *he*, whatever he is, has hold of her. I think he has used my sister to create this ...,' she spread out her arms, 'this barrier. Somehow, he has warped time.'

There was a collective gasp, mostly from mages ... a mage who wove time?

Amber spoke again. *'He* has her and he uses her, she is in utter misery. If nothing else, I must help her, I must find her.' She broke down now, the thought of that creature using her sister, tears forming. Dane held her, kissed the top of her head.

'She's number one priority dear, I don't think we understood before.'

Estrién nodded agreement, gently held her hand, then took White Star from its sheath. It had been whining softly ever since they neared the barrier. He walked up to the wall of nothingness, lay his head on one side, then slowly pierced it with the sword. White Star entered partly, the whining louder and louder, then he retrieved it. It seemed fine, a little cleaner on the edge maybe. He touched the end where it had gone through the barrier

'Hmm, ice cold and a little blunt.' He took out his whetstone to sharpen the edge, 'otherwise seems fine - but I wouldn't try that with anything else,' he warned. 'White Star isn't like any other sword.' He sheathed the weapon. 'We need to find your sister, and fast.'

*

Colonel Mackenzie read the missive from a Captain Fields, written 'near Manecaestr'. He couldn't believe the contents, sounded like gobbledygook, utter fairytale, but it appeared the city was cut off from the rest of Mer'edrynn, by '*an impenetrable barrier, not physical, never seen the like*'. He was particularly annoyed because there were one or two highly politicised and articulate men in that city, possible contenders for Leader. He sent word to several alchemists he knew - men just on the edge of magedom, close but not quite, enough to save their skins - clever at manipulating chemicals and the like, but without the ability to use magic. They would have to get their collective brains together on this one.

He also sent out missives to convene an Extraordinary General Meeting on the Isle of Glasse to all Adammite commanders and political thinkers. No time must be wasted in the investiture of a new Leader.

Then he packed his kitbag and took a warship to the Adammite-held small port of Herringhold, some miles south of Grimmpool, directly west of Manecaestr. He needed to see this phenomenon for himself.

*

If those outside the city of Manecaestr could not see in, the people within were also unable to see out. The grey and shimmering mass hung like a pall around the city, blocking, not merely any exit, but also the sky above.

Manecaestr looked up to a never ending grey sky, a cloud that was not a cloud, non-shifting, non moving, without variation in shade or hue, just a strange and colourless shimmer. They didn't mind grey clouds, there were often grey skies, and admittedly, it took some time before those in the centre of the city actually noticed it.

But the night hung as grey as the day, just a slight reflection as the torches of the city blazed. That soon became a problem as there was no wind to blow away the sooty flecks and the atmosphere became thick with smoke, like an inn on a feast day, cloud-heavy with leaf roll and pipe leaf. It soon became choking and guards were issued orders to douse every torch.

The city at night, without torches, moonlight or starlight, was black as pitch, while during the day, as misty grey as the land of the Fae.

The Fae ... those strange riders who enter our world for the single purpose of stealing youths or children or babe-in-arms to take to their dull and miserable realm as their own children, their lovers, or merely to draw the life force from fresh healthy bodies. They do not eat, although they perhaps drink a little wine, for wine is intoxicating, neither do they drink the blood of their prey, for they are not vampires. But still, the life force is slowly imbibed nevertheless, and the youthful body grows old, weak and feeble.

And so they keep their youth, surviving for centuries in their grey and colourless world.

In fact, deep in the Fae world, the elder Fae felt the change, subtle by nature, although far-reaching, understood the barrier, for it was very similar to their own barrier between their dark underworld and the life pulse of Mer'edrynn. It was also huge, whereas the portal they used was small, only a few riders went through at a time. This was large enough to open several portals at once, send many Fae through, capture many beings.

The only question was did they have chariots and baskets enough to bring back their prey?

The silver-haired leader turned to his consort, the one of the gossamer threads, his smile feral with pleasure. 'Bodies for the taking,' he laughed, 'open and available ...'

She too nodded, her pale grey eyes gleaming at the thought. They had lost several of their kind the day that human female and her three male followers had escaped. She wanted revenge, particularly on humankind. Besides, they'd had to kill the bears, such a waste, they had been amusing, in many ways. But how had this been created?

'Who ... why ...?' she asked him.

'I am unsure ... there was *one* ... many centuries ago, dost thou remember? He came among us, he was ... unsettling ... corrupt, even by our standards. We merely take the life force, yet he wanted more, the very soul. He did not stay, for we had little to offer such a being, we are too alike, and there was nought he could offer us. Yet, he had powers, possibly enough to create such?'

Even so, he wondered if that were true?

She nodded, agreeing, it must be so, *that one* was kin yet not kin to Faefolk. What did it matter anyway, he had opened up the city to their need. There were few single travellers at this time of year, the nights were icy, they rode little. The Fae were hungry - in many ways.

She was still a little unsure, 'we do not normally take our prey like this, we will be open to a large city, full of beings - some will have weapons. Also - beware - we do not normally show ourselves ... we hunt in the night and keep to ourselves.'

Her consort nodded in agreement, 'yet,' he persuaded her, 'think of the numbers we can take on one swift hunt - enough for years. The opening is there ready for our use, therefore let us use it, take what we can. Then we disappear for decades until we are nothing but a memory.'

The old Fae female accepted this, yes, so much prey available in one go, perhaps several trips? 'Take as much Fae dust as possible,' she warned. But her mouth was watering, already savouring the possibilities.

They quickly called the group together and gleefully mounted their misty-white steeds, eyes filled with expectant pleasure.

A human city filled with delectable beings, and passage directly into it...

... Delicious!

Chapter 4

A few days after the battle of Draecastle.

Eamonn Norland sat somewhat uncomfortably in his plush red leather chair, placed the quill down on the small glazed plate he used to protect his oak desk from being stained by ink drops, and pushed the manuscript he had been assiduously writing away from him. Unconsciously, the Minister in Charge of Ordinance and Supply tucked a lock of his greying hair back over his large round ears and gazed curiously through the window.

What in Mer'edrynn was that? He stood uncertainly, strode to the window, peered upwards. It looked like cloud, yet ... utterly uniform, no varying shades, no movement, not light or dark clouds with sun peeping through, or at least, attempting to peep. It kind of glistened too, like rain drops, yet, it was the strangest shimmer he had ever seen. It took him some while before he realised it wasn't cloud, at least none he knew of and was probably below cloud level.

His first thought was, 'what have those damn mages done now?'

He marched downstairs to the foyer of the Council Chambers, once ornate, now a plain affair stripped of its gold-leaf embellishments, and through the heavy oak doors, to the cobbled street outside, the cobbles being a recent and welcome innovation for horses and carriages.

He wasn't alone. Across the wide road, Lefwynn Hydeman, another council member and Master of the Saddlers and

Leather-workers Guild also stepped out of his equally plush offices on to his wide wrought iron balcony. He too could be seen staring at the sky, in fact, down below, the road was soon becoming full as more and more people left the comfort of their Merchant Quarter stores, workshops and offices to stand and silently gaze upwards.

None could understand it. It was there, yet not there, could be seen, yet not be seen. There was a strange silence too, no wind, no late Endurance icy gales as they blasted down a narrow street turned wind tunnel if the wind came from the north. Neither was there rain or sun. It looked like it ought to rain at any moment, yet nothing happened.

Worse, it didn't move - clouds *moved*, dammit, didn't they, even an overcast sky bloody well shifted!

It just hung there, and those in the centre of the prosperous city, a city teeming with life, looked on in wonder.

Those by the outskirts of the city saw it differently, particularly those on the ramparts of the city walls and in the guard towers, as close to the phenomena as they could get.

One guard peeked his head over the ramparts into the greyness. The other guards pulled him back quickly, but it was too late. He'd died of old age brought on in an instant. Word was passed and orders hurriedly given - *Do Not Touch the Phenomenon, by Order.* Not if you valued your life, that is.

Rambolt, Colonel-in-Chief of the Adammite Militia in Manecaestr, hurried to visit the edge. It was difficult as all roads and streets were crowded with curious onlookers, he returned to the barracks where he picked up a whip and a large black and white Shire horse, usually used for pulling carts and ballistae. He was a heavy, thick set man, broad of both chest and arms, and the horse suited him well. It took time to find a large enough saddle, but he finally mounted and rode his way through the well-guarded gates of the military headquarters, shouting at both the horse and anybody in his way, neither was he afraid to use the whip on both the horse and the annoyingly obstructive citizens. After a few shouts and cries, people learned to get out of his way and he made it to the outer walls in good time.

'What the fuck is it?' he asked. No one knew, but he was quickly told about the dead guard - a Hellboy too, waste of a good crossbowman. He was taken to the site where the guard had died, shown the body lying in the gatehouse, shook his head as he examined it.

He used the short, sharp language known to all combatants. 'Fuck, fuck, *fuck*!' followed by, 'who did this, bloody mages?' It was always mages, it had to be. 'I want a full sweep of the city, there are mages here still, hiding their dirty little butts somewhere. Try the sewers, look in empty houses and hidden tunnels, find them and bring any you collect to me.'

He stood for a while studying it, looking up, down and around querulously.

Like Estrién he took out his sword from its scabbard, walked slowly over to the grey haze and carefully poked the end through the mist. It was covered in rust as he pulled it out again. 'Get barriers up,' he told the soldiers, 'keep everyone away - and if you find any sodding mages, keep them alive - we need to get the fucking truth out of them.' He marched back to the waiting Shire, quickly mounted and pushed his way back through the milling throngs to his headquarters.

Once there he wrote out a note to his beloved leader, Mordecai von Adamm, explaining their predicament, requesting troops be sent down from Draecastle, and informing him he was doing everything he possibly could about the phenomena. He hoped to use carrier pigeon to send it, not yet understanding there was no way out above either.

Neither was he aware that von Adamm was dead, and Draecastle in the hands of the new young King Duggan, a true Merrievian, all Adammites gone from the fortress and the city. The barrier had gone up swiftly, even the fast-galloping horses of the First Adammite Messenger League could not travel the nearly two hundred miles between Draecastle and Manecaestr in so short a time, especially with the bad weather.

The courier arrived, as did Estrién and the others, too late to enter. He looked, he queried the few local yokels from the nearby farm who warned him it was dangerous - showed him a dead fox that had tried to enter, and like many others, he scratched his head. Then the rider from the messenger service turned his horse west to the small outpost half way between Manecaestr and Herringhold to inform the garrison there and get word to either the Isle of Glasse or Mere'garde. There he informed a Captain Fields who immediately despatched him to the coast with a note for Colonel Mackenzie on Mere'garde.

Colonel Rambolt however, knew nothing of this, only that if that barrier was the whole way around the city, then he had a city effectively under siege. He had thousands of mouths to feed and order to keep, and if nothing and no one could get out, then equally, nothing and no-one could get in.

He quickly sent for Eomann Norland and Lefwynn Hydeman to discuss supplies, they would know the current state of affairs here, both Council members. Their meeting was brief, word was quickly sent to every store and warehouse in the city to ration everything. Lists were quickly drawn up, efficiency being keynote within

Adammite realm, tickets and passes were supplied to essential staff and soldiers, they would have first pick of food and supplies. Unessential human males, not involved in war work, bar keepers and the like, came next, then females, unless with child by an Adammite father, followed by the lesser races.

Norland suggested they could be allowed to starve, although, he considered they could also be looked on as a food supply, should the state of emergency last that long? Colonel Rambolt agreed, although that might cause disagreement among some of the nobility and wealthier citizens who had paid good money for their elven or dwarven slaves. But still, the choice was there if this continued.

Briefly he wondered what an elven steak might taste like. He would have to try it some time.

Meanwhile he convened a full meeting of all Council Elders, Guild Chairmen and officers of the militia at Candlemaker's Hall for the following morning.

The night was long and dark, the street torches were quickly snuffed when it was discovered they polluted the air and used essential oxygen and Colonel Rambolt, along with many others spent a miserable night under cold sheets in icy fireless rooms. The wood smoke from home fires also polluted the atmosphere inside the closed dome of Manecaestr, people began choking, word was sent around to use only essential fires for cooking at designated places.

Rambolt made his way to Candlemaker's Hall the next morn, the day merely a few shades lighter than the previous night. It felt very cold in the city; he wrapped his cloak around him, chill, but airless, and decidedly damp. Others too made their way to the Hall, Eomann Norland, Lefwynn Hydeman of the Saddlers, and a host of Guild-masters of the city. Many people were out and about, still curious, still trying to fathom out what was happening. The streets in fact, were full.

Then they came, strange portals opened, the silken-haired riders with the streaming gossamer cloaks on their misty steeds, flying down, swooping through newly-opened silver holes in steel grey skies. It seemed the air was filled with frost breathing horses and clanking chariots, the sound of silver spurs and silver chains clinking their death knoll.

Now people looked on in fear as childhood stories and bedtime tales came true, mouths open in astonishment. The chariots pulled silver baskets to carry home their prey, all riders held the gleam of greed and lust in their eyes, and a sickly smile of triumph. The thin, but impenetrable haze of no time was not impenetrable to those who lived outside of normal time.

Humans, elves, dwarves watched the skies en masse, one people, one set of frightened people. Race or sex had no preference; youth and health were what concerned the Fae. Blood, rich blood, the streaming life forces of youth, pulsating in vibrant young bodies was all that concerned them, if anything the sweetness of an elven youth was preferable to human.

There was no time for any kind of defence.

Silent gaping mouths turned to screams as the first Fae dust hit and whole groups went down. No one ran to help, but many ran away, rushing into homes or buildings, anything, anywhere to escape. Bodies were pushed down and trampled upon, children kicked to one side as soldiers too scuttered terrified from a battlefield they could not control. No one cared who was taken, as long as it wasn't themselves.

And the Fae laughed, as more and more holes appeared in the sky and more Fae poured through, taking advantage of the extraordinary situation. A path had opened from their realm to the city, not exactly the type they were used to, but definitely adaptable, small tunnels created through the spherical barrier. Ice cold, out of time, airless tunnels, but still, short enough for their ride and for their comatose victims to live through.

They collected many fine specimens, particularly children, took them back to their dark and miserable realm and imprisoned them. They laughed, danced and feasted, gorging on life forces, such a feast they had not had in centuries. They took the young men and women and indulged their particular sexual proclivities with each and everyone; there were neither boundaries nor shortages, merely abundance. Some died that first night, some held out, a few were chosen to join them. All were enjoyed.

The children were kept as their own, groomed to become like themselves, they would turn eventually into Fae.

They returned every few days, the skies dancing with prancing horses and triumphant riders, eyes gleaming, silver hair streaming, gorged on youth. Fae dust was thrown down quickly and bodies were leisurely collected.

Normally their rule was to remain hidden from view, carefully collect everything they could from the unwary travellers out in the hills or byways. They would remove anything personal in order to wipe his or her existence away, leave nothing behind for others to ponder - their way was to work quietly and clandestinely. They were legend and folk-tale, mystery and secrecy, hidden from view, known only in dreams. The traveller had simply vanished, perhaps been taken by bandits, drowned in a lake, moved on to another town. Nothing was left behind that would suggest the Fae were responsible, for if their routes were known - and there were only a certain number of these - people might lie in wait, there might be ambush or attack. The advantage of surprise would be gone, and the fearsome tales would diminish.

So they usually travelled in the depths of the night, the pale nights of late summer, when victims could be seen from the skies, yet most people were sleeping. Only revellers and the occasional ploughman taking advantage of summer light sometimes saw them from afar, wondering if what they saw was true?

Legend they were, and legend they wanted to stay - *until this* - this was beyond their wildest dreams. The temptation to swell their numbers by so many in such a short time was too great. Thirst, or hunger, or simply craving, proved too much, and so they took advantage of the suddenly available mass entrance to a heavily populated city.

But what they feared was also true, for on the third hunt the Adammites were waiting for them. Colonel Rambolt ordered all human citizens to stay indoors for the next few days, and collected as many elves as he could. He penned them into several large squares of the city, allowed others to simply walk the streets, not wanting to make it seem obvious that they were bait. Around each square, however, his Hellboys were waiting, some on the ground, some on top of buildings, some inside with their crossbows pointed at both the squares and the skies.

The ill-treated and half starved elves were afraid, but could do nothing. When one tried to escape he was quickly stopped with a crossbow bolt in his back. No one else moved; to be truthful they weren't sure that living with the Fae could be any worse than living under the Adammites.

As the strange gaps appeared in the grey haze, and the Fae triumphantly flew through, the Colonel gave the word. Bolts were shot immediately - no point waiting for Fae dust to fill the skies and knock everyone unconscious - shoot now and take out what they could. It would be a warning if nothing else.

Several flying horses fell, several riders were knocked off, dropping to the ground in limb crunching sickliness, only to be kicked and beaten by heavy Adammite boots. None that fell lived, although that annoyed the Colonel as he wished to question them, he couldn't however blame his soldiers, they were doing their job. The rest of the Fae quickly understood their feast was over, streamed upwards and disappeared as quickly as they came through the ice-cold tunnels.

The tunnels vanished with a sudden finality.

As the elder silver-haired rider jumped gasping off his sweating horse, the old female Fae shook a long talon-like fingernail at him.

'We were fools for lust, were we not?'

Her consort agreed. 'We keep to the old ways from now, as we should. It was tempting, too tempting.' Then he grinned, 'we have lost some, but the prisons are full as are the larders. There are babes, many babes, human and elven. Wouldst thou like a new child, my heart?'

She shook her ancient head. 'Nay, no more for me, my paps will not feed. Besides, two of my children were downed this day. I thirst only for nourishment, not pleasure.'

But the gleam in her consort's eye told her he had many set aside for his personal use. He briefly held up his hand, massaged two of the fingers, the ones broken by the red haired human female, they ached this day after such a ride. 'I hoped *she* would be among them, referring to Amber, 'I specifically requested the search for her, and that group of annoying males with her. One day I will find them and punish them.' His consort sympathised with him, agreed on the necessity of capture and punishment.

It seemed that whatever the world, Amber, Estrién, Dane and Tamlyn, were on the Most Wanted lists.

… Not that they cared.

*

He remembered the Fae, remembered his short sojourn with them. He had thought, at one point, that he might have use for them. *He* quickly understood he was wasting his time, these were lazy, good for nothing beings of pure pleasure, dilettantes all. Worse than Merrievians, they merely drank, slept and fornicated throughout their long lives, created nothing, took everything. There was nothing to corrupt, nothing to feed off, nothing to use.

… No soul to take pleasure in destroying. The loss of a few of them by the Adammites was simply irrelevant.

He had placed Manecaestr in isolation, not because he cared about his dubious army, but because he was afraid they would, like von Adamm and those at Draecastle, be beaten by the Merrievians. They had gone over to *him* en masse in the city, they had performed as he required. He did not desire their return to the Merrievian fold, to life and laughter, joy and love. His desire was for disassociation, to split people apart, first from the other races, then from each other, man against wife, friend against friend, child against parent.

The last was a particular desire, the utmost corruption against bloodline and family. Notices were up throughout the city, indeed in all Adammite towns, *'Children! Do not let the corruption of your elders corrupt you! Inform your teacher or youth leader if you see any one of your family partaking in the old festivals or rituals. Your duty lies with von Adamm.'*

Or, *'Is your sister a mage? Is your father an elf friend? Follow the path of Truth and tell us now, before you too are tainted with this evil.'*

And so forth. *He* took satisfaction at the thought. Divide and destroy, a most excellent weapon of war.

True, these people cut off from the rest of Mer'edrynn were of no further use to the cause of Death in the rest of the realms, but the insidious deaths inside the city as it slowly starved would be near perfect for his purpose. Besides, the Adammites had failed up at Draecastle, a degree of punishment was necessary, a warning about failure.

Admittedly he had originally done it because of a brief and unexpected moment of anger, somewhat alien to his ice cold system, that a small group could so easily penetrate his defences and kill his General, his protégé, thereby ruining years of planning. He wondered if he should have cut off Draecastle as punishment instead?

He quickly understood his reaction had in actual fact been near perfect, a city of many lost souls all waiting for release. Once the Adammites had fled, the other citizens of Draecastle, that is, those of a kinder disposition, ruled by unwritten laws of respect, charity and understanding, would have fought back, worked together, harmonized; even as they died, they would not have suited his purpose, martyrs all. Whereas, Manecaestr, or part of it, had gone over to him, at least, the leaders and Masters of the city had been bribed, blackmailed and generally persuaded and conditioned one way or another. They were ripe for the taking.

He savoured the thought ... ripe and ready. He wondered whether to go soon, hasten their end, but decided the better way was the slow annihilation and degeneration of the once proud city. Starvation as supplies ran out, thirst as the wells dried up and eventually the choking sound of people gasping for breath as the air became tainted and used up. Add the sounds of screams and anger as they attacked each other in their desperation, Adammites, he well knew, chosen particularly for their lack of humanity rather than the other way around.

Yes, the slow creeping death leading to a final frenzy. Every unwholesome act and untimely death was mana to his being. He was proud of his creation, satisfied that what had once been a decent, law-abiding city full of life and laughter, had been reduced to this ... a city waiting to die.

He stood inside the circular tower of Anaïs' home, once her shelter, his eyes, or rather, the eyes of the human he inhabited, gleamed red with pleasure. Yes, he would wait to enter, the stench of fear and death would be great in his nostrils, the sound of weeping sacred to his ears, the sight of all those lost souls satisfying to eyes that held no compassion.

Anaïs watched him ponder the situation; apart from the gleaming red eyes, there was no other expression to signify if he delighted in his thoughts, he merely extrapolated the data. She knew it satisfied his need and she was aware of his hunger, she understood his power grew as souls became corrupted, as bodies died, particularly a violent death, as sickness crept throughout the land.

She knew that she had somehow to stop him, that perhaps she could repair the tapestry, but he would not let her. To be truthful, she was not sure if she could fully repair it, she could only try. She certainly could not give back that which had been taken. The city floundered in time, out on a limb, cast off like an island in the centre of nowhere. The city would never be the same again, would always retain a little 'otherworldliness', it's people touched by the strangest of strange and evil magic.

She wished she was not alone, the whole pain of the world upon fragile shoulders, shoulders bowed down by the weight of his being. She remembered she once had parents, how they sacrificed themselves trying to save their village from the overwhelming numbers of Alderfolk. She remembered her sister, how she had looked after her those months, often taking beatings on her behalf. She knew she offered the ultimate sacrifice to set her free, for the Alderfolk may well have executed her for such a deed.

But, no, she was sure she lived, for some nights ago she had dreamed of her, dreamed she was in danger at *his* hands, that Amber was ill, near death.

What Amber did not know that night, was that her sister too had fought for her, that her screams and the pain she felt, were those of a young woman battling *him* to save her soul, willing to sacrifice herself for the sister who had sacrificed for her.

When *he* returned from Draecastle he punished her sorely, her body battered and bruised even beyond the norm. But not broken, for that would end the feast, the torment must continue.

He allowed her that final and greatest of all liars, the last of the ills of the world when Pandora opened that box and set them free, the one souls cling to despite all evidence to the contrary.

He allowed her hope.

Chapter 5

The month of Icefall can be hard, roads slushy from sleet and winds still bitter, made worse by hearts hoping for the end of winter, looking for the light in the darkness.

The shorter route home across the north of the Bollands and through the Drell Moors was now impassable, the companions took the long trek south around the outskirts of Manecaestr. They looked therefore to reach the border between Segantium and Mercantia and then turn east towards Thornsgate and Ravenscroft Hall, there being decent roads and the weather was still bad

Lady Violet stayed along with her entourage and she wanted Garrett with her for a steady flow of information between herself, Lord Black and Estrién's group. Three mages also stayed, Richelda and Jaxon because of their illusion magic to test the phenomenon and Sylva was needed as a healer if they managed to break through. No one knew what conditions would be like inside, but the city was effectively under siege and supplies would eventually run out.

Merrie alone knew what would happen then in a city already at war with itself.

They followed the Long Ride to the border at the lower edges of the Bollands hills. At the junction of the two roads, three more mages left the group to report to Lord Black on events, before joining King Alexis. That left the core mage group of Dane, Salli, Trevaine and Robson.

They stopped off at the coaching in by the junction, noticing the Wanted poster in the window, four familiar faces on display, four people to be caught by any means and put to death.

Estrién actually smiled as he marched inside, grabbed the poster and threw it down in front of the landlord of the inn. Briefly he stared into his face as he tore it in two, then handed him the two parts.

'You may not yet be aware, von Adamm is dead. I ... with the help of my friends, killed him,' he stated briefly before scrutinising the various pumps on the bar, his smile widening. 'Hmm, I'll have a pint of your Spiced Amber ale, if you don't mind.' There was a general agreement, it was a chilly night. 'Make that eight pints please.'

The barman gave an apologetic grin and poured out the ale. 'No charge Sir, I think you've already paid enough.'

*

Amber thought the old Hall looked wonderful under its white mantle of snow on their approached. Warm lamps were lit in the windows as they turned through crystal-covered gates of Ravenscroft Hall, having taken a quick stop-off in Thornsgate for food and supplies. The two old elven retainers would not be ready for eight people arriving, they would fuss and be upset. Estrién knew to smooth the way with offerings and apologies.

Betsy and Tilly were just glad to see them all alive, they'd been kept reasonably well informed of events, had tried to keep the hall ready and waiting for them, so beds were all aired and clean. 'So glad to see you, young master Estrién, and,' Betsy turned beaming to Amber, 'and you, my Lady, we were so worried for you. But you're home now ...'

'We're not staying long,' Estrién replied, 'just here to recoup a little, Amber was hurt in the fighting ... although,' he quickly continued as he saw their worried eyes, 'she's much better now. No, we need to find out some information, then we move on.' They took off their cloaks and weapons, everyone making for their old rooms to relax.

Betsy held Estrién's arm, 'a moment sir ...' she whispered.

She turned to the oak dresser in the entrance hall, picked out what appeared to be a parcel of leaves secured by a band of leaves and twigs twisted into a circle. She handed it to Estrién.

'This arrived a few days ago sir, a *Lady* delivered it.' There was a distinct emphasis on the word lady, and it clearly had a capital L.

'What exactly do you mean?' Estrién was curious.

'Well ... she was odd sir, very odd. She was very, oh how can I put this, she wasn't *all there*, if you see what I mean.' Estrién started to laugh, she continued hurriedly, 'no, I don't mean you know, wanting or simple, no, I mean she wasn't *all there*. She looked normal, then she didn't, she was very beautiful, but sort of shimmering. I could almost see through her. She was very delicate, pale as the moon, and her voice was sweet as wine or - no, as sweet as the freshest water from a mountain stream.' Betsy stopped, surprised at herself, she didn't usually wax lyrical. 'She wasn't human or elf or even tree or water nymph, she was ... more like spirit. But she left me with that parcel there, said to give to *your hands only*, then she ... disappeared sir, and the next thing I saw was a beautiful doe running towards the forest. Fair took my breath away,' and she sat heavily down upon a finely carved chair by the cloaks' hooks as if to emphasise the point.

Estrién scratched the back of his head. 'A doe, you say ... hmm,' admiring the natural beauty of the small parcel.

'Yes, I think I do know, let me get my cloak off and take this to my study.'

He wondered, could it be, was it from him? He of the antlers and the golden torque? Yet he had said their paths would probably not cross again. He sat down at his desk and carefully removed the small parcel from its arboreal bracelet. He unwrapped the leaves, they smelled clean and wholesome; sycamore infused with pine and linden, cedar and lavender. Inside were two tiny saffron-yellow cakes, and a small sprig of sweet amber, still blooming with yellow flowers and the reddening fruit in the centre, fresh and bright as if full summer instead of deep winter. The leaves of sweet amber are cleansing and healing, often called heal-all, but the fruit turns black and is deadly.

Rather like Amber.

He understood, showed the gift to Amber. 'Will you come to the forest with me tonight, I think there is someone who would speak with ... thee.' He realised he spoke the old terminology, it seemed fitting. She nodded, of course, odd as it sounded, if Estrién wished this there would be a good reason.

Amber turned to the kitchens to organise meals with Betsy, twelve or more mouths to feed that night, depending who was currently working there. She ran into young Furbis, he was helping unload the cart.

'My, you've grown,' she exclaimed as the boy stood proudly. 'I see your ears have healed well, Betsy is clearly looking after you.' Furbis just smiled and ran inside with a sack of dried peas and lentils. He spoke only with Betsy and Tilly, answered the groom when spoken to, but was too shy to talk to anyone else, especially the Mistress of the house. He was happiest with the horses. Amber continued to the kitchens, the feeling that she had 'come home' ever present.

A quick inspection was due, part of her duty, Betsy wouldn't forgive her for not doing so.

Everything naturally was in order and immaculate, and praise was duly given. 'Hope we've brought enough supplies with us, we are likely only to be a few days. Can you do pies? They love pies.'

Betsy smiled, of course they loved pies, men always loved pies. Thank goodness the new mistress wasn't one of those fussy ones wanting plain boiled fish or fancy duck terrine. Men needed *real* food.

Later that night, when all were asleep, Amber and Estrién crept quietly out of the house towards the green glow inside the forest near his home. Amber knew a little of his last meeting, but he was unable to tell her everything, other than, 'I think he gave me some of his strength.' It was mostly a little hazy.

The land between the Hall and the forest lay white and pure, they left a trail of footsteps as they approached. Estrién knew he was correct in his assumption when he saw the white hare and the white doe, followed quickly by the silent white whippet, camouflaged against the snow as they ran. Were they part of some ritual, he asked himself? Whatever, the night hung silent, the frosted forest shimmered under a waxing snow moon and their breaths clouded the clear air.

There was no sound as their boots trod the crisp snow.

Amber glanced curiously at Estrién. 'What is ...?' she began, but he shushed her and put his fingers to her lips. Instead, he took her hand, beckoning her, moving slowly towards the strange green fire in the heart of the forest.

A figure approached, fleeting and iridescent, crystal gleaming, the snow lay rainbow around her as she moved.

As Amber approached, a fragile hand reached out, clasped hers. 'I wanted to talk to you,' she softly explained, guiding them both deeper into the forest.

He stood to greet them as they entered the grove, pale green with unearthly fire, his huge antlers reflecting the emerald flames. The snow was gone here, winter was banished, albeit temporarily, the air warm around them, yet there was no heat from the blazing fire. He nodded graciously to Estrién and bowed deeply to Amber. Both returned his greeting.

'Madam, I am happy to see thee.' He turned his stately head towards Estrién. 'I thank thee, my son, thou has done well. The counter-strike has begun. But thou has still much to do,' his gaze now turning to Amber, 'as I think thee knoweth.' For a few moments he studied her, then nodded. 'My wife speaks true, thou art of the blood, thee and thy sister.' He bowed again

Amber's eyes widened, 'my sister? What do you know of her, can you tell me anything?'

'Speak with my wife, she knows her, she keeps an eye on her. I and my kind have tried to protect her, we kept him away for some time. But he broke through the barriers and the deceptions, he found her. We have only been able to watch and support her since. We and the local inhabitants make sure she has food and supplies; we take care of her as she enters the forest or climbs the mountain paths in search of her dyes. We can keep her safe from everything ... except *him*.'

'You know where she is then? Tell me - I must find her.' Amber was distraught with worry.

'Speak then with my wife, she will take thee to her - but the question is, art thou ready? *He* will know as soon as thee finds her, and if thou art with the Wielder of Light,' his eyes briefly searched Estrién's, 'then *anything* can happen.'

He did not know Amber, he knew fully the worth of men, but his understanding of womankind was limited. He studied her again, taking in her essence. 'Thou art at the centre of this, Amber, thou art the magic that makes the weave. Others may wield the magic, but thee and thy kind create it. Thou art the beginning and the end and without thee, there is no tomorrow.' He stopped and spoke instead to Estrién. 'Take care of her, the future lies within.'

His wife reached out once more, took Amber aside, they spoke softly together, female to female, empathic and benevolent, gifting, giving and sharing. 'I will take thee to her,' she finally said, 'I will wait at the entrance to the forest tomorrow. Look for the doe, I will lead thee through. Come on foot though, there is little room for horses, and the path can be cruel.'

They were offered spiced mulled wine to warm them, the night was cold, a toast to the recent victory and to the uncertain future. Estrién hesitated, remembering the last time, but it was simply wine, blood red and rich. Once more pipes were played, sweet music through the forest, and the night creatures gathered round, cowering in corners at the great figure, but eager to hear, to enjoy the gentle rhythm.

Amber and Estrién walked slowly back to the Hall, it seemed a long distance, the moon lit their path. As they climbed into bed Estrién realised it was still early, or perhaps better to say the night was late.

No time at all had gone by.

*

She stood quivering by a holly bush, still red with berries bright against the snow, her pale flanks merging with the forest. The forest here, Shirewood-named by humans, was mostly mixed woodland, oaks and elms, shrubs of various kinds, a few firs dotted here and there. Right now it was devoid of leaves, rowans, ashes and whitebeams blended together indiscriminately. Mostly it was just white, only the holly stood green and clear. She munched on a crisp leaf as she waited.

She was afraid of humans and elves, or dwarves for that matter, not that there were many in the Foraes Dair. They were loud and brash, they cut down trees, hunted her kind, but then, they needed food, warmth and shelter, she forgave them. Worse though, they were so emotional, she could feel their excesses, it discomforted her. Anaïs on the other hand was gentle, such a sweet nature. She loved her, especially when she had thoughtfully put some hazelnuts out for her one winter, despite the young woman being hungry. She took them and pounded them into flour, made special cakes for her, left them as a gift. Young Anaïs only saw her in her doe form, or only acknowledged her as that. Perhaps she knew otherwise, for she knew so much, perhaps she also knew that it was her favourite form; four legs and a strong body gave her a freedom the other did not.

She had done her best to protect Anaïs; in normal times, this would have been enough. The doe was afraid of no beast, and the forest was her companion. But *him*.... no. He was not life, he destroyed life. Like those Adammites running through Oakleigh forest down in what the elves termed Elvinhaeme, she knew of them, she felt them. That was both her power and her weakness. If her husband was the sheer spirit of the land, then she was its heart, and hearts could be broken. She wept for Oakleigh, was glad that Dane had the power to mend it, he and his oaken staff were of the land. She thought she might like to meet him.

And here they were ... eight in all; the sister of Anaïs, stronger than Anaïs, firm and capable, her handsome and equally strong husband, the Wielder of Light, followed by their two companions, Dane the Mage and ... oh, he was laughing, his eyes bright and cheerful, Tamlyn ... did he know he was starlight and sunshine combined?

Behind him, yes, the kind older mage, he of water-and-willow, her nymph sisters told her of him, music-flowing, soothing, sleeping and gentleness. He brought the opposite to *him*, that savage reaper of souls, this one brought a quiet and peaceful end. He too was of the land.

A young woman then, she of the hawk, she knew of her, good hunts-woman yes, but fair, in all ways. Yes, she already knew her, an independent young woman, strong and kind. She maintained the balance.

Then, finally, two young men, clearly mages, the elements ran through them. They had yet to be formed, but the company they were in should keep them true.

Yes, she could accept these people, she would take them through. It was a long way to go, longer if you were uncomfortable with your company. Hmm, yes, a long way to go, and who knew what at the end of it?

Dane saw her as he was crossing the sloping no-man's land between Ravenscroft and the Foraes Dair. Or rather, he felt her, before he saw her, trepidation and concern, mixed with a gentle strength and deep courage. He understood, approached her carefully, reverentially, gave a deep bow and spoke gently.

'We thank thee ma'am, for thy kindness. Thou do us honour. We will try not to disturb your forest as we pass through, but we need to reach Amber's sister as soon as possible, as you well know.' He bent down on one knee, placed his oaken staff at her feet, he knew he must offer it to this ancient being of the forest.

For a few brief moments he saw her in her true form, pure spirit, bright and shining, she smiled upon him. Then she took human form, always difficult, not her natural self, but she needed to speak.

'Thank you Dane, I accept thy gift, truly of the forest, but return it to thee, for it belongs to thee. The tree from which it came is now gone, and those beings who killed it are under attack themselves. Yet, *he* controls them now, and *he* will be worse than his deputy, von Adamm. He is in his true state now, his strength growing daily, and his ultimate goal is to remove all life. The Adammites were just a means to an end, there to foment hate and anger, greed and lust on which he feeds and grows. I do not know how you combat those, but I do know this staff is best held in thy hands. Therefore I return it to thee, and remember, Dane, this staff bears the gift of life as well as death, balance in all things. Wield it well, Dane.'

She picked it up from the ground, handed it to him. He stood shocked as a clean and clear power passed from her to him through the staff. His eyes queried her.

She smiled benignly upon him, 'it holds the gift of growth, a gift from the Mother. Thou may find it has uses. But Dane ... these gifts are not from me, they were already given to thee by thy mage father and thy dryad mother. I have merely cleansed the staff so it is wholly thine and not of mages past. Thou will find it answers purely.'

Dane bowed once more, 'I thank thee, my Lady.'

She returned to her doe state, led them into the forest, the ancient Foraes Dair. The forest covered the land from north to south, held powers both good and evil, some of manners long forgotten, some sleeping, some yet to be born, a few like the awakening spirit in the Bard's Fells, best left untouched. The forest lived and died, grew and was cleared or harvested by the folk who lived there, something of an uneasy alliance, yet a beneficial one; people needed the forest and the forest needed tending or it would grow unchecked and choke itself.

She led them along paths known only to her and her kind, the secret ways of the forest. They walked solemnly through the grove where just the night before a great fire had blazed, a fire without heat. Estrién and Amber gazed in wonder for there were no signs of the fire, just an empty space in the centre, no sign even of the large logs upon which they sat. The snow lay pristine, but a few white and green snowdrops bowed their heads, the first taste of spring-to-come. The doe was saddened however; spring would be late this year, for *he* held it back. His very presence was an abomination to nature.

The forest here was quiet, most creatures tucked up for winter, snoozing quietly through snow-chilled days and icy nights. Some would not make it to spring, would sleep into oblivion, more this year than previously. Still, there was movement around them, a few red foxes scampering close, not particularly interested in them but her, the doe. They were blessed by her presence. She whispered her way through, treading carefully, for ought could be under the snow and she would harm nothing. She did not tell the others, but she felt uneasy, not because of the somewhat garrulous and noisy races surrounding her who often seemed to chatter for no reason at all, for they were quite quiet and respectful of her. No, the forest here - and perhaps all of it now - was perhaps a little *too* quiet. She caught a glimpse of yellow and black eyes peering at them through undergrowth, felt a shiver as something - she wasn't sure what - and that alone was uncomfortable for she should know - slithered its way through soft snow.

A little further in and the silent forest was suddenly pierced by a loud and raucous caw as a carrion crow took off from the top of a stately cedar, its velvet black wings shaking snow from the bobbing branch. She shook, trembling along her flank, her uneasiness growing. This forest was now filled with spies, that was certain, for she knew not the crow.

Why should she feel so alien in her own forest?

Then she felt not one, but two hands caressing her doe-form, gently soothing her. Calming magic from Dane's hand fluttered along her spine and the other one, the bright one, Tamlyn, he tenderly stroked her, sweetly soft and reassuring.

'We are with thee, be not afraid. It is our job to protect,' he whispered. It was kind of them, yet she did not tremble with fear, but the imbalance around her and the pain of the forest became hers. She was far stronger than they knew, had powers they could not guess, but it was good of these people to care. She longed for spring to burst forth in all its glory, the full weight of growth and fertility to push back the growing darkness in the land, the rising sap to stir and enervate.

Let the dance begin!

One day she would look up at a hilltop and there he would be, her husband in all his glory, proud and strong. She would rush to greet him, her heart filled with happiness and expectation, then a mad chase of joy, the breath of life in their nostrils, hearts bound in bliss, a wind's dash to renew and reinvigorate the land.

And spring would come.

Soon, my husband, soon. But it would be later this year, for the cold seeped strong.

She led them deeper into the Foraes Dair, always moving north and east when she could, found a small clearing where they could camp for the night. She left them, she would not sleep among them, but assured them she would return on the morrow. 'Be up as dawn breaks, for we must waste no time,' she warned them. Then, in the wink of an eye, she was gone.

The group were silent as they set up camp, the snow thin on the rocky ground here, a canopy of green fir above them. Dane set to drying twigs and dead branches, made a small cheering fire for everyone. Tents were erected, Amber set up her cooking spit and two cook pots - easier to carry two than one large, since they were on foot. Soon a warming meal was ready, but it was a quiet meal, everyone busy with their own thoughts. The gentle doe they had followed was clearly the heart of the forest, they were sensible of the honour she gave them. But they all knew the heart was troubled, her sorrow was theirs.

It touched Tamlyn more than anyone, his home was the forest, always would be. He loved Ravenscroft because it was just inside his beloved Foraes Dair, the main bulk of the forest mere metres away. He felt the doe's pain.

He took out his small lute, always carried it now, a fine sabre at his belt and a lute on his back; Tamlyn: warrior, lover and troubadour in one. He played a gentle tune, *'in este Foraes honorum,' an* ode to the forest, he told them. Its soothing harmonies drifted on the wind.

'I tread thee softly, forest fair,
I breathe the incense of thy air.
I lift my eyes to Foraes Dair,

My home lies there

From root to tip of forest fair,
From elven babe to rook and hare
Mother-fed by Foraes Dair,
My home lies there.

No foe shall harm thee, forest fair
Nor shall they of thy bounty share
I raise my sword for Foraes Dair
My home lies there

I am the blood of forest fair
Leafling-born and raised with care
I give my love to Foraes Dair,
My heart lies there,
My heart lies there'

Amber softly kissed Tamlyn as the delicate sound of his lute trailed away. 'That was beautiful dear, but I don't understand. If the title is in Elvhen, why are the words in Plaintongue?'

His laughing eyes danced at her. 'Because the words just came to me liefl'en, and I felt the need to sing them. I tend to think in Elvhen, but I have been with you all long enough that sometimes Plaintongue is closer to me, certainly closer to my heart.' He smiled softly, took her hand, brushed his lips against the back of it, then turned her hand over and gently kissed the palm.

He did not know that the doe was close by, sheltering under a fir for the night, keeping a protective eye upon them. Nor could he see the tear that formed in an eye, nor the peace that came to her heart, the heart of the forest.

*

The land rose as they travelled eastwards, the doe followed a river, Clement by name, clement by nature, its source the icy but refreshing waters from the tips of the mysterious Greylumings. It ran clean and clear through the forest, bubbled and laughed according to the season, silver fish flashed and flickered through its waters, for it was rich with food. The banks of the river too were fertile, even now as the group softly trod its course.

Dane, as usual, was on the lookout for potential herbs or medicinal plants, he noticed a few hellebores growing, white heads with yellow stamens, sometimes a pink variety, good as a purgative, and a few shoots and leaves of wild garlic were pushing their way to life. But mostly the forest was damp and dismal, ferns and flora, what was once bright yellow and purple iris down by the water, all reduced to slushy brown fronds. As they moved further in, the snow cleared and the ground became heavy mud, hard going and unexpectedly treacherous in places. Dane's foot went through the pink heather he had trod upon, up to his knee in mud and a sharp pain as he twisted his ankle.

'Damn and blast'!' he shouted, the sound ringing through the forest, as he dragged himself across to a large stone, pulled off his boot and massaged his ankle. He tried shooting healing light into it, but it's hard for a mage to heal himself. Salli bent down, touched his leg with his wand, soothing the aches. Took out fine linen bandages, wrapped them tightly around the ankle. 'Keep it straight and tread carefully,' he told him.

They continued following the doe, as she wound her way past the river banks, a wide detour around a water-logged meadow through a gap between trees. It was there again, the few bubbles told her as it slid and slinked its way through the slime. Neither was it alone, there were other bubbles rising, more slithers and slipping, somethings eel-like, coiling and curling, hissing through the shallow and foetid water.

Whatever they were, they were *his*. The doe shuddered, these were not natural, but infestation, parasites in her land. They would feed and take, but give no return; poisoning as they went; only their death and decomposition would nourish the land, and to be sure, she wasn't even certain of that. Like their master, they were not of the weave.

Only fire would purify, the Adammites said that, but somehow, the Adammites had besmirched the cleansing properties of fire, misappropriating its nature. Still, she wondered, perhaps somewhere in their psyche they had understood; fire, that first tool of mankind, symbol of both life and death, they merely ignored the balance.

Whatever the case, she knew this, if these infestations were not destroyed they would multiply and devour her land, they would impoverish the soil and infect the waters. The natural wildlife would die from starvation, just as the elder races were dying at the hands of the Adammites.

He was slowly taking control.

There was one bright ray of hope in the darkening world, as King Alexis brought home his Queen. They rode into Orlandium in a carriage borrowed from Lord Black, the carriage spacious with long open windows for the royal family to be seen by the welcoming crowds. The child, Anna'laeth waved ecstatically at everyone; her innocent smile charmed them all.

At first, Neria had considered wearing a wide hat or cap to cover her mutilated ears. She discussed it with Alexis.

'I'm ashamed of my ears now, my love, those people have deformed me. Yet, I do believe if I hide them, I've let those devils win. On the other hand, I don't wish to scare the children, or see the looks of pity in people's eyes.'

Alexis looked on her, both pride and pity in his own eyes. 'Darling, you bear the scars of war; you have taken punishment from those bastards for no reason whatsoever but their own cruel pleasure. You were brave and strong, my love, and you did your best to protect our daughter. I say, let the world see what they did, let them understand the savagery of those Adammites. Yes, people will stare and will pity, but that is natural and it only shows a love for you, a kindness in their hearts.'

His wife nodded, accepting, yes, she would ride in with her clipped ears bare for them all to see. She would also leave them bare if there were meetings with officials, but she thought a light cotton cap, a few frills around, would be best indoors normally. It would comfort her, people's stares would be hard to take on a daily basis, and the tips, or what was left of them, were often sore. Humans just did not clearly understand the delicacy of elven ears, even her loving husband.

'Do as you wish my dear,' he replied. 'I know whatever you choose, it will be the right thing. I'm just relieved to have you home and safe by my side.'

And so she sat in the borrowed royal carriage, waving at her people, smiling and cheerful as they returned home. There were many looks of pity that day, some were shocked, but all understood the bravery of the woman.

It only made them love their queen all the more.

Chapter 6

Foraes Dair, northern Floriénne, month of Icefall.

Kielan reigned in his horse, then made quietly for cover behind a group of firs. There was a sound he did not like, a sound alien to the forest. The Foraes Dair here in the northern region was well tended, typically Floriénne, well kept, wide pathways and bridleways suitable for horses or the odd carriage, deciduous on the lower slopes turning coniferous as the land rose. Small villages peeped through the trees, a large clearing signified a market traded here every few weeks, it was clean but the ruts of wagons could be seen in the soft winter ground. These were managed woods where people lived and lived well, the Sylvanii. To all intents and purposes, here in the south west of Mer'edrynn, the woods were safe and secure.

People like Knight Captain Kielan Penlachl'en patrolled them daily. A Courtier knight, yet expected to spend part of his time patrolling the forest, keeping peace, making note of problems, taking care of the odd wild beast that ventured so far south, wolves, boars and such. He, like Tamlyn was expert with both sabre and bow, a fine horseman and very often, also similar to Tamlyn, something of a poet and singer. The strange idiosyncrasy of Floriénne elves was in him, beautiful in form, beautiful by nature, but deadly in spirit.

He had a tendency to sing a hymn to the fallen as he killed - whether it on the hunt for game - in which he excelled, the death of a fierce and troublesome bear, or the demise of an enemy. Like most elves of Floriénne he wore elven braids in his flaxen hair, his deep green eyes were filled with pleasure as well as a little sharpness, his lips were both sensual and strong. The sharp black and silver doublet of the Dair Chev'al suited him well, the armour designed as much for style as purpose. It looked well at Court.

Unfortunately, it was not chosen for a deal of protection.

The sabre cat came at him before he could respond, swift and silent, pouncing with the kind of leap only a such a cat can spring.

Kielan's horse reared as a talon raked through leather leggings, a fortunate occurrence, for it allowed the rider to kick back quickly. The next spring was directly to the horse however, a massive bite to the neck, and the horse dropped, a horrible jagged gash through its throat. Kielan jumped off, his leg in agony, scrambled as he could while blood from the gaping rent in both leggings and flesh poured over leather boots.

He managed to take out his sabre before the cat sprang again, slashed and hacked at the hide of the beast. It jumped him, teeth biting straight through the padded leather arm of his doublet, he felt flesh go and a bone break. A talon reached up and slashed his cheek, more blood flowed. He grunted and shoved, the hot breath of the tiger in his nostrils, he pulled his head back, desperately trying to pull away from the creature. With an almighty effort, he pushed the sabre-toothed tiger off his body, giving him barely enough time to aim for the cat's neck. His own sabre sliced sharply through the throat of the sabre cat, as more talons clawed through leather armour and raked down his chest.

Kielan was dripping with blood, one eye part closed where the cat had lacerated his cheek, the feral cat smelled blood and was in a frenzy.

So was Kielan, life for a life, his own or the cat's; he lifted his agonised arm and one more desperate but well aimed slash with the lethal blade put paid to the sabre cat. It dropped in front of him, warm blood welling up, spurting on what was left of his ripped armour as it died. For a moment, the moment of relief, he understood what his ancestors of old must have felt, bloodied by the blood of the prey, a prey more lethal than any game he had quarried in the Foraes Dair.

'A sabre for the sabre,' he softly sang, although the words were Elvhen, *'bloodied in battle, beaten in field. Sharpest of steel 'gainst sharpest of claws, neither would yield.'*

Then he collapsed, his own life blood staining the battle ground as red as the tiger's.

The villagers came to help now, the small and peaceful elven village close by. They had watched in horror as the knight was attacked, yet helpless themselves to aid. They took his almost lifeless body to the nearest home, tended his wounds, let him sleep. He was alive, just, but it was unlikely the Knight's Captain would be able to bear arms again, certainly not shoot a bow.

Then they went back to the clearing where the cat had pounced upon both fallen horse and the knight. They looked on in horror at the great beast.

There were no sabre toothed tigers in Mer'edrynn. They had been extinct for over a thousand years.

*

The Dûchesse looked down with sadness upon what had once been a beautiful knight. The scars of battle held no honour or glory for her, she merely saw a badly disfigured face. Kielan was alive, talking, chatting even, glad to speak of his adventure with his admiring fellow knights; they patted him on the shoulder, cheered him and brought gifts of good cognac and fresh grapes. Tamlyn's own father sent a case of rich sweet red wine, fortified with herbs, *'to help strengthen him and cheer his convalescence,'* the accompanying note said.

But the Dûchesse was hard and unyielding. True, he had beaten a sabre-toothed tiger - she wouldn't have believed it if they hadn't brought the cat back for examination - but still, the scars would remain. It would not suit her Court at all. She considered pensioning him off, or no perhaps giving him the charge of a troop she was preparing to send to Westerling to help King Alexis against the Adammites in Elvinhaeme.

Yes, that would probably be kinder; true, he was rather young, but he was intelligent and now was probably useless as a warrior, command would suit him, and it was clear he would be a hero in the eyes of the young elves.

She congratulated Kielan on his bravery, his victory against the fierce creature and his miraculous escape from death.

'Not miraculous, Your Grace, strength, the utilisation of skills taught me by our own fine swordsmen, and a good sword served me well. I am only sorry about the loss of my poor horse,' he replied modestly.

She nodded, sympathetic, wondering if there was a good mage around who might heal the thickly ridged scars? Even so, some would still remain; they were very deep, bone deep. 'We will provide a fresh horse for you, my warrior,' she offered. 'I have a suggestion, if you would care to think on it. It will be some time ... if ever... before you gain back your old fighting skills.' The knight nodded, smiled ruefully and a little lopsidedly. She continued, 'I need someone to command a group to join King Alexis' troops, someone brave like yourself for you will face the Adammites of Elvinhaeme, not in the front line, but rather to organise and help prepare the campaign.' She had no one in mind for the position in any case, her Knights worked usually in small patrol groups, not battle armies. 'You organised the troop that helped at Pennyport, you probably have as much experience as any,' she continued.

The young knight lay back on comfortable pillows, he was exhausted from loss of blood, his broken arm and he would probably limp the rest of his life. He knew his left arm was practically useless, unless the mages could help, but he didn't wish his fighting days to be over. Neither did he wish to see his face in the mirror, but that was another matter.

Like Tamlyn, he still felt he had a need to prove himself.

'I would be honoured, your Grace,' he replied. She bowed and left, grateful that he had still a reason to be among her warriors, but glad he would not be shocking her Court. She would award some bravery medal, they always liked that kind of thing, he could wear it with honour.

Knight Commander Kielan Penlachl'en sent out to the libraries for books on military history and famous campaigns - pretty old ones at that, for there had been none in hundreds of years. Still, they were something to read during his convalescence.

*

He wasn't the only one to find wild and ferocious beasts in the more northern parts of Floriénne's Foraes Dair. The small village of Muilefloré, famous for its mulberry trees, was attacked by marauding wolves one night, including possibly two werewolves. There were few archers here, spinners and weavers all, for the trees were the home of the silk moth. The werewolves, berserk with madness and ferocity, brought about by who knew what ill magic, tore down the trees, gnawed and clawed the trunks, killed several of the villagers.

The elves did their best to defend themselves against these beings, their screams eventually heard by two patrolling Dair Chev'al officers. They galloped to the scene, but the pack had gone, taking with them a child and a young man, their screams rending the air as they were taken. The village gave chase, lost them in the forest, the two horsemen searched for days, found a trail of blood that led to nowhere and only gave up when it was clear the trail had disappeared deep into the thick tangle of the wildwood.

Three of the villagers had been bitten by the wolves, they were afraid - would they be infected with this terrible disease too? The Dair Chev'al left to find healing mages, hoping they would know something about wereblood. As Estrién had said previously - werewolves had not been heard of in centuries, or even if they ever actually existed outside of tales.

*

Further north-east, deeper into the forest, but still within the boundaries of Floriénne, a young boy and girl enjoyed a snowball fight in the cold morning. There had been a flurry of snow the previous night, rarely seen in Floriénne; it had to be a damn cold winter for snow. The children were up bright and early to take advantage, build a small snow-elf - carrots for nose *and* ears - then enjoy hurling tiny snowballs at each other.

'Ha, that's three hits for me, I win,' the boy shouted triumphantly to his sister. She pulled a face at him, then threw a snowball back right into his face. He fell, laughing, before pulling himself up, brushed himself down and carried on, two snowballs in quick succession.

As his mother came out to call them in for breakfast, he heard a strange whirring noise, the sound of many wings flapping together, a cackle and a caw, shrieks and screams of a mass of flying birds. The two children and their mother watched the skies in horror as they turned black with flying creatures.

A massive battle was happening above them, rooks, starlings, blackbirds and several magpies, fighting in a ferocious mid-air battle against ravens, gulls, buzzards and sparrow hawks. Where the gulls - huge grey and white gannets - had come from was anyone's guess, perhaps they followed the rivers northwards through the forest?

The elf girl screamed as a black crow dropped at her feet, bloodied and lifeless, then the garden seemed filled with dead black-feathered bodies, the white snow staining pink.

The mother wasted no more time, what was up there could come down, possibly attack them. She grabbed her children and hurried them inside, then dashed outside to close the wooden shutters as an extra precaution; the thin leaded glass would not be much protection against such a mass. As she wrestled with the catch of the shutter - she'd only opened them to let a little winter sunshine in - one gull swooped down to attack her. She screamed in pain as it bit the back of her neck. She tried to brush it off, but its claws were in her hair, scratching her scalp, blood already oozing.

The young boy heard his mother cry, saw her frightened face at the window and ran outside. Quick thinking, he bent down and gathered snow into his hands, beating and moulding it into a small but lethal snowball before throwing it at the gull. It did not harm it, but it startled it, when a second hit it in the eye, it had enough and flew off. The grateful mother ran inside with her son, slammed shut the door, proud and thankful of her little hero. She hoped her husband, deeper in the forest at his craft's table in the small cabin he used to store wood, was indoors and safe.

They waited until the shrieking noises above moved on and the air was quiet before they peeped outside. The garden was thick with dead birds, a mix of species, both sides of the battle. She took a large brush, swept the bodies into a pile at the edge of the garden, her husband could burn them when he returned. It was a nasty, unwholesome sight

She had seen brief battles in the air before when birds flew into other bird's territory, trespassing on their tree top homes, the larger species acting as guards, shooing away the intruders, the smaller birds safely flying around the outside calling courage upon the bigger and braver.

But she had never seen anything like this, so many, so fierce, nor so many deaths. Like many others, she wondered what was happening to her world?

Throughout Shirewood, or the Foraes Dair as it is called by the elves, similar battles were taking place. Many birds and beasts had gone over, not whole species, but nevertheless, enough to cause havoc among the creatures of the woods.

He looked on with pleasure, the forest pulsated with life, he wanted it dead. Now, during the lean times, the quiet of the year before it fully awoke for spring, when the smaller animals still slept, or were slowly awakening, weak and hungry, now was the time to attack.

The destruction of Shirewood would be a superb victory against this land.

*

Further north in the Foraes Dair, much further north, where the forest is known as Shirewood, three elderly maiden sisters peered through the ill-fitting windows of the large, but ramshackle cottage they called home. It was built of stone, had been well made, originally, but had pretty much disintegrated over the decades, mostly due to lack of care. Doors and windows rattled in their holes, bits of masonry fell off on a regular basis thanks to sharp northern winds and rain, several shutters were nailed up closed, others hanging off, and one room was permanently closed off thanks to a gaping hole in the roof. The entrance gate in the front wall was also decidedly squiffy.

The chimneys however were well swept, warm fires kept blazing at all times of year in the main rooms and the gardens were immaculate. The sisters were excellent gardeners, grew plenty of vegetables, fruit and herbs, '*for a variety of purposes*' as they put it.

They eked out a living in the deep wildwood as people occasionally sought them out for healing potions, a few poisons for garden pests, and the odd, and most lucrative, 'Lottie's Special Mix,' a herbal/fungal mixture with decidedly hallucinogenic properties. Certain mushrooms grew very well in their damp cellars.

Dane's herbal rollies were tame by comparison.

Anny, Lottie and Em had spent the morning with irons in the fire, curling their somewhat sparse locks, in case customers, guests or 'suitors' came around. They rarely did, but it wouldn't be polite to look a dishevelled mess, although Lottie was happy to merely tie hers straight back into a stiff bun. The sitting room held the delicate aroma of singed hair as well as the highly spiced ham stew they were having for lunch. The ham was a bit old, so near to winter's end, the fat a bit whiffy, and the spices covered up the strong flavour. It was still edible, just about, and the sisters had steel stomachs in any case, especially if a few glasses of usquebae were knocked back before, during and after the meal.

They weren't exactly good cooks, but the way they looked at it, throw in a few spices and preferably as much alcohol as possible, then *anything* became edible.

Anny wondered if she should pop a little of her homemade dandelion cordial (60 percent proof) into the stew? Anny was a very good alchemist, it was smooth stuff, would probably kill off anything nasty. Killed off taste buds too. She looked patiently out at the whitened garden, still snow here, it was the rainy month - where was the rain 'to thaw the frozen lakes again?' she wondered. She wondered a lot, thought, considered, pondered. She was the quiet one of the three.

Em took the curling tongues out of her thinning - and greying - hair. The youngest of the three, she patted her hair coquettishly as she watched the path outside carefully, still hopeful of a suitor. One might turn up ... one day. She rather hoped he would be handy with hammer and nails, the house so desperately needed it. Or rich, preferably rich. Rich would be good.

Lottie, the eldest, sighed with displeasure, she wanted to get outside and get that garden turned over for spring, perhaps dig in some pig manure, there was plenty out in the shed, and the midden had rotted down nicely, add to the mix. Her strong and stout leather boots were sitting waiting patiently by the door for her eventual use. But the garden was frozen, bloody annoying. She placed her hands on ample hips and grumbled to her sisters.

'Spring's effing late!' Her sisters nodded agreement, no need to reply, Lottie did all the talking in any case. 'I'll never get my potatoes planted - and those bloody cabbages are rotting out there.'

None of them actually liked cabbage, but they grew well in the garden, so Lottie always planted them. The young spring greens were supposed to go awfully well with young spring lamb, if you liked that kind of thing. They slurped up the lamb with delight, then dutifully stuffed their mouths with cabbage for the sole reason 'it did you good'.

At that moment, Lottie dreamed of eating a nice bit of tender young lamb, but as she so accurately put it, spring was late, or rather winter was still holding on well. *Icefall* had turned into *Shroving,* time to get sowing, or at least digging, but there was snow on the ground and ice cold winds that chilled you to the bone.

It was the time of year when you think spring is so close, just around the corner, and the odd fine sunny day with a touch of warmth in the air fools you into throwing off that sad old woolly cardi you've been wearing for months as you dash out into late winter sunshine.

Then catch a chill.

Well, the sun was there this morning, but no warmth, Lottie looked out at the one lone daffodil bravely rearing its head in the corner of the garden and decided they were 'a waste of bloody space.' She might as well have planted onions there, but Em liked a few bright flowers. Personally, she thought Em was a bit of a softy, but hey ho, Em was her sister, blood kin and all that, wouldn't do for everyone to be the same, would it?

Still, if the sun stayed out a little longer it might thaw out that garden a bit, she could get on with some digging.

She heard Em give a loud gasp as she threw open the window and craned her neck to see out. Lottie therefore did likewise, saw the group of people walking along the path through the forest, just south-west of the cottage.

Hmm, quite a large group, mixed elf, human and definitely mages.

They were following a beautiful doe.

Em hurried to the door and rushed outside. 'Oh, you dear people, you look icy cold, do come and enjoy something hot with us,' she gushed. Hospitality was expected in these out of the way places, and Em took advantage of every wayfarer that passed. She loved giving parties.

By the time you had been questioned thoroughly about every aspect of your life, the latest news from the city, what the new fashions were and what the latest gossip was, a traveller had definitely paid for his lunch.

She gazed at the doe, who was watching her expectantly, Em was unsure how to address her, something a little odd there ... 'I think we have some nuts,' she said finally, 'we have plenty of cabbage and there's fresh milk from the cow ...?' Frankly, she had no idea what to offer, but offer she must. She felt rather silly talking to a doe and yet ...

She almost collapsed when the doe briefly turned into a human female, began laughing and replied, 'that is kind of you, but I have no need of anything, thank you,' her eyes twinkling. For one moment she smiled into Em's eyes, the smile more delightful than any Em had ever seen. A small blessing passed from her to the human, a warmth unlike anything Em had known.

'*Oh* ...' stammered Em.

Anny merely stared thoughtfully, both at the doe and her two-legged followers. She noticed a hawk hovering close by, it had odd markings. She made no comment.

'Humph!' snorted Lottie, taking in the situation, 'we've only got some plain fare, end-of-season stuff, you'll have to make do.' She wasn't having any fuss made here. 'But you're welcome to join us,' she finished, remembering her manners; visitors were guests and should be treated accordingly. You turned no one away out here in the wildwood.

Estrién, Amber, Tamlyn, Reave and the four mages were glad of the welcome, they had been travelling for many long days now, the cold forest hard going. Game was sparse here, besides they didn't really like to hunt in the presence of the doe, they existed mostly off fish when there was a river, a few berries and the remaining dried beans and pulses they carried. Estrién spoke on everyone's behalf.

'Thank you for your invitation. We have been travelling for some time, searching for my wife's sister, who is missing. Supplies are now getting low and we would be glad of your hospitality.' He was good at formal stuff. 'We understand however that at this time of year your own supplies are equally low, but if we could just use your barns or stables for a night, it would be preferable to sleeping in tents. We still have quite a journey to go, or so we believe. Tents are not the warmest of shelter at this time of year.' He smiled encouragingly, he had a lovely smile.

'Nonsense!' returned Lottie gruffly, eyeing her sisters. 'We have a couple of spare rooms, if you don't mind bunking down for the night.' She counted the number of males in the party - six of them, all armed one way or another. She always protected her sisters. 'But just a warning ...' She moved over to the fireplace in the sitting room, took the large double-headed war-axe down from the wall, went back to the door and brandished it in the air. 'No funny business, OK? I'm pretty good with this and well prepared to use it.'

They could easily believe her.

It was no wonder poor Em was still single.

Tamlyn hastily came to the fore, spoke in his gentle and gallant way, his best Court smile playing his pleasant features. 'Madam, or perhaps, I should say Miss?' he smiled again then carried on, 'I am Knight Captain Tamlyn Taenghelin of the Court of Floriénne, more recently of the esteemed group now known as the White Shield, it would be an honour to enjoy your hospitality and we would be delighted to use the rooms you have offered. We are in sore need of a good night's sleep under a proper roof, and thank you wholeheartedly. I give you my word as a true Knight, we shall cause you neither trouble nor offence.' He bowed his head.

'Hmm, fancy speech, typical elf ...' Lottie began, but then she relented as she watched the fern green eyes twinkling and laughing. Why did he have such big eyes, she wondered ... and those bloody long lashes...? 'Well, come in then, and wipe your feet ... all of you,' she replied gruffly.

Eight people walked gratefully into the big warm and comfortable sitting room of Harefax Cottage, every one of them making for the cheering fire.

Em and Anny dashed into the kitchen to put the kettle on the hob and to turn off the stew. They didn't want their guests suffering from food poisoning. Cheeses, bread and pickles were hurriedly brought out, the guests took turns toasting the bread in front of the fire. Anny found overwintered apples with the least brown spots to offer her guests. There weren't that many, so she chopped them into quarters and added some nuts to make a more wholesome plateful. It was a bad time of year for guests. Lottie offered some home-made ale, brewed just a couple of weeks previously. Like most home brews, it was pretty strong.

It turned into a very convivial afternoon, the three sisters learnt much of the 'war effort' as they put it, gave the travellers a few tips as to what to do with those scandalous Adammites and Anny took the four mages off to her distillery when they expressed a real delight in her Dandelion Cordial.

Later, all guests enjoyed a little of the Lottie's Special Mix, and it became an even more convivial evening, lasting into the early hours of the morning as Tamlyn played his lute (when he wasn't dancing with Em), Salli his flute (when he wasn't dancing with Em) and Reave her tambourine (she didn't dance with Em). Gertie the Hawk stayed in the barn, enjoying a few mice sheltering from the snow.

Em had the night of her life dancing with every male in the party. Even Lottie was persuaded, by Tamlyn of course, to join in the dancing.

Estrién, Tamlyn, Amber and Dane took one of the, admittedly rather damp spare rooms, the three mages the other, and Reave was offered a comfortable bed on the sofa by the warm fire.

And the following morning, the group took time out of their journey to fix the draughty doors, windows and shutters, chop up some logs for the fire, straighten the squiffy front gate and for the mages to easily haul tiles up to fix the leaky roof. Dane even warmed a big patch of garden for Lottie with gentle fire magic. She actually smiled.

Anny gave them a large bottle of Dandelion cordial to take on their journey, Lottie offered a little of her Special Mix, giving the mages strict instructions on its use, and Em gave them a big bag of currant buns to help them on their way.

Three sisters watched their guests depart, each sighing heavily as they left. It had been one of the loveliest nights they'd known, and each felt proud that they had finally done something to help, as they termed it, 'the War Effort'.

Em watched long as they walked away, her elderly hand waving still, even after they were out of sight.

*

The paths wove and wound through the ever-changing landscape of Shirewood. They crossed a hill, then down through a valley with a gushing river and across the most rickety bridge they had ever seen. Ahead the forest grew thickly, pine trees shuffled for space.

The doe felt them before she saw them, those perverted creatures *he* had created. She stepped into the thick forest, firs all around, little light underneath and it was a dark day, rain threatening. The forest felt wrong, very wrong.

Then the stench hit them, rotten and malevolent, mind choking filth, so bad it made you dizzy, wanted to heave. Everyone began coughing and spluttering, eyes watering. Now they could see them, writhing and slipping, sliding around the branches of the pines, choking and strangling. The doe saw one, a foot long greenish-black creature something that was neither snake nor worm, a cross between eel and leech, little suckers that clung to the branch, pointed tail waving and curling below. She looked on in horror as it spat a putrid pus-green slime onto the pine needles. She realised all the branches in the forest were dying, many eaten by the over-sized worm-creatures.

Several dropped on to Reave's head. She screamed and shook it, grabbed at the over-sized worms and threw them on to the ground, stamping and shouting. 'What the hell are they?' she cried.

They all stepped back, out of the trees, the smell under them was abominable, but it seemed confined to the forest itself.

Everyone was taking in breaths of air, clearing their lungs.

'Dear Goddess!' exclaimed Amber. 'That's unbelievable; it smells like a cesspit has exploded over rotten eggs and vomit.'

Estrién stepped back close to the trees, he seemed to be listening. He looked green when he finally returned, stood aside and was promptly sick. He took out a bottle of usquebae from his pack, drank swiftly, wiped his mouth. 'Sorry about that, that smell is poisonous.' He sighed, shaking his head. 'Tried communing with them, pointless of course, they are all mindless, all I gathered was eat and sleep, no other reason for being. That pus softens the pine needles.' He looked ill, never encountered anything like them.

Briefly the doe turned human, nodded her head. 'They have no place in my forest,' she replied, 'they are not of my world.' For a few moments she entered the forest, stood quietly before returning, shaking a clinging wriggling form off her pale gold hair. She spoke sadly, 'they bring death to my home - all other beasts are gone or lie dead, and there are no birds. They feast too on dead carcases, parasites all.'

Dane shot fire at the beast as it dropped to the floor, watched as it writhed and blackened. He too was saddened, always concerned for his beloved woods. 'Come spring they'll be at the deciduous trees too as the young leaves come out, the oaks and elms will go. They have to be destroyed.'

The others looked at him. Tamlyn asked, 'how? They've infested a whole forest from the looks of it,'

'We'll have to fire the forest - there's no other way, but we must keep it from getting out of hand. There are small copses close by and many shrubs, bushes. Then they stretch into a much larger section of the Foraes Dair, can't let it spread. How far does this particular section of woods stretch?'

The Lady studied the forest ahead of her before replying. 'About half a mile, probably a couple of miles wide, then gaps. But there is more forest behind, we do not know how that is,' she replied. *How much of my forest is destroyed*, she thought, or worse, *how much will I have to destroy*?

'My Lady, if it has to be, then it has to be. We have to sacrifice a part so the infestation does not spread to the whole. My problem is how do we contain it?' Dane had no wish to burn the whole Foraes Dair. He wished he had more mages with him. 'Trevaine and Robson are elementalists like me, they can help set fire to the forest, but it will take a huge amount of mana to fire it, it's pretty damp at this time of year, even if they are pines. It's been snowing on and off for months. There'd be little left to contain it once it catches and it would only leave Salli to somehow provide a watery ring fence around a large area.

'Is there no other way,' asked Amber, 'can we poison them?'

Dane and the other mages shook their heads. 'Can't leave anything of them, they are pure poison themselves, their remains will just kill more life. Dammit, those are resinous pines, they're antiseptic and these blasted creatures are feeding off them - and they still smell like that! No, it has to be fire, but I only want to burn that which is necessary.'

'Leave the fire part to me,' suggested Reave, 'perhaps with Amber and Tamlyn. We can shoot flaming arrows into the forest, make it catch fire. You mages can use your ice and water skills to contain the fire as it reaches the outer edges.'

The Lady of the Forest nodded, 'good thinking Reave, and I can help too. We cannot allow the whole forest to go up at once, it would spread beyond itself, but we can perhaps do a section at a time.' Surprised looks from all, how did you fire merely a part of a forest? 'I can direct the flames with wind. I cannot stand outside the forest and make the wind keep it contained inside, for the wind cannot blow in every direction at once, but I can go to the very centre of the forest, ensure the wind blows the flames towards you. If I guide the wind in small arcs, like a cone, you can contain the fire as it reaches the outer edge, and we can circle our way around the trees.'

'Won't you be harmed?' asked a very worried Tamlyn.

'No, I can use my doe form to escape the fire should it turn back towards me, believe me, I run swift, for I am no ordinary doe. That does not worry me. As for those oversized larvae ... that's another matter, I have no idea ... but it is my forest and my land. I cannot allow this infestation to continue.' She had said everything she needed to say, she turned back into the doe form, looked sadly upon the looming forest.

Salli looked thoughtful. 'Give me a moment,' he said, marching off across the valley to the water course in its centre. Like Estrién, he was seen to pause, to stand thoughtfully, his hands held out in soundless entreaty. After a few minutes he returned.

'I spoke to the river spirits, there are a few water nymphs hidden down there, I explained the situation. They were already aware, many afraid of the creatures in the trees. But they desire to help you, my Lady. They have agreed to detour the river, at least keep this end, the south-western end of the forest fire confined. It will help.'

Estrién watched his group, all ready to help. Again, he was proud of them their combined ingenuity, their multi-skilled ability. Yet he wondered what he could do, his sword was of no real use against such a foe, and he was no bowman. He decided to cut down a clean pine branch, if he could find one, go into the forest with the doe, use it to sweep the elongated worm things from her, they would surely drop on her. He placed his hood over his head, tightened it, went back to the trees and looked for suitable branch on the very outskirts. He lopped a branch with White Star, shook it vigorously, then came back.

'I'll go with you my Lady; keep them off you with this.'

Dane looked up quickly, 'don't be stupid, you'll be poisoned, that stink is lethal.' He stopped to think. 'Perhaps I can make a cleansing potion for you to drink, keep it by you, something fresh, blood-purifying. Give me a moment.'

He too went back down to the river, filled his small teapot, came back and searched in his pack for herbs. A quick flash of fire and the brew boiled, he let it stand for some minutes, before pouring it into Estrién's half full bottle of usquebae, the two could work together. 'Drink it if you feel dizzy or very sick, but come back out when you can, that stink is probably cumulative, it could knock you out, possibly kill you.'

Estrién nodded, thankful.

Amber rummaged through her pack, came out with a silk scarf. 'Tie this around your mouth and nose,' she offered. Dane took it from her, poured a few freshening oils on it, passed it to Estrién.

'Best we can do - don't stay in there too long though.'

Estrién took it from him gratefully, wrapped it around his face, tied it at the back, pulled his hood back over, then took off his belt from around his leather armour, buckled it instead around the outside of the cloak, tightening it to him. 'Don't want them slithering down my neck,' he stated, voice muffled by the scarf. He stooped, tightening laces at the top of his leather boots, pulled on leather gloves, tied the hood of his cloak even tighter. He handed his backpack to

Amber. 'Not taking anything in with me they could sneak into, keep it safe dear.' She nodded, of course.

He stood ready, the branch in his left hand to clear the worms, White Star gleaming in the other, useful for lopping branches, perhaps slicing a few of the stinking, squirming forms. All that could be seen of him were two angry and anxious emerald eyes. He looked like a highway robber on a bad day.

Tamlyn bent down to the doe, stroked her flank. 'Be careful, my lady,' he whispered, 'the forest needs you.' She nuzzled her head into his hand.

The mages were already lighting a small fire, ripping up bandages and soaking them in grease, then pouring oil onto dried moss - all mages always carried some, moss being useful as antiseptic packing in a wound. They wrapped the moss and bandages around arrows in readiness.

'How will we know when you are in place?' Amber asked.

'You'll see a light, a bright light,' Estrién replied, 'shoot your arrows in that direction, then wait for my Lady to direct the wind. After that, it's up to the mages to contain it.' All looked querulously at him. 'My Lady told me,' he explained.

He picked up a water skin, emptied it over his cloak. 'Might help a bit against the fire if it comes my way, also make it a bit slippery for those bloody big worms if they fall on me.' He filled it again, attached it to his belt, then marched off into the forest with the doe.

The rest continued preparing arrows, awaiting the signal.

It was strange, but regardless of the fact the large worm-like creatures had no vocal chords, the forest was filled with a peculiar hum. Perhaps it came as they spat out the slimy pus on to the pine needles, perhaps it was just their breathing, but it became more tangible as Estrién and the doe ventured further in.

Almost as soon as they entered, Estrién was hard at work clearing the creatures from the doe. They dropped quickly from the trees, spying something more edible than pine needles, spitting green pus over her flank. He poured water over her, cleaning the acidic pus, brushing the offensive things off her, while they squirmed over his own head and cloak. He shook himself, used the branch to push them off his back, before returning to clean the doe.

They hurried through a shower of two foot long, fat slimy worms, the stink getting worse as they ran, Estrién batting away the creatures with the branch. Soon he had to stop, the stench unbearable, he was retching inside the silk scarf. He grabbed the potion Dane had made, lifted up the scarf and took a swig. He shook his head, the poison already getting to him, making him dizzy, light headed. Under every tree the creatures fell upon them, ravenous for more food and both Estrién and the doe were clearly a welcome prey. Estrién looked down to find several snaking around his legs, he kicked them off, swiped White Star through them. The chopped up worm things slithered and wriggled, determined to still live regardless of a lack of head or tail. He stamped upon them, all the while still trying to sweep them off the doe.

She ignored every one, occasionally shaking her head if one fell upon her muzzle. Like Estrién she trod upon the beings, kicked out as one landed close by, all the while running towards the centre of the forest. She didn't run ahead of Estrién, despite her four legs, she kept pace with him. Together they approached the centre to find much of the foliage gone, the trees bare and the ground pulsating with squirming, wriggling forms and stinking from acidic pale green pus.

'If I ever get out of this,' thought Estrién, 'I need new boots and a new cloak.' The pus was etching into the leather, the soles disintegrating. The doe's hooves however were far stronger, she seemed unperturbed. One coiled itself around Estrién's wrist, he grabbed it and threw it down, stamped on it, a vile stench emitting as it squelched under him.

Suddenly she stopped, the very centre of the infestation, here no worm things fell upon them, the trees dead, the branches bare, every bit of green eaten or disintegrated. But the ground was covered in writhing forms all blindly searching for food. Now it was Estrién's job to stop the creatures on the ground crawling up and over her.

For a moment he watched fascinated as she took her own form, pure white, radiant light. He held up his hand against his eyes, so bright, she was so bright. He felt her warmth entering him, clean, pure; utterly beautiful. It filled him with peace, joy and courage. As he looked down, he saw the ground around them become still, the wriggling worms seemed lifeless. The creatures were not dead, for *she* did not bring death, *she* brought life, she was of the Mother, and death was not part of her. But they lay still, quiescent, almost as a babe lies quietly as her mother sings a lullaby, except no woman could ever have given birth to such abominations.

There was a moment's stillness, a hush upon the forest before Estrién saw the first flaming arrow and heard it thwack against a branch. It was obviously Reave's for she would not miss, then came another, some from high in the air, some falling on the ground, but nevertheless, constant. The arrows came down, a few trees flared then sizzled, then died, the moisture on the branches fizzling the flames. More arrows came down upon the forest, they too fizzled out. The trees were wet through with winter rain and snow and would not burn.

The group outside shook their heads in disappointment, it was going to take a concerted effort to do this, more mana being used when they needed to conserve it.

Dane looked thoughtfully at his staff. He remembered the anger when he was at Sunstones, the sheer power that came through the oak staff as it poured out electric bolts over the singing stones.

He could but try.

'Stand back everyone,' he demanded.

He stood facing the stinking forest, alive with creeping, wriggling forms. He hated it, it was an abomination, he let the feeling go, from his head to his arms, his fingers, to his staff. It was a process, one mages learnt from an early age. *Use the power, use your emotion, but use it wisely, then filter it, shift it from self to staff, push it through ... and let it go.*

He concentrated.

Suddenly a massive lightning bolt shot from the end of the staff towards the forest, almost as powerful as the one at Sunstones. Maybe not quite so powerful, but it was enough. It crackled and fizzled over the trees in front of him, spread across and hit the branches. 'Now!' he shouted, as the three archers let loose their arrows.

The forest lit up in flames.

Estrién and the doe watched the trees, wondering what was happening? The forest was quiet, the flames fizzled to nothing but smoke, smouldering before they died out, the smell even worse than before. It caught in the throat and choked. Yet nothing seemed to happen for a while, all was quiet, the whole forest silent, even the humming stopped.

Suddenly a massive crackle of amberic lightning hit the forest, then a barrage of fiery arrows, and he watched as the pines shot up in flame. The forest then caught quickly, the pus ignited and burnt the trees and the sickly slimy creatures among them. 'Well done everyone,' he thought to himself. So ... the pus was flammable.

He now stood in the centre of a flaming forest, the fire catching and spreading, the heat growing by the moment, the stench unbearable. He stood choking and coughing, the fire approaching rapidly. He wondered how *she* could control this, it would catch the other trees, they would be surrounded.

Then behind him, out of nowhere, came the wind, as bitter cold as a late winter gale can be. The Lady of the Forest turned swiftly into her human form, holding her arms wide, began directing it, almost as if she was herding it, the Lady holding her head on one side as if listening. As the fire approached, she guided the wind like a funnel, keeping part of the forest free from fire, pushing the fire outwards, back towards Dane's group of mages. All the while she listened, concentrated, waiting for the knowledge that the fire had been contained at the edge of the infestation.

When she was sure, she turned, waited a little for the fire to begin to die out, charred and blackened stumps remaining. Then they moved northwards where more wretched wriggling beings were trying to crawl up their legs, some dropping thickly on them from overheated tree branches, suckers clamping onto skin. She raised a delicate hand and pushed them off. They collapsed and lay still, but were alive.

'I cannot kill, even such parasites as these,' were her words. 'it is not my place. I rely on thee, Estrién, thou art my warrior.'

He understood, bashed and stamped and sliced at the creeping and slithering creatures, several winding around his own legs, his feet now beginning to feel the acid through the thick leather soles of his boots. It itched and burnt.

As the fire began to die she fanned the flames northwards, her hands waving in the air, the wind blowing the lessening flames back into life. Those on the outside must have seen the change in direction, for more amberic lightning suddenly crashed among the trees and fiery arrows fell from the sky.

She stood firmly, directing the wind as the fire spread, holding it and keeping it within a small arc. As the trees near them caught flame she began to push the wind outwards, away from themselves and towards the mages, the fire spreading through the arc of trees. Eventually every tree caught fire.

Estrién did not see the bitter tears rolling down her cheeks, bereft at the loss of her forest.

She was the heart and the heart wept.

Dane meanwhile was directing the mages outside the trees.

'Run north, quickly, she's moved on,' he screamed, 'get some arrows flying!' He waited until Reave, Amber and Tamlyn shot several arrows into the trees, then did as he had previously. Huge bolts of lightning shot from the end of his oaken staff deep into the heart of the pine woods. He'd realised straight-away that a few flames would not do the trick, there had to be extra, literally the spark to start the fire.

'Quick, it's coming our way.'

Four mages hurried to stop the flames before they spread to other parts of Shirewood. The gap between the woodlands wasn't large, they froze the very ground between the woods, they cooled the air on the outside of the forest. The ground behind them, to the south-west was now wet through, the river overflowed and flooded the lower end of the valley, protecting the rest of the valley from fire. But it could not flow uphill, as the ground rose upwards, that job belonged to the mages.

For this, Salli was at the forefront, his staff guiding the other mages. From somewhere he found a well deep underground, forced the water upwards until it burst through, drenching the hillside. The other mages took their cue, froze the water, blocked the fire.

Then again the fire moved, north east this time, on they ran past the tor of the forested hillside. Not so much need to fire the trees now, it had taken hold well, as forest fires do, the pine sap had caught, containment was the problem.

Trevaine found rocks, hurled them in the air. All four mages guided them towards the edge of the flaming trees, a wall to block the fire. Suddenly rocks were flying everywhere as mages gouged out the hillside and found stone. Smoke too, drifting towards them from the forest, the wet branches steaming as they caught. It smelled of burnt corpses, rotten to the core, everyone coughing, retching.

If it's this bad outside, thought Amber, *how much worse is it for Estrién inside?*

Estrién had got past the choking, retching, coughing stage, he was numbed with poison. He simply moved soundlessly, unable to think of anything other than protecting the Lady.

The creatures now seemed to realise they were being attacked and finally understood who was attacking them.

They dropped from the trees and snaked and slithered en masse for them both. Hundreds of wriggling, squirming forms attacked, sickly yellow green pus shooting from their mouths.

He dropped the branch, it was disintegrating, held White Star in both hands. He didn't use it as a sword, chopping as before, he swept it from side to side, batting the large worm-creatures away as the pair moved north east and to the next section of forest. Up and down, sideways through the soft squelchy bodies, choking at the smell, dizzy from the poison. He cleared a small section, stopped to drink another swig of Dane's potion, watching as they squirmed their sickly way towards him.

Up, down, a great sweeping arc, they whizzed through the air, while the Lady fanned the forest and guided the wind. The last section now, she only hoped the mages outside had enough mana left to control it. Estrién looked green, she wondered how he continued, she could taste the poison herself. She needed to maintain this form for just a short while more, just enough to guide the fire through the remaining trees.

The land to the south, west and north of them was burnt charcoal, the remains of the trees looked tortured. She wondered if it could ever return to health, or if this place would always be blighted? She did not know, it was outside her world, outside the cycle.

She followed Estrién as he swept the beings aside, once more called the wind, once more directed it as the forest flamed, the final section. She could see Estrién was on the edge of collapse, his cloak was in tatters, his boots ragged, his gloves shredded from acid. The stinking worm things surrounded them. She stood firm, held the wind aloft, this cone of wind, made sure the last section was fully alight, and pushed the fire outwards.

She heaved a sigh of relief when it eventually began to die down. Only the centre here, where she and Estrién stood, only here was the infestation still alive and wriggling.

Estrién was still bravely batting at every creature, he let none touch her, yet many were climbing up his legs, over his boots, clinging to the shreds of his cloak.

She walked over to him, her work was done, sharply she clapped her hands. The worm creatures fell off, stunned, sleeping on to the floor.

He looked dazedly at her, managed a smile, opened his mouth to speak, realised he couldn't speak, the poison affecting both his vocal chords and his brain, his ability to speak gone.

He couldn't say a word.

Dane's group were still trying to contain the final flames, freezing the ground in front of them. They would still have to check the forest when it had all died down, set fire to anything possibly still alive, including trees and branches that may have escaped the fire somehow. Every single thing in what had been a thriving forest must be turned to blackened charcoal in case of infestation, eggs, larvae, spores, or whatever was the creature's young.

The forest remains would need to be checked for some years to come, just in case anything could live through such a conflagration. With beings like these, who knew?

They weren't born of the Cycle, they weren't of nature.

Soon it became clear enough to see the figures of Estrién and the Lady through the blackened stumps. They made their way towards the pair cooling the ground in front of them as they walked, checking around them, watching carefully for anything alive. Occasionally a mage would shoot fire at something, alive or not, best to be careful.

They saw Estrién standing still, swaying slightly from side to side. The smell was not so bad now, more a charcoal smell, cleaner, if a little stifling, but becoming worse as they walked towards the centre.

The mages saw the circle of now quiescent forms surrounding the Lady and Estrién. They watched as she took him by the hand and led him gently away from the blackened forest, he seemed to be stumbling. He smiled briefly as he passed them, but did not speak, instead he looked stunned. Amber turned to follow them, Tamlyn too, there was something surely wrong here.

'He has been poisoned,' were the Lady's only words.

Dane and the mages flamed the rest of the creatures, then fled the centre as the stench hit them. They too were choking and gasping, Robson and Salli stopped to be sick. Estrién had survived this?

Outside, on a green hillside, where the air was fresh and clean, Estrién stood gulping air into his lungs. 'I ...' he started to say, then nothing, nothing would come out. He looked weary, his skin grey, covered in tattered armour and stinking filth.

Amber helped tear off the cloak, his boots, gloves and the silk scarf around his mouth. She threw them to one side then offered the remains of Dane's potion to his lips. He drank gratefully, but still unable to speak, to offer thanks. He sat heavily down on the damp hillside, staring into nothing.

The Lady too seemed to be doing the same, taking in pure air, her head raised to the sky, her eyes closed, her lips set.

After a moment or two she looked sadly at Estrién, then spoke.

'Thou art my brave warrior, Sir Estrién, a true knight in all ways. Thou stood by me, protected me when I needed a firm and trusty hand of protection. I could name thee as thou deserveth, *Trueheart*, protector of the wildwood, but thou already hast been named *he who wields the Shield of Light*, and so thou art. And the rest of you ...' turning to the others, the mages now returning from the centre, 'thou has all worked to protect my land, I give thee utmost thanks.' She turned back to the sitting Estrién, took him by the hand again, helped him rise and led him a little way down the slope of the hill, away from the others.

'Stand still my dear, fear not what I do, for it will help thee.'

He just stared dazedly into her eyes and gave a lop-sided nod.

She poised herself in front of him, arms outwards, hands upwards, then came a flash of brightness as she became pure light, pure essence, radiant and beautiful to behold. The light sparkled as a thousand diamonds, all colours of the rainbow, streaming outwards towards Estrién. He didn't move, mesmerised by the light.

The others watched amazed as the light slowly moved through him, as he began to shine as she did, his face suddenly alight with pleasure, a blissful smile spreading across his features. As the light moved onwards and left him, he stood silent and speechless...

... but this time with delight, he had never felt so clean and pure and healthy. For a few moments he held the feeling, the bliss of her touch, the strength of her, the love she held for all in her creatures, her forest. She turned back into her female form, and he gazed gratefully into her eyes. He dropped down on to one knee, bowed his head.

Then he went straight to Amber, took her head in his hands and kissed her lips, passing the radiance into her. Now he spoke, his voice regained, he felt blessed.

'I had to share that with thee, my love, thee and I are one, a gift for us both.' He smiled across at the Lady; she nodded and smiled back, her eyes laughing. Then he went to Dane and Tamlyn, hugged them both, clasped their hands, before shaking the hand of every member of his team. He cleared his throat before speaking, relishing the freshness of air around him, his head clean and clear of the poison he had breathed in.

'You all did so well, I am so proud of you all. I wanted to give each of you a little of what *she* gave me. I have never felt so good in my life.' He turned to the Lady. 'My Lady, I thank thee with all my heart.'

For a few more moments she held her human form. 'Nay, Sir Estrién, I thank thee, for all thee and thy group have done. I thank all of thee.' She stopped, pointed north. 'I must leave thee now, thou and thine must go northwards, thou can see the mountains ahead, the Greylumings. If thee keep to the north-east paths and passages, eventually thou will see a tall grey tower in which the Weaver of Time doth dwell. It is but a few miles from a small village of Wildlings, they know of her, take offerings of food and ale to her, all they can spare. They are rough folk, with even rougher speech, but they are not bad people and they give her kindnesses. They are very afraid of her, but they respect her too, unlike the terrible being who rides or walks there sometimes.' She stopped to sigh deeply. 'Thou no longer require my aid, and I have much to do - here alone, and in other places, I must bring life back. I must bring in the spring, for the season turns although it turns late. Every one of thee has helped, for this is a true victory over the death *that one* desires.

I and my mate thank thee with all our heart.' And with that she turned back into the gentle doe, lifted her head to them in acknowledgement, then ran back into the dead forest.

With every step, she left a trail of sweet purple violets, even among the grey ashes and the cinders.

Chapter 7

The core members of the White Shield, or Nim'randuel, as Estrién preferred, left the doe in the ravaged remains of the forest and travelled northwards over the hills for a couple of miles, away from the devastation, before setting camp. Everyone was exhausted, mana depleted, and Estrién had come down from his initial exhilaration. No one wanted to eat, Dane made a clean herbal brew for everyone, then they all slept for several hours. Sick to their stomachs, none could eat that day.

Wherever they went during the next few days, it seemed they were always watched. Whether this was by friend or foe, none knew, but the birds of the air seemed to fly off quickly at their approach. Since the doe had left, they all felt a little friendless, despite the company of each other.

Reave now took advantage of her bow, brought down several woodcock and the odd rabbit. She spotted a roe deer through the trees, knew it would be a long time before she could hunt one again, she let it be. That Lady, goddess, whatever, the spirit of the woods ... no, she could never forget her. The rest of the party were appreciative of a little meat in their diet.

They carried on northwards and eastwards, keeping the grim Greylumings in their sights whenever there was a gap or a hill to keep track. *He* must have known they were close, for often he sent the wild beasts to stop them

He was not aware however that Estrién had the power to soothe them. Bears came, crazed by his will, Estrién and Salli stood at the front of the group, the bears snuffled and turned away, pacified by their particular kind of magic. Wolves too, a large feral pack, came running. Estrién wanted as little slaughter as possible, not now they were nearing Anaïs' home. He lifted his arms and concentrated, waving weird signs and sigils, as Salli waved his soothing wand. Tamlyn too took out his lute, played soft melodies, it seemed fitting. The wolves howled then turned away. Some fell asleep across their path.

Once or twice Estrién spotted a dragon's flight across the tips of the Greylumings. That was natural, as it should be, he wondered if one was the dragon he had saved, who, in turn had saved him? He decided they had not gone over, wondered if that was even possible, they were a law unto themselves. Proud, majestic, graceful and self-contained, they lived outside the normal world, a species beyond.. They would only attack for food, the hunt of life, essential, yet did not attack cities teeming with life. That was the province of the more vociferous creatures, the two-legged ones with bows and arrows; the draconae had enough sense to leave the cities and villages alone.

Yet woe betide you if you encroached upon their territory, then you were fair game.

They were creatures of great power and magic, yet they were still of the Cycle.

Dane saw them and shuddered; he'd had to make his way through Draconia when he left the Isle of Glasse. There were not that many dragons, but it had been a very unsettling experience. He found caves to sleep in during the day, travelled only at night, the thought of becoming dragon food decidedly unpleasant. He hoped there weren't too many near Anaïs' tower.

With each day's travel towards the mountains, they could see Amber grow more anxious and restless. Her sleep too was disturbed, her dreams, when she slept deep enough to dream, were troubling, something, or *someone* always on the edge, threatening her. But more than that, she worried over her sister, wondering what was happening to her, what was *he* doing to her?

He however, was not at the tower; *he* was roaming the land, fomenting hatred and division. He rode swiftly, changed horses and bodies as necessary, left a little misery and mayhem wherever he rode. Unlike the doe, his steps left the land barren. It wasn't that he wanted a permanent winter, for that, like death, is an ending and a cleansing. He did not require a land filled with pure snow and crisp ice. Nay, if anything he would prefer the miserable world of the Fae, ever a soul saddening grey twixt dark and light, dull and depressing.

He merely did not wish life to renew itself.

Evil is a strange beast, wreaking havoc, creating imbalance, animosity between friends and family and fomenting hatred.

… The lure of power without responsibility or sensibility, lust without love or respect, wealth born of greed and easy money instead of hard work, his hand lies in all of these.

... A world where half-baked ideologies are declared as undeniable truths, yet benefit only an elite few.

... A world over-burdened by regulation, yet without the understanding of self-discipline or self-control.

... A world where sly rumours are whispered into eager ears, yet hold no fact.

... A world where grievances or grudges are implied, yet have no substance.

... A world where slick slogans spout from lips, yet have neither depth nor consideration.

Divide, break down ... and rule, *his* methods, mean, cheap and underhand.

He now rode south over the crumbling paths at the base of the Greylumings, shale and grit, sharp grey flint and dark granite, pushing the horse ever faster. Thence he rode westwards, finding one of the few good paths through the Foraes Dair, leaving filth and infestation in his wake, a toxic mix inflicting slow death upon the forest. But the forest was large, he could not destroy all of it.

Then he moved down to Mercantia, spreading more dissension and division.

Lord Black sent his guards through the city to remove any Sons of the Blazing Sun cultists, for they were entering the city again, this time in quite large numbers. He was annoyed, he and Lady Violet had always promoted the freedom of speech in the city, dammit, he liked a good debate, but this sect was fomenting pure hatred. Violet was still north, still trying to understand the circle of no-time around Manecaestr. Lord Black asked the universities and great libraries to seek out whatever they could, find some solution. He didn't hold out much hope.

More to the point, would his city be next? Who knew? Life was changing daily now.

It was as if the death of von Adamm had galvanised the death cult with even more hatred, rather than its pacification. Perhaps it was like a tree when you lop off a withered or diseased branch and two or three grow in its place. Or, more pointedly, when a cancer is cut out yet that strangely promotes more cancer. Whatever the case there were many ugly rumours being passed around his city.

Several women came forth and said they had carried his unwanted 'love child', two of whom he had never seen in his life before. He simply told them he would get mages to verify parentage, if they were his offspring, he would make reparation, but that would only be for those older than his own children, for he had looked at no other woman since he married. He had been a philanderer in his youth, true, he had certainly sowed wild oats, yet it had been done in a spirit of pleasure and joy. He never wished harm, merely that he was a highly sexed young man seeking a good woman as a mate.

Violet stopped his philandering, took him in hand and made a man of him. He loved her to her core.

Yet women passed rumours that he was having affairs 'on the side' with them, cheating on his wife while she was away, had taken to gallivanting, nights out on the town, drinking and visiting brothels.

They were using his past weakness against him.

Word sneakily passed north to Violet without his knowledge, politely informing her of the antics of her errant husband.

She scotched them immediately. 'Utter bollocks!' was her verdict. She sent him a letter via Gracie.

'They tell me you are missing me so much you have taken to visiting the whorehouses. That's OK darling, but please don't bring back any nasty diseases. Love you, Violet.'

He returned with, 'what the...??! Haven't been in a brothel since ... actually, don't think I've ever visited one ... never needed to!! Love you, Black xxxxxxxxx. PS I do miss you.'

Violet merely smiled to herself and blew a kiss in the general direction of Mortia.

There were rumours too of anarchy and subversion, the overthrow of the 'unfair, cruel and greedy hierarchy of the city', namely *Evil* Lord Black and his 'parasitic family and hangers-on who live off the fat of the land while the people starve.'

'Can't help my family name,' he thought, 'don't care what they think of me, but no bugger threatens my family.' Besides, his city was wealthy through trade and craft, most people were sleek, well-fed and prosperous. The Adammite war had brought more wealth to the citizens as Lord Black opened his own coffers to commission large supplies of armour, weapons, war machines, defence measures, enlarge his armies and hire mercenaries. There was no unemployment at all.

Lord Black combed the city, scotched the rumours and made sure he was seen regularly, full armour, going about the city on his jet black destrier (naturally called Ebony) his sword, Gutthrust, at his side and a full complement of guard behind him. He believed a show of force was necessary; he took part in many a sweep of dissenters and cultists. Lord Black came from a long line of ancestors who did not hide behind walls while others fought on their behalf, nor did they take prisoners.

The bodies were taken outside the city walls, pits dug and left for mages to fire.

It gained him the respect of the citizens, the fear of the Adammites and it put a stop to further dissension, at least in the city.

Yet Lord Black was amazed at how quickly it had spread through his city, despite his earlier attempts to quash it.

His army continually patrolled the rest of Mercantia, had always done so, there to keep the peace and to accompany the Circuit Judges as they travelled and settled disputes, grievances or judged crimes. But there were more now, many more. Lord Black doubled the number of Judges as he doubled the number of patrols.

He hoped it was enough.

*

The forest thinned out as the land rose and fell towards the Greyluming Mountains. Thick wood turned into copse and moorland. Hillsides grew sparse with vegetation, rocky outcrops of the mountains. The cold winds blew fiercely across open plains.

No one knew what lay beyond the mountains, they were impassable. They rose jagged, stark and bleak, a clear boundary across the whole of Mer'edrynn from Fenland in the south, even through to Vikénar in the northern lands. There were tales that only dragons lived beyond them, and then the land turned to everlasting sea, the end of the world.

No one had been, no one knew, or if they had managed the ascent, no one returned. They weren't the kind of mountains you climbed and came back from, at least not *whole*.

When first they saw them, everyone held hope in their eyes, the snow capped mountains looked rather grandiose and even beautiful; they seemed quite close. But sight can be deceiving for they were bigger than anything they had ever seen, they were in fact many, many miles distant.

There were moors, hills and valleys to cross still. Small villages came and went, eking out a miserable existence on the edges of civilisation, the Mountain people they were called, the Wildlings. Yet they were civilised enough in their own way, peaceful enough amongst themselves and fairly hospitable to strangers. They mostly lived in round beehive shaped huts, dry stone built, the stone chosen for shape and packed perfectly together, much like Salli's although not so comfortable, and the roofs also were stone, not thatch. Few willows grew here, there were no fancy tables or bookcases, no basket chairs with soft squashy cushions, or pretty baskets filled with dried herbs - their furniture was basic, necessary and rough hewn. These people lived off the land around them and had not changed in a thousand years or more. Like their ancestors, they made use of their surroundings for all their needs, their tools mostly made of flint, slate or bone, or a very basic iron, their clothing of furs and leather, sheepskin and goatskin mostly, for these lived off the mountain grasses.

Often they hungered during the winter months, especially these last barren ones. Just as the people of older days thought they had offended their ancestors, they too made sacrifices as peace offerings. The ancestors were important, barrows could be seen here and there, graves marked out by small crosses or small juniper trees. The junipers were also useful, the dried berries added flavouring to pickled meats and strong alcohol - genièvre - and the leaves and branches were medicinal. But only a little could be taken, a polite request and a prayer to the ancestors for approval was necessary.

Sometimes groups of strong hunters went into the far forest for food, several days hike, returning two or three weeks later with their spoils, including tree trunks and logs as well as game. Then feasts were held, the game used in every possible way from meat to skin and sinew, and nuts brought back from the forests were an added treat. Again, every part was used, just as the Lady Merrie had done, back on Norfrost when the land was inhospitable and cruel.

Yet like the Lady Merrie, none thought to leave, to find a city and dwell there in more comfort, perhaps luxury. They knew the cities existed, occasional travellers came and went, even some of their own travelled and came back. Yet this was their home by the mountains, for all its impoverishment, this was where their ancestors had lived and died. This was where they would stay.

When the company came across the small settlement near a gushing river that swept coldly down from the Greylumings, they felt they had gone back in time. Perhaps it is so, perhaps the Greylumings themselves, inert and timeless held back the years.

Two long haired children were down by the river holding fishing poles that appeared to be made of bone, catgut lines fastened on to the ends. Two bearded men held on to the ends of a large fishing net, while a third appeared to be pushing, or at least persuading any fish in the river towards the nets. They must have caught something for the men were seen to quickly scoop up the net, silver flashes of scales shimmering. There were smiles and shouts from the bare-chested men, a good supper tonight, and the long fish bones were so useful, sharp and pointed.

All wore nothing but furs or skins, pretty rough looking too, although they were adorned with belts made of thick iron rings; various bone or iron utensils and implements attached to the rings by leather thongs. Their chests were bare, if you could call it so, for they were thickly covered in hair. Amber and Reave were seen to smirk and smile at each other, a slight nod, *not bad...*

The men marched out of the river, picked up short fur and leather boots and had pulled them on before they saw the group of approaching strangers.

They stared at them for fully a minute, inspecting the company as they walked down the hill, before shouting to them in Plaintongue, heavily accented but understandable.

'What ye lot want 'ere?'

Amber quickly spoke up. 'We are travelling through sir, we make for the Greylumings. A Tower, if you have seen it.'

The dark haired male stared at her for some time, then conferred with his fellows before speaking.

'Ye Amber?'

She stood astonished; here, out in the back end of beyond, they were expecting her?

She saw no point in denying it; if they were friendly they would no doubt help. If they were enemy, it would be yet another fight, undesired but unavoidable. She nodded.

'I'm looking for my sister.'

'That sorceress lass yer sister? W"hay, bugger me!' The conversation ended as he nodded to all of them, motioning them to follow him.

'How did you know ...?' Amber began.

'News travels,' was all the reply. He took them across to the settlement, people already coming out of the round stone huts to greet and to inspect. Like the fishermen, all wore furs or goat skin tunics. The tunics looked better made, embellished with beads and feathers, or intricate runes and designs done upon them in poker-work. All wore similar short fur boots like the fishermen, and both men and women kept their hair in plaits trimmed with beads, although one or two women piled their hair high, kept in place with fine netting and decorated fish bones.

An old woman joined them, her hair piled up on her head, pure white, a thick sheepskin around her shoulders to keep out the winter chill, her eyes shrewd and piercing. All the menfolk stood to attention as she approached, heads high, shoulders back, respect clearly shown upon their faces.

'Welcome strangers, be welcome 'ere.' She put her head on one side, studying them before speaking again. 'Summat's up,' she declared, 'summat's 'appening out there, and I want to ken what it be. I've seen the signs ... and ye lot ... ye lot can tell me.'

All members of Amber's group eyed each other - what was she - the soothsayer or something?

'Ye needn't look like that,' she tersely informed them, 'I'm nae witch or mystic, just the Auld Mother. Aye, most of this village be me offspring one way or another. But I ken nature, and all's wrong.' She put her hands on her hips then beckoned. 'C'mon in afore ye catch yer deaths out there in them daft cloots.'

She led them into an overheated circular hall, very roomy, a large fire in the centre, strange smelling, certainly not wood, the forest too far for regular collection.

Dane inspected the fire, roundish black cinders and cobs, very hot. He noticed that there were hessian sacks at the side, black stones tumbling out. He picked one up, examined it.

'Hast'a ne'er sin call afore?' the old woman asked, her voice rose up and down, sing-song, thick with local accent.

'Call?' Dane replied, 'no, we use wood where I come from. This looks efficient.'

She smiled, 'aye that it is, we add some peat and a bit o' heather fer kindling.' She nodded to two hefty looking men, 'they picks it out't hillside, hard job, dirty clarty work. Now sit ye down and tell us truth.' Her word was final.

The floor was stone flagged, like a crazy paving, but swept well. There were several benches, shaped from tree trunks dragged back to the village from the forest, covered in goat skins. Other goat skins were placed around the central fire, probably also used as sleeping mats. Decorations of beads and feathers adorned the dark walls. It was basic, but solid.

All sat down as told, large stone mugs were brought, each filled with a heavy brown brew, the infamous 'broon dog' of legend. It was thick, heady, and tasted horrible. This wasn't the tourist brewed rip off they had drunk in the cheap bars Longshanks had taken them to in Grimmpool. This was the real thing.

It blew your head off.

The locals watched as they drank, sussing who was man enough to take it, or who wasn't worth their time.

Every member of the company drained their glasses, even Reave.

Amber wiped her mouth, 'grand stuff that,' she offered cheerily. The old woman refilled her mug, watched as she downed half of it, before explaining who and what they were and the reason they were in their part of the country.

Most of the village were now crowded inside the round stone hut, squashed at the sides, everyone listening intently. Eyebrows were raised constantly, and many openly scoffed when she explained about the big city of Manecaestr being cut off by some kind of time cloud.

'No, it's true,' Amber continued, 'all too true I am afraid. It is why I must find my sister ... she ... she is,' she stopped, how did you describe such a person?

A young man raised his hand. 'Canst I speak, Mother?' he asked, his voice respectful. The old woman nodded. He continued, his accent thick but understandable. 'She be the Weaver, that's what she is. Sin 'er once, up on't fells, she were after goat's hair and wool left on't sharp stones and rocks by passing beasts. Me goats go up there, y'see, I go up to check 'em,' he explained. 'Sin her looking for 'erbs and grasses too, stuff for her dyes.' Others nodded they too had seen her sometimes.

All left her alone.

'The Weaver?' asked Estrién curiously.

'Aye, that's what she's known as roond 'ere. She's a sorceress, scary, saw her flashing lights once, lightning coming out her fingers.'

Three mages chuckled. 'We can do that,' Dane replied, ' there's four mages here, all different, good healers too if you need any healing.' It was a kind offer.

All shook their heads. 'I thank ye,' the Auld Mother replied, 'but we're strong of flesh and bone out 'ere - we have to be or we wouldn't survive.'

'Can you tell me where she is,' asked Amber, 'where lies her Tower?'

The young goatherd answered. 'Yonder north yet, there be a tangle of forest some days north of here, then to the east, some miles on, a tarn close by. Ye can't miss it.'

'You've been then?' Amber was surprised.

'Aye, Auld Mother 'ad me tek stuff to her, some food, goat skin, some wool for her weaving. It were quite a trek, I tell ye. Didn't go up though,' he added hastily, 'left the sack at bottom't steps like rest of stuff. Nay, I'm not that fond. It's a funny place that, gives you the heebies.' He stopped, took a sup of his own brew, he'd said his piece.

Some days north, not so far now then ... Amber's thoughts were broken into.

'Watch out, there's fell beasts about, even the birds of the air - bloody fighting each other,' the Auld Mother told them. 'Ask more when ye get to the villages closer than 'ere, they'll tell ye. There's death in the very air.'

They were offered mats for the night, more Broon Dog and a tasty dish of 'Aggerty, which consisted of sliced 'tetties' and onions, cooked in a big flat iron pan over the coals, goat's cheese melted through. It was very tasty. There were rough iron spoons to eat it with, all implements and tools made by themselves, a little iron ore close to the coal deposits. None were iron smiths, but the coal burnt high, they fashioned what they needed.

They thanked them warmly, had little to offer as payment, but none was expected other than the usual payment of stories, news and gossip. As with the three old sisters, Salli, Tamlyn and Reave played their instruments for everyone, turning the meeting into an occasion.

But the Auld Mother looked unhappy. Amber questioned her. 'Aye lass,' she confessed, 'I've sin things, things I niver wish tae see again. Summat travels through, summat bad - leaves death and filth in his wake, proper laidly he be. He goes in the direction of her tower, where ye be going. I've been watching ye all night, and there's summat about all 'o ye that's special. But only the Gods know what'll 'appen when ye meet. I'm just sorry I'm no witch as ye thought, I can't offer ye magic tokens or amulets. But I'll pray for all of ye, that I will.'

Amber thanked her.

The following morning they set off once more, hope in hearts, but more than a little apprehensive. No one knew what lay ahead.

*

They stayed overnight at another two of the Hill people's settlements, accepted cordially, if a little warily at each. Huge jugs of Broon Dog were offered as if some kind of test, and questions were asked, the villagers needing answers.

'Corruption,' the Auld Mother of the next settlement stated, "he brings corruption everywhere. Evil to the core - I've felt it. Wouldn't like tae be in yon sister's boots,' she added finally.

'Ee brings madness too,' a young woman told them, 'took me bairn ... we heard 'im ride past one night, felt 'im, felt the badness, little bairn did too. Began crying, took sick, cried itself to death. None knew what troubled it, t'weren't a normal sickness, nowt like we'd sin afore. It ne'er stopped crying from moment that thing rode through, 'til little mite took its last breath. Aye,' her face and eyes were sorrow-filled, 'aye, that bad'n took me bairn.'

Her mate walked across to her. 'Then don't let it tek ye, love, get well and we'll 'ave more bairns, ye'll see,' he tried to comfort her. It was plain to see how she was pining, dark circles under her eyes and she was thinner than the other females.

Salli moved quietly over to her, took out his wand, touched on the shoulder. She looked startled.

'What have ye done?'

He smiled gently, 'a little ease, that is all. You will not forget your daughter - yes, it was a girl-child was it not?' She nodded, 'but you have no need to carry such a burden forever. Have peace in your heart and remember her with love. That one has touched the lives of many, ourselves included, there is no need to blame yourself. Your mate speaks true, the best thing you can do is to get well, move forward.' His voice was as gentle as his smile.

Estrién spoke on behalf of them all. 'We come to end this, at least we can end your suffering here. Once we find Amber's sister, we'll take her away. *That one,*' he emphasised the term, 'will have no reason to ride through here again. We can offer you that at least.'

The following morning every member of the village came to solemnly shake their hands before they left. Equally solemn faces watched them depart.

At the final settlement, closer to the small forest nearer the Tower, the villagers came out of their stone roundhouses en masse to greet them, but this time with hostility.
Stones were thrown, even an arrow landed at their feet.
The Auld Mother stood fast at the front of her people. 'Get ye gone, yer not wanted 'ere. Go fiends, go back where ye belong.'
Amber moved to the front of the group. 'We come with peace in our hearts Auld Mother, we wish no harm. I seek my sister, the sorceress in the Tower, we seek to help her.'
The Auld Mother moved forward a little. 'Come 'ere then lass, let me see ye proper.'
Amber moved towards her as the old woman peered into her eyes. She took her time, examining her, almost as if she saw though her. 'Aye,' she eventually conceded, 'ye speaks the truth. That lass is yer sister?' she added, sucking through her teeth, not waiting for an answer. 'Aye, there be a favour, same eyes, but ... well, ye'll see.'
As with the other villages, they were beckoned into the main beehive-shaped dwelling. It was richer and more comfortable looking than the other dwellings, closer to the forest for wood and there was an abundance of local iron ore, a smelter could be seen - and smelled - just outside the village.
Metal sconces adorned the walls, torches burned brightly, a huge cauldron was on the coal-filled hearth and a big metal pot was ready with boiling water. The cauldron was filled

with some sort of pork stew, pigs and wild boar roamed the nearby forest.

The people looked well fed, if ruddy cheeked, a freezing cold wind came down the valley. Like the other settlements they too wore goat skin tunics and furs, the Auld Mother wore a thick woollen cloak, a big collar of sheepskin to keep warm. She motioned to them to sit down.

'What can you tell me?' Amber needed information, whatever she knew.

'Nay, tell me first what ye ken.' The Auld Mother was unsure, and in any case had no wish to speak of either the Sorceress, or that which rode past and went to the tower.

'I believe my sister is held in that tower, that she escaped there to evade this evil being who rides through our land. I believe he found her and is using her. I believe she has immense powers, powers that are to do with time.' Amber explained about Manecaestr and the strange zone around it.

The Auld Mother nodded, accepting her words. 'Aye, I can believe that. The mountains, the Auld Greys we call them here, they are beyond time. Strange things 'appen up there, people come, mainly to find the mountains, mages and the like. There are other towers in the mountains, Merrie only knows how people live, but I suppose mages have powers for all their needs.' She stopped to take a deep draught of her dark ale before continuing.

Amber noticed she used Merrie's name, not the gods, or the Auld Gods. The village leader continued.

'Aye, as ye get near them, ye'll find things aren't quite so ... normal. It might be yer sister of course, we know her to be some kind of enchantress, but I've seen things me whole life. Those mountains ... they touch ... they touch something strange. When I took me place as Auld Mother I had to spend a month up there, by meself. Not a good experience, I can tell ye. Cauld and cruel, them mountains. Right glad I were to come down, back to hearth and home.' She filled Amber's mug and her own. 'Now *he* comes there, a thousand times worse, leaves badness. But, ye know, I don't think the mountains like him either, he's not part of them. So, aye lass, be careful up there, be reight careful.' She would say no more.

It only worried Amber all the more.

The following morning she saw them off. 'Go north through the woods, then turn right, ye'll see a path. Follow it, don't turn off, it'll bring ye to the base of the mountains. Keep east and eventually ye'll see yer sister's tower. ... probably. Sometimes it's not there, so keep yer 'e'en open. And time's odd, it might tek a short time, it might tek days. Be careful on them mountains, specially this time o' year, rains coming down, wet and slippery, bloody treacherous. May the Blessings of Merrie be on ye all, and may Lady Luck follow everyone of ye.'

She turned away, went straight back inside her dwelling, she would not watch them leave.

*

It wasn't far to the forest, half a day's hike, no more, but the forest was large. They could see where the villagers had been, felled trees, broad stumps. It was clearly managed, young saplings replaced the old trees. They heard a sound of sawing, two young men pushing and pulling at a big saw across a hefty tree trunk. The young men waved at them, they waved back, they had been at the meeting the previous night, but were up and out earlier than the group.

'Tree's rotten,' one shouted, 'yon bad'n is killing this land.'

Dane walked across, inspected it, the same sickening as in Oakleigh. 'I can heal them,' he said, 'done it before down south.'

There weren't many deciduous trees here, most were firs, pines. Nevertheless he spent time testing each tree they passed, holding his oak staff to each and every one. 'Not so bad as at Oakleigh,' he commented, 'the trees, like the people are hardier.'

They decided to make camp, allow Dane to spend the afternoon healing the forest, they had no idea what it would be like later. Every tree he healed would be a blow against the sickness in the land.

They came north to the edge of the forest early the following day, vast moorland, heath and possibly peat bog to their east. There was a path of sorts at the edge of the forest, they took it. It led across the moors. It was obvious why the Auld Mother had said to stick to the path, a low lying mist wisped and curled across the freezing moorland, misleading a traveller, luring them into bogs and pits; any step could be fatal. They walked single file, Salli leading, he seemed to be good at path-finding, for it disappeared every so often, weathered into nothingness by harsh winters. At some point it would be repaired, but that was for the spring days ahead, not the thick winter ones.

For two long days they walked, making camp by the edges at night, still the Greylumings looked no nearer. Forbidding greyness topped with white, a never ending windswept vista of jagged rocks and crags. The path below them echoed the mountains, rocks crushed to a mud coloured gravel, yet the purple heather over the moorland was a welcome sight.

By the third day there were outcrops of the mountains, the land began to rise, although it had looked level across the moors. It became hard walking, they were glad of thick boots. Estrién had bargained for a pair of strong looking boots and a goatskin cape from the last settlement; his own were in shreds from the acidic green pus of the slimy creatures in the forest. The goatskin was slightly itchy, but warm.

In places the slate and granite mountains had been quarried, sharp stones poking their way through soles, extremely difficult to walk through. Some of the rocks were igneous, sulphur smelling and others sparkled with minerals. They weren't completely grey, the brown patches across the hillsides told everyone there would be grass come spring. Rivers and waterfalls gushed their icy way down the mountainsides. The small sheltered vales too, a few corries made by the circular motion of ancient ice, held woods and copses, lakes or tarns. Hardy flora existed up here, flowers peeped their heads and summer brought an abundance of hardy plants like rock cress or soapwort, rock rose and thyme.

Each day the mountains loomed larger, higher than anything they had ever seen. They were vast, bold, spectacular, beautiful and terrifying. They weren't devoid of life, birds flew, kites and kestrels, Reave spotted a hawk, so did Gertie.

She didn't wait to find out if the other hawk would defend her territory, she had been trained to kill. She flew off into the bright, morning blue sky, tucked her wings back and nose-dived at the other hawk. The other hawk was older and bigger than her, but she had the advantage of surprise and speed. There was a flurry of grey brown and red feathers and the older hawk dropped. For a few moments Gertie soared around the sky above them, triumphant in her victory, marking the territory as her own.

Surprisingly the other birds kept away, she had established her strength, her skill. The company watched as she flew down, came back up shaking wet feathers and a silver fish in her mouth, a river to the south of them.

The mountains were flowing with rivers, most swollen by winter rain and snow, ice cold from the tips. Small lakes filled vast hollows, rich with wild brown trout, perch and a few huge pike were spotted. They stopped to fish, to feast on a cook pot filled with perch. They cleaned and gutted them, stripped the scales and fried them on the skillets over a hastily built camp fire.

They filled their waterskins from the fast flowing rivers with some of the purest and coldest water they had ever tasted. One sunny morning Dane couldn't resist the lure of them. He stripped off and dashed in, quickly lathering his body with soap, just managing to rinse before he ran out again.

'Bloody hell, that's cold,' he laughed as one of the other mages blew warm air around him. He swiftly got dressed. 'I feel fantastic,' he crowed. The others just smiled, *very nice, if you like that kind of thing*, their patient smiles told him.

They passed spectacular waterfalls, the roar strumming through their bodies, the mountains humming around them with rushing water frothing white as it hit the stony floor.

On a blue-sky summer's day, bright with sunlight, sweet grass growing and the smell of heather or gorse in the air, the mountains would be glorious. Treacherous, but glorious.

But early spring is a fickle fellow and the next day the rains came and the cold wind blew, walking became difficult, mountain paths slippery. A mist came down, impassable. They stopped, lit a fire, crept under tents, the bone-chilling cold swirling in, breaths icy, sat looking out at nothingness.

The following morning they crept out of the tents to a clear sky. They packed and carried on up the hill eastwards. Then the whole company stopped.

There, ahead of them, standing proudly on a crag in the distance, rose a majestic tower, sparkling grey, lighter than the darker grey of the mountains around rising behind the tower. Estrién took Amber's hand, 'there it is dear, look, down there, the tarn they spoke of,' all eyes turned to the tarn, it looked dark and still, a few trees and shrubs around the edges. Then they looked back to the tower.

But it wasn't there, it had been there, it was no longer there.

Everyone blinked their eyes and shook their heads. It had been there a moment ago. They stared at the place where it had been, trying to see the tower.

Five minutes later it reappeared.

'Trick of the light,' declared Trevaine, 'depends on the sun's rays. It's got some kind of reflective stone or mineral in it, when the sun shines in a particular way you can see it. Otherwise it blends in with the background, perfectly camouflaged.'

'How do you know?' asked Dane, intrigued.

'Mage trick, knew a mage who did this back in Segantium, made a packet at festivals.'

Amber agreed. 'Yes, sort of thing we'd do in the circus too, especially in the side shows, the crowds loved it. Can't tell you how it's done though.'

'Well, we need to keep in mind the exact position,' stated Estrién. 'Between the disappearing act and the rain and mist, we can easily lose it.' He looked down at the tarn. 'Keep that to our right, shouldn't go too far wrong.'

They agreed, kept the tarn in sight, continued eastwards.

But they weren't quite correct about the now-you-see-it, now-you-don't tower.

There were other forces at work here.

Chapter 8

The path looked straight. At least, at first it looked straight, then it didn't, it curved and waved and took them around unexpected corners. It was straight, in the same way that a circle looks straight if you were on the perimeter, before you discover it's an infinity sign. The tarn they were 'keeping to their right' often appeared on their left, and like the tower, sometimes disappeared completely. Yet the road remained long and yes, *straight*.

After a half-day's walking they decided they were further away from the tower than when they had seen it that morning. They considered leaving the path, taking a direct route to the tower.

All the mages shook their heads ominously at that, *no straying from the path* - they knew what that could do in land like this. It was agreed, and in any case they had been commanded by the Auld Mother to not stray from the path. They followed its peculiar route.

Time and space were odd here, intermingled, played little jokes with each other and wrapped you around their respective little fingers. Only the path knew the way to the tower.

The Greylumings hold secrets and power, 'tis wise not to mess with them but go with the flow.

They came upon the tarn unexpectedly, it suddenly appeared to their right, a good place for it to be. As the clouds moved, so did the tarn change colour, greens, blues, slate grey and dull brown. Sometimes it reflected the sky, sometimes not, clean and clear, laden with rainbow-hued fish and gracefully swirling fronds of aquatic flora.

Then it changed and became deepest black as the world suddenly turned dark around them, fully black, totally black. It might have been night, but it was a solid wall of black. The company stopped moving, Robson lit the end of his staff, a bright blue swirling flame, yet apart from the faces around him, it lit nothing, not even the path.

No one moved, no one dared move. The tarn was just to their right, they knew that, at least, kept that knowledge. It was *probably* still to their right. They listened, usually there were lake noises, fish popping out and splashing the water, a few ducks, a whoosh of lakeside leaves.

Nothing, total silence.

The group sat down on the path, some in front, some behind, all facing the way they were going, or had planned to. They held hands and kept quiet, waiting. There was nothing else they could do. Robson held the light on his staff for as long as he could, then total darkness.

No one spoke for a while, then Amber began to worry that everyone was there. She made each speak their name, just to check, sighed with relief when all responded. Estrién took out a rope, each curled it around a wrist, looped around all of them, securing them together. Somehow, it felt safer. He held White Star high in the air, it shimmered, but had nothing to reflect, yet it cheered the company.

Then the light suddenly returned, and no, it wasn't daylight, just dim evening light, stars beginning to twinkle above them.

While they had a measure of light they quickly gathered a few twigs and branches from shrubs by the tarn, still roped together, one always remaining on the path to pull them back if necessary. The land could not be trusted.

Dane lit a fire, brewed tea, no one was hungry. They erected one of the tents, slept in two groups, four in, four on guard. Gertie perched herself on Reave's arm, then tucked up under a tent flap for the night. She too was wary. Bird or hunter, mage and man, all were subject to the Greylumings' own laws of nature.

The mist around them the following day was worse. Not so much the mist, the strange noises, calls and cries and odd bodies floating or drifting through the grey. Something ... someone walked up to Amber, tapped her on the shoulder and ran off. She shrieked, *what was that?*

They weren't ghosts, they were real, they lived. It was just that people had been this way before, and would come this way after. Time was odd here, curled in on itself, a Möbius strip, attached to itself without edges.

Here, everyone passed through at the same time, the mist similar to the one around Manecaestr, but all-time not no-time. Bodies came and went, some passing through their own bodies, one swept Reave aside as he hurried along the path. He didn't touch her, she couldn't feel his physical body, but there was a force, strange and unyielding. It was clear that each saw the other, but there could be no conversation, cries and gasps were heard from who-knew-when? They called back, but speech did not cross the aeons. Words were separated by centuries, sound is slower than light.

Amber considered that it was perhaps good that the mist around Manecaestr wasn't like this, the city would become jammed with people.

They decided to carry on regardless, walk steadily along the path, not stray, keep roped together. The path soon turned silent, others had trodden this path before, become, like them, mute with surprise, or fear. They too passed through bodies, ethereal in this time space, solid in their own. This was a lonely path, one few would follow unless necessary, yet it was filled with anxious, serious people, all intent on their own task, all acutely and uneasily aware of everyone else.

Then they heard Amber's name being called through the mist. It sounded like her sister, but she couldn't be sure. It could have been called now, yesterday, months ago, or tomorrow.

Still they walked, determined to push onwards, the mist would rise, all mists moved on, maybe the mist around Manecaestr would too?

But that mist had been created, this was natural, if such could be called so. It was simply a product of the mountains, the Greylumings, ancient and splendid, power beyond understanding.

As the day tracked towards noon and a spring sun beamed down, the mist began to die away. Bodies became fewer, further apart and the cries became quieter. Eventually the mist lifted, only for them to find that the tarn was now on their left and they were facing westwards. At some point during the blackness or the mist they had turned around. The tall tower looked further away, far distant.

'Fuck and blast!' Dane was heard to say, profane when angry.. They stopped for tea, the mages brought slippery-strange fish out of the tarn using their magic, they ate in silence. But it refreshed them, they marched off eastward diligently. By nightfall they had made up the ground and passed themselves. Perhaps they had actually passed their earlier selves in the mist earlier, who knew? But the night was crisp and clear and they continued as long as possible, sparkles in the path reflecting the bright moon.

Eventually they camped, Estrién lay his sword down on the path, the point facing forwards, the direction they needed. Amber too lay a dirk facing the same way, taking no chances this time. Again they took it in turns to sleep, eyes watched carefully all night for strangenesses, but the night was uneventful.

Tamlyn found Amber weeping in their tent.

'What ails you, liefl'en? Tell me, let me help?' He put an arm around her shoulders, held her hand. 'Is it your sister? We shall find her, take her home, we shall, I promise you.' His voice was tender.

She looked up, wiped her eyes. 'Just thinking of her taking this path, so desperate to get away, to hide. This terrible, lonely path, she walked it by herself, faced whatever dangers, finally found her sanctuary, then *he* came and violated it. She made her way to the end of the world for nothing.'

Tamlyn nodded, held her close. 'it may be that for the Weaver of Time as they call her, the path was not so terrible. And the Doe said they watched her, tried to help her. She was not alone, dulc'esta mea, have no fear of that.'

Amber agreed, that was true, yet her sister would not have known, she would still have felt alone and troubled. Dane and Estrién entered the tent, felt her anxiety, they too held her close. Hugs and kisses always help. Yet all slept a troubled and restless sleep that night.

The path kept to the edge of the tarn the following day, straighter and more predictable, it seemed to obey the normal laws of time and space for once. The sometimes sparkling tower loomed closer, as did the mountains. High and gloomy they became, almost blotting out the noonday sun, and the air grew cold as the sun disappeared. Sometimes the tower disappeared too, popping back into view ten minutes or so later. None knew if it was light or time or magic, or just a reflection of the minerals in the stone?

By afternoon the land had become jagged, raw grey stone, sharp and merciless. There was an odd smell here too, similar to the coal seams they passed near the settlements of beehive huts, ferrous and sulphurous, something unclean. Vegetation fled from this place, nothing grew between these rocks. Yet birds flew back and forth, from the tower itself, making for the trees around the tarn, the only patch of greenery. Many chattered above them, once they saw a fight in the air, magpies and ravens versus a group of rooks. No one knew which side had turned, which birds fought on *his* side, it was impossible to tell. Only when Gertie suddenly flew up, joined in the fight on the side of the magpies could it be seen the rooks here were *his*. She brought several down, turned the tide of the fight, the remaining rooks fled. She flew back triumphantly to Reave's waiting arm.

Somehow, many decades, or possibly centuries previously, someone had hewn steps in this jagged rock, had carved a rough passage up the hillside to the tower above. Flat slate grey stones were laid, easier on the feet that the shale and rubble of the hillside. The group followed the steps, part of the path – no straying - keep to the path or who knew what might happen? The steps too curved and shifted, taking them the long way around the hill, almost as if there could never be a direct route there.

A little way up and they came across a small shrine, obviously to the mage or enchantress who lived above. It appeared to be made of granite, much darker, carved with patience and attention to detail, symbols of sun and moon, leaves and flowers carved into the stone. A small candle sat in a hollow stone bowl next to a small wooden carving of the Lady Merrie. Sacks were left, also some dried flowers and grasses tied with flaxen twine, a few bulrushes from the tarn. Someone had left a tiny doll dressed with care, a likeness perhaps of a child or babe, hoping for a blessing from the Weaver.

They carefully collected everything to take to Anaïs in the tower at the top of the hill. Amber peeped in the sacks: a little corn, some pulses, dried fish and meat, one sack was simply goat hair, one of sheep's wool. The Wildlings had tried to help her. Amber tried not to break down again, but her heart was touched by these simple kindnesses.

Estrién turned to Amber, took her hand, reassured her. 'Soon, dearest, soon. We'll help your sister, see, others too have helped her, she hasn't been alone.' Amber nodded at him, yes ... soon.

The first few tentative circuits around the base of the hill remained quiet and peaceful. Why the path had to meander so much was anyone's guess? Perhaps the people - or mages - who had created it had simply found it the easier method. Perhaps it started off straight and steep but the Greylumings considered otherwise. Whatever the case, it slowly trundled its painstaking spiral up the hill to the tower.

But as they rounded the steps a few minutes later, something changed, the mountain turned silent, the atmosphere flushed with electric expectancy.

Within seconds dark clouds loomed from the west, a light rain began to fall. The clouds quickly turned darker and the air colder, soft rain turned to sharp hail. The hail lashed down its small, painful white missiles, beating the tops of heads mercilessly. The steps became lethal as they quickly turned white, halted everyone in their tracks.

Cries of 'what the hell?' and 'oh bugger,' amongst other more profane statements could be heard, mostly from Dane. All peered miserably at the slippery, sliding white steps.

Then came a long, low and ominous rumble. Hail, it seemed wasn't enough. The sky lit up and thunder rolled in, the hail momentarily stopping before the rain bucketed down, a deluge of water. Clothes, cloaks, hair was drenched, cold-splattered to the core. It lashed down mercilessly, flooding the stairway to the tower, rocks and boulders tumbling perilously, an icy river flowing swiftly down the steps making passage impassable. Amber was knocked in the shins and knees by the passing debris, cries and yelps were heard.

The path turned treacherous.

None of this was natural.

He knew they were there. *He* would stop them at all cost.

There were more cries as Reave and Salli lost their footing as the flood hit them and they began to slide downwards, backwards to the bottom.

'Grab them!' Estrién shouted. Hands quickly took hold, and they all clasped arms and hands, trying to keep upright in the flowing water and stay together. Estrién took the rope out again, passed it around, everyone lashed themselves to it. If anyone fell, the others would keep hold, not let them go.

... Or all go together.

There were more crashes of thunder and now lightning began to strike around them, glancing off rocks and steps. It seemed to be deliberately aiming for the waterway of the destroyed stairway, directed by some unseen hand. The group scrambled quickly off the over-flowing steps onto craggy and equally slippery rocks, before the lightning struck the waters and electrocuted the lot of them. Electric bolts crashed and flashed one after another, thunder growled and roared, all of it aiming for the companions.

The three elemental mages worked together to throw up a joint protective circle around them as a lightning bolt arced its jagged way down, directly above them. It glanced off harmlessly, but then came another and another. They worked relentlessly as bolts came down one after another, after another.

He was many miles away, but he knew they were there. He could not come physically immediately, the distance too far but he could send emissaries and weather was easy to control. *He* could not let them reach Anaïs.

Dane understood this was no normal storm, he could feel the magic, *he* had done this. He wondered how long it could continue, how long their mana could hold up the circle? Not long enough, he decided, they were mages with a finite amount of mana merely defending themselves against an enemy with unknown resources. Defence was OK but defence never won a battle, when that mana ran out there would be no defence at all. He steeled himself, an idea he would test, whatever it cost him. He had to try.

'Let me out!' he shouted to Robson and Trevaine, quickly removing the rope around his wrist. They gazed, startled at him ... *out* ... in that? He nodded, 'give me a portal to get through.'

They did as told, he was the master mage of their group.

Dane dashed through the opening, they closed it as he ran. He clambered, sliding constantly, further up the slope along the sharp and jagged stones, keeping away from the streams of water coming down the steps. He finally perched himself on a higher rock some way above them, a reasonable distance, made sure his footing was secure, that the ground beneath him was flat enough for his purpose. He concentrated deeply, a mage concentration, inside and yet outside, one with himself and his surroundings, before holding up his oaken staff and shouting out, *'you're not the only one who can control lightning mate!'*

He held the staff high in the air, his arms spread out, for a moment he closed his eyes in readiness. Then he took a deep breath and began to twirl around and around, waving the staff in a circle, a mad whirling dance.

The oak staff began, as oaks do, to attract the lightning.

Under the protective canopy mouths gaped open as the silver blue flashes turned from them and streamed towards Dane, making for the staff, as lightning makes for the lightning rod.

Amber screamed, her hand on her mouth in fear of her loved one. She tried to get out to help him, Estrién held her back.

'He knows what he's doing love. Let him concentrate.'

Dane however didn't act as a lightning rod does, he didn't earth the zig zag bolts, they didn't go through the staff, through him and finally into the rocks around them. Instead they streamed *into* the raised staff, one by one by one, flash by flash. He stood firm and strong as the lightning shot into the oaken stave. Eventually, it began to shake and shudder as the power flowed inwards; Dane had to hold the staff with both hands to control it, each power surge making the staff more difficult to control.

This was the very opposite of the event at Sunstones.

For a full five minutes Dane held the staff high as the lightning poured in. Now he was shaking as the staff shook, he wondered how long he could take it? This was more powerful than anything he had encountered. The determined and resourceful mage stood strong, he would overcome this at all costs, even if that cost was himself.

Yet the staff held, the clean and purified staff made wholesome by the Doe.

The lightning began to dwindle as it disappeared down his staff. The thunder calmed, was finally beaten and went rumbling and coughing its way down the mountainside. The lashing rain eased, was neutered into nothingness.

Finally there came calm, just a little wind whispered through the mountains.

Eventually Trevaine and Robson took down the protective circle and ran to Dane as he collapsed exhausted on the ground above them.

Hell's bells!' he was heard to say. 'I'm effing charged with the stuff!' He extended an arm from his prone position, electric bolts shot out. 'Think I took in some residual lightning, the staff is absolutely full, it was overflowing.' He shot out a few more bolts from trembling fingertips. 'Keep away everyone, let me get rid of some of this or I'll electrocute you.'

For a minute or two he shot amberic bolts into the mountainside. 'Whew, that's better, but I'd still keep clear of me for a while, I'm buzzing!' He smiled cheerily at them all.

Amber shook her head in amazement; only mages could perform such a feat as that. *Truly amazing.* 'You're incredible!' she shouted to him. Dane just grinned and waved.

They waited for the steps to dry out before moving on.

'He knows we're here,' Dane remarked, 'he threw that at us, it wasn't natural.'

There was a general agreement all round. 'He knows we're close to my sister,' commented Amber.

Estrién stood firm. 'We stick together, we beat him,' he announced, his melodious voice determined and passionate. 'Every one of us must hold true to each other, to our land, to the Lady Merrie. Keep her love in our hearts and *he* cannot break us.' He was strong in his conviction.

Amber took hold of his hand. 'Let's find my sister,' she said, 'get her to safety - if there is such a place.'

They continued the long climb up the steps to the tower. They were ill-wrought affairs, the hail and storm loosened them and there were rockslides in places. Many steps had gone leaving nothing but steep slope and rubble.

The younger mages made it their job to create a useable path, shifting and flattening stones. Dane did little, he was exhausted, but Trevaine and Robson worked tirelessly. Everyone helped remove boulders that somehow mysteriously blocked the pathway, lodged exactly in the places calculated to hold them back the most.

Yet even as they were nearing it, the tower disappeared from view.

'Not again!' they all cried, although Dane was heard to shout something rather more profane.

Then the light disappeared again, complete blackness came over and covered the craggy hill. Either *he* was determined they should not reach her, or the very mountains decreed it. Perhaps it was just an effect of the Greylumings, a simple, natural but somewhat erratic phenomenon. Regardless, everything turned pitch black yet again.

Once more they stopped walking, stood still. Once more Robson lit the end of his staff and bright blue starlight shone from it. Yet it did not penetrate the darkness, just a light that all could see. Again the ropes came out, again they attached them to the group. No one moved ... no one dared, there was a long drop below.

They stood in weary silence as the darkness filled the mountain sides. On it went, on and on, never varying. Dane flashed fire out into the void, nothing could be seen but further darkness.

They sat down, wondering how long it could go on for?

Five minutes, ten minutes, the time stretched out, one hour, then two and more.

'We've got to do something ...' Estrién stated. 'So damn near, so close.'

The darkness carried on. The group sat together in heavy silence, unable to move, the hillside a mass of loose rocks brought down by the flooding. Dane was heard swearing and complaining in frustration.

Amber thought she heard something, looked up, 'what's that?' she asked, hoping it wasn't more of *his* magic thrown at them.

Hey all saw it, the light in the darkness. It seemed friendly somehow, not born of a misshaped evil but kindness. A small light, a flickering light, no more than a candle, wavering and drifting inside its little glass lantern.

Through the thickened air came a weak but clear voice, a voice unused to regular speech, a voice fragile but resolute.

'Is that you Amber? Is that my sister?' The words came soft and gentle on the air.

A young woman, aged with care, slowly crept into view, a small but welcome lantern held in her hand. The lantern's magic glow - for it was no ordinary light - cleared and cheered the darkness around her, or perhaps it was the woman, not the light.

Everyone watched as she carefully made her way towards them.

'I will take you up to my tower,' the quiet voice told them, holding out a painfully thin and trembling hand, beckoning them. 'Follow me.'

Amber's eyes filled with tears, her heart weeping, as she watched the bruised and battered form of her younger sister tread slowly ahead of them. Her once golden hair had turned completely white, her body bent in pain as she limped and hobbled her way slowly before them to the place that had once been her refuge.

They had found the young woman known locally as the Weaver, Anaïs, the Weaver of Time.

*

End of part One.

Mer'edrynn Book 3

SeamRipper

Part 2: Wyndecraft.

Adammite HQ, Isle of Glasse, month of Shroving.
Colonel Mackenzie stood at the end of the conference table and called the session to order.

'Firstly I would like to hold a two minute silence to commemorate the sad passing of our beloved leader, Mordecai von Adamm.' It was, he realised, the first time he had spoken von Adamm's name in full.

The rest of the Adammite top personnel around the table, a mixed bunch of military, administrative executives and political leaders nodded, all stood and bowed their heads. During the silence it dawned on Mackenzie that von Adamm's name was somewhat contrived. No one could surely be born with such a portentous name? The man had clearly taken it as a pseudonym, a pretty good one. He wondered what his real name had been ... or perhaps if it should be kept as the hereditary title of the leader? Whatever, he wasn't paid to think, he was paid to perform, let the next leader consider the matter.

Time stretched as it always does during moments of inaction and imposed contemplation. At least feet didn't shuffle nor did anyone sneeze or cough - trained soldiers stand quietly.

Eventually he held up his hand to break the silence. 'We all know why we are here, we intend to install a new leader of the Adammites, to continue the work started by Commander von Adamm to create a fully Adammite-controlled land throughout Mer'edrynn. Von Adamm has gone, defeated by this bloody annoying White Shield group, a mixed set of troublemaking misfits if ever there was one,' he grumbled. 'Our leader is dead, a new one must take his place.

I have no intention of offering myself here, I have arranged this meeting purely as his second-in-command, leader of his armed forces at Draecastle.' He shook his head, 'I am a good soldier, a damn good one, despite what happened that night when our supposed allies turned against us, but I know my limits. We need someone with foresight, strength of purpose and an ability to sway others. I hereby offer the chair to anyone who believes he has these qualities.' He sat down with relief, duty done.

Colonel Grey rose immediately, no point letting anyone else get a word in first. *See the opportunity, grab it, take out the competition,* was his motto.

'Before I speak, I'd like to offer our grateful thanks to the man who made our movement possible and for whom we mourn this day. Von Adamm led the way to a new understanding, a belief in ourselves as masters of this world. It can only be our duty to carry on this work, to fulfil that belief.' He raised a fist high in the air. 'Three cheers for von Adamm,' he shouted, 'Hip hip!'

The various Colonels, Chiefs of Staff and Administrative Officers around the long oblong table cheered loudly.

'Thank you, my friends and colleagues. Our humble respect is due to our fallen leader.' He stopped to stare each member in the eye before continuing, a trick he had learned from the 'great man' himself. He'd spent years watching him. 'We *must* carry on ... and we *will* carry on. Our leader created an indestructible machine when he created the Adammites, we are bound together as one, one goal, one purpose. We have an excellent and ready-prepared set of rules and regulations to follow, his great words of wisdom are already spread throughout the lands. We require someone capable of imposing those rules, capable of leading men.

For several years I advised von Adamm from a military standpoint until he moved north to Draecastle. As an experienced soldier I personally believed we should consolidate our position in the south east and von Adamm left me in charge to do so. It was right for him to ally with King Kyneweth, an Adammite sympathiser, a very wise political decision. Von Adamm was a great thinker and speaker, his ideologies and ideas the very centre of our beliefs.

At some point, the general plan was for our troops to move northwards and the northern troops to move south, thus taking the whole centre of Mer'edrynn between us. Thenceforth, once the main centres of civilisation were ours, we could move on to the removal of the elves from Floriénne, followed by the instigation of Adammite rule in the northern realms of Vikénar, Picantés etcetera. In other words, the complete imposition of Adammite rule over the whole of Mer'edrynn. That was his ultimate goal

However, von Adamm was not a warrior, he had never trained as a soldier. Both I and Colonel Mackenzie advised him continually in military matters. Unfortunately he did not always listen.' He could see Mackenzie nodding vigorously. 'As a soldier I believed it was not wise to take so many of our men up to Draecastle, splitting our effective forces, nor was the decision to try to take the southern ports of Westerling a good military move at that time. I offered him my advice, he ignored it, as was his right. He was our leader, the decisions were his to make. Events have since proved me correct. I lost too many good men at Pennyport.

Despite this, I have not only been able to consolidate our position in Elvinhaeme, I have taken the capital city and made it our own. Elvinhaeme is now correctly termed *Mordecia* in honour of von Adamm.' He raised his eyebrows and smiled. Everyone around the table cheered.

'I think I have already proved my capabilities. I had little resources remaining once von Adamm had left, and the debacle at Pennyport. Yet I recovered, I planned and I worked. In proof of this, I currently sit on the throne of the palace in Belcast'el. Believe me, gentlemen, I intend to take all the cities of Mer'edrynn, and cast off any who perch their pathetic Merrievian backsides on their respective thrones.' He paused to allow them to take in his remarks, something Von Adamm would have done.

'We can work together to take Mer'edrynn fully, When politicians, military and the whole administrative machine work as one, this is clearly possible. But we need to plan carefully protect what we have and steadily take more .We have already planted the seed of unrest in many towns and cities, we must continue taking advantage of that fact. But from now on we must act militarily, we must use our own excellent forces to take this land. We must realise there are no allies, as with Kyneweth, there are only Adammites. Allies can turn, can betray, as they did at Draecastle. My enemy's enemy is not my friend, he may even be another potential enemy. The only trust we can have is trust in ourselves. The only truth we know is the Adammite truth, the belief in ourselves.

I can assure you I have that belief and the knowledge, the experience and the damn dogged determination to do not just as Von Adamm did, but more, to lead you into the glorious future of an Adammite-controlled world.' He stopped, he'd wasted enough time chatting, time now to get a move on. He looked up and nodded at the door.

Two dozen of his fully armed and highly trained men swept through and arranged themselves behind the chairs of everyone present. Each held a hand to his sword, awaiting the Colonel's orders. There were enough to take out everyone sitting at the table in one swift move. Two guards holding lethal-looking crossbows stood by his side, each pointed generally at the assembled.

There were some seriously startled eyes around the table.

'May I introduce you to my personal guard, gentlemen?' He stopped and smiled at the company. 'I fully intend to take over as sole Commander of the Adammites, a name I also intend to retain. Does anyone wish to dispute that?' Each guard took one menacing step closer. He watched the raised eyebrows, then saw the grin and a 'thumbs up' from Colonel Mackenzie, who immediately stood and began clapping his hands. He briefly nodded to him, an understanding between two military men. The assembled group looked to him, then also rose from the table, began applauding, aware they had been outflanked in more ways than one.

The Chief Executive of Administrative Affairs, normally stationed at the Isle of Glasse, spoke up on behalf of them all.

'You're just the man we're after, Commander,' he declared as the applause died away. 'You'll be ideal.'

*

Little could be seen as the group followed Anaïs up the final stretch of hill to her tower, only the wavering light of her lantern, lit by one small votive candle. They followed her shuffling footsteps, wary of treading out of the narrowly lit path into absolute darkness. Yet the short journey took time, her pace painfully slow, Amber could hear her laboured breathing and panting, Dane and Salli could only wait patiently until they reached her home, both straining at the bit to give her some ease, to help heal her, their mage's souls sorrowed by such agony as she must feel.

As they circled round the hill, the tower suddenly sparkled into view, glinting and glittering, lamps could be seen in small arched tower windows, and further around, a warm glow through a tall arched doorway.

The group heard a small voice, clearly pleased. 'It always does that, it lights up when I come home,' Anaïs pointed out. 'I think it likes me.'

They followed her through the doorway into a well lit circular room, torches in sconces on the walls, barrels and wooden boxes, sacks and baskets scattered across the floor. The locals, many of whom were at least a day or days walk away, had left plenty for her.

In a niche of the room blazed a fire in a circular brazier. It was hot, extremely hot, yet had no smoke. Neither did it smell of burning wood or the local coal. The flames seemed to rise from one large, possibly oak log in the brazier. A cauldron above held water for washing.

A circular wooden bath hid behind some of the boxes, soap and a towel neatly placed on a tiny table next to it. Two wooden buckets stood by the fire ready to collect water from the outside rain-barrel for bathing, easiest here on the ground floor, no more steps to climb with heavy buckets.

On a slate bench sat a big washing bowl, a few dishes and a couple of wooden spoons drying at the side. A smaller bucket on the floor held a mixture of water and urine, traditional for cleaning raw wool.

'This is the store room,' she told them, 'come upstairs, there are several flights.' Quietly the slight grey robed figure led them up stairs that circled the tower wall, stopping every few steps to take breath; she would turn and smile encouragingly, but pain covered her features.

They came to the second floor where a spinning wheel sat resting in the centre as well as a variety of carding implements. Sacks of wool lay around; a table was covered in spools of plain thread awaiting use. Here she combed and spun the thread for her tapestry. She dyed only that which she needed, small amounts at a time, the dyes difficult to come by.

Across the wooden floor, then more steps along the wall of the tower to the next floor.

The third floor was her bedroom, sparse and simple. A small wooden bed with a gay patchwork cover, rush matting on the floor, a candle in a stone basin on a tiny stool by her bed. There were no mirrors or any feminine accoutrements, just a brush for her hair on a wooden wash stand where a bright yellow jug stood next to a small white basin. A dish held soap, and a towel hung on a wooden peg in the wall.

Just across from these was a tiny shrine to the Lady Merrie. A rush mat lay in front of a table on which stood a small soapstone statue of the Lady, hands out in welcome as always, candles in soapstone dishes at each side of her, a wooden tray in front with offerings of dried flowers.

Amber wondered how often her sister had prayed for help at that shrine?

Another slow climb to the next floor, clearly living quarters, an ancient and battered dining table and two chairs , a small stool with a beautiful embroidered cushion upon it close to another small fire set in a niche in the wall, the heat in here stifling. Here Anaïs cooked her solitary meals in a cauldron hung from a spit across the fire. Again it seemed to consist of one log of some sort, nor were there other logs nearby to make up the fire. A small chimney took cooking smells out, as downstairs, there was no smoke at all, only a little steam from the soup in the cooking pot. As with the bedroom, it was plain and simple, the grey stone walls were devoid of any embellishments other than small torches.

'Please sit down, would you like some ale?' the small voice asked, politeness learned at her mother's knee had not been forgotten, words spoken hesitantly, as if the art of speech *was* forgotten. It was clear the effort of reaching them had exhausted her, yet here she was playing hostess to her sister and seven strangers.

The company could plainly see her eyes were troubled, traumatised beyond fear, she looked shocked, her body trembled.

Amber broke down, ran to her sister, held her in her arms. For a few moments the others watched as two sisters wept and hugged each other, before Estrién spoke. He was angry and shocked at the state of affairs, but he kept his temper, his voice gentle.

'My dear sister-in-law, we have come to take you home, to help you and to protect you. I only wish we could have come before. Nevertheless, as soon as it is light, we shall gather everything necessary and get you to safety.'

Anaïs' eyes widened. 'Sister-in-law? *Oh*, of course ...' she added cryptically, then looked at Amber, 'how lovely for you Amber, and you look so strong, so fine, but then you always were.' She sat heavily down on the small stool by the fire, unable to stand a moment longer with her pain.

Amber laughed amidst her tears, 'yes dear, Estrién is my husband but,' she gave a sly grin towards Dane and Tamlyn, 'it's a little more complicated than that!'

The two stepped forward, bowed to Anaïs, each echoing Amber's grin.

'We are her bondsmen,' Tamlyn explained, 'we are all part of one bond.' He was Tamlyn; he took her fragile hand and gently kissed the back of it. Anaïs smiled, her eyes suddenly bright.

'What lovely men, Amber, and it is very kind of you, but I cannot go anywhere. I could barely walk to meet you all, I can go no further than that.' Her softly spoken words were almost matter-of-fact about it. She seemed distant from all of them, her world was here, not out there. *He* had been but recently, he hadn't destroyed her will as he intended, but her body was broken.

Everyone shook their heads, she wasn't remaining here another day.

Dane moved close to her, his mage senses trembling at her pain. 'We are your brothers now, your welfare is in our hands. We'll stay tonight dear, get some food and a night's sleep. Tomorrow we take you home, you tell us what needs to be taken, we'll carry everything. You are coming with us if we have to carry you every step of the way.'

'There's a lot to take, I thank you with all my heart.' She suddenly smiled at the company, a sweet smile from a pale young face lined with pain, eyes that held horrors unknown and a mane of long, prematurely white hair.

Salli now came forward, he too bowed; everyone felt there should be both formality and politeness in her company. 'I am a healer mage, as is Dane, will you let us look at you, we can give you some ease.'

She shook her head, spoke in her gentle voice. 'I think your magic is unlikely to work upon me, but if you have any potions that soothe aches, they would be welcome.'

They took her downstairs to her bed chamber on the floor below, came back some minutes later. 'She's asleep, she's exhausted.' Dane had given her a soothing sleeping draught. 'She's right though, our magic won't work in her, she's too powerful.'

Salli agreed. 'Never felt anything like her, and her body has been broken in many places. Don't know how she remains upright.' He stood seething in the wavering light of the wall torches. 'I'm a healer, not a warrior, but if I ever come across the individual who has done this I will personally tear him apart with my own hands.'

There was a general agreement among the company.

'I'll carry her home, she can hardly weigh anything,' Tamlyn stated. 'From this moment her life changes for the better.'

'Yes,' agreed Amber, 'as long as we *can* get her out of here. It's been quiet since we arrived, but who knows what the morning will bring?'

She took a torch from one the wall sconces. 'There are more floors above, let's look what's there.'

Carefully she climbed the stairs to the next room, an odd smell now permeating down the stairs, something smothering and unclean.

Tables filled the circular room, littered with bottles and potions, an alembic or two, dishes filled with dyes and herbs. Dried grasses and flowers filled rush baskets. This was the room where Anaïs created the alchemical dyes for her wools and threads. It didn't smell good. Dane went over to a set of jars on one of the tables, opened one and sniffed carefully. He stepped back coughing.

'Holy Mother, what is in that?' He quickly replaced the lid before the smell permeated the whole room.

But that wasn't where the foul smell was coming from. Amber stood at the bottom of the stairs to the top tower room. 'It's coming from up there,' she told them, moving upwards.

She took hold of the black metal handle of the door and unlatched it. As it swung open she hurriedly stepped back, gagging. 'Goodness me!,' she complained before taking a deep breath and peeking in. It was dark night, there were no torches lit on the walls, but Amber could see a little with the torch she carried.

The room was filled with a large sewing frame, a chair in front, a table at its side covered with threads and sewing implements. Huge spools of plain thread stood at the side, the base for the weave. It was too dark to see the colours of the threads on the tables,, but the smell of them was abominable. A small dish looked like it held blood, but Amber couldn't be sure.

The sewing frame held the tapestry Anaïs was creating.

She moved over to the tapestry, an ill-odour emanating from the cloth.

Inside the frame was currently a blank canvas, about three feet high by three feet wide, the tightly stretched warp awaiting the weft threads to be woven into the next scene. To the right edge of the frame the finished tapestry rolled onwards, curling over itself, yards upon yards upon yards of it. From what Amber could see in the dim light, it was in clear sections, each separated by a small cream panel, possibly flax, an edging of simplicity that stitched the frames together. A brief look showed it depicted scenes from the events in the world, the story of Mer'edrynn over the past few years. It was mostly woven, but some scenes were embroidered upon the basic weave, stitches on top of stitches, as if the weaver had changed her mind or wanted to emphasise something in a canvas that could not be altered once woven. The final weave it seemed, must remain untouched. Whatever the case, foul-smelling as it was, she could see that even in the dim and wavering light of the torch, the tapestry was magnificent.

She saw the fortress of Draecastle, men in bright armour fighting outside, flashes of mage light in the sky. The wall walk of the inner keep was displayed separately, two people with arms stretched high, as a figure fell below them to the ground. A dark horseman had been embroidered in a corner, watching as his General fell. He was not of the weave, stitched outside the cloth, but his form still disturbed the pattern.

She could see a huge city depicted in detail, beautiful and intricate work. There was a tear in the fabric around the city, no more than a thread wide. Amber understood, it was enough to cast Manecaestr adrift. Even so, it seemed held together, there must be fine stitching somewhere, it was still part of the weave. There, yet not there.

She peeked at the last scene just beyond the sewing frame. To her surprise it showed Amber and the group climbing the mountain. Someone looking like Dane held a staff in the air as lightning struck. She had depicted him well, even the look of concentration on his face.

Had she seen them from her tower, had this been woven as they approached - or had it been woven previously - *before* they arrived?

Whatever the case, the new canvas in the frame itself lay bare, long lines of taut warp threads awaiting the weave, waiting for events to come.

*

The group made themselves comfortable overnight, got a big stew going in the cauldron, arranged their sleeping mats. Dane, Tamlyn and Estrién went downstairs to see what could be recovered from the barrels and boxes. Several held beans, grains and pulses, they would fill their sacks and pouches with what they could carry, food being pretty scarce in the mountains. There were a few bottles of usquebae as well as the local 'broon dog', many covered in dust, obviously Anaïs was no drinker. It was clear the local people - not that local either - had ensured Anaïs didn't starve. Dane was interested in the various herbs, but decided to leave it for the morn to check them out.

The night was quiet, the morning dawned clear and bright and when Amber peeped out of one of the arched windows, the mountain looked clean and fresh. She could see a nearby waterfall sparkling its way down the mountainside. It was hard to believe the events of the previous days.

She went to wake her sister, found an empty bed. Hurriedly ran downstairs searching through rooms but couldn't find her.

She eventually took the steps to the tower room. The sunlight hit her as she entered, the windows were large and many in this circular space. They were open this morning, fresh mountain air breezing through, cleansing the foul smell of the night before. It was a bright room, and as in her sitting room, a cheerful fire blazed in the corner. Like the fire down below, there was no smoke.

Her sister was sitting at the loom, quietly stitching.

'Hallo Amber, it's so good to see you.' She looked calm and, like the room, bright and cheerful, as if nothing had happened. 'I have no pain this morning, that draught Dane gave me was powerful. I must thank him.' She carried on weaving as if her life depended on it. Perhaps it did.

'We need to get a move on dear, we need to get going.' Amber kept her voice gentle, clearly her sister hadn't taken in what they were planning. She watched as her sister's nimble fingers swiftly wove a pattern, pushing the different coloured threads down the warp as she wove to pack them tightly.

'There is time ...' her sister replied softly.

Amber looked over her shoulder, a pattern already beginning to be displayed. On the lower part of the tapestry a small border could be seen. At first Amber thought they were splashes of blood, but then realised her sister was creating the beginning of a border of red and white roses. 'They're lovely ...' she commented.

Her sister sighed, 'yes, they will be. There will be a border of them all around this section. I woke this morning and wanted to get this started.'

'I came up here last night,' Amber confessed, 'I saw part of your beautiful tapestry, but ...' she trailed off. She tried to be tactful. 'It, well, it smelled pretty badly in here, is it the dyes or something?'

Her sister shook her head. 'Only partly, it's always worse at night. There are bad things in the weave.' She looked sorrowfully at her sister. 'I had to put them in, *he* made me, no choice, he has too much strength for me alone. *He* put his blood in there, and slit my wrist to mingle with his blood - neither should be in.' She continued her weaving, her hands moving with tremendous speed over the tapestry.

'Can't you remove them, or cleanse the blood?' Amber asked.

'No dear, once a frame is complete, it cannot be altered. I can add a little embroidery - but that alters time itself.' She smiled now, 'Time ought to be constant, there are things that shall be, they are ordained. Once it is placed here in the tapestry it is written. Yet there are people who themselves change time, they change the pattern of the future.' She gazed oddly at her sister before continuing. 'Cleanse it? I don't know...' she shook her head uncertainly. 'But I have done my best to keep it true, there are so many flaws, so much evil has entered the world. I have tried to hold it back, tried to repair that which has been shredded. It's been hard sister, so hard.'

Amber could see the panic in her eyes.

Anaïs whispered to her, confiding. 'I could not have gone on much longer. Then it would have been *his* will, the future *he* ordained, outside of time. I would have been forced to put him in the frame, directly into the weave. That would be the end of the world as we know it.

Still, I always knew you would come. But you know, I was never sure if I truly knew, or if it was just wishful thinking ... You cannot foretell your own future.

Let me be for now dear, I must continue. I leave the move in your hands.' She turned back to the tapestry, continued weaving, totally engrossed. The world outside no longer existed other than in the frame.

Amber kissed her cheek and left to organise the move.

They found her later still stitching. Estrién gently removed her from the loom. 'Come dear, it's time to go. We'll carry your loom and the tapestry. Can they be separated?'

'Technically, yes, in reality, no. All the sections have been woven separately as this one, but all are stitched together.'

She looked firmly up at him. 'It wouldn't be right. I'm sorry, but they must be carried together.'

He looked at the tapestry on the floor, once rolled fully it would be quite some weight, add the loom and it would be pretty heavy. Still, there were mages to lighten the load.

There was also Anaïs to carry, as well as her wools and silks, various dyes, and the dried foodstuffs. Plus tents, sleeping mats, weapons, water bottles and a whole host of other paraphernalia necessary to keep nine people alive and well in the wilderness.

No problem then...

Everyone did their share and Tamlyn was true to his word. He picked her up and marched out of the door with her in his arms. 'You're no weight,' he whispered to her, 'come, little sister, just you cling on to me.'

Amber carried her bag of wools and silk threads, and a pack containing her few clothes and possessions. She slipped the small embroidered cushion from the stool before the fire into her bag. It was sweetly pretty, flowers and leaves interlaced together, a shame to leave it behind.

The tapestry was tightly rolled up and secured to the loom, blankets tucked around to keep the rain off. The four mages carried the loom and the tapestry between them, none wanted anything happening to it. They regarded it as a sacred trust. They left the liquid dyes, but took dried herbs and coloured powders ready to be used for dye. None wanted the stink of some of the dyes in the bottles and Anaïs had given no instructions for these.

Estrién and Reave took what they could with them from the stores.

Amber looked at the fire, wondered how to put it out, cover it with ashes perhaps?

There were no ashes.

'Leave them in,' Anaïs told her. 'The fires were lit when I arrived, they've never gone out. It's mage fire, secret and sacred, eternal in form. This and the two downstairs must be left for the next mage who arrives here.'

The mages inspected the fire, shook their heads, it was beyond their capabilities. Dane considered using ice magic to douse it, decided it was best held in respect, left as it had been.

They prepared to leave. Everyone hoped there would be no need to fight, over-laden as they were.

Yet the first problem was getting down the narrow winding steps of the hill, the storm had blown many of the treads away and the rocks on either side were treacherous. It was slow going, often the loom was seen to be hovering in mid air as it was manoeuvred down.

Tamlyn was afraid of slipping with his own precious burden.

Yet the weather held, nothing appeared to halt their progress as they descended. They stopped to make camp as the day turned dark; they had made it near the tarn - to their left this time. The loom was given space in one of the tents, kept covered in case of rain. Anaïs slept with the loom, preferring to rest almost as soon as they made camp. Dane went in to check on her, offer her more herbal painkillers. He always carried oils, massaged her spine with a soothing mix, she fell asleep immediately. He tried to enter her in his magical way, to heal, but the barrier of her own magic stopped him. Still, it was a little less strong than the night before, maybe the painkillers, maybe she just trusted him more.

He was disturbed. It reminded him of the night he met Amber, how he had checked her body, found the bruises, the beatings and the internal sprains and wounds. With Anaïs, it was already obvious from the outside, but what he could discover internally, was horrendous. Her physical suffering must be terrible. More to the point, he worried about her psychological problems. There was something not quite right, she was shut in upon herself, the world outside blocked. She had been polite with them all, yet kept herself separate. Although, he admitted, with the power he felt in her, it was probably necessarily so.

What was it with these sisters? Who chose to hurt two such lovely beings, to harm and maim them?

But he knew who, or more precisely *what*. Amber herself had said, *he* seemed to be there all her life, somewhere on the edge, high on the horizon. Barely seen, but still... *there*.

Clearly determined to punish the two sisters in as many ways as possible...

He took Amber aside for a quiet word.

I didn't want to worry you last night because I wasn't sure. She is in a great deal of pain and her spine is out of line. Now ...' as Amber looked up shocked, 'we can help there, manoeuvre the spine back, massage and use supports to guide it back over time. I could do it more quickly with magic, but that's not possible with your sister. It's fairly recent, a few weeks or less, he must have given her a real beating to get it like that. There are other things too, various ribs have been broken in the past, they've healed but he's punished her beyond belief.' He stopped, looked Amber in the eye. 'That's not actually what I'm worried about, all of this can heal over time, given the right conditions.'

Amber stared at him, a worried frown across her features. 'What is it Dane, don't hold back. Is she dying?'

'What ...?' He shook his head, 'oh no, she'll live, after a fashion. But she's completely traumatised, that will take a lot longer to heal. She ... there's something wrong ... I can't figure out what, she feels ... *strange*. She seems to have retreated into a world of her own. She speaks, she answers you, but she's somewhere else. I'm not sure if we can bring her back from that.'

'She needs time and care Dane, he's broken her in too many ways. But you know...' Amber smiled up at him, 'we females are stronger than you think. She's had no one to trust in years, she has to be brought gently back into our world. I'm not casting off my sister yet, she's hardier than you know. She's never been like the rest of us, you can't fit her into a normal set of rules, so don't try.'

Amber walked off to prepare a wholesome broth for her sister, a little cupboard love never went amiss.

*

They continued down the mountainside the following morning. The tarn mysteriously remained in place and the path oddly ran straight. Maybe having Anaïs with them kept time at bay, maybe the tapestry had something to do with it. True, the peculiar mist came down again, voices were heard, both near and far, even the occasional shape flitted past, but Anaïs seemed in control here. It certainly didn't worry her. She asked Tamlyn to put her down, she would walk for a short while.

She stood squarely in front of them and held out her arms in supplication, her face peering upwards to the sky.

The mist shifted, became dawn, although it had been mid afternoon when the mist came down. It didn't matter, it was clear, they continued on their way. Tamlyn could not bear to see her hobbling, he picked her up again after a hundred yards or so.

'Come little elain'ae, it is too much for you.' She smiled up at him, put her arms around his neck. 'Put your trust in me, let me help you.' She nodded, put her head on his shoulder and fell asleep.

It was possibly the first truly peaceful sleep she'd had for months, if not years.

The group struggled down the mountainside with their burdens, but the struggle was a natural one, much to carry and a difficult path. The path remained quiet, and although *he* sent a few minions to watch their progress, he did or appeared to do nothing to impede it.

Which of course, was strange.

Yet even the spies and watchers he sent foundered. A barrier had been set around Anaïs, similar to that around Amber as she lay ill after the battle at Draecastle, perhaps more so.

The juxtaposition of the Wielder of Light and the Weaver of Time kept the world around them in balance. It wasn't spectacular, couldn't be seen, there were no stars or rainbows or mystical marvels.

Estrién was the latest of a long bloodline, strength, courage and compassion came together in him. Warriors scattered before him and beasts were pacified by him. He was one with the structure, one with the world.

Anaïs was time's representative, a link between that which was, is or could be. Time wove itself around her and she gave it place. She grounded time into being: the *now*. No one as yet knew what her other powers might be other than as the Weaver, setting a structure for events that were or are to come.

May be she didn't know either.

Whatever ... the beasts he sent to attack cowered in fear and ran, the birds of prey flew haphazardly, lost their bearings, wandered on the wind. The land sighed with satisfaction at their passing, something was finally right with the world, if only momentarily.

For a short while, *he* lost sight of her.

That alone was disturbing.

He was also aware that it was not only a matter of Anaïs and Estrién. Amber, Dane and Tamlyn were also part of an immutable pattern, a perfect form and shape. Love creates a formidable structure.

The question is, can love, or even hate, overcome cold, calculated indifference? The tapestry, whilst not including him fully, held his essence, the stink of corruption. As his powers grew, that corruption grew also. Mer'edrynn was at a crisis of her existence, a finely honed knife edge with a chasm on either side. One side led to the world they knew, but the other to a world of indoctrination, separation, and the rule of a dictatorial state.

He enjoyed that thought, the ties of family, blood or friendship were an anathema to him. And *he* had plans for all those emotional and irrational beings. The Company of the Shield, Nim'randuel, were merely irritating flies in the ointment.

As they neared the edges of the sharp and rocky crag, they heard the sound of hooves beating across the stones through early morning mist. Estrién looked up, he knew that sound, knew it well.

'Elara!' he shouted across the moors, 'here, Elara,' he gave a shrill whistle. She replied with a whinny and galloped towards them. She stood perfectly still by him while he stroked her neck. 'What are you doing here? How did you know?' She shook her mane as if to tell him to hush, then walked over to Tamlyn, nudged Anaïs.

Estrién understood. He quickly got a blanket to put over her, slipped her bridal on, always carried in his pack. Tamlyn helped Anaïs on to Elara. 'Have no fear,' Estrién told her, 'she will keep you safe, she will not let you fall.'

The young woman smiled shyly and took the reins. Elara stood still, she still didn't move, as if waiting for something. Again Estrién understood, she would take some of their burdens, Anaïs' goods, she would help. They strapped packs behind Anaïs, until the horse was satisfied. Then she walked slowly along, her delicate burden would not be harmed.

Some miles further on, they reached the small forest north of the Wildlings settlement.

A great antlered-being stood awaiting them. He took one look at Anaïs and bowed his head. 'Madam, I am honoured,' his voice rich and mellow. 'Thou ar't truly of her, thou ar't filled with the Pattern.' He addressed the company. 'Come, follow me, I have a place of safety for her, somewhere she will be permanently protected.'

'We were going to take her home,' protested Amber.

'One day, that may be so, but not now. You have work elsewhere, much is happening. You will not be there to protect her, she will be at his mercy. She must gain her strength and ...' he stopped himself, would say no more about her. 'Besides, I think, Sir Estrién, you do not wish your home desecrated or destroyed by *him*, for he will do that. '

Estrién had to agree. 'But where are we taking her?'

'To safety. First we must go north, for the forest is difficult to the west. It thins out a little many miles north, then there is a good path westwards. But I cannot say more ...' he looked upwards to the trees, 'there are spies everywhere. They will follow, but I have called my own, they will try and destroy the enemy.'

'We have seen few since the Tower,' Estrién told him. 'They seem to keep away.'

'So much the better,' he replied.

Amber was unsure, her sister needed sanctuary, a place with familiar faces.

'She will have both peace and sanctuary. Come, there is little time. *He* is occupied right now, Lord Black is busy undoing all his works in Mortia and he takes the fight to the rest of Mercantia.' He stopped to look at the loom and the tapestry. 'Strap that upon my back when I am in my beast form, it is weightless to me. It will be my honour to carry it.'

He spoke no more, like his mate he turned swiftly into his stag form, his favourite form. Spring needed bringing in, wherever he stepped he would renew the land. The fact he had the Weaver of Time and the Wielder of Light with him would only invigorate it more, not to mention carrying the tapestry upon his back. He was part of the weave, Anaïs had woven him deep into its core.

The barren lands would truly become fertile.

They followed the Great Stag northwards, and it was as if a fresh spring air followed him. The cleansing air seeped into the tapestry, oxygenating the weave. During that ride, the people of Manecaestr breathed deeply, wondering where the fresh air had suddenly come from? Alas, it was but temporary.

For a short while, hearts in Manecaestr raised in hope, humans returned to the friendships they had known, whether with fellow humans, whatever their politics, or with the enslaved elves of the city. Even a few Adammites began to wonder about the strictures of the new regime there? Politics or otherwise, free human or enslaved elf, it was irrelevant.

Every being was held prisoner in that city. Every person was to be punished for the loss of Draecastle and the loss of Von Adamm. If anything *he* wished the most punishment upon the Adammites themselves for they had failed him.

He considered himself invincible, at least during his long and destructive existence he had been so. Wasn't he immortal? He always assumed so. He had been since the beginning, whispered the first words of dissent, of subtle lies and subversion into innocent ears. He had broken down the structure of Mer'edrynn as fast as it could be made.

The old gods, if such they were, ruled with an iron fist, demanding their sacrifices as a right. Or, at least, they did until the Lady Merrie came, a balancing of the forces, an offering of love and life. Did she really exist? Or was she simply an allegory, an imaginative explanation for a change in understanding, a natural evolution of people as weather structures warmed and brought fertility instead of ice?

Did it matter?

She was never a religion, but an outward expression of the natural world. No one worshipped her, but all contemplated her and respected her as a force of nature. As a child loves its mother, so did Merrievians love her, desiring to make her proud of them, of what they could achieve if they kept her love in their hearts. They were one with the world.

He might have left a corrupting grain of sand inside a soul, but the Mother left a nourishing seed to grow, blossom and bring forth good fruit.

At the moment however, they followed the stag across wild country and dense woodland. Elara seemed to know the direction, she found paths among the tangled trees of Shirewood, she kept moving north and ever westwards.

She arrived at her destination just on the first day of spring. It was in an area thick with hills, the kind you climb and think you've arrived at the top, only to find another just beyond. The Windvale hills they were called and a braw wind could truly blow through them. But they also held sheltered and hidden valleys; secret places, rich, fertile and gentle.

The great river Setaia tumbled down from these hills, the stag's own river as he called it. All the land around that river was verdant and lush. They stopped by a small wood. The stag raised his head, offered his burden of the loom back to the mages, before changing into a more human-looking form.

'Take this now, there is not far to go. I will leave you here, my place is not in the village. They are expecting you. Take care of her ... for all our sakes.'

They collected the loom and the tapestry and he swiftly disappeared into the woods.

They saw what appeared to be a small village ahead of them through the trees. Dane understood almost immediately. He saw the guards at the gateposts standing proudly in their fine armour under white surtouts adorned with a red cross and something roundish and white in the centre. Dane realised what it was.

It was a white rose.

Here was the counterpart to Rosewater; here was the White Rose temple.

'Hail fellows and my ladies, well met,' the guard greeted them. 'Welcome to Rosevale.'

*

It was the exact counterpart to the Red Rose temple, an entrance hall with stained glass windows depicting white roses rather than red, leading directly into a chapel. The priests of the temple were standing in line, waiting for her, for Anaïs, each held head bowed.

The High Priest Lord Aldergard came forward, gave a deep bow. 'Be welcome here, my lady, come, rest and take your ease. We have quarters ready for you, a pleasant bed chamber and a good sewing room for the loom and your tapestry. Rest assured we will guard you and the tapestry with our lives. There is also a room set aside for preparation, please let us know whatever you require, we will endeavour to procure it for you.'

He took them through to rooms on the second floor for safety, a quiet corner of the living quarters. Everything was as she needed, light and airy, and a pleasant smell of roses and lavender pervaded the rooms.

'I was given a vision, three nights ago. A great antlered stag came to me and told me to prepare, to make ready to receive you and I have been asked to protect you. I know who you are and what you are. It is my great honour to serve.

Over a hundred well-trained brothers of the White Rose stand ready to guard you from the evil presence that has pursued you and tried to harm you. One of our brothers is a mage, a physician, he has been given orders to aid you in every way.'

He left them to settle in, rooms were prepared for them all. The mages placed the loom in the centre of the large, light room, left the tapestry on the table prepared for it.

Amber saw Anaïs was weeping. She ran to her, hugged her, 'You're safe now, sister.'

Anaïs nodded, 'I know, these are lovely people.' She looked up, her eyes wandering around the room. 'I shall stay here for the rest of my life, I know that. If they agree, I shall make this my home.' She carried on weeping. The men knew to leave her, they were tears of relief. Tears are good for females, they heal.

Amber understood, here was the best place for her, a quiet and contemplative home, a sheltered valley, the delight of the gardens - she knew she'd want to help in those later, when she was well - and most of all, Merrie's own warrior priests to protect her.

No, she couldn't have given her anything better; the Stag knew her needs well.

Dane went to talk to the mage physician, Brother Elyan, who pre-empted him. 'I am aware of her needs. My Lord Aldergard spoke to the God of the forest, some kind of waking vision. We do not question these things here, they are part of our lives.'

'You need to be careful with her, she's on the edge to say the least, she's been through hell with that fiend.'

'I know she requires my aid, that she has been used badly by this creature, whatever or whoever he may be. I know that peace, quiet and security are essential right now. We will protect, that is our role. Have no fear for her.'

Dane could ask no more of them.

Later, Lord Aldergard joined them at their table for dinner. Anaïs was sleeping, she would have meals in her rooms for now, whatever she chose. 'This is very auspicious., Lady Anaïs has arrived on the day of the Mother, the first of spring, we welcome her with heart and faith. We have been given a sacred task here, both a great pleasure to serve her, and yet a difficult undertaking to protect her. I believe we have prepared for this day for years, for what else are we if not Her warriors and providers?' He looked them all in the eye. 'I give you my solemn promise we will fight *him* to the death.'

Eight glasses were lifted in toast to him.

Anaïs did not join them, but the evening was given over to feasting and pleasantry, the spring festival. The meal was fine but simple, the wine delicate in flavour - an elderflower wine made by themselves, the music played by the brothers was pleasant, there were jokes and some songs, but no dancing. Amber and Reave were in fact the only females there.

Lord Aldergard explained. 'We are a little stricter here than the Red Rose temple, we tend to be celibate, we are more inhibited, given over to meditation and contemplation. We are of course some miles from the nearest town, we do not encourage fraternisation. You understand, this is not imposed, any man here is welcome to visit the town any time he chooses, if he desires a female friend that is up to him, but few do. Neither do we discourage homosexuality, but to be truthful,' he confided, 'we all prefer the simplicity of friendship rather than a more complicated relationship; it is less stressful. We are still warriors, we practise our combat skills and of course we work hard in the gardens, but we tend to live a more monastic life here, it suits us. I think the quiet atmosphere here will be ideal for the Lady Anaïs.'

Amber remarked on the beautiful roses on the tables. The first of spring, yet each table held a glass vase containing a white rose in full bloom, a symbol of the purity of the new season. The priests explained the roses were kept in pots inside during the winter, nurtured and kept warm, brought to bloom in time for the equinox. The cut rose was offered as a simple sacrifice, a thank you to the Lady Merrie.

'These are the purest of our roses, the whitest and most fragrant,' Lord Aldergard told her. 'We grow many here, not just white, but pale pinks, pale peach, creams and the palest of yellow. Like the Red Rose Temple, there are many variants. We also grow such things as white currant and snowberry, a field is given over to meadow sweet for its medicinal purposes and we have a garden purely for medicinal plants. You have been enjoying our own wine tonight, grown from our elder trees on the estate. Like the Red Rose temple we also grow lavender, but we grow the sharpest and most medicinal varieties, cleansing and antiseptic. We enjoy experimenting with the palest flora of nature in our pursuit of simplicity and purity of form. There are also simple water gardens on the estate, areas deliberately created for quiet contemplation.

I hope ...' he continued, 'I hope the atmosphere here will help heal your sister, help calm her. It would be good to see her weave gentle colours into her tapestry of life, perhaps bring some peace to Mer'edrynn.'

They stayed a few days to settle her in. Tamlyn often spoke with her, acted as go between, she trusted him, he was kind and gentle. She did not leave her quarters, but as the group wandered the just-awakening gardens, breathing in the clean pure air, they often saw her smiling down at them from one of the upper floor windows of her tapestry room.

The family were relieved that she had a place of safety, but there was much care in their hearts for her well-being. They hoped the gentleness of the temple would heal her.

On the morning they were leaving, Anaïs saw them in the gardens, came to say goodbye. Her limp was noticeably better.

Amber gazed softly upon her. 'We leave you in good hands dear. Are you happy enough to stay here?'

'Yes,' her sister replied as they hugged each other. 'I am content.'

Yet tears fell down each sister's cheeks.

'Take care out there, Amber,' said Anaïs. 'Come back for me in a few week's time, when I may feel a little better. I am the only one who can save Manecaestr and I am unable to do this right now. I must go there, it cannot be done from here. I can only pray they hold on for such a length of time.'

Amber looked startled. 'You can do something?'

'Possibly,' was the enigmatic reply?

Chapter 2

The priests of the Rose Temple lent them a large carriage, took them across to Lakeside where they were relieved to find King Duggan's troops in charge.

The town was in chaos, buildings burned – by both sides - homes ruined, families and friendships destroyed. The Temple of Merrie had been the first to go, acts of savagery committed against the priestesses and the inside of the temple gutted. As they entered the town, a crowd of people stood in a nearby field holding a memorial service. They had buried their dead, tried to repair their lives, only now had they come together to mourn.

'We are just coming to terms with this,' one explained to them, a local miller. 'It's been hard, too hard for us ordinary folk. Those Adammite bastards stormed in, took over and killed our town guard. There were those inside ready to greet them, folk you never knew were like that. They killed the mayor, took his house and used the council chambers for themselves. They … they made us watch while they burnt people, held us back.' He stood silently shaking his head, traumatised by the experience.

Everyone they spoke to was the same. It was a town in turmoil. Many Adammites or collaborators were imprisoned, awaiting trial; King Duggan wanted to be seen to be fair, wanted to impose law and order back upon the land. He wanted neither witch hunts nor mob rule. He left soldiers in the town to keep order until tempers calmed.

The company felt compelled to stay and help for a while, the small town seemed shattered by the experience. They took rooms in an inn close by Kelpie lake and for several days they helped rebuild, the mages particularly useful for lifting heavy posts and roof beams. Amber wanted to stay in any case, she could help out here while waiting for her sister to recover a little.

Estrién, exhausted after a hard day's work of fetching and carrying, took a long gulp of Umberland Bitter ale as he sat by a roaring log fire. They had all wanted to assist in the repairs, if nothing else other than to offer encouragement to a distraught populace. He looked out through the inn's windows as dusk descended over the lake. The scene seemed incongruous with the devastation behind him.

The view from the inn was peaceful enough. Spring had broken out in all its glory; daffodils waved their sunshine shades all along the shore of Kelpie lake. A lone swan glided across the water, its graceful shape leaving ripples in its wake. The purple hills behind rose majestically, winter snow lay still upon their tops, yet large patches of yellow gorse added a welcome of the season. A couple of fishermen were silhouetted by the edge of the lake, hoping for an evening catch; whatever happened, they still had mouths to feed.

Nature had moved on, regardless of the war. Estrién wondered if the townsfolk could move on as easily? Forgiveness was not an easy virtue. He considered that, like the ripples on the water behind the swan, the consequences of this war would continue spreading long after it had passed. Indeed, the swan was lucky to be alive, Adammites deliberately hunted them. They ate their flesh with relish knowing they were sacred to Merrievians, protected by them for their grace and beauty – a pure white symbol of the Lady. No one, not even the King or Lord, ate swan. It had been another act of desecration.

They wished to break or destroy all the old customs, the very culture of Mer'edrynn. The thread of a nation that held its varied people and species together had unravelled and broken. Estrién felt it to his core, and wondered if it could ever be repaired?

He was fidgeting, he needed action, carrying logs and stone was all very well, but he was anxious to get on with the fight; his role was warrior, not labourer. He made up his mind to leave.

'Look, Amber, I realise we need to wait for your sister, but that doesn't necessarily mean all of us. You stay here with Trevaine and Robson, maybe keep Reave with you to communicate with us. I personally want to get down to wherever Duggan's forces are now, he's probably taken back most of the towns, but I need to help. We'll see as we carry on down. We'll hire horses to get to Manecaestr, wait for you there. Failing that, we'll get word to you via Reave's hawk, Gertie.'

Amber agreed, but Dane butted in. 'No, I'll stay. I'm concerned for Anaïs ... and there are people here who need our help. Salli particularly is needed, there's too much trauma here. There's something else too, there is a disease in the town, maybe from the drinking wells, I'm not sure, but some kind of ague is spreading. It will need mages to stop it, to heal. I don't like the feel of it.'

The other three mages agreed, there were several mystery illnesses around, they couldn't leave. He turned to Amber. 'You go dear, you are most useful with Estrién, I'll bring Anaïs down when she is well enough.'

The four mages and Reave stayed. Amber, Estrién and Tamlyn took to the road.

*

They found King Duggan and his troops further along the Long Ride near Cragbottom. Estrién was surprised to see the young King.

'I've left my younger brother Oswain in charge temporarily,' he explained, 'he and Longshanks are busy settling disputes. I need to be seen here, I need to show my people that I am in charge, that I care. I need to show them I can risk my life on their behalf, not merely sitting on my backside pontificating on petty problems. In short, Estrién, I need to prove myself to them.' He seemed to have aged in the last few months, but it was more a maturity than weariness. 'I follow my Knight Commander's orders of course, he knows combat much better than I do, but I'm learning. I have joined them in the past – Dad sent me up to the Picantés border for a while, but those were only skirmishes, this is something else.'

'We'll give you any help you need.' Estrién pointed to White Star upon his back. 'We also found Amber's sister – she might – and I mean might, be able to do something about Manecaestr, although she's pretty ill and it's very tenuous as yet.'

The young king nodded, he had too many worries upon inexperienced shoulders.

The Adammites of Cragbottom however had already heard the news about Draecastle and Lakeside falling. They picked up their belongings and fled to the small fishing port of Herringhold where Colonel Mackenzie was returning after giving his report on Manecaestr to Colonel (now Commander) Grey. He had been, seen, and left his own spies and researchers outside of the city. Like Lady Violet and the mages, they had attempted to enter the Circle by various means. Several elves had died during their experiments, enough for him to explain to Commander Grey that the phenomenon was currently impassable.

MacKenzie needed to be there, and preferably with a large force, he wanted to see what was happening. He brought his own to the port of Herringhold, and this was considerably swelled by the numbers fleeing the smaller towns on the Long Ride. He desperately needed to keep hold of the port, now their only access to Segantium and therefore took but a small select group with him to Manecaestr. He carefully avoided the King's troops as well as Lady Violet and her entourage, set up camp to the north west of the city with his spies. At the moment he wished to avoid battle, he was between two enemies, King Duggan, and Lord Black. Yet he needed to know about the city, the phenomenon. He had never seen anything like it in his life, it fascinated him.

Cragbottom therefore was easily taken; quelling the riots and stopping the backlash afterwards was another matter. The king sent his forces throughout the town, imposed a curfew and ordered town elders to meet at the Council chambers.

'We will imprison the community leaders who collaborated with the Adammites,' he told them. 'We will give them fair trials, listen to what they say, hear full evidence. I've got to return this land to a semblance of order, got to show them that we are far more civilised than those damn invaders with their false promises and seditious slogans. I will not have heads rolled or stuck on stakes – that is not my way of leadership. There must be an understanding,' he continued, 'there has been division for too long. I want peace in my land, and that can only be brought about by rule of law, fairly made and fairly dealt.'

The Town Elders watched on, aware there was a wise head on these young shoulders. Gourien had taught him well. They quickly organised a Town guard, quelled the riots and took the ringleaders into custody.

'It's been like this everywhere,' Duggan told Estrién and the others. 'They want revenge, obviously so. But if we do the same back to them, how different are we to the Adammites?' He knew he was treading a fine line, the people needed a show of strength, but what was strength without compassion?

Amber suggested getting the Temples of Merrie up and running, get any Adammite prisoners chain-ganged into rebuilding them, make them physically pay for their crimes, money and goods included. It was spring, so put them to work in fields that needed tilling, use them positively, to be seen to be punishing them, but practically rather than vengefully.

King Duggan thought it was a good idea. Execution was not the answer for civilians caught up in Adammite religious frenzy, or bullied into acceptance of Adammite ways, and in any case, imprisonment cost money – especially in a land riven with war. The old ways of Outcasting a felon could not be used either – they would simply be free to return to the Adammite fold. No, he had to think of better solutions, ones that showed both fairness and strength.

He was young and idealistic. He would, as the Lady asked of him, do his best.

They sent word by Gertie to Dane; she had been flying back and forth constantly as they travelled: the roads were safe, it would be possible to bring Anaïs whenever she was ready. Amber, Estrién and Tamlyn moved down to join Lady Violet.

*

Dane and the other mages meanwhile were in the thick of epidemic. There were flu-like symptoms, a rash of suppurating sores, vomiting, diarrhoea, and ultimately death. The first cases were now dying, the incubation period probably a couple of weeks, the illness itself long and drawn out. People had thought they had colds brought on by winter chills, maybe the wells had been poisoned and so gave them food poisoning, everyone had different symptoms and different periods of incubation.

'We either have several plagues happening at once,' Dane concluded, 'or we have one plague that adapts itself to the body, perhaps picks the weakest point.'

Salli agreed, he felt it was adaptable, he would treat everyone accordingly. Trevaine and Robson weren't exactly healers, but followed Dane and Salli's instructions, they worked with the local remedian, helped to make up different kinds of medicines according to the symptoms. The whole town felt wrong.

The town mourned for the loss of their Temple, the loss of their priestesses, considered this was a punishment given by the Lady herself for not protecting them enough.

Dane quickly stamped on that. 'Do you think the Lady Merrie would ever take revenge as such upon you? She has always offered light and love, kindness and generosity. She would not bring this upon you. No, the Adammites have left something here.'

He knew who it was, that *he,* that being beyond evil, had produced this, but he could not tell these people that. The Adammites were enough for them to cope with, let them keep hope in their hearts. 'Besides,' he offered, 'don't you think the Lady Merrie sent us here in your time of need?

We will work with your remedians and we will beat this together.'

They saw the truth of that, followed the orders of the mages. Dane ordered them to boil all water, burn the clothes of any who were dying and to commit the dead to the pyre rather than burial.

Almost every person in Lakeside saw symptoms, some lesser, some greater, somehow the mages healed them. Each was treated differently, Dane and Salli particularly worked non-stop, it seemed mages were naturally immune. Healers arrived from the White Rose temple; Anaïs had sent them, had understood the trouble at Lakeside. She sent apologies for not being there to help, she wasn't yet well enough.

The priests brought cleansing herbs and medicines with them. They took over the Adammite barracks and used it as a temporary hospital and quarantine area. Any citizen seen to exhibit any signs of ill health – however slight – was to immediately present themselves there for quarantine and treatment. More brothers arrived simply to see to the dead.

Dane heaved a sigh of relief; it meant he could work on the problem itself.

He inspected the well waters; there were many wells in the town, also connected to the lake, none seemed clean, some kind of impurity. 'Unnatural,' he thought, 'definitely *his* work.' If the lake itself was polluted, that would be disastrous. He could cleanse each well, but not if it was permanently being re-infected. He got Salli to check the lake, went with him to the banks one morning and watched him strip off by the shore before wading in.

'I can feel it better naked,' Salli explained.

He walked in until he was covered by the water, it was icy cold, Dane saw him shiver. Then he watched as Salli swam out towards the centre. Salli trod water for a few moments, thinking, feeling, sending magical streams through the water. There was a breeze that morning; like the swan it left ripples upon the lake, Salli drifted southwards. Suddenly he turned and swam quickly back to the shore.

He hurriedly got dressed, he looked sick.

'Dear Goddess, Dane, I know what it is. I must have disturbed it as I searched with my mind and senses. You remember those damn slimy worm creatures in Shirewood? There's something in the lake similar in shape, only it's enormous. I saw it in the bottom, long and dark with a bulbous head. I saw a gaping mouth with huge fangs – a real predator. It's like some massive sea serpent from the old tales and legends. I could feel the evil, the sickness and decay all through it. It seems a slippery creature, it clearly saw – or felt- me too, and burrowed its way deep into the mud of the bottom. How we'll find it or kill it, I've no idea.'

'It's polluting the wells then?'

'Oh yes, and any fish we catch, although the lake water is relatively clean, it seems to be concentrating in the wells. Maybe the creature lives under the lake, possibly in caves linked to the underground wells. But it's there, definitely there.'

'We need to draw it out, catch it, destroy it.'

'How?'

'Some kind of bait, something pretty big. You said it is a predator, meat on the end of a line, half a cow or something.'

'*Poor cow*,' replied Salli.

'*Poor* people of Lakeside, and the small villages around it,' retorted Dane. He went to the Elders of the town, explained the problem, it had to be caught and killed.

The fishermen consulted together, talked to the carpenters, came up with an idea.

Two days later the carpenters rolled out a huge and heavy wooden crane designed to take the weight of the creature. The crane would act as an enormous fishing rod. A local farmer sacrificed a cow for the bait. Everyone hoped the beast, sea serpent or whatever it was, liked beef, none wanted to think that *they* might be the preferred meat of choice. The blacksmith had a long coil of Dwarven cord, he used it for special items, had cost him a fortune. It too was sacrificed, it would be the 'fishing' line. The expensive cord could not be used afterwards; no one would want to touch it. The war had already cost him dearly, he and the other blacksmith had both been forced to work for the Adammites, and the pay they had received had been minimal. He'd hidden the Dwarven cord, hoping to make up his losses after the war, but it seemed the war hadn't yet ended here. He sighed and grumbled, measured out the cord and fashioned a large hook for the end.

The townspeople came to watch as the fishermen rolled the crane to the shore, following it through the town. Wooden jacks were put under the crane and the wheels removed, the crane further weighted with stones, and several beefy and burly men took hold of long ropes attached to the crane to help hold it down. A ratcheted pulley system held the cord, it would reel out smoothly, but each turn backwards would hold the catch little by little.

The mages stood by the shore as the local fishermen took charge. They took a large boat towards the centre, uncoiling the dwarven cord as they rowed. The remains of the cow were attached to the large hook and pushed over the boat into the water. Then they rowed as quickly as they could back to shore and the awaiting mages. Several boats were ready to take them out, get the mages closer to the creature.

Bowmen stood by the shore to help with the catch, Dane had provided poison for their arrows. None knew what it would take to kill the creature.

Then they waited, a town slowly dying from poison, a town on the edge, people nervously shuffling, worried faces, angry faces, grim-visaged and determined. Many had lost loved ones to this creature, to its venom or whatever had polluted the water.

They waited ...

And waited ...

An hour or more went by, two hours; the day was turning dark before the mages felt a rumble under the water. It came from further up the lake, deep underground. Then the lake seemed to quiver, the evening light on the surface glimmered and trembled. Something disturbed the muddy waters at the bottom, the surface turned black, dead plants and fish rose to the surface.

There was sudden movement as a long pointed tail-end rose from the lake, a blue green shimmer, oily and greasy looking, then crashed heavily back down again. Water splashed everywhere.

The bulbous head could now be seen below the surface, making a direct line for the bait as the body undulated to and fro behind it. It was massive, thirty feet long or more, somewhere between fish and snake, yet neither, the big brother of the forest abominations.

The enormous mouth opened, revealing sharply pointed and blackened fangs, a grinning wide open maw of death. Hungrily it snatched at the remains of the cow, took it in one gulp.

The cord hanging from the crane suddenly became taught,

The fishermen quickly rolled back the cord over the pulley, several clicks were heard with each turn of the wheel. The massive head of the thing shot out of the water.

'Now!' shouted Dane, as archers raised their bows and shot a volley of arrows into the globular head. It pulsated sickeningly. More of the body was seen as the fishermen heaved and the crane pulled higher, each turn ratcheted so it could not pull away. Dane and the group of mages now took their cue, the rowers took the boats out and the mages stood uncertainly in rocking boats, each shooting lightning bolts into the air. The deadly bolts found their target and the crowd watched horrified as the creature jerked and jolted, trying to escape from the hook, wriggling and squirming to get away from the amberic lightning. More poisoned arrows were let fly into its streaky slimy body. Still it shook, trying to rid itself of the hook, desperate to escape.

The crane suddenly shot forwards and collapsed. More men arrived to grab the ropes and keep the line steady. They held on grim-faced as the beast reared and squirmed.

But it was mindless, like the foul pestilence in the forest, it only held on to the thought of eating and sleeping. Salli had radiated some kind of power as he swam in the lake; the creature had felt it, cowered from him. But it smelled the meat and therefore came to find it. It had no cunning, no skill. It pulled away, only to find the hook sinking further into the roof of its mouth. The body rose and fell in undulating crescents, the tail lifting high and splashing down again, the waters of the lake heaving and the boats shaking back and forth from the waves. Yet the mages stood still, none moved as they sent another round of zig zag bolts into the creature.

The poison from the arrows must have been helping, it seemed to slow down, the waves stopped crashing around the boats, the head gave one last massive shake and then dropped. The thing didn't float; it dropped heavily and vertically, the point of the tail scraping the sand at the bottom of the lake.

The fishermen slowly reeled it in to the shore, pulled it onto the shingle of the beach.

It smelled abominable like the creatures in the forest, yet everyone crowded round to see.

'Keep away, it's poisonous, leave this to the mages,' shouted Dane. It filled the beach, an abomination, an offence to nature. It smelled of putrefaction and death.

There were four elementalists, they poured down fire upon the creature until only ashes remained.

'I hope that was the only one,' Dane asked Salli.

'Yes,' he replied, I felt only one such being. I never want to feel such again.'

Between them, Dane and Salli, they spent the next week using magic to cleanse the wells, and purify the lake. Dane was glad of the pureness of his oaken staff, blessed by the lady of the forest, cleansed and whole. It returned the waters to wholeness.

Salli used his special magic to ask the spirits of the lake to bless the waters, he believed they answered, the lake felt clean again.

The healers from the White Rose temple stayed to help until the town was well again. 'This is our duty,' they told Dane, 'we must all help.'

There came a day when Dane was satisfied the waters were clean, he was ready to leave. As Dane and Salli entered the inn later, two priests of the White Rose stood guarding the inn door. They were startled to find Anaïs sitting comfortably in a large chair by the log fire, waiting for them.

'I hear you have done good work here. Will you take me down to the lake to look, please?'

They took her down to the shore; she spent moments in concentration before speaking to them.

'Yes,' she agreed, 'it is cleansed, it is whole. You are fine mages, both of you.' They all walked back to the inn, a slight limp was noticeable, but she walked much more steadily, albeit with a stick one of the brothers had fashioned for her. 'Brother Elyan had done well; he has worked with me daily. I'm ready, at least as ready as I'll ever be,' she said, 'take me to Manecaestr.'

'Are you sure?' asked Dane.

'No, but no more time can be wasted, those people will die if I don't go soon. There will already be unnecessary deaths, I cannot waste more lives. My body is still weak, but that is irrelevant, my mind is strong. ... And yes...' looking pointedly at Dane, '... stronger than you think, my brother, there were – are – reasons why I am not wholly myself, but that can keep. We need to go, and we need to go now.'

They took her carriage down to Manecaestr.

Chapter 3

It smelled inside Manecaestr, suffice to say it ponged something rotten. The air, what there was of it, was greasy from fried food and high with the stink of dung heap, sweat and generally dirty bodies. The wells were running low, washing was kept to a minimum, water needed for drinking, the rationing barely holding out. The dead were quickly buried before they added to the general stink. It was the other smell that bothered people though. The air had become damp, mould grew everywhere and wooden structures were visibly starting to rot. Mushrooms grew well, providing a new if unpredictable source of nourishment. Some mushrooms were edible, some exceedingly poisonous. There were new varieties and none knew their properties until they were eaten. The Adammites could have tried them out on animals, rats perhaps which were plaguing the city, but no, they used elves as testers.

There was desperation in the city never felt before.

*

In Belcast'el, Commander Grey took stock of his war machine. He checked the supply books and the armament ledgers given him by his Chief Executive., shaking his head as he did so. There simply weren't enough ships for purpose, nor were there enough trebuchets or ballistae. He needed more war machines, including massive battering rams. He needed fast carriages for his army, and horses to pull them.

The horses he could manage, elves seemed to like them; there were plenty in the surrounding countryside. Timber however was a different matter. There was little left on either the Isle of Glasse or Mere'garde.

In short, he needed Oakleigh forest. He therefore made up his mind that it was now time to take it, root out the rest of the elves there. He would need something special for those Freowulven archers though, they had defeated his men in the last sortie.

But now he had the Hellboys with their crossbows, more than a match for Freowulven bows and arrows. He smiled to himself, left Belcast'el under the charge of his Captain, newly promoted to Major, and gathered his troops.

The journey was not quite as easy as he thought. The first village en route defended itself, being well fortified; Amber and the company had been through here previously. Beacons were lit and other villages warned. The few mages had, as instructed practised their elemental magic, they had learned to become war mages.

Two Hellboys were immediately struck down by flashfire and the metal parts of the crossbows struck by amberic lightning. Commander Grey raised his eyebrows in surprise, this was not expected. Elves did not retaliate, they were too soft. He withdrew to a safe position and ordered the battering rams.

They pushed their way through the wooden defences of the small villages, slaughtering as they went. The elves fought with axes, picks, scythes and pitchforks – the tools of their trade, for most were farmers or gardeners – they fought with the determination that comes from defending your home, your people. The mages fought with them, helping deplete the Adammite forces.

Yet that only slowed down the eight-square formation of Commander Grey's troops. It was efficient and lethal. One small village could not defeat it. He ordered the Hellboys to aim for the mages, get them out quick, then take the rest.

It didn't take long and he left a line of slaughter behind him.

He didn't burn the village, there was no time for that, nor did he take the main route to the forest. Instead he ignored the other villages and went cross country. He wanted as full a complement of men as possible when he reached Oakleigh Forest. He would come back later and remove the rest of the elves. The houses and buildings he decided he would leave intact, all Adammites needed homes after all, and these were particularly pleasant. But the elves would pay, by death or slavery, he didn't care which.

The beacons had been lit however, and the Freowulven had seen them.

Woodmoss saw the Adammites first as they approached the forest. The big old satyr heard their movement and the creak and roll of the war engines and carriages filled with men. Neither were the men silent, they were full of bravado, exclaiming how many elves they would kill that day.

'Not if I can help it,' he thought, pulling a huge tree trunk he had felled earlier towards the small lane they travelled along. He angled it across, wedged it between trees. It would stop them awhile, the forest thickened here. The men would have to leave the carriages, walk through the forest, more importantly, their eight square formation was impossible through the woods.

Swiftly he moved towards the Freowulven settlement. He didn't mind speaking to the Outlaws, he had no quarrel with them. He knew what it was to be a loner, an outcast, although he had done nothing wrong in his entire life. He simply did not fit in; he was one of the last of the satyrs and a dying species. He had done a little trading with them during the winter, his finely crafted plates, bowls and goblets in return for freshly caught meat. He'd helped shift logs and the odd dead tree trunk for them, even been to a local village to get medicines for their sick children since they were not allowed to trade.

He hurried along the path to meet Jovan, the leader of the Freowulven group. Jovan stood watching the heavy pan-like creature dash with surprising grace towards him. He scratched the edge of his skin below the eye patch; the remains of his eye irritated him today. A scuffle with a mountain bear had taken it years ago, infection set in, he was lucky not to have lost the other eye. The bear was somewhat unluckier, his sword saw to that. He looked what he was: mean, lean, and dangerous, a wolf to lead the Freowulven.

'Careful,' he shouted to Woodmoss, 'remember the paths.' Woodmoss took note.

'They're coming,' he said, 'I've tried to delay them a little.'

Jovan nodded, he wasn't really a talker, he used speech when necessary, kept to himself otherwise. He had organised as best he could. His archers spent their day camouflaged in the pine trees awaiting events. Now they were ready.

Commander Grey reached the outskirts of Oakleigh forest and immediately ordered the felling and lumbering of trees. That was after all what he was here for. The carriages full of soldiers carried on into the forest itself, the paths becoming irregular and narrow. They came across the huge log left by Woodmoss.

'Get some bloody axes here, get that out of the way!' he called. 'The rest of you go on foot, I want this forest taken quickly. Get your crossbows ready.' He was annoyed they could not move in the square formation he loved, they would have to go singly. Still, he could use the carriages to take the lumber back to Belcast'el and Hollyporth.

They moved warily, unsure of the forest, wondering what was hidden in the trees. Once or twice they stumbled, jagged tree shoots catching them as they gazed upwards for hidden foes. Bolts were fired at unseen targets when the wind whistled through the trees and branches creaked. They moved onwards, closer to the thickset forest, to the civilisations that lived here among the trees, wondering why they had as yet not been challenged?

They understood when the first group fell into a long pit and arrows quickly rained down upon them. Like Commander Grey, the Freowulven had also spent the autumn and winter preparing. The elves had lent them tools, they had dug large pits and channels around their part of the forest, covered them in nets and dead bracken. It looked fine in winter; although it would look a little odd as the spring continued, fresh grass or ferns would have to be placed daily. Paths, of a kind, were marked out, maps given to the elves; they knew not to step on the bracken. Jovan considered placing sharpened stakes in the pits, but if a child fell in there would be hell to pay. Now they watched as Grey's fighters fell into them.

'Down!' shouted their Commander to the rest of the militia, before they too fell into the pits. 'Get under cover!'

It was too late, for suddenly behind them the earth moved and Freowulven charged out of half a dozen camouflaged tunnels.

They were ready with sword as well as bow; they charged from behind and shot arrows from ahead. The forest quickly became filled with the sound of steel upon steel, cries of anger and pain as sharpened blades struck home, and arrows met their target.

'Hellboys, shoot ... get those fucking elves!' Commander Grey cried, quickly realising that battering rams and ballistae were a waste of time here, only mud to stick in and trees to shoot at. There were no walls or fences, only the natural barrier of the forest itself. He was particularly annoyed when a large trebuchet fell sideways into one of the trenches.

He watched in amazement as Woodmoss picked up one of his own battering rams and threw it back at his troops, unable to believe the strength of the satyr. He shook his head, he had foolishly underestimated these people, their strength, their wit and their courage.

But he was no fool, he quickly pulled back, not wishing to lose more men. Under any other circumstances he would have smoked out these people, fired the forest. That could not be, since the forest was paramount. The Freowulven gleefully watched them retreat, taunting and shouting as they left.

He vented his anger on several small villages on the way back to Belcast'el. Oakleigh forest might be safe for now, but his concentrated fire-power annihilated the tiny settlements, leaving death, destruction and the smoking remains of hamlets in his wake.

His army was excellent in cities and on wide open plains, but he understood he would need a different kind of soldier to take the forests. Or perhaps, he thought, a different kind of warfare? He needed the forest, but those living there were inessential, more than disposable. He decided to consult his alchemists and physicians, wondering if they could somehow use poisons to kill off the offending populace of Oakleigh?

Whatever, he would pay them back.

*

The tiny figure stood bent, hands clasped upon the walking stick in from of her as she observed the phenomenon. The curved back, the stick and the pure white flowing hair presented an aged figure, until she turned around and a young and beautiful face could be seen. An oval face, similar in shape to Amber, yet with deep brown eyes, soulfully measuring the circle, or more correctly, the sphere of no-time, the strange cloud-like phenomenon around the city. Her full lips were pursed and her eyes frowned as she studied, her head bent to one side, deep in thought.

As she moved forward, her long dove grey gown almost blended into the circle, she and it seemed one. She bent close, listened, or appeared to be listening and placed her right palm onto the cloud formation, before turning the palm to her face and studying it. Then she placed both palms upon it, bent her head again and closed her eyes.

The company watched, all were there, Amber, Dane, Estrién and Tamlyn, the other three mages Salli, Robson and Trevaine. Reave had met up with Garret who had been stationed with Lady Violet, quite a reunion, and the two Morus hawks, Gracie and Gertie were flying around each other above them. Lady Violet and her entourage, a group of mages, alchemists and guards, were also there, including Anaïs own Priests of the White Rose; all eyes were on Anaïs. No one spoke, all held baited breath.

Eventually Anaïs came out of her reverie, walked back towards them. 'I need to enter it, but I cannot go alone. I have not my full strength, I need help – there are bad things in there. Estrién...' she paused, searching his face, 'will you come with me, please? Your sword and your skills are valuable.'

'Is it possible?' he asked, 'I know my sword can enter, but can I?'

She nodded, 'yes, with my help, we can both go in. But if I can ... *deal* ... I don't know how else to term it, with this time corridor, it will leave the land it covers bad – wasted and ill - I don't know what will be left behind. Frankly, anything could come out of there while we are in, so everyone here must be on the alert, we cannot go killing everything inside, and to be truthful, I'm not exactly sure what will happen. And Dane...' her eyes glanced hopefully at him, 'once the circle is gone, we shall need that staff of yours, the land will be barren, or ailing. I couldn't even tell you how thick the barrier is. I think,' here she bent her head to one side again, 'I think no more than a field's width, but it will need healing.'

Dane nodded, his oaken staff was ready and waiting once the circle was gone..

Estrién turned to Amber, kissed her fully on the lips as he said goodbye, then moved forwards to the barrier, awaiting Anaïs. Amber took her sister's hand, hugged her. 'Are you sure dear?'

Anaïs shook her head. 'No, but it must be done now. I hear cries in the city, cries and moans. We must go, if you do not mind lending me your husband for a while, I value his skills.'

Amber laughed, 'take him and welcome dear, just bring him back in one piece, please.'

Everyone watched as Anaïs stood close to the barrier, concentrated, then waved her hands in the air, signs and sigils, almost like the ones Estrién used to pacify beasts. To their amazement a small opening appeared and she stepped through, followed quickly by Estrién, his sword drawn and ready.

Then the hole closed up and the time circle swallowed them.

At first he thought he was flying, like the night he flew from Mere'garde to the mainland on the dragon. He kept tight hold of White Star, ice cold in his hand. Everything around him was mist and he could not see Anaïs ahead of him. He wondered if he was alone here?

'Anaïs are you there?' he shouted. It sounded like he was calling through glue. For some moments he heard nothing before a soft voice hailed in the distance.

'Estrién, I'm here, walk towards my voice, you are but a few seconds out of time behind me. Walk closer, enter my time stream.'

He moved towards her voice, shuffling through a sea of treacle, the current constantly against him. 'Where are you, I can't see you?' he shouted again. The air around him was thick, breathing was difficult.

'Here... no, here, I can see you, turn to your left, it's not far. .... oh no ....' her voice trailed off.

Estrién turned to her voice but was swept backwards, time pushing him out. He did not belong here. He fell, picked himself up, waded across towards her voice. Still he was swept away, fell heavily, twisted an ankle, briefly swore, then stood and limped slowly in her direction. He still could not see through the mist, 'shout again Anaïs, where are you?'

She continued calling to him, he continued pushing against an unrelenting tide of time, somehow becoming thicker and more solid with every step.

Eventually he took out White Star, held it in front of him, slashed at the mist. It shone and sparkled, although where the light came from he knew not. Miraculously the mist parted, he could briefly see her in front of him, before the mist closed in. He continued hacking and slashing with White Star, cutting through air with the consistency of treacle or custard, thick and gloopy.

Eventually he made it to her, to the quiet space around Anaïs. 'You OK? he asked her.

'I'm fine, my brother, but you are not,' motioning to his ankle. 'Stay close, at least until I can expand this circle around me. I have as yet no idea how to remove this, but I think we must travel through and find its core.'

Yes, that seemed correct; there must be a centre to this … whatever it was.

He examined the space around him, strangely it was no longer misty grey. There were many colours and no colours all at once, glinting and gleaming with fluorescent essence; greys greens and golds multifaceted with purple, yellow, silver, midnight blue and pearl grey. One colour, many colours, moulding, melding, separating and condensing constantly as he looked.

Anaïs smiled at him. 'time changes,' she said cryptically, 'you follow me, keep close,'

She had no mage staff or wand, the stick she carried was for physical purposes only. There was just Anaïs, a small boned, tiny female, physically abused and broken by *him,* limping gently along the time corridor, her soft voice almost inaudible.

None of that mattered, what was inside her mattered.

She held up an arm, palm outwards towards the multi-coloured mist. 'You ready?' her voice was almost a whisper, sound swallowed by time.

'Let's get this done with,' was the reply.

She moved forwards, and time winked out.

The blackness of the universe surrounded them, birth of a universe, before time. Stillness and silence were bed mates, a rushing of nothingness in ears and a sense of falling.

Only two heartbeats could be heard, Anaïs' and Estrién's, the pulse of two lives beating, the proof of existence. Then Estrién briefly heard himself cry as he was pulled downwards. Something swirled ahead, cloud-like, star-like and a sun came screaming into being.

Now there was light, blinding, flashing, heat searing light, Estrién steadied, the falling stopped and he held his arm over his eyes to block the brightness. White Star shone like the star she had come from, the star she had been born of, mother star, father sun. She glittered with a thousand diamonds into the sky. He heard her sing sweetly.

With gentle and graceful movements as hands upon a harp, Anaïs drew the universe towards her. It answered her, it came forth, it burst upon them, rainbow circled, a shower of rain, a gust of wind, a breath of purest air.

And somewhere in the distance a babe woke from its slumber, wept, crying for its mother's breast, tiny tongue searching for food, the stuff of existence, nourishment and love. It was a night cry, a hunger cry, pain and fear, a need that never ended.

Anaïs sang a lullaby, sweet mother dreams entered the child; she shushed, pacified. Now the universe coalesced, settled itself into being, hunger and need satiated. A path formed, Anaïs took it, followed the path of light, the one the mages saw, like the paths around Ravenscroft, silver secret into the future ... mage paths of destiny.

The path circled and curled around sand and stone, through dust filled skies and gaping chasms. It spiralled upwards, became a stairway, they stepped on, it moved of its own accord. Up and up into the blue as forests and mountains grew beside them, green, grey and chestnut; the intense smell of resins, cedar and cypress, pine, the sweetness of sandalwood, the brightness of an apple and the bitterness of the sloe.

Flowers formed, unfolding into huge overblown blossoms, bright and bonny, reds, pinks and purples, their scent overpowering; roses, heliotrope, peach blossom, jasmine and violet, suffocating the air with sweetness.

And in the flowers, the putrefaction, the death decay, the dying leaves crumbling, flaking, crisp underfoot. The seeds of tomorrow's blossoms floated in the air softly upon feathery stems, showering themselves over Anaïs and Estrién.

He held out his hand, caught one, saw the universe in one small seed as time began again.

A sun sang softly as dawn broke, Anaïs held her head in reverence and her arms in supplication. The pale amber beams shone over her, golden gracious, deep and delicate, strong and powerful, glowing as the sun rose in the sky.

The moving stairway halted at a lush meadow, rich and ripe. The grasses danced, oats, barley, rye waving in the summer breeze ... careless, carefree, the dance of life, happy in those final moments before the scythe came down and the cycle moved on. Anaïs and Estrién stepped off the stairway as the meadow waved and undulated around them.

But the waving meadow was the sea of time where silver fish swam aimlessly into the void and sorrow ruled the world. Everything changed; joy ran, love was lost,
They sank down into depths unfathomable, the weight of the ocean upon their shoulders. Hearts crushed, hope wained as they wandered bewildered along the sandy sea bed, Anaïs wept with weariness, no compassion here in the depths. Her body bent even more under the weight of water. Estrién cried out loud for Amber, his love, where was she? He could not find her. He knew he would never see her again; they would never leave this desolate place. He was nothing here, no-one, a shell upon the sand.

Then a huge fish, shark-like and vicious, came at them, sharp rapacious teeth searching for food. Estrién saw, was challenged and now knew his place, his role, there was no room for either self pity or compassion here in these depths; kill or be killed.

He hurried before Anaïs, slashed through the liquid at the shark, White Star gleaming, the light in the dreary dullness, his warrior heart beating a drum of war against the foe. Back and forth, slicing through the jaw of the fish until blood swam in streamlets around them.

It lay at their feet, scales glinting in the water.

'First foe down,' Anaïs muttered as she flowed through sea-space, her hair floating and cascading behind her. Sea anemones danced as she passed, white flowers sprang upon the bottom of the sea bed. Eventually she found a cave, they entered warily as the sea slowly ebbed behind them and shingle and sea shells gritted underfoot.

Molluscs clung stubbornly to damp walls and something shining shrank in a corner. There was a sound of popping as air squeezed out of wet stone and sand. They crept towards the back of the cave seeking a way out. But the cave narrowed, became tunnel and they crawled into hollow darkness, sharp edges of rock biting and scratching. Creeping became crawling on bellies until the way ahead became blocked. Again Estrién used White Star, this time as a tool, poking and pushing until the sand and rubble shifted. Air turned suffocating, smell of soil, earthy, mustiness, close and confining. More tunnels, more blockages, push against them, use White Star, crawl through to freedom.

They burst into an underground hall lit with new born stars, sunlight dancing in the distance. Life in all its forms writhed and wriggled on the damp earth, a birthing chamber of existence. Yet it was all natural life, it cried, it wailed, it laughed and fought, seeking the best it could. It was symbiotic with Mer'edrynn, part of the pattern.

It felt Anaïs, parted a path for her to walk, shrank back as she passed. A reverent hush came upon the chamber and the pair walked gently through to the light beyond.

But the land outside was white with the pale ghosts of warriors fighting an infinite battle; cries and screams rent the air. Men eternally dying, yet never at peace, Adammite or elf, human or dwarf, none mattered only that their pain filled the air. Here was endless war.

'You must end this,' she asked Estrién, 'for I cannot. They need a warrior's touch, the final thrust of blade.'

Estrién understood as he raced across the crowded battlefield, White Star singing and piercing the hearts of men too proud to die in battle, too brave to surrender, bound by duty to honour their code, their country, their King. He gave them rest as Anaïs sang of strength, courage and love to the falling heroes. Finally peace came to their hearts and the dancing sun turned blushing upon quiescent land as the battlefield turned into a thousand red poppies and a myriad of cold, white bones.

'*He* was here,' she said, 'he would not let them rest. *He* wanted their pain, eternal balm to his own mean soul.'

'*If* he has such a thing,' Estrién remarked.

Time passed, it wandered and wove, it whispered and wept. The pale mist wisped around them, returning with vengeance, became cold and sharp. Anaïs took them both through it, Estrién close behind, he had no wish to lose her.

Images played on the edges of the mist, memories, time past. Anaïs saw the Alderfolk once more, their Aldervetch screaming and chanting oaths upon the air as her parents defended her village. She watched as arrows flew and her parents fell. She felt the touch of her sister, holding her after she had been beaten by them, heard the love in Amber's voice as she vowed to free her. That was the last gentle voice she had heard, for things happened afterwards that Amber did not know.

She saw the madness in the eyes of young wild men, the group who raped her as she travelled through a lonely wood. She heard the cry of hungry wolves as they pursued her naked and terrified, yelping and biting at her feet. She felt the greasy, grimy calloused hand of the farmer who let her sleep in his cattle-shed in return for her favours and a day's work in the fields.

And every one of them lay dead behind her as she slowly understood her powers. The Weaver of Time holds death in her hands; human or wolf; each died of old age.

All the images she saw were sad, heartbreaking for she knew no kindness after she escaped the Alderfolk's camp. Only did she find peace once she found her mage tower deep in the unpredictable Greylumings ... a place where time stood still or moved on at will, weird and unaccountable. She had felt comfortable for a short while, before *he* came. The people too, strange, yet solid, they were kind, or merely they just feared her, but they helped her live comfortably in her tower.

Here, the images danced and played upon the mist, only the bad memories, for she could no longer remember the good. Yet she wept not, it was past and she must be strong.

Estrién saw other memories; his life had been happier, well cared for, loving parents and a kind uncle. He saw himself as he sneaked through sacred halls towards his goal, his sword, while people feasted above him. He saw the glass case and the sword slumbering inside, waiting for him to open it and awaken the blade.

He saw, or rather heard the sword sing as he used it to slice through three members of the Dair Chev'al when they came to kill him. He regretted that they gave him no chance, but it he had no wish to die and the sword offered him life-through-death.

He gasped as he watched the moment he first saw Amber as she walked through the forest, realising he had loved her from the beginning.

He saw the two of them in the wayside inn's bedroom, the sun setting, her skin glowing as he took her naked into his arms for the first time. He smelled the perfume of her hair and the sweetness of her flesh, tasting her; her kiss, the kiss of eternity.

He felt the love of her flow around him, warmth seeping through him; delirious with passion, he cried her name into the wind, it rang through the mists of time. Yet he felt a desperation in his need for her, the loss of her, she should be with him …. where was she?

Then he fell on his knees and wept as he saw her fall at Draecastle, blood seeping on cold stone, his heart racing, his own blood turning icy cold as he pursued von Adamm.

Again he cried her name upon the void, wondering if they could ever leave this place, if there would ever be an end, if he could but return to her?

Anaïs understood his pain and took him by the hand, 'come, Estrién, we cannot stay here, we will weep unto death in this place. *He* is here too, his wiles and wickedness, he brings sadness and loss. He turns good things bad and bad things worse. Come, hurry, we cannot stay. Besides, we are close now, close to the meaning of this.'

With all speed they ran through the mists of time.

They arrived at the centre, a huge arena, where bodiless faces mocked at them, bears roamed the circle and slaves stood shackled awaiting their fate. There was a huge cacophony of sound, horns blaring, drums banging, a constant crash of cymbals. Children sat hungry in the stalls across, their arms held out begging for food, their faces weary with hopelessness. A clown with a grinning face ran over and threw a bucket of silvery fae dust into their faces, the children cried out in pain.

Estrién looked up and saw Amber swinging high on the trapeze above him, but she slipped falling to her death. He ran, arms outstretched to catch her but she disappeared as he held her in his arms. The bears growled menacingly and frightened the children, they screamed as they neared and the slaves in shackles stood helpless as they sniffed and pawed at them. One bear trundled over to Estrién, up on two legs, claws out ready to lash and slash.

'I will kill you' it told him, yet he raised his arms, his hands, he spoke gently, he pacified the bear.

It dropped on all fours and wandered away, disappearing as Amber had done. He stood calmly in front of the others, waving signs and sigils and with peace in his heart. The bears moved slowly out of the arena, somewhere, who knew where in time or space? This time, last time, sometime never; they were gone.

Anaïs stood calmly in the centre of the arena, her arms held out, her palms upwards, concentrating. Slowly the sound died, the beating and clanging, all became still in the arena, even the children stopped weeping. She walked over to them, her arms filled with good things, food and love and warmth. They took them from her, nourished by her, they sat quietly as their big round and trusting eyes watched her curiously, before they vanished slowly, one by one. The last child stared solemnly into her face, the hope of his future, before he too disappeared.

She walked to the group of waiting slaves, held her hands over them. Their shackles fell to the ground. Slowly they left the arena, a single shuffling file of freedom.

Everything became absolutely silent and the world waited. For some moments time held still.

Then the floor of the arena turned blood red.

Anaïs stood in the centre, curiously surveying the ground, then cast her eyes at Estrién. 'Do something for me, please.' She held up her arms high in the air. 'Use White Star to cut my wrists.'

'What!' He shook his head, no, that would kill her, too much blood.

Her eyes begged. 'Do it,' she pleaded. 'It needs blood, my blood. Blood of life, blood of death, blood of sacrifice. *Do it!*' It was an order this time, not a plea.

He walked slowly up to her, held up White Star. He clasped the back of her right hand while he slit one wrist, watched as blood gushed out, then did the same with the other. Rivulets ran down the dove coloured gown, little streams of scarlet against the pale grey.

She put down her arms, held out her wrists over the arena floor. Droplets scattered, mingled with the blood red of the floor, disappeared into infinity. She moved to the northern end of the arena, then west, south, east, to the centre again, then all points in between, dripping, dripping, dripping, life-liquid losing, until she collapsed back in the very centre of the circle.

Estrién ran to help her, but she was disappearing as he ran, body fading, light fading, clarifying into nothingness. He put out a hand to hold her, keep her there, but she vanished even as he touched her. It was almost as if she had bled out of existence.

He was alone in the arena, no Anaïs, and no idea how to get out.

*

Outside there was some consternation. Amber for one thing was anxious; she had faith in Anaïs, but had no idea what the Time Circle would do to Estrién. She worried and fretted, quietly offering prayers for the safe return of her husband and her sister.

The fact that she alone heard her name called upon the wind did nothing to ease her worry.

Dane and the other mages stood close, they could hear something happening inside, but were unsure whether that was in the circle or inside Manecaestr itself. The noise became louder, they realised it was the sound of running hooves, barking dogs and the braying, champing, jittering, clacking, clucking sounds of various animals.

There came a clearance in the mist, small but large enough for two donkeys, three goats, several horses, dogs, geese and duck to dash out from the circle, followed by a smothering host of white moths. The noise came from inside, for as they passed them, running who-knew-where, there was no sound at all. The circle thickened again as quickly as it cleared.

The mages raised a collective eyebrow and studied the region they had emerged from.

'Well, *something*'s happening,' Salli offered helpfully.

'Estrién's sword probably scared the life out of them,' retorted Amber.

Now they watched with curiosity as the circle turned pale amber, then pale green, pink, blue, violet in a rapid series of flashes. It seemed to shimmer, grow larger, sink in on itself, before returning to its original state. Yet it was not the original state, there was something different, it seemed brighter somehow.

When a dozen warriors dashed out, all clad in the armour of hundreds of years gone by, they went on alert. The warriors seemed dazed, but angry, very angry. Their bronzed helmets resplendent with magnificent red plumes shone in the midday sun, their bronze swords gleamed hungrily and the leather tunics and arm guards were decorated with bright brass platelets.

'Death to Macedons!' they cried as they charged at the company, mistaking them for the enemy they had been fighting.

'Oh shit,' shouted Dane, 'get ready everyone!'

The mages, Lady Violet's included, shot amberic lightning at the breast plates and the helmets. Archers, including Reave and Garrett took aim. Reave aimed for the neck of one, realising there was little else to shoot at. He went down gurgling, she never missed. Another charged near her, two rapid arrows to the knee stopped him, and Tamlyn finished him off with his sabre.

The momentary hesitation as one peered curiously at Amber was enough for her to dig him in the ribs under the breastplate, and issue a slice to his neck as he fell.

The rest were taken down by Lady Violet's guards, all well experienced and also in full plate armour. Movement in plate armour was heavy going, but fine for guard duty and close combat. It came in handy now as the bronze swords hit. A dent or two was all that was taken, and their steel swords proved superior. The company stood around the dead bodies, curiously inspecting them. Who were these warriors, more importantly, *when* were they from? It certainly wasn't now, nor did they look like anything Mer'edrynn had ever produced.

'They look ... *foreign*,' was the general opinion. The mages studied them with relish.

*

Estrién dropped to his knees in the centre of the arena, disbelieving. She couldn't just fade into nothingness, could she? He called out her name, but no-one answered. Then he realised the floor beneath him was going, fading as she faded, he was dropping, falling, hurtling down into nothingness.

On and on he dropped, arms flailing as he tried to catch on to anything available. There was nothing to hold on to. Then the light of sunrise surrounded him, he saw spring green fields, quickly changing to dark forests, shimmering lakes and a blood moon night.

It dawned on him that he wasn't falling, but time around him was rising. He watched lovers kiss and dance under the velvet night sky, a child was born, grew to womanhood, aged and died, a hundred children, grandchildren and great grandchildren mourned her death. He saw an entire nation rise and fall, warriors with plumed helmets fighting under a red hot sun, the birth of kings, the death of queens and the march of an army across a gentle land covering it with blood. He sat clutching his knees, White Star in one hand, eyes wide at the procession of time. It had to settle some time ... hadn't it?

*

'Welcome to my world, my dear.' The words seemed pleasant, if the sensation of ice-cold crystal shards piercing soft female skin can be regarded so.

He stood across from her; an ethereal emanation of pure evil. He was the shadow on the horizon, the haunter of dreams and the scent of decay, the serpentine voice in innocent ears.

This was his realm, his world and his word was power. Here the Adammites were dust in the wind, the rest of creation even less so.

Anaïs writhed from the pain of his voice, trying to ascertain what had happened, trying to protect herself from *him*. She held it together until the stabbing pains passed, little by little as echoes fade into nothingness. She stared up at the being from her prone position on the floor. It was difficult to determine exactly what it was, perhaps pulsating red energy around some vaguely human shell, might describe it? She was exhausted from loss of blood, lack of food or sleep and her mouth was parched, her tongue swollen. She neither remembered travelling here or arriving. Neither did she know what time had passed, if any.

Time was relative here, or non-existent.

There was no room or building around her, neither walls nor floor. She saw stars in the distance, only strange shafts of light close by, all interspersed by blackness, a void of nothingness. *He* trod one of the beams of light, she was on another, there were several.

'*Mage paths,*' she thought.

He spoke again. 'I finally have you Anaïs, the *real* you, your centre, the Weaver of Time. I have waited long, too long. You belong to me, you must know that, yet you escaped me long ago. Why did you do that Anaïs? It served you no purpose.

Now, finally, you have come, I knew you could not resist the time circle we created – together, you understand, it was created together. I knew it would bring you here, to my world, outside of time. I led you … I led them all … to this moment.

Just as it takes two for creation in your world, thus it takes two for destruction in mine … and here you are... my prisoner.' The sound that followed might have been mistaken for laughter, had it not felt like steel daggers in Anaïs' flesh.

She would have spoken, refuted his words, but no sound came out of her mouth. She could not speak.

'So now,' he continued, 'since you are finally here, I can complete my plans. You and I will blend as one and complete the pattern, *my* pattern, not your chaotic organic pattern. There is but one structure, mine, and you will create it, removing the other from its miserable and pathetic existence. You are here to weave the end of your world.'

His voice held the satisfied smugness of victory as he continued. 'I will punish you severely for eluding me for so long; you require correction before you die. I shall enjoy your pain as you weave; your sorrow, your bitter tears and the anguish you shall scream into the void, sweet music to my ears. Scream loud, Anaïs, for there will be no-one to hear you and I shall certainly not care.'

He paused to let it sink in before continuing, appearing to relish explaining her future existence. 'This is the end for your kind and the beginning of mine. You will witness your fellow humans die, your loved ones, your family. They will die painfully Anaïs, I assure you of that. You will breathe the stench of their deaths into your nostrils, you will feel every moment of their anguished passing. I will feed you the poisoned flesh of the unborn and we will drink the heady blood of dying warriors together, bitter on your tongue.

This you will weave into the pattern.

Then there will only be yourself left alive, you alone - the final representation of your wriggling, stinking life form. Your tapestry will thus become meaningless; there will be nothing to record; it will therefore collapse and disintegrate. Then, you and I will join together, here in my realm of death. You will feel my breath pierce your pathetic, weak body and you will lie, like the tapestry, in shreds. I will watch your skin whiten as your life force seeps away, dripping from our marital bed into the empty void around us. But it will not bring life Anaïs, for my void is death.

You too will slowly die, Anaïs, slowly disappear from existence as you disappeared today in the Arena of Time, the last being from your putrid world.

Then the worm of death will triumph, the cold of the tomb will prevail.

You are mine Anaïs, you *cannot* leave my world.'

He laughed in cold triumph and it was acid upon her skin. She tried to stand but could not. He stepped across the paths of light towards her, red eyes gleaming with anticipation.

Chapter 4

Commander Grey pulled back to Belcast'el and considered his next step. He arranged a meeting with his alchemists and physicians to test various poisons, liquid or gaseous, on elven slaves. He wanted something fast acting, he didn't care if it meant death or simply slumber; they could easily take out an unconscious elf or two. There was of course no honour in such a deed, but that was irrelevant; the ends were more important than the means. You only took honour from combat if your foe was worthy. Elves and the like were mere vermin. Soon, he would own Oakleigh.

He decided in the meanwhile to push on northwards. King Alexis seemed intent on protecting the southern coast of both Westerling and Floriénne, the ports, and of course he had a full garrison up at Sunstones. Nevertheless, a push as far as the Whitecap Mountains would keep his men on their toes, secure the Bay of Gulls and the forests at the lower slopes of the mountains which thankfully were no longer full of Freowulven.

Yes, time to push out the boundaries of what had been Elvinhaeme, to make the new Mordecia larger, perhaps get as far as Rhiannon's Vale in Westerling itself? Troops were pouring in now, groups that had been separated by Von Adamm to hold the various towns along the Long Ride; they came with hearts of anger that they had been betrayed by Draecastle. The villages here no longer needed constant watching, so many elves were either dead or taken as slaves, and Belcast'el could be safely kept as a garrison town.

This was his land, he had taken it, von Adamm had given him men's hearts, but by guts and determination he had honed his army and crushed the populace.

Still, it didn't seem that much of a victory, hard steel against pitchforks and a few soft silly elves. He had fought poets and minstrels, farmers and craftsmen, not a worthy foe.

He had to admit, as he had taken this land, he hadn't realised how many humans lived side by side with the elves. He thought the land was elven only, yet they had lived here happily, were ready to fight against other humans for an elven land. Like the elves they lived with, they too were soft, non-combatants, market gardeners, carpenters, writers, musicians and the like. They were useful, he captured those he could, but there were no true warriors among them.

No, he needed to fully test his troops now; his army was ready, angry and hungry for battle and for victory. He knew, if given the right conditions, he could win, easily defeat King Alexis' troops out in the field. He needed to plan when and where he would meet his troops, manoeuvre him into the weakest positions.

To kill a King would be a delight, the 'crowning' glory of his life. He chuckled at his own pun as he went to meet with staff and make preparations. He sent word north to leave a garrison at Herringhold, enough to protect passage for all troops and possibly Adammite leaders or dedicated personnel out of Manecaestr if it ever became open again. He considered they would be in a sorry state by now, would need help. The others, civilians of the Adammite persuasion or otherwise could flee or fall, he didn't really care; he just wanted his Hellboys home.

The rest of the troops should pull back either to the Isle of Glasse for further training or to Mordecia. In the meantime he would further consolidate his position here.

He sent out his Hellboys to execute unruly natives, take captive the weaker ones and clear villages for the future use of Adammite families.

*

'Blast and damnation!' exclaimed King Alexis. He had heard about the attempt on Oakleigh, was glad to hear it had been repulsed, Estrién's idea of using Freowulven had been the right one. But now he heard the Adammites had moved forward and up towards his own borders, indeed had fully taken the western shoreline of the Bay of Gulls. It had always been problematic due to its vicinity near the Freowulven-held areas of the lower Whitecaps. It hadn't particularly mattered because the Freowulven had previously seen to Adammites coming in that way, a threat to themselves. He had been happy to use them as unpaid guards; they were after all, felons, most having escaped the hangman's noose.

But of course they were now protecting Oakleigh, and the Elvinhaeme militia weren't there any more to see to the coast. Within a few weeks Commander Grey not only moved up as far as the border between Elvinhaeme and Westerling, he marched further north and had taken the main highway to the coast, right up to the edges of the Whitecap mountains.

'Good luck to him there,' thought King Alexis, knowing the difficulties of the forests there. If the bears or wildcats didn't get you, it only took one small dragon to devastate a unit of troops. It was why he had never used the Whitecaps for lumber, too damn dangerous. 'He's welcome to lose some of his men to gain a few logs.'

But the loss of part of Westerling affected him. His troops were concentrated further along Mab's Bay, just north of Oakleigh, partly to help if Oakleigh got invaded, but mostly because the main route from Orlandium to Belcast'el ended just at the border. It was a good place for defence, unlike the plain to the west and the road to the coast.

The rest of his troops were stationed on the south coast, his precious ports were not to be taken. Dair Chev'al accompanied his troops to the south; they sat tall and proud upon their steeds, swords and spurs shining, the buttons and buckles of their black uniforms gleaming.

King Alexis had more ships patrolling, his land would not be taken again from the sea. He patrolled the coast of Herne's Bay too, a thank you to the Dair Chev'al, keeping Floriénne free from intruders. But he did not have as many as he wished, could not afford to build more. He hoped he had enough for any further planned maritime invasion. Occasionally ships had come through, von Adamm insisted on harrying the coast. But, from Mab's Bay in Westerling, to Herne's Bay in Floriénne, they worked together to maintain the coastline; between them they repulsed the Adammites wherever they landed.

There had been little since the death of von Adamm though, all troops seemed to have pulled back to Elvinhaeme. This new leader seemed more of a soldier than a politician, it had taken him but a short time to remove the Dûc de Luxonne and place himself on the throne. The news was devastating, he felt sick at the thought of the fate of the elves inside the Dûcdom.

He was also unsure about the numbers of Adammites seen to be along the western coastal route, all marching easterly in his direction. His troops did not have the advantage of the eight square formation of the Adammites, nor those new-fangled crossbows. He would never forget that the battle of Pennyport had almost been a disaster. He'd held on by the skin of his teeth and some incredible good luck –

the intervention of the Dair Chev'al and those four young adventurers, now the centre of the main resistance, the *White Shield*, or in Elvhen, *Nim'randuel.*

Everything revolved around them, he understood that. There was more to this than mere Adammite revolution. They were fighting something deeper, behind all this unrest, something evil to its core.

'And good luck to them,' he thought, 'May Merrie bless them eternally.' Meanwhile, his problems were more mundane, physical, in the shape of a large and looming invasion to the west. He did not know if this new Commander intended drawing his troops to the west while more ships invaded the south, or merely if this was a full scale invasion. He couldn't take the chance; he had to leave enough troops to guard the coast.

He polished his sword, called his Knights to him, his prized *Corps de Lyons* and left to join his troops amassing to the west.

*

At the edge of a farmer's field to the north of Manecaestr, Colonel Mackenzie shuddered as he stared curiously at the weird phenomena known as the time circle. It fascinated him. Everything in his life before could be solved by the use of two things: cash or hard steel. This was beyond him, beyond anything he had ever known and he was as curious as the mages further south. There was a small group with him, two alchemists, an astronomer, a physicist, and a 'holistic remedian,' he called himself. Plus, of course, a dozen fit young Adammite soldiers, including four Hellboys.

They had taken over the farm, kept the farmer and his wife and son currently trussed up In the stable. It was an arable farm given over to oats and rye, recently sown. There were no cattle, no farmhands to arrive daily and it was pretty deserted around the area - a good place to camp, the farmhouse too was comfortable and useful. A couple of dogs barked for an hour or two, but that was easily remedied with a crossbow bolt.

He'd watched the spherical structure shimmer and change hue, wondered what was going on? The alchemists threw various minerals at it, tried to see if they could replicate the changes but nothing happened. Then it returned to the same grey shade with the odd unsettling sparkle, a slightly eerie spectacle.

Mackenzie watched now in amazement as a portion of it grew lighter, a hollow appeared and a dozen large brown bears shambled their way out of the sphere. Quickly he ordered his Hellboys to fire their crossbows, and his swordsmen hurried forwards. A few minutes later, despite some yelps and cries from the swordsmen, it was all over and the bears lay in a heap.

As with the mages further south, the alchemists and scientific officers crowded around inspecting this new phenomena. One of the alchemists was actually a mage, but he kept it quiet, self preservation uppermost. It was difficult, so often he wanted to simply raise a mage hand and use one of his elemental powers, stopped himself just in time. He'd come with them from Mere'garde basically in order to escape, but still hadn't found the opportunity. One night ... one night he would go.

The bears proved all too real, solid, physical. 'Where the hell did they pop up from?' Colonel Mackenzie asked. It was a rhetorical question, there was clearly no answer.

He asked the same question a few hours later as a long line of mixed elves and humans staggered slowly through. They wore the cheap and simple garments of the slave market, but they looked different, ethereal and free. True, they seemed dazed, obviously in shock at the release from ... *wherever* ... but there was something uncanny too.

Colonel Mackenzie was about to order his men to execute them, they were after all, unarmed, but he saw the looks in his men's eyes.

They were terrified.

He left the people alone, allowed them to simply walk away. As they disappeared into the distance – literally faded away despite remaining in plain view - he understood his men were correct. Things, beings, were emerging from the time circle that shouldn't appear here and he didn't like it at all.

For the first time in his life he shivered, and it wasn't from the cold.

*

Lady Violet sent word to Lord Black that things were happening to the time conduit or whatever it was. He sent a company of mixed horse and foot soldiers, as many archers as he could spare, plus the usual paraphernalia of war machinery for their support. Lady Violet was particularly pleased to see the camp cook, Sunny Blackthorne arrive; she had learnt her craft under Grimwold Serf, finally there would be some decent food to eat. The messes Lady Violet and her personal guard had made, mostly blackened and tough meat char grilled on their makeshift campfire, had done nothing for her digestion.

Young King Duggan also arrived at the time sphere with another company of soldiers. They were well prepared for whatever they found should the circle become open.

Dane looked at the newly assembled company and smiled. After what he and Salli had seen when they went to Manecaestr, there couldn't be enough troops to retake the city. Dane was a kind man, always had been, brought up to love and kindness, and Salli was gentle, a non-combatant, he used his powers to ease, not give pain, but both wished revenge upon the Adammites of Manecaestr for what they had witnessed. Salli now wore a sword at all times, he declared he was happy to use it inside the city. He didn't particularly like the idea, but he could also use his willow wand to bring death if necessary.

'I use it to give a quiet end to those suffering; I have rarely used it to kill, apart from that night at Draecastle, to end von Adamm's dominion. Now however, once tha Time zone disappears, I go in for revenge on these people, I've never felt anger like this before. Somehow, that diminishes me, and I am afraid it will infect my wand with hatred.'

'Not if you go in cold,' Dane replied. 'Stay cool, be logical, take hatred out of your head and use your wand and your powers as just punishment. Those bastards have given up their humanity, there must be a balance, it's payback time and you are Nemesis. You can do it, Salli. When that circle thing opens, we move in and we strike on behalf of every poor bugger who has been murdered, displaced or enslaved by them. I looked into their eyes, Salli; they have forgotten what it means to be human, so when I kill, *as I will*, I'll feel nothing.

Maybe that makes me like them, but it's all they deserve. Now if that diminishes us, as you fear, then so be it. Besides,' he laughed and grinned at Salli, 'they're damn good fighters, it will be mostly self- defence, you won't have time to even think. You can salve your conscience that way if you wish.'

Salli nodded thoughtfully, 'as you say Dane, but it's here and now that my conscience pricks me.' He walked away, a little quiet meditation would help, then stopped and turned back. 'You've matured Dane, you are becoming the mage I expected you would. Just make sure that you leave a little humanity inside you too.'

Dane watched him go, realising that the tables had turned; Salli had given him comfort when they had been inside the city and he was the emotional one. But time had allowed him to consider and he knew that cold revenge worked best for the task ahead. Frankly he didn't dare allow his feelings to get the better of him, they were way too strong. It would affect his judgement and his abilities in Manecaestr if he let go. He would leave the anger for afterwards; use that energy to help the victims.

He heard Amber cry out and he hurried across to her. She was pointing at the circle, there was an opening appearing, it was thinning. They could see someone, or something hobbling through the mist towards them. Each drew swords; no one knew what might appear next.

*

He lost count of sunrises and moon-rises, so fast they made him dizzy. He held on to White Star, the only solid thing near him, held on to it for dear life, wondering if he let go would he swirl up into the ether, would he disappear on time's arc?

Then it settled as quickly as it started and the pale grey cloud of the phenomena surrounded him again. Estrién stood, despite there being no floor, the mist seemed to dissipate a little, surely it was lighter around him? Was that the sun overhead? He definitely saw a clearing, a patch much lighter than the rest; he walked towards it, walking on nothing but air. Time steadied itself, he could see Amber and the others through the opening. He walked … slowly, for time stretched again and it was like walking through clear honey towards his loved ones. He called, but there was still a barrier to sound. He sliced through the air with his sword as he had done to reach Anaïs. It became easier, thinner; he breathed fresh air as he neared the exit.

Amber gave a cry as she watched Estrién stagger out of the mist. His skin seemed as grey as the time circle, he limped a little from the twist to his ankle, but he was otherwise unharmed. She ran to help him, to hug her beloved husband, to welcome him back into her life. It felt as if he had been gone an eternity, which perhaps was true.

He held up a hand to stop her. 'I've lost her,' he cried, 'I've lost Anaïs … she just disappeared.' He briefly explained how she seemed to evaporate before the arena too faded around him, leaving only the time circle. 'She just faded away...' He hung his head in shame. 'I'm sorry, Amber, I'm so sorry.'

All eyes turned to the strange circle of time around the city. What had happened to Anaïs, was she dead?

They gathered together, watching and waiting.

*

Amber stood by Estrién's side staring at the time circle. She remembered a day, some years ago. They had a fortune teller in the circus, a strange woman, she read cards or a crystal ball, sometimes the palm of your hand. Over the first few weeks she joined them everyone went to her to have their future told, except Amber. Eventually it was her turn, her friends persuaded her, the fortune teller was good, very good, she had told them all kinds of things about their lives, past and future. She was truly worth a visit.

Amber became curious, decided to give her a go. She went inside the gaily coloured tent, sat down at the circular table across from the mysterious veiled figure. The coverless table was cheap pine, darkened with age. One meagre brass candle lit the centre of the table, but a couple of carved elven candelabra stood close by. A curtain behind the woman closed off her sleeping area and there was little else to see.

The table held a small crystal scrying ball and a large pack of richly decorated cards.

The woman studied her for some time, then took hold of the palm of her hand, scrutinising it carefully. She shook her head and let go, then pushed the pack of cards across to Amber.

'Consider what you wish to ask me and shuffle the cards, then blank your mind and cut them twice please.' The voice was crisp and clear, there was no fudging or wheedling in her manner.

Amber did as she was told then passed them back.

The woman picked up the cards and began laying them on the table in front of her. Amber saw a wheel of life with people clinging to the sides as it circled, a card that looked like a dark, horned devil, a grinning skeleton waved two bony hands at her and a tall circular tower, a fortress, tumbled apart, what looked like terrified people falling down from the top as the fortress collapsed.

The soothsayer stopped, shook her head. She turned the rest of the cards to her and slowly looked at them. Her eyes widened and she gathered every card together, closed the pack.

'I cannot read your future,' she solemnly declared. 'Do not ask me.'

'Cannot ... or will not?' Amber asked.

'The future is only yours to see,' she replied. '*And yours to choose*. The cards merely indicate the path you travel. What happens on those paths is up to you.'

She would say no more and Amber left

She remembered her now, the fear on the woman's face, the consternation on her own as she wondered what it meant ... if anything?

But now she understood; the paths she trod had been hard, dogged by that damn creature, that evil being, only the love of her men had supported her. Her life had changed, again and again, and death had insidiously played its treacherous role. When Estrién stumbled out of the misty circle without her sister, everything collapsed before her. The circle was still there, her sister gone.

The tower had fallen, time, death and the devil played their part; there was no hope, no future. Amber felt more desolate than at any other point in her life.

*

In Floriénne many elves would have agreed with Amber.

There had been a bad winter and now it was spring but nothing was growing. Floriénne was a fertile place, rich in both flora and fauna. People lived so well here, the forest and the fields provided everything from wines to silk and perfumes, from well-fattened cattle and wild game to fine timber, the seas and rivers brought in fish and they even had a small silver mine for their own jewellery. True, they bought weapons and armour from the dwarves of Hammerhold and the steel-smiths of Mercantia, but they weren't actually a war-like nation. The females particularly hated war or the paraphernalia of war, although it has to be admitted, they couldn't help admiring the Dair Chev'al on their beautiful steeds, resplendent in black and silver armour.

By this time in the year the woods should be a carpet of bluebells and the wild garlic should be shooting up, leaves uncurling on mulberry bushes and shrubs and trees bursting into blossom.

Nothing was happening, worse still, Lord Taenghelin inspected his vines. They weren't dead, but they were ailing, attacked with a vicious fungus. 'Noble rot' was one thing, this was quite another. He called for a mage, he'd never seen this before. He knew what it was though, his son had kept him informed over the past months. He hadn't given any military information, but he had written at length about some being who dogged them, hated the world, wished to destroy it. It was behind the Adammites, he told him. They were fighting it, and *'not to worry, Papa, I am with the very best people you can imagine. I am proud to be their friend and their bondsman. Whatever happens, we go together, we fight together, we love together, and we will win over this evil. Do not worry about me because, even if I die, I die knowing I have done that which is right.'*

He put down the letter and wiped his eyes, this war meant sacrifice, but he hoped it didn't mean the loss of his only son.

He also hoped his son might quicken up the end of this creature a little, preferably before he lost all of his vines …

The Dûchesse of Floriénne however wasn't quite so forgiving. She blamed Estrién for the loss of the sacred sword and for bringing disaster – as she knew it would, as foretold – upon Floriénne. Somehow, the Adammites passed her by, there were none in Floriénne and they hadn't attacked either via the Foraes Dair or the coast, although that was mostly thanks to King Alexis' naval patrols.

Nevertheless her land was dying, the forests, the crops, even animals ailing. The folk watched groups of wild beasts attacking each other, great aerial battles as birds made war, never sure what was on which side. Like the rest of Mer'edrynn, her people too suffered ailments and illnesses never encountered before, she herself had a cough that wouldn't go. She longed for a proper spring to appear, the air was damp and cold. She longed for summer sunshine.

It was Estrién's fault; he had brought this upon them as the legends said. She wanted that sword returning, the life blood of her nation. He had taken it and now … this. It was too much, she would send out her knights again, find him, kill him, bring the sword home where it belonged …

She sat down heavily on the delicate chaise longue. It was no use, Estrién was right. He hadn't caused this, nor had the sword, she reflected. It was a tool to be used at the right time, and that time was now. Good luck to him and may Merrie take care of him...

…*And the sword.*

She turned her attention to more mundane matters. A missive from the Dair Chev'al informed her that her new commander of the war forces, that elf with the dreadful scarred face, the one who had beaten that sabre toothed tiger, Knight Commander Kielan Penlachl'en, had joined forces with King Alexis' own forces near the river Tethés. She shuddered at the thought of his cheek, deeply scored and warped from the cat's claws, and that horrible one on his neck, he was probably enough to terrify the Adammites into submission.

But she understood he would make a good commander. She sent for her military advisers to hear the latest information on the deployment of forces around Floriénne. At the moment that was much more of a concern, along with acquiring as many remedians, healers and mages as she could, to somehow normalise her beloved land.

She called a meeting of farmers, gardeners, gamekeepers, grounds men, botanists and herbalists, and of course, foresters, along with the requisite mages and medical people to discuss in detail what, if anything they could do to counter the situation.

It might not be sword and steel she was facing, but she had her own war to fight, a war against nature itself. *He* had decided that Floriénne was a blight on the world, too rich to continue to exist. He sent his minions of death to destroy it. The Adammites would not touch it, at least not as yet, but they weren't the only forces at his disposal.

There would be no spring here, *he* would watch it die, and as it dropped and dried he would send his crackling flames to cleanse this putrescence from existence. Only when the huge forest, the very heart of Mer'edrynn lay as grey dust and blackened charcoal would he be satisfied.

But right at the moment, *he* had other things on his mind.

Chapter 5

Month of Oestra, Manecaestr, Segantium.

Back inside Manecaestr, civil war had broken out, led by a group of females who called themselves the Women's Army of Retribution, or W.A.R., although some men insisted on calling it the Wenches Army. Didn't matter what it was called, these were tough northern women, not used to being at the beck and call of a few 'male tossers', as they succinctly put it.

It had started immediately the Adammites took over Manecaestr, not so much a revolution, more a *'just you try it, mate,'* to their husbands when confronted with the 'I'm joining the Adammites' speech. It worked for some time too, few older married men signed up. But the lure of weapon training and legalised bullying proved too much. Men joined and came home wielding not only a damn big stick and strutting in a fancy uniform, but also carrying a sharp sword. Add city wide curfew, slave markets, a ban on meetings other than Adammite controlled, and the inability to move about in public as a single female, not to mention public whippings, beatings or the ducking chair, as well as the infamous pyres, life for human females in Manecaestr became extremely difficult. Life for females in any Adammite controlled area was difficult.

But the ladies of Manecaestr were neither soft nor stupid. Under the pretence of 'bread-baking for victory,' meetings (which due to the nature of bread making could go on for hours), or 'soldier's sewing circles', and the infamous 'vest-knitting wives and girlfriends,' (a particularly lethal group) the women offered tea and sympathy to their long-suffering friends. They also offered valuable information gained via pillow talk which they passed to the underground movements, and learned a few self defensive moves should they need them. Eventually this came to the ears of Lady Violet's spies who smuggled in knives, daggers and swords, although, as many a woman said, a good rolling pin can just as easily crush a man's skull, or knacker his lower regions. Poison, too is a particularly useful tool and the VKWAGS put it to good use.

They practised combat and guerrilla warfare in cellars and underground rooms, finally emerging as what became known as W.A.R. The ex-Women's Jousting team which had met bi-monthly at Manecaestr Arena joined them, as did the ex-Female Archers of Manecaestr (groups 1 and 2) who had won blue ribbons at various tourneys. All, like 'Meredith Grimes and Daughters, Blacksmiths and Metalworkers' had been threatened with execution if they continued with their 'unseemly' ways. They and those like them therefore took their skills to the W.A.R.

Some sneaked out at night after ensuring their loved ones were snoring from a sleeping draught in their late night hot-milk-and-usquebae. They rescued many a woman and her children from a particularly abhorrent mate, took out various guards around the city and the prison guards were peculiarly susceptible to certain female charms, enabling them to free elves, humans and a few ailing dwarves from the stinky and lice-ridden cells.

There was a rise in prostitution in the city, not particularly needed previously, but the influx of many soldiers rendered it both necessary and also, quite lucrative. The Night Angels, as they called themselves, were taught combat skills in case of attack, and they brought a great deal of inside information to the W.A.R. war table, plus ten percent of their fees.

Those who couldn't fight used the various innocent sounding groups to bake extra bread, make clothes and blankets and create medicines for the poor and helpless or for Escape Parcels.

These of course became unnecessary when the Circle appeared. No one got out, not a bloody soul. So they kept the Escape Parcels as Famine Relief Parcels, knowing exactly who would be first to get food and who would be far down the chain. There was no further discussion between outside parties and the inner underground, but because of the situation, they worked together with certain anti-Adammite groups and the few mages who still lived in the city. They worked however in cells, or small groups, it was essential word did not get out to the Adammite hierarchy.

It is probable that at one point over ninety percent of females in Manecaestr over the age of fifteen belonged to one of the subversive movements, but thanks to the cell grouping, few were discovered.

Of those who were the central core of the movement, they remain to this day unknown. They wore hoods and black leather masks to hide their identity as they quietly co-ordinated the various groups. But, they were ready and waiting to create a full scale attack alongside their male counterparts when the opportunity was ripe.

As life deteriorated under the spherical dome of the Time Circle, they became more and more necessary... also, more and more bold and adventurous. They broke into warehouses, killed guards and took food, medicines and essentials to their underground lairs to be distributed to the needy. They made a list of the worst of the Adammites, sent assassins to deal with them, and at one point managed to poison the food in one of the army barracks. Quite a few Adammite soldiers died before the poison was traced and the cook was blamed as an Elf sympathiser and executed. None In the W.A.R. movement mourned his loss.

When the Fae attacks began, they looked on it as fate and while the Adammites were occupied with setting up defences, they took the opportunity to raid several guard houses along with armourers, weapon smiths and fletchers and actually booby trap their equipment.

They could not however, control their anger against women who had capitulated or openly flaunted their relationship with the Adammites. Many were found tied to a tall street torch in the mornings, tarred and feathered from top to bottom. Some in the W.A.R. found this petty, but others applauded. As they said, their name was Retribution.

They were secret and (mostly) subtle, they were strong and intelligent. They kept up the spirits of the women of Manecaestr throughout that long winter and the dark, and somewhat sweaty days of the Phenomenon.

In short, they were the heart and soul of a proud city reduced to a hell hole of misery under the power-tripping rule of a misogynist death cult. They would not give in.

*

King Duggan's and Lord Black's troops weren't the only ones arriving at the Time Circle. A large group of the Rover clan arrived, complete with the sharpest and brightest steel axes Amber had ever seen.

'Hammerhold made these 'specially for us, their strongest steel, added a few enchantments too.' Big Joe Ironhand pointed his massive hand towards a cart they had pulled down with them; it was filled with wooden crates. He opened the tops of a couple and showed them the contents. 'These were supposed to be delivered to that Colonel Grey down in Elvinhaeme, but he doesn't stand a chance in hell of getting them now. Here, make use of them.'

They were filled with wood and steel crossbows and steel bolts.

Lady Violet's personal guard gazed curiously at them took a few to practise with.

'Fucking hell, these are good,' they announced, rapidly rationing them out to the interested parties of both King Duggan and Lord Black's archers.

They quickly made some makeshift targets of straw and sawdust, measuring distance, speed, accuracy, depth of penetration and the time it took to recharge the crossbow. There were fewer bolts per minute as compared to arrows, a mere two, but that was outweighed by the speed of flight, accuracy and deadliness.

Reave too was interested, she took one, examined it and tried it out. It kicked a little, she missed her first target, took that into account. She spent time examining the sights of the crossbow; there was a square to look through and various marks to show distance. She centred the crossbow on one of the marks, put her foot through the wooden stirrup and pulled up the strong hempen rope; it felt odd, a little sticky. The Rovers explained to her it was steeped in glue for extra strength, helped in the rain or the rope would loosen.

She nodded, yes, a good idea. Once more she sighted the bow, cocked it back and slotted the rope into the notch. She popped a steel bolt into the barrel channel and aimed at the target. She pulled the wooden trigger, the crossbow jumped slightly left and again she missed her target.

She was annoyed, but would not give up so easily. She reloaded the crossbow, it took time, far more than her longbow, that would need addressing. She then crouched down on one knee, used it to steady the bow and sight her quarry. It felt better, aimed easier; she took breath and pulled the trigger once more.

This time it went straight through the makeshift target with a vengeance, ended up in the bole of an unfortunate tree somewhat further along the field.

'Wow!' she declared, 'Holy Merrie!' She stood up. 'Right boys, I want as many of you as there are crossbows and we need some good swordsmen with bloody big shields to protect us while we recharge. Any takers?'

A whole row of eager men stepped forward.

Reave's Avenging Marksmen and Sharpshooters, otherwise known as 'the Rams', was born.

*

King Alexis' company met with the Dair Chev'al close to the southern end of Rhiannon's Vale. The Whitecap Mountains loomed ahead of him, the wide and beautiful river Tethés separated his forces from those of Commander Grey's. There was a long narrow bridge here over a steep ravine, the main road carried on along it, wide enough for one wagon or carriage to cross, not enough for many troops at a time. Yet they were there, across, even a few arrows and bolts flew occasionally, just to remind each side they were enemies.

The two sides stood at each edge of the huge ravine and glared at each other.

The morning was warm, spring was in the air here, unlike Floriénne, and Knight Commander Kielan Penlachl'en took off his cap and gauntlets as he jumped from his horse to meet the King. Momentarily, King Alexis stood shocked, the face of the Knight Commander had been horribly ravaged, but quickly manners overtook the initial distaste and he hurried to greet him. Briefly he examined the scar, the mark of some fierce claw, must have been a hell of a fight, yet the man still lived. He meant 'elf' of course, yet a fully grown male elf was still a man, still held manhood in him, this one clearly more than most.

'Glad you're here,' he stated warmly, '… that must have been a rare fight,' he smiled, pointing at the Knight Commander's face. He wasn't going to ignore it, pretend it didn't exist; besides so many men had scars from the recent battles. This was worst than most though. Anyway, he wanted it out of the way, they had other stuff to consider, that bloody Grey and his invasion.

The Knight Commander's face cracked a little as he laughed. 'Yes, it was pretty fierce. There aren't too many sabre toothed tigers around these days, it was me or him, and my own sabre won.'

King Alexis' face dropped. 'Single handed?' Kielan nodded, it was so. 'Holy Merrie, I'm glad it wasn't me. … Hey, must have you next to me in a fight, you can clearly take care of yourself! C'mon,' he continued, leading him to the Field Command tent, where the rest of his staff waited, 'let's talk shop and get this bloody thing underway then we can all go home.'

There was a rustle among the military men as they entered, followed by a general air of respect given to the elven Knight. The king spoke to the assembled.

'There is a large force of Adammites, led by their new Commander Grey, sitting there across the water waiting to invade the rest of my kingdom. There are probably around five hundred presently and that's just a fraction of the numbers to the south, more arriving daily. They have already taken Elvinhaeme and the western end, the somewhat wilder wastes of my land. Regardless of numbers, they are taking no more, it is time to fight and push them back. We need to cross the river and strike.'

He put his hands down upon the table; a map lay in front of him. 'There are only two bridges across,' he told the assembled company, 'unless we row over the Tethés which is rather stupid as we'd be sitting ducks; one of which is the Concorde Bridge, which lies some miles further down. That bridge marks the boundary crossing point from Westerling to Elvinhaeme. It ...' the king smiled, 'it means a lot to me, I and Neria were married there. I came to the edge of my kingdom and set up a wedding camp. I watched my beautiful wife, her family and entourage walk over that bridge, I met her in the centre, our families stood on either side while we were wed, then I picked her up and carried her off to my camp for the damn biggest party there's ever been there.

Whatever happens, that bridge must continue standing, it's a symbol of the love and friendship between our nations. No doubt this Grey fellow has left a large force there to stop us. I'm awaiting my spies now to give me information.

The other bridge, this one here, is too narrow. It was deliberately left so, never wanted invaders from the coast, but I didn't send a large force over there because of the Freowulven. They kept the coast clear, even smugglers didn't come further inland to Westerling because they traded with the Freowulven, wins all round. I can easily keep this bridge, this crossing, but it doesn't repel that bugger sitting over there.

I can't come in by the Bay of Gulls and catch him from the coast because he has too many of his own patrol boats and warships. I'm still fortifying my own, still building and a few months on, I might go at his ships.

So it means using the other bridge; we leave men here, keep him thinking this is where we are, but I've also got troops amassing further down.

So the only way is down, then up, but the plain is flat there, we will be wide open. Frankly, I'm at a loss, he has far more troops than we have. We will be sitting ducks as we cross that bridge and even then, he could easily surround us, take us out. It appears an impossible task. C'mon guys, give me some ideas how to rid ourselves of those bastards.' He sat down on the camp stool, he didn't bring fancy chairs or paraphernalia with him, never bothered about comfort, and gazed hopefully at the group of knights, personal guard and war chiefs he had around him.

'So there is currently no battle plan then?' Kielan asked.

'Never had a proper battle plan in my life. I'm not a bloody Adammite; I'm a king of what was once a peaceful country. People need saving, we have to save them. Plans are good, but hey, you have to be adaptable, shit happens. Nearly got killed taking back Pennyport, only got through that thanks to those four White Shield and you Dair Chev'al. I pretty much winged it on Mere'garde, took a chance or two, still got my Nerry home. Besides, their troops are fucking good and they use a formation far better than anything I could create. They've practised this for years on that bloody island of theirs, we haven't. No, we can't beat them in open combat, so let's have something a little more constructive than me losing hundreds of men for no reason at all, in one big battle. I'm not doing it. Let's look at something more creative, huh?' He had mages with him, hoped they could come up with something interesting.

Beers were passed around and the group settled to do some serious thinking, when a message came through.

'*Heard you are here. If you are willing, we can join your troops west of Concorde Bridge near river. I can offer some damn good archers and I have a few ideas – we know this country well. I want that bastard.*'

It was signed Jovan, leader of the Freowulven.

*

The Great Stag crossed the river Tethés and continued westwards across Rhiannon's Vale towards the mountains. He picked up an unusual amount of fellow wildlife along the way. They were all his, few had turned, it seemed *he* was concentrating on the Foraes Dair. They eventually gathered in a wood near the plain to the south where Commander Grey's forces were camped.

He was pleased, there were many, everything from wolves, foxes and bears, other stags and deer, along with smaller animals, including rats and water voles, could be useful. He checked around him, yes, all the birds were his, he called down a hovering hawk, then turned into his more human form, took a small piece of ancient parchment and wrote a few words in charcoal, before attaching the note to the hawk. The group of animals stood back at his change, he was at his most majestic, most fierce, he frightened them. He changed back, reassured them, they preferred his stag aspect.

The hawk took the note to King Alexis, '*the beasts and birds await your command.*' It was signed with a flourish, the name illegible yet immensely powerful. Something noble and proud entered Alexis as he read it, some indefinable characteristic of manhood, deep, strong and old as the hills. He felt empowered. He had no idea what it meant, but he knew there was an army he had not even considered ... and they were on his side.

Somewhere behind this was, he knew, the White Shield, and he wished they were down here with him. But they had work to do further north, that peculiar spherical time whatnot.

Still, his army was not only slowly growing in numbers, it was expanding, no longer concentrated in one place. He took hope.

*

Two figures were seen approaching King Alexis' camp, they had large packs on their backs and each seemed to be carrying something that looked like a sack with sticks hanging out of it. They were stopped from entering by one of the guards.

'Tell yon king there, he might want us with him if there's to be a wee battle,' said one.

The guard looked at him, 'you bring arms, a force with you, or perhaps great battle skills?' he asked.

'Nay, none o' that,' replied Jack McJock. 'We bring something much better… something to stir the blood of our boys and scatter a foe … *Bagpipes!*'

'Aye,' replied his cousin, Jock McJack, 'this'll terrify any bloody enemy. Always brought these into battle did our boys … scares the shit out o' people.'

They took out the pipes and played a well-rehearsed battle theme together.

The whole camp stood up, wondering what was about to come and crush them? It sounded like a massive wild animal crying and screaming.

King Alexis smiled and went to welcome them both, he actually loved bagpipes, damn stirring stuff.

'Just want we want as we go into battle,' he declared, 'welcome aboard my friends.'

'Aye,' they both replied, 'but only if ye've got a decent bottle or two of Glenrite 'Ard.'

'We'll find some somewhere,' the king assured them.

*

Further north, two brothers approached the daunting spectacle of the Time Circle. They had arrived the previous night at the camp, part of Lord Black's troops, but it was a pitch dark night. Now this morning they were exploring the makeshift camp, and wondered what all the commotion was about in a field ahead of them. Several other soldiers were standing by the hedges watching on, all were south of the practice targets, well away from harm. Cheers often went up as bolts severed targets or shredded them to pieces. The brothers nodded admiringly as they neared the field, these men were pretty good with this odd weapon.

They stopped in their tracks when they saw their sister, their baby sister as they always called her. She still wore the pigtails of old, but she was ... grown, adult. A mature woman was across the field from them, practising on one knee with the weird-looking bow and occasionally standing up to give orders to the large group of men in the field with her.

One brother looked at the other. 'Can't be little bowmaiden, can it?'

'Nay, we left her at home, keeping the place straight for us to come back to when it's over.'

'Doesn't half look like her though and ... shit, that hawk's aiming straight for her ...' hey, Reave!' He shouted across and made to run to help.

He watched incredulously as the hawk settled on her well-gloved arm and she fed it a tit-bit before carefully taking a note from the collar around its neck. The brothers made for the entry to the field, but were stopped by a burly-looking guy who also wore a heavy glove and a thick leather cap on his head. The sword by his side looked well used, but so were their own swords.

'What you two after?' he said, 'this field's out of bounds to anyone but the Rams.'

Rams? There weren't any rams in the field, they shook their heads, confused. 'That's our sister,' they said, pointing at Reave, 'we've just come up with more of Lord Black's forces.'

'*Captain* Reave, you mean, these are her forces, the Rams.' The pride was clear in his voice, Garrett enjoyed watching the group, he had little to do at the moment and his role of Hawker couldn't be altered, he couldn't really become a Ram. Besides, he wasn't really keen on the crossbow, not his style. In any case, he was technically her superior officer, at least at Court. No, it definitely wouldn't do to become a Ram too, not in that sense anyway … he chuckled quietly to himself.

The two young men stared at each other before a wild cry was heard and Reave dashed across the field towards them. She jumped over the hedge and flung her arms around them, the hawk hovering menacingly above her.

'What …? Never thought I'd see you guys again,' she laughed. She introduced Garrett, 'Chief Hawker of Lord Black, he had trained her … he was also her 'beau', she added sheepishly. Garrett grinned, kissed her hand, briefly shook theirs.

The brothers looked at each other again, their little sister was all grown up.

'Come on, I'll introduce you to my friends, the White Shield. I've told them loads about my brothers, I was so proud when you two joined Lord Black's forces. But,' she added sorrowfully, 'you know our other brothers are dead, don't you?'

Both brothers nodded, yes, they'd heard. She took them over to meet Amber, Dane, Estrién and Tamlyn along with the rest of the crew.

It's seemed their little sister hadn't just grown up, she now moved in big circles too.

*

The arrival of the Rovers with the large consignment of crossbows had enlivened the camp, and the instigation of the Rams was a welcome diversion to everyone, including the four core members of the White Shield. They cheered on Reave, even though they knew she would be leaving their group. This was more important, Reave had her own purpose in life.

When her brothers arrived, everyone was happy for her, but if anything it added to Amber's sense of loss. Where was her sister? Amber couldn't bear to think.

Later that night, in the tent the four shared, Amber lay in Dane's loving arms. He had awoken in the deep dark velvet before morning comes, heard her softly weeping. He moved over to her.

'My love ... tell me?" he asked, 'is it your sister?' He felt her nod on his chest.

'I try not to think of it during the day,' she whispered, not wishing to wake the others. 'But there's little to do, I thought we would be inside Manecaestr by now. Instead, there is nothing, no end to that bloody circle and my sister is gone.'

'You seem positive enough during the day, you keep up all our spirits.'

He felt her nod again, 'yes, I try, it's important. It just comes out when I think no-one's watching. I'm happy for Reave, she's found two of her brothers, but it just seems to make the loss of Anaïs all the worse. Where is she, Dane, what's happening to her? Does she even exist anymore?' A tear trickled on to his bare chest.

He put his hand under her chin, lifted her face to him, gently kissed her cheek. 'My mage senses tell me she is still there somewhere – honestly, I'm not just saying that to comfort you. I think if we have lost the Weaver of Time - and your sister definitely has powers beyond anything I've ever known – then I think the whole world would know. It would affect us badly, so far, nothing has happened.'

'That is true, she is so … *special*, isn't she? But I'm still afraid for her Dane, I can feel *him,* he's mixed up in this.'

'Then if that's so, and he's currently intent on your sister, maybe we should take advantage of the fact. Get on with dispersing these Adammite fools, take back our world while he's busy. For all we know, perhaps that's her role, to divert him from what's happening on this world?' He was guessing now, he had no idea as such, but a few positive events seemed to be taking place recently.

Amber shook her head, 'no, that's not right. If he has Anaïs …' she trailed off. The thought was unbearable. She knew what even a shadow's presence of him was like… She shuddered, 'no, that cannot be, no one could be in his presence long, you would … you'd disintegrate.' She considered her sister, locked in eternal battle with him, or running forever pursued by him, all to save this world from his clutches. No one, not even the greatest martyr or the worst murderer deserved that. Dane heard her sigh, it saddened his heart.

'All I know is that he is slowly ripping apart the seams of our world, tearing the fabric into pieces and shredding its structure into rags,' Dane waxed angrily.

'Hmm, that's pretty poetic Dane, nice similes, if it wasn't damn tragic.'

'Yes,' he replied, 'don't forget I'm a mage, I feel this right through my bones.' He held her close, 'come here love,' kissing her, 'sleep easy, dear. We need little Anaïs to patch it all up again and believe me, we'll find her if I have to go into that damn time circle myself.'

'If only we could...' she replied sleepily.

They slept tucked in each other's arms the rest of that long and weary night.

Chapter 6

Jovan explained the situation to the Elf Father of Oakleigh. The Elf Father didn't want to hear him, still pretended Jovan didn't exist, yet he was immensely grateful when the attack by Commander Grey had happened. He was aware that most of Elvinhaeme had gone, yet their ancient forest was untouched. The elves lived peacefully, and since Dane had cleansed the trees the dryads, fauns and the older races had begun to thrive again. True, the forest had not given up its bounty quite as easily as in the past, and the winter had been harder than any they had known, but they still existed. Unless there were others in the wildwood, the Foraes Dair, Oakleigh was the last known home of the elder magical races.

He wasn't pleased at what he heard.

'I'm sorry to have to tell you, but we are leaving, temporarily you understand. The King of Westerling – and I've nothing against him because he allowed me to live – is gathering forces north of here. That bloody Grey is invading Westerling now, thinks he can take the whole blasted land.

Personally I'd like to go down to Belcast'el, but I haven't enough forces, nor can I communicate with any of the other elves. Even so, we have to make our stand. King Alexis is happy to meet us near the Bridge of Concorde, it's now or never. I'm sorry, but you're on your own for a while, we'll return as soon as we can. Get your own elves in the trees here, you can see we've fortified it, we repulsed that bastard easily enough. His forces will be taken up with ours and the King's so there won't be that many left. Besides, they can't march eight square through the forest, you have a chance if he sends any troops.'

The Elf Father nodded, he would deploy his own archers; they had practised, they would try to defend the forest.

Jovan meanwhile moved north with his troop of Freowulven, calling for Woodmoss on the way.

'You ready?' he asked, 'we are going to make our stand against these bastards. You in?'

The old Satyr grinned lopsidedly, 'just try keeping me out,' he replied, grabbing an enormous axe. 'Fashioned this specially, take a few heads at once, this will ...'

Jovan patted his friend on the back and together they marched off to war.

Neither the Elf Father nor Jovan were aware that Grey had no further intention of invading Oakleigh that way, or that his own special forces were currently making their way to the forest complete with deadly poisons to remove every elf, dryad, naiad, nymph, faun and all the wild animals that lived there.

*

Commander Grey deployed a thousand troops close to the Concorde Bridge in the south and a company of foot soldiers, along with a large troop of Hellboys near the narrow bridge on the Western highway to the north. He had another two thousand encamped between, a few hours away, ready to be deployed according to whichever bridge he took first.

Currently he and a couple of hundred of his personal guard, all elite troops, were with the Hellboys, looking at the northernmost bridge and the steep ravine below it. His spies told him the king was across the water, but this was not a good place to attack.

It was clear he could not simply march over the narrow bridge, not while King Alexis had his own troops on the eastern bank of the Tethés. It didn't however look as if there were too many across the ravine, but it didn't make it any easier.

'Damn and blast!' he said to himself, 'why did they build such a bloody useless bridge?' The bridge was long and narrow, one carriage wide. People could walk across, but carriages going west or east waited patiently until it was their turn, paying a small fee to the Tollman before crossing. The banks were steep gorge, difficult to climb, any horseman would be a sitting target and in any case the river was pretty wide at the bottom.

He understood however that traffic wasn't exactly busy along the western highway and it was eminently defensible. He considered the matter, four abreast with full length shields in front? That could work, as long as the king didn't have those effing mages with him, then they were sitting ducks. He looked to his war machines, perhaps a tall mantlet in front of the men? A mantlet was a huge shield on wheels, often simply made, wooden or even woven. He could perhaps create a makeshift one on top of a cart?

Then he realised that would be a bloody waste of time, the mages would simply burn it.

Fuck it! He wanted Westerling, and to take it he had to destroy King Alexis.

Briefly he considered moving his men further north along the valley between the Tethés river and the Whitecaps, make for the bridge at Sunstones, but - no, just *no*. Alexis had that fully protected, at least for now.

Dammit, bridges were a bloody nuisance!

He sent out spies who went up river, past a wide bend and took a boat across overnight. He couldn't send all his troops that way, too easily spotted, even by night, but one small coracle looked like a couple of fishermen.

They returned with, 'yes, there were mages and a company of troops.' Dammit, he could see that from across here, the mages were practising flashfire, seeing if they could send it all the way across the bridge – they couldn't. 'But', they told him, 'the king isn't there, he's gone south with the main bulk of troops.'

South, huh? That meant the Concorde Bridge, just a few hours south, less on horseback. So Alexis had decided to meet him there? Well and good, there was a wide plain on both sides able for him to deploy a full complement of forces in their glorious eight square battle formations.

Perfect.

Three thousand and more against Alexis' puny set of troops.

Nevertheless, he would leave this bridge fully covered. If he couldn't cross, then neither could the enemy, it was stalemate. Besides, with his Hellboys in place here, the Westerlings would not have an easy time of it, they could continually harry those across. A few Hellboys, by which he meant a couple of hundred or so plus their relevant shields bearers, and a trebuchet or two to shoot along the bridge, would keep the other side occupied. He could easily keep this bridge and once he had taken the Concorde Bridge, he would come up from behind and take out those troops across.

That was a very satisfying thought.

When he took Westerling, he would double the width of the bridge, open up the Bay of Gulls, perhaps have a small fishing port there. Of course, there would be no such thing as Freowulven to harry trade, neither would he continue the tradition of Outlawing a felon. The death penalty swiftly and permanently put paid to any future trouble.

Meanwhile, he had a king to kill...

Accordingly, Commander Grey climbed on his horse and sped southwards through the night with his company of personal guard to join the forces mid plain, move them down to the Concorde bridge where the rest of his force was waiting. Between them, he had more than enough forces to oust the king's troops. Oust them? *He had enough to annihilate them.*

It was early morn, although still dark by the time they reached the plain near the bridge, a gentle incline up to the river. They had made good time and he allowed his troops, now the rear guard, a few hours sleep and a good meal. He too ate a brief meal but did not sleep, never seemed to need it when he was keyed up for battle.

He received word from his forward troops closer to the bridge; the forces of King Alexis were amassing across the river. 'Good,' he considered, 'finally a reasonable battle,' although he didn't think that much of the king's army. 'I'll have that bridge by nightfall.'

He considered what Alexis had, couldn't be more than a few hundred. Frankly, Alexis was an idiot to take him on.

'Stupid fool,' he conjectured, 'if he fights as he did at Pennyport, he'll fight to the death. Stupid, elf-loving fool.' Still... he'd wormed out of it that day at Pennyport, and he had managed that rescue of his wife on Mere'garde ... plus there were rumours he'd gone himself. 'May not be quite such a fool, better not to underestimate him.'

He contemplated the various scenarios:

He considered luring Alexis' forces across the bridge, pretending he was retreating, then a pincer movement as his own troops came from both north and south on either side of him. Somehow he didn't think he'd take the bait.

No, better to sacrifice a couple of hundred of his own men during the first wave across the bridge, they would see to the mages and some of the archers. The bridge was wide, meant for a carriage on either side, eight square across could do it easily. There were always casualties in war, sacrifices, numbers that were nothing but battle fodder. It was tough, but the end justified the means. Yes, the bridge was wide enough to fight on.

Then the rest could swarm over, remove Alexis' troops and carry on into Westerling.

He had to admit he was somewhat disconcerted when his spies greeted him with the news that neither the king, nor his elite troops were actually with the forces across. *'Whereabouts unknown'*, they told him.

'Well fucking find him!' he shouted angrily, 'I want him dead and preferably by my own hand. … And don't tell me he's in hiding somewhere; he's not the sort to do that!' They left to seek the king.

They did not return.

*

'Commander Grey and his private guard have gone sir,' the young scout reported to King Alexis. 'There are probably around three hundred across, although many are Hellboys.' It was late night, a new moon, only camp fires could be seen across the water.

Alexis considered the latest information. 'Thought so, can't mistake the sound of troops moving, too many creaky sounds and horses neighing, even from this far across the river. I knew he was after me, he's made this personal. I take it that you successfully reported I'd moved south to Concorde Bridge?'

The young man nodded, 'yes, we met the spies they sent, gave them the news.'

Alexis smiled at the young man. 'Well done, Hodgkins, keep up the good work. I'll continue with the misinformation as long as possible. If they can do it to me with my own advisor, Filby, then I can do it to them.'

'That's all very well sir, but my comrades in the regular forces are beginning to suspect me as a traitor.' The young man was keen to be of service, but he was also fond of his good reputation.

'Just keep this up for now. You make a damn good fifth columnist and I need people with your skills, you are extremely good at infiltrating.' He sighed. 'I trust no one after the Filby fiasco, I can only trust myself, so you report directly to me.' Alexis placed a hand on the young man's shoulder. 'If I live through this, I want you at Court, you have been extremely useful, but right now silence is everything.'

The double-agent grabbed his horse and quickly rode south with his false orders and troop movements to give to his Adammite cohorts. He knew every spy currently sneaking in the King's camp, they thought he was one of theirs. He looked forward to the day he could expose them, and preferably 'take them out' himself. Still, they were useful ... for now.

Alexis watched him go, '*brave man*,' he thought, then looked up and saw the hawk hovering just above his tent. He considered it was no ordinary hawk, although it didn't look like his own Geordie, the Morus hawk. He didn't think tying a note to its neck was a good idea.

'Tell him *now* would be a good time,' he offered, feeling somewhat foolish. To his surprise the hawk gave an odd screeching sound and flew off, a mere shadow across the moon as it flew.

He ordered the small company he had with him to be ready to move. Small yes, but many were his own Corps de Lyons. Normally they wore court armour, looked splendid with red surtouts on which a golden lion passant was emblazoned. Now they wore simple but strong field armour, as he did himself, battle ready. He picked up his shield, heavy steel, and like the Court surtouts of his Corps de Lyon, bore a gold lion 'passant guardant' on a scarlet (gules) background. The lion looked like it walked proudly while leering menacingly at you. Strictly speaking it was his great grandfather's shield, slightly battered, although it hadn't seen a great deal of combat. He hoped he wouldn't dishonour it.

He stood watching the campfires across the bridge, waiting. He had no idea what would happen, but he trusted whoever had sent him that note. He took it out of his top pocket under his armour, briefly read it again by candlelight … *'the beasts and birds await your command'*. He couldn't help it, but a shiver ran down his spine.

'This is more than I could ever have considered,' he thought.

Around half an hour later there came a strange rumbling of hooves, a shrieking, screeching, yelping and yapping noise across the water. He heard a huge flapping of wings above him, all making for the Adammite encampment.

It was followed by the astonished screams of men as they were attacked by hundreds of wild animals and birds, the wolves, bears and large antlered stags to the forefront, hawks, kites, eagles and falcons leading an army of rooks, jackdaws and magpies from above. The Adammite forces were taken completely by surprise; none could have imagined such an attack.

'Now everyone, move!' he shouted as they ran across the bridge while the Adammite forces were fully occupied.

True, some of the Adammites collected themselves and shot at his men as they ran. The Hellboys were good, very good.

But not so good when the eagles swooped and made straight for their eyes. Nor was their eight strong formation too good when attacked by the claws of hungry bears. They lifted their arms in fear to fend off wolves who threw themselves up to rip apart their throats, while wildcats clawed savagely at their legs. The stags moved in, bent their many-antlered heads and tossed the shield bearers in the air like rag dolls. One, an enormous beast with a proud fiery head, made light work of any Adammite soldier he crossed. He seemed to shine in the night, and he was glorious to watch.

Soon King Alexis' troops swarmed upon them too, finishing off with cold steel what the animals had begun with tooth and claw. The battle was short, Alexis own numbers swelled by the birds and beasts.

'Now follow me, boys!' he cried, leaving the bodies to be picked over by the wolves. They were probably a couple of hours behind Commander Grey; he would quietly follow them down to the Bridge of Concorde. He hoped he could get there before dawn, but he would take his chance. What he hoped for most was that his other troops were safely in place, otherwise he was stymied. He had his plan, but he never trusted plans.

'Bet I'll be winging it as usual,' he considered.

He was pleasantly surprised to find that a large group of wildlife followed his troops, all led by the biggest and most stately stag he had ever seen in his life. It seemed to him that as one king led his troops, so here was another king leading his unlikely army. King Alexis saluted the stag, the stag threw back his head proudly and nodded in return.

King Alexis came over the plains just as dawn broke, he hoped to goodness his so-called battle plans were in place. They wouldn't be, he was sure, although it was simple enough.

The river Tethés was the main line of defence between him and the Adammites. He'd sent almost all of his troops to guard the wide Concorde Bridge, stop Adammite forces swarming over into his land and overpowering it. But guarding the bridge was not enough. Like Grey, he knew he had to take the bridge, get his forces over and face Grey's army.

It would be one final stand.

There were more than three thousand troops between, many were already in their eight square battle formations, lines of men with sword and shield followed by crossbowmen, some simply swordsmen, even pike men, alternate lines of death. Every one of those groups pointed towards the bridge and Alexis' main force.

Somehow his smaller troop had to distract the huge mass of blasted Adammites while his own main forces moved over the Concorde Bridge. He had to make space.

It would take time for Alexis' main army to cross over; there were Grey's troops and trebuchets, massive ballistae, even a battering ram in between. He already heard the mighty crashes as boulders rained down upon troops and bridge alike. 'Please don't destroy my bridge,' he thought, making for the eastern-most end of the enemy, the eight-square formations nearer the bridge. Somehow he had to turn that force, distract it, break it up, whatever. He didn't care as long as he manoeuvred some of those forces away.

Give his army a chance, even a small one.

It was a race as to which side would cross first. He had to turn that force to him, stop them attacking the bridge and somehow keep them occupied.

Alexis shrugged back his shoulders, took a deep breath and gave a nod to the two pipers. 'C'mon guys, let's get this started.'

Jock McJack and Jack McJock smiled happily at each other, brothers-in-arms now. Admittedly the 'bloody big mace' was still carried at Jack McJock's side and his cousin now carried the equivalent size axe. They were ready for anything. The sound of bagpipes suddenly filled the air, firstly with a sheer cacophony of sound calculated to terrify the opposition, followed by a stirring battle hymn.

The Adammite troops nearest to the King all turned their way, wondering what the hell was going on? Alexis merely smiled and shouted, *'charge …!'*

It is safe to say the two pipers played throughout the day, they stayed near the king, helping to push his troops forward, filling them with blood frenzy.

Alexis and his small, but somewhat disparate army rushed in, a decoy force, his Corps de Lyons elite troops leading the charge, determined to at least protect the King until other forces arrived. As Alexis said, he was no battle master, but he was damn good in a skirmish.

The Adammites however easily kept the attackers at bay with hundreds of crossbow bolts. They were deadly killing machines, and the King's troops were stupidly running over a wide open plain. It was an easy task for the Adammite army.

'A noble charge,' thought Grey as he watched from the centre of the plain. 'But damn stupid.'

Alexis also watched as many of his troops went down, pierced even through thick armour, through plate armoured cuirasses. As the blood of his people began soaking the broad plain, Alexis wondered if he had made the right choice? Perhaps it would have been better to simply defend the bridges, concede the west of Westerling to the Adammites, save all these souls?

But that would have meant he didn't care, he had already left it too late, he had allowed Elvinhaeme to go, *all those elves* ... his friends. Not that he could have done anything, he decided, only now did he have a semblance of an army. Only now could he try, although he wondered even so if he had come too early, he should have brought more troops. Yet that probably only meant more people would die.

Question .... when was an attack appropriate? When you finally had enough forces, but an entire people had died while you gathered them? It looked like he still didn't have enough; they were going down in their dozens. Animals too, their pitiful yelps as the crossbows took them rang in his ears. 'Bless their souls,' he thought to himself.

He was beginning to wish he hadn't started this. Like Pennyport, too many good men were dying. Yes, they had saved Pennyport, but the cost had been high, and only by the skin of his teeth. But there would be no further help this day, he only had a finite number of forces, although he had his battle plan, *if* it worked and that would be that. He bloody well hoped his plans were in place or he was done for.

All told, including his main forces across the river, he had precisely half the forces of the Adammites, and they were tucked up in their impenetrable square formations in the few more defensive areas of the southern plains. He watched as his forces went down, dead or injured by those lethal bolts of Hellboys. True, some of his got near, were met with massive shields and there were groups of melee around. But he had no idea how to penetrate the bulk of that formation. He didn't even really want to penetrate them, that would be suicide, but to run, harry, pull back then keep up the charge. He did just that, he sounded the retreat, pulled back a little, gathered his small force and pushed in again.

He wanted the group by the bridge to turn and come for him, stamp out this little flea that was biting their legs. He was bait, he knew Grey would want to challenge him once he found out he was here. He merely wanted to keep that bastard occupied as long as he could.

But he heard the shouts of his most loyal forces as they rushed to protect him from the deadly bolts. He heard their cries of pain as they fell. He saw the Great Stag lead his army, and wept as he watched wolves, foxes, even bears go down on an already bloodied battlefield.

Still, nevertheless, he carried on, he had to keep these forces turned to him while his own came over the bridge ... whatever the cost.

*

The company of Dair Chev'al had crossed Mab's Bay by boat at Croftcoats, even fishermen had loaded them onto their own boats to accommodate all the horses, and they entered Elvinhaeme south of the Tethés river, before moving north through Oakleigh. There they met up with the Freowulven, joined forces. Kielan, Knight Commander of these troops, didn't give a damn alongside whom he fought, as long as they were crack troops. Neither did he really care about the fact the Freowulven were Outlaws, their crimes had been committed in Westerling or Elvinhaeme, not Floriénne. Floriénne had its own set of laws.

They left their horses just north of the main forest of Oakleigh and quietly moved through the small outgrowth, a wood of some splendid firs, taking advantage, as did Commander Grey, of the dark night. They eventually stopped just south of Commander Grey's rearguard forces.

They were hidden as only elves can hide in a greenwood, even one as small as the pinewood near Grey's camp. They watched more Adammites arrive during the night, quite a noisy affair.

'Shit, just how many troops has he got?' Jovan asked the Knight Commander.

'Our spies say over three thousand including those by the bridge,' Kielan replied. 'We come with a couple of hundred to add to your Freowulven. I know we are not many, but we are all good archers and I think your men, like mine, are also good with the sword. We also have the benefit of surprise, and of course, we are not the main thrust of the attack.

No,' he explained, 'we are simply another diversion while the rest of the army crosses the bridge. Think we can do it?' he asked.

Jovan turned his good eye towards him. 'Well, we can but die trying ...' he replied. 'What about you?' referring to the limp and the almost useless left hand of the battle-scarred Kielan.

Kielan lifted his right arm, 'my sword hand is fine and I run slightly lop sided, OK? At least I've got *two* eyes ...' he wryly observed.

Jovan laughed and clapped him on the back, 'Only just ...' he returned, the left eye being almost closed by the heavy scars. 'Anyway, only need one eye for my bow.'

'Well, we can just about manage between us then ...' came the reply.

As the rosy fingers of dawn waved over the horizon, the elves decided it was probably a good time to move in. King Alexis had said 'dawn,' and dawn it was.

Commander Grey heard the shouts and screams of his men as a massive volley of arrows shot at them from the nearby trees, *behind* his troops, not to the north of them where King Alexis was now charging. What the hell was happening? When a messenger brought one of the arrows he realised who and where from. They were elvish, finely made, cedar shafts, goose feather fletchings and a small, lethal steel tip, the very best.

He quickly arranged his rear guard troops into some kind of order, a long line of shields in the forefront of the eight square formation: shield bearers then swordsmen, plus Hellboys behind overturned carts and wagons.

'Get those effing elves!' he told his troops, 'get rid of every stupid, grinning, green-eyed elf! Now get moving!'

The air became thick with an exchange of arrows and bolts, and his battle formations charged towards the trees to quickly deal with the offending elves.

*

As Alexis heard the sound of battle from the south he knew he was not alone. '*Good men*, I knew that Jovan character would keep his word,' he thought, *'they are in place.'* He sent his Morus hawk across the plain to his main army across the river; it took but a few minutes. *'Now!'* the note ordered.

'Again!' he shouted to his men, *'with me, boys*!'

He and the wild beasts charged again from the north as the group of Dair Chev'al and Freowulven attacked from the south.

A huge flock of birds could be seen flying high, their shrieking calls sounded across the battlefield. But the birds of the air did not attack the main group of Adammites. They swerved in their flight and made towards the Adammite groups defending the bridge, they swooped down on the defenders, clawing, biting, scratching, seeking weak points: faces and eyes, confusing the troops, wings fluttering and battering, halting the war machines.

Alexis was surprised to see the massive figure of Woodmoss hurtle himself across the southern end of the battlefield and throw a huge tree trunk at the group by the bridge. Nor did he stop running, despite crossbows being turned in his direction. Adammites hurried to attack him as he ran. He took the enormous axe from his back and swiped at everything in his path.

Nor was he alone, there were mages in the first push over the bridge and two with Woodmoss, keeping a protective barrier around him as he ran. Fire and electric suddenly shot into the battlefield, and many a boulder was stopped in mid air, turned and thrown back at the Adammites, just as the mages had done at Draecastle. It became mayhem, the Adammites confused; *rocks did not just turn and come back at you*! It gave time enough to allow Woodmoss to reach the troops by the bridge, pick up one of the ballistae, and smash it into the Adammite lines. Then he picked up the tree trunk he had thrown and swiped another whole row of troops out of his way.

For a short while, the bridge was open.

Elemental mages dashed across shooting fire and electrum in the face of any straggling Adammite, clearing the way.

King Alexis' forces swarmed over the bridge towards the central plain and the massed forces of the Adammites.

King Alexis' small but determined army moved in their respective directions; Freowulven and Dair Cheval northwards, he and his Corps de Lyons plus the wild beasts to the south, the main bulk of his regular army plus more Dair Cheval westwards towards Grey and his huge square army of troops. The massive force that had been designed as an attack force now it found itself on the defensive.

It didn't really matter, attack or defend, it was still a lethal formation. For the King's forces it was like charging into a brick wall.

The horsemen of the Dair Chev'al now rode in on their splendid steeds and with bow or sabre aimed for the enemy. Elven black and silver fought Adammite black and red. Shouts, screams and horrible gurgles filled the air. The horses moved on, let the infantry take the rest, like the Corps de Lyons, they wanted to reach the King, protect him.

Elemental mages, having helped take the bridge, now attached themselves to each company of foot soldiers. They moved forwards, the foot soldiers followed. Flashfire and amberic lightning first, to start the fight and put fear and pain into the foe, then they would retreat to keep protective barriers around their respective forces.

Dane had taught them well.

But the tightly knit groups of Adammites held them back. True, there were screams as shields were set ablaze or met with lightning bolts, but the return fire by Hellboys was lethal. Soldiers went down, mages were the first to be aimed at, to take out, Grey's orders. The lines of King Alexis' troops were far easier to destroy than Grey's formations.

Alexis' worst fear began to come true, bodies heaped upon the battlefield.

He knew he hadn't enough troops, even with the one battle plan he'd ever had. He knew it wouldn't work, but by the Merrie, he'd had to take that chance. He saw his lines weakening, saw the pleasure on every Adammite face as they hit another of his troops.

There were just too many Adammites, even with his surprise attacks. He watched as his men reached the Adammite formations, yes, they made inroads, but too slowly, he just didn't have enough forces.

Shit! He wished he hadn't begun this, but knew there had been no choice. This was one of those moments when a stand had to be made, dammit, he had to try. You had to try your best, hadn't you? By the Merrie, that's all you could do.

No matter what they would still make this a day to remember, they would take what they could, perhaps halve the Adammite numbers. It would be up to Lord Black, he had soldiers, perhaps he could finish off what Alexis had begun? Perhaps... although right now he was occupied up north with the White Shield.

Dammit, Alexis wished they were here right now. He was losing it, in more ways than one.

Then the enormous stag ran to him, stood by his side, lifted his head high and bellowed into the air, an odd sound, like a cross between a grunt and a war horn. Alexis took his cue, took heart, raised by the sheer energy of the stag next to him, lifted his own war horn to his mouth and sounded the call. The two pipers followed, and then in unison, all four called together.

The cacophony rang across the plain.

Alexis' men rallied to the call, raised their swords and threw themselves into the fray. The Dair Chev'al raised their bows, arrows flew, before they jumped off their horses and ran to help Alexis' forces, sabres gleaming in the morning sun.

Wild beasts arrived from every corner of the plains, north, south, east and west, they made for legs and throats, anything visible. The smaller beasts, foxes, squirrels, wild dogs, even beavers and badgers squirmed their way through the legs of the Adammite cordons, biting and clawing from the very inside of the formations.

Then the flocks of birds returned from the bridge to swoop down from above and scratch and tear at skin and leather. Alexis watched amazed as crossbows were snatched out of hands by the claws of eagles and hawks, as magpies, rooks, and ravens landed on Adammite heads to peck and shred. He gasped as bears knocked the huge shields away and smashed into the cleverly contrived formations and the antlers of huge stags drove inroads into the battle groups.

The fancy formations began to fall apart and Alexis moved in with his Corps de Lyons, his own elite troops, while a group of Dair Chev'al on horseback circled protectively. He had one thought on his mind, reach Commander Grey, seek him out and meet him face to face ... end this slaughter one way or another. No point fighting until every bugger – on either side - was dead, a scrapheap of bloody flesh and bones.

The great stag remained on the outside, calling and organising his own forces. Grey belonged to Alexis, not him, it was not his battle, but he would continue helping the human and elven forces of the King. Yes, sometimes these were his enemy too, hunters of animals, yet that was no more than many in the animal kingdom; brutal but necessary. He did not blame a wolf for needing meat. All belonged to the cycle, even if it was an uneasy shuffling around each other for survival. He was only concerned that the balance was maintained, and these people were of the balance, the natural way.

His lethal antlers continued their deadly path through Adammite lines.

To the east, closer to the Concorde Bridge, the Westerling forces also began to push through the now floundering lines of Adammite troops, a crash of sword upon sword and shield upon shield. The golden lion passant on the red background fought bravely against the black and red blazing sun of the Adammite shield. They crashed and slashed, they screamed and fought, they shouted and swore. Woodmoss was almost a troop of his own; his axe flailed back and forth, heads rolled. He eventually met Alexis, now in the centre of the plain.

'Keep behind me, your Majesty, I'll help you make your way to their Commander.'

Alexis nodded approval; he'd no idea how he was to manage reaching Grey. He said he always winged these things, played it by ear. He hadn't even known about Woodmoss. Gladly, he followed him through the lines, his own troops surrounding him; he didn't really fight as many Adammites as he wanted to, but neither were they able to reach him, despite their constant attacks. Truth to tell, it made him feel a little cowardly, hidden inside his circle of troops, when he wanted to lead, yet he knew what lay ahead for him. This day would take all his courage.

His small but lethal force steadily moved towards the very centre of the battle where Commander Grey was organising his troops. First went Woodmoss with his accompanying mages, then several Corps de Lyons defending the King directly behind. After that came more rows of Corps de Lyons and further outside like a huge V formation, Dair Chev'al on horseback with their deadly arrows.

The V formation began to make inroads upon the Adammite forces, although the last thing they wanted was those same forces to come behind them in some kind of pincer movement. But Alexis didn't care, he only wished to get to the centre, to meet bloody Grey.

South, the Freowulven and the other company of Dair Chev'al, also on foot, hidden in their position in the small forest, were slowly but surely depleting the lower end of the Adammites. As the Adammite troops moved south towards them, lethal showers of arrows rained down upon them. Nor could they keep their battle formations as they neared the forest. As Commander Grey had hoped to draw Alexis' troops across an open plain to defeat them, so did the elves draw the Adammites towards the forest for the same purpose.

Jovan knew once they were in the forest, the Adammites were done for and he grinned evilly at the thought of how many human throats he would cut, or hearts he would pierce that day. He was filled with anger, blood lust and the thirst for revenge; it had built up over years.

He let go, threw out his pain, this was the day of reckoning. Soon, as he sliced savagely across an Adammite neck, he was heard to shout, *'that's for my wife you fucking bastard!'* and to another, *'and that's for the child that was never born, may you rot in hell!'*

He continued in this vein for several hours, somehow his anger got in the way of their swords, their crossbows, somehow he took out more Adammites than anyone that day, even Woodmoss, and he vented his grief upon them all.

Meanwhile, Alexis pushed forwards, or rather inwards, where was that bastard?

Time moved slowly as bodies fell around him, slow-motion deaths, blood-curdling, long-drawn-out screams, a rush of blood in his ears, sounds from far away. He heard an elongated shriek as a gull swooped, on and on it went, he saw his own sword pierce someone, he didn't know who, looked curiously as the soldier dropped, carefully stepped over him, almost reverentially. Wondered what he was doing among all this pain and hatred? Who started all this ... and why?

Eventually he saw him, Woodmoss knocked every soldier out of the way, created a path for Alexis to follow. Time became normal, work to be done, honour to uphold, truth to maintain and love to cherish. A King's strength must be seen, or he was no king.

In the centre of the battlefield a small but highly essential battle of its own began to take place.

King Alexis looked across at Commander Grey. The Commander was unaware, but two hawks hovered overhead, Alexis' own Morus hawk, and one belonging to the Great Stag, a General of his forces had they but known it. Both poised ready to strike, to ravage the Adammite commander with their claws, yet Alexis looked up and shook his head. No, whatever the outcome, Grey was his, this was his fight alone.

Other members of both sides momentarily stopped fighting; here was the culmination of the battle. The two leaders stood forth, eyed up each other. Whoever lived, their side would be the victor this day, regardless of how many forces had been taken out.

...A dutiful and loving Merrievian King, versus an extremely experienced and ruthless Adammite warrior.

King Alexis had only recently known war, he could count the number of battles on one hand, although he had taken part in many skirmishes, helped put down the rebellion in his land.

But he had never fought someone with Grey's skills. The Commander watched him with distaste, he even sneered.

'Come on whelp, I've more battles tucked under my belt than you've had women,' he laughed.

Alexis considered that was probably true. He'd played around a little when young, but he had soon met the love of his life, his Nerry. Never wanted anyone else since.

And somehow, that off-the-cuff and somewhat cheap remark started a blazing anger in him. Like Jovan, he had seen his beloved wife hurt by these people, they had taken her and his only daughter, kidnapped them and imprisoned them. Little Anna'laeth still had nightmares and his wife was much quieter these days. Nerry didn't like being seen in public, her confidence had gone, she was ashamed of her ears and she trusted no one, not even her own handmaidens.

He shook his head as he thought of them, his wife and child, something blazed inside him and he screamed out loud his anger. Quite unthinking, pushed by bloodlust more than anything, he ran across the intervening space and rammed his shield straight into Commander Grey's face.

Grey reeled back, but the experienced fighter quickly took stock and knocked the offending shield straight out of Alexis' hand. He carried no shield, but he did wield a damn big sword, a great two-handed bastard sword. Alexis' own broadsword was a typical knightly sword, double edged, dangerous but short enough to be worn on his belt, well over a foot shorter than Grey's bastard sword.

Grey now held his sword in both hands high in the air, aiming to swipe Alexis' own sword out of his, before striking and killing. Alexis saw the slice coming, jumped backwards, that sword had a far longer reach than his own. Perhaps he could get his shield back? But no, Grey was already coming at him again, he staggered backwards away from the blade, sidestepped as the blade swept downwards again in an arc and then he jumped over the blade itself. Quickly he turned and hit at Grey on the back with the pommel of his broadsword. Grey staggered from the blow.

Alexis took the opportunity to gather his shield again. He ran, bent down and grabbed it just as Grey turned and once more came at him.

There was a loud clang as steel sword met steel shield. The golden lion of the shield looked dented and there was a large scratch across its flank. Alexis struggled to push Grey away with the shield, but he managed to bring down his own sword as he fought. He struck Grey on the arm and blood gushed out. Now it was Grey's turn to stagger away. He briefly looked at his arm and wiped his mouth before charging in again. The whelp had managed a hit, pitiful really, not enough to maim.

There was no finesse on either side, no polite fencing moves or shouts of 'touché' or whatever. This duel to the death sounded more like two animals grunting and heaving as they fought. The crowd around were now silent, they could not join in, even if they wanted to. Woodmoss held people back with his massive axe, threatening everyone, both sides.

They came together again, clashed and shouted obscenities at each other. Alexis now seemed to be dancing around a small arena, jumping from side to side, twirling to keep out of the way of the huge sword, Grey grunting heavily as he followed. Alexis had danced regularly with Neria, he was light on his feet. Grey ran forwards, determined to catch him; he was no heavyweight either, although he was slower than Alexis. He struck wildly at Alexis' dancing figure with the long reach of his bastard sword, a slash to his thigh; blood ran down the king's leg.

Alexis staggered a little, reeling as Grey began to catch up with him. He tried to move away, that damn sword was reaching again for him, but he was limping now. Another slash came down on the same leg, more blood bubbling over his boots.

Grey knew he would cut him down and as he fell, take off his head as he took the Dûc de Luxonne. He watched with pleasure as his enemy weakened.

The dancing slowed, Alexis could not outrun the overlarge sword, his waltzing and prancing stopped. Alexis hobbled backwards as Grey smiled triumphantly, his prey was weakened, he could soon finish him. Then he would take Westerling, sit on the throne at Orlandium.

'I'll make it quick,' he told the King, 'you deserve that much,' as he raised his sword and moved in for the kill.

Alexis looked curiously at the oncoming figure, blood oozing down his leg. It was probably on fire with the pain, yet he felt nothing although it didn't seem to respond to him, kept buckling under him. He wondered how his life had come to this? There could be but a few seconds left now, he could no longer keep out of its reach.

Perhaps he should have had a better battle plan, but then, they just weren't his forte.

Then he stood still, calm in the centre of the storm as if he had made up his mind. He held up his shield as if to defend himself and momentarily looked at it.

It was heavier than the sword, much heavier, in fact it had always been a bit of a nuisance to carry it. But his father had told him when he was a young man, your *sword can kill a man, but your shield can save your life. Yes... so true.*

One last go...

With all his might and strength he threw the weighty shield, not at Grey himself, but at Grey's sword. The heavy shield flew through the air and knocked against the bastard sword. The sword wasn't knocked out of his hand, but the combined weight pushed Grey sideways.

Alexis staggered forwards and struck a surprised Grey across his neck, slicing through the thick leather neck guard, then struck again, and again before the Commander could recover. Grey fell down on the ground, lifeblood pouring, but still Alexis hacked at him, neck, arms, any place there wasn't metal protection. Then he began kicking him fiercely.

'You stinking little shit of an Adammite, die you fucking bastard!'

He continued kicking him, 'that's for every elf you've hurt, you steaming pile of dung!' He kicked his face, blood rush thrumming through his ears, his heart pounding, the heartbeat louder than the silent crowd around him. 'That's for Neria,' he screamed and kicked, 'and that's for little Anny you fucking excuse for a man!'

By the time he died, Commander Grey had little face left.

The Adammite troops surrounding them ran, terrified of this King gone berserk. Alexis' forces turned on them, triumphant, broke the back of them. There was consternation among the ranks, confusion and despair. They were being attacked on all sides, even from the air, and there was no Commander to order or rally his troops.

All who were left routed, ran away from this strange battlefield of humans and elves and mages with their terrifying flashfire or lightning, beasts with massive teeth that bit through thick leather, and birds that flew down and clawed out your eyes. They ran to the coast, ran all the way to Hollyporth to claim sanctuary, or take ships back to their stronghold on the Isle of Glasse.

In the centre of it all, King Alexis heaved a sigh and collapsed on the ground from loss of blood. Woodmoss promptly picked him up and proudly carried him to the makeshift field hospital where the healer mages were already trying to save the wounded.

He wounds were staunched and healed, but he was utterly exhausted. While his troops celebrated their victory that night, he slept deeply, the sleep of the just.

Later that night, when it was all over, Jovan too sat exhausted under the fir trees of the small forest he occupied. He had no room in his heart for celebration, he was weary with hate. He sat with his back to the tree trunk, sipping usquebae from a small bottle he carried, pretty raw, strong stuff too. It burnt his throat and he sat in silence, staring at nothing. Then, for some moments, he began weeping, crying out the name of his beloved wife, something he had never done during the intervening years since she had died. He had stayed stone cold sober and dry eyed in all that time, but now … now was the time to mourn her. He felt he had avenged her at last. He allowed himself his outburst before taking one last gulp of the fiery liquid. Then like Alexis, he too slept the sleep of the just and there were neither dreams nor nightmares.

The stag also left the battle field, he was proud of his forces. It had been a great blow to *him,* perhaps a final blow here in Elvinhaeme. He solemnly and proudly thanked all the beasts and birds for their help that day, every one as much a soldier as Alexis own' forces.

But later, as he moved deep in the greenwood of Oakleigh forest, the stag looked on the woeful sight of sick and ailing elves, some already dying from the poison that Grey had sent by his secret forces. He had poisoned the small rivers and watercourses of the forest.

It all lay silent; there were piles of dead birds, the little ones, the songbirds, the sparrows and larks, the chattering chaffinches and the friendly robins. They lay, like the small animals, the rabbits and hares, voles, mice, dead in their hundreds.

He heard the cries and moans of sick elves.

Victory had come at a dear price.

Chapter 7

When she was younger, Anaïs led a pleasant life. Her mother and father were kind to her, her home was comfortable and the village she lived in was peaceful. True, her older sister sometimes teased her quite mercilessly; Amber was always so active, played with the village lads on the green, sang loud, often funny songs, while she quietly stayed home. She loved her father, he knew so much, a fine alchemist, he taught her well. Her mother taught her the more sedate and homely skills, cooking, needlework, weaving, also some healing; she enjoyed nature walks with her mother as she showed her flowers or herbs and shrubs, explained their healing powers. Their house was filled with tomes about such things as philosophy and the stars, what the universe might be made of, botany, biology and treatises on elemental magic. She studied everything.

It was strange really; perhaps they were preparing her for when she came into her powers? They never said, just offered her good things. Neither was she aware she had magic until the Alderfolk captured her and her sister. She was in shock for a while, perhaps that was the catalyst? But she came to understand there was something as deep and old as the universe inside her and the day Amber set her free was also the day it became clear.

She couldn't use her magic to also set Amber free; it was too young, too raw. She simply had an understanding that she and the universe were one, that she understood time. Other people could see time as it was, could perceive backwards, memories of events. She perceived time as one whole mass, yesterday, today, tomorrow. She saw events from long ago, and events in the future. But ... and there was a big 'but' ... they were only *possible* outcomes, all along a line of probability and all of them according to the pattern. They fit happily into the fabric, the stuff of life. Some were definite, had to be, others were still forming; these involved the shapers of the universe, people on whom the future depended.

The world would evolve according to their decisions. *No* ... they didn't need to be the 'great' people, 'important' in the eyes of many. It only took one person in the right place at the right time, to do or say the right thing ... or not ... and the future changed accordingly.

Whatever it took however, it included love, courage, honour and yes, a little faith.

Later she learned that she could do far more than merely watch time, she could control it.

Anaïs understood the fabric of the world may have begun with the tight warp threads, all rigidly formed in straight and logical lines, but then the tapestry began, the whirling, wisping, writhing weave of life. Life danced and sang, loved and cried, was happy, sad, and angry, delighted by turns, despondent by others. It was unpredictable, and the pattern with all its hues, sounds and scents mingled and blended in chaotic confusion.

Some happily joined in the merry dance, some were pulled by the scruff of their necks into it, while a few simply Watched, for the pattern had places for the Observers too, yet each had their own role. All were separate, yet all fit harmoniously into the weave. ...Or maybe *almost all* ...

A few did not fit so harmoniously and *he* not at all, the most outside of outsiders.

He had been since the beginning when the world was new and beings came into formation. Some were perfect forms, others not so perfect. One, *him,* was not born, but an unnatural creation composed of the unforgiving screams of childbirth, the night fears of children weeping in the dark, the unattainable desires of men and the irreparable regrets of the aged. Yet largely he was the result of cold, calculated indifference, for that is most damaging of all. It all mingled in the void, *dammit, it had to go somewhere* ... and it coalesced into *him*. He was wrong in every way and had no wish to be otherwise.

He, who had neither father nor mother, loving or otherwise, dwelled in his shadowy realm that held no place in this world. Perhaps it is safe to say he lay on the edges of consciousness.

He also knew time, knew it well. But, like time, he had been created and could not be dissolved. Nay, his existence grew more powerful as time moved on.

It remains unknown the moment he discovered he was a god in the minds of men. He observed the phenomena with scientific precision, tested and tried the variations of his powers, comprehending that the suffering of these beings actually gave him a perverse pleasure.

He therefore studied their pain with relish, watched with cold curiosity and observed their dissolution with a calculated interest.

He offered them the suffering by which he had been created, declaiming it would lead to power, possible godhead. It was a lie of course, an experiment in manipulation. The people believed him and appointed priests to guide them.

Thus the ancestors worshipped him, their priests sacrificed their newborns to appease him, pacify him. They lay themselves down and let him trample upon them, fearing his wrath. They ruled and repressed their own people with an iron rod according to his laws, even as terror ruled their own hearts. They called it ancestor-worship, but they kept the secret of their wrathful god. Deep inside them, the priests knew the truth: if they ever entered *his* realm it would mean disintegration of body, spirit or soul ... annihilation of one's very essence.

But that was until Merrie came, and she balanced the pain with the joy. She was irrepressible, too full of life to worry about death. She was a bright sun filled with love.

For a little while in the scheme of things, the Lady Merrie pushed back his evil. *He* watched with distaste as her children danced and sang under a brilliant blue sky, praising the delights of the world she gave them. As that world prospered *he* hated it more and more, watching from his realm of shadow, his cold lair of death.

He searched and found its weaknesses; every being, every thing bears its own Achilles heel for *him* to exploit. Slowly he infiltrated it again, let his essence seep into those willing to accept, even bodies willing to host him. He began to triumph once more.

He created the Adammites for the sheer pleasure of disrupting a world in harmony. He had no political desires, didn't give a damn. They were simply a means to an end ... *the* end; they would annihilate themselves. If they could not accept his rule, then he would destroy them all.

True, there were those who opposed him, annoyances mostly. Some however held powers of their own, born of the pattern, offspring of the Lady. Some were the movers and shakers of the world, some were the Creatives, some were simply the Watchers, enjoying vicariously the lives of the rest. *Hmm, he considered... that White Shield set... they would have to go soon.*

Now, in any case, he had the means to do so, the means of destruction in his own hands, waiting here in his own world. Here in his own realm across the pale beams of light, lay Anaïs, that ultimate of the Watchers, the one who could observe time and weave it into being.

It was gratifying to note that the end of the world was near. He would use her, take what she had into himself, infiltrate the weave and disintegrate its very fabric. The world would finally become ordered and rigid; *his* variation of the pattern held only death; a world without people, a forest without trees, a garden without flowers.

No life, love or laughter.

He now gazed with satisfaction upon her prone body lying upon the mage path of light across from him and smiled with delight; she was helpless in his realm. He taunted her with his intentions, explained how she would suffer, enjoyed the pain on her face as she realised her failure, the final death of her world.

For a few moments, if such time existed here, he gazed upon her pain-racked face before he stepped triumphantly across to her...

... and found his way blocked as a scarlet wall of blood streamed down from the Time Circle above him, Anaïs' own blood, her blood offered in the Arena of Time as Estrién slit her wrists. It poured through the floor of the arena, the infinite red floor of the arena, a floor that already held the blood of innocents, the blood of sacrifices gladly made and freely given, the blood of brave warriors fighting for heart and home, the blood of a loving woman as she carried a child into existence.

The blood of life poured through into his realm of death.

Anaïs struggled to her feet, stretched out her arms, her hands touched the rich red torrent. She smiled; she was strengthened, nourished by the blood of her mothers and their mothers before them. Now she could speak, yet unlike him, she was neither taunting nor triumphant.

'You will not touch me,' she called. 'You cannot cross the blood, you will not destroy me. Only by entering my own realm can you hurt me, but that is only my physical body. You did well there, you chose powerful and cruel men to host you, they broke my body in many ways. Yet you did not break my spirit and you never will.' She spoke with a great sadness. 'It was foolish of you to enter them, for you became a part of their existence, you left your essence inside.' She gazed across and spoke firmly. 'Even if you could cross that barrier, you will not hurt me.

You took me did you not, a desire not born of lust but power, the will to hurt and destroy? Again and again you abused me, raped me, and yes, you even took my blood to mingle with yours and create the Time Circle.

But blood will have blood, and time will tell, as the old sayings go. Even when you come to my world - as you will for your war is being lost while you tarry here – you will not touch me. I guarantee that you will not dare to harm me.' Her smile was of the Gioconda, secret and satisfied, yet like all women, it held a shadowy fear of the unknown...

...The great unknown, the leap into the future.

He was curious. 'Why, what are you saying?'

'The last time you came to my tower you left me with child. I carry both the seed of the body who hosted you and a spark of your existence. The babe is yours and somehow, I do not think you would wish it dead for it is your one and only chance of creation.'

The rivers of blood cleared a little, enabling him to see through, although he could not pass.

'I have taken other women in the past, as other men hosted me. This has never happened, it cannot be, none ever bore a child. *I* do not give life.'

She merely smiled her enigma smile again. 'You have often offered a grain of yourself into both men and women, did they but know it. You were a slippery psychological serpent, misdirecting their lives towards evil. This has happened with all the regularity of clockwork and it will continue to happen. But no, you could not give life.

Yet I carry the seeds of *time* inside me, and they are infinite. Merrie herself smiled upon me the day I was born and gave me this gift. I and time are one. I alone am able to bring *your* child into existence, although I have no wish to do so. Yet life is life and I will not harm even this miserable creature.' She took a deep breath; fresh air somehow seemed to be permeating into the realm.

The strangely gleaming figure briefly glowed fiery red. He was surprised and yet…? He considered the possible outcome.

'If this is so, then I will enter the very fabric of your world. He will be my spear point, the Commander of my forces, the king of my dark realm.' He sounded smug, yet he was not sure if he had triumphed or failed? He had taken part in creation, the stuff of life. He mused on the thought, but was interrupted by Anaïs.

'First you must find me, then you must try to take him. I will not allow that and I will watch over him, keep him from harm. I will quash your very essence from him. You will not have him.'

She opened her hand and fine strands of pure gold wove across the paths of light, the mage paths upon which she and he stood. The broken threads of time mingled together, roamed and wove their merry dance; they laughed and sang and were repaired. In a flash of white radiance, Anaïs disappeared from his world. She heard his cry of anger as she left.

All at once, the Time Circle cleared and took its place in the infinite void where it belonged.

Anaïs stood alone upon a blackened field, the final result of the anomaly. She held a quietly triumphant smile upon her pale features, and for a few moments offered a small prayer of thankfulness to the Lady, to the gods, to any spirits that might just be watching – whether they existed in truth or not.

The diverse groups both outside and inside Manecaestr stared in shock at the sudden disappearance of the Circle and the appearance of a young woman with bloodstained hands and hair as old as time. She saw her family running to greet her, her faithful guards from the White Rose temple hurrying to protect her, others rushing to meet her out of sheer relief or curiosity.

She smiled upon them all, but they halted in their steps, wondering why her smile was as enigmatic as the Temporal Abnormality itself.

'Quickly, there is no time to waste!' she shouted as the others ran to her. '*He* will come soon, save them, save the people of this forsaken city!'

Amber was first to her, hugging her, shaking her head at her, 'you did it Anaïs, you did it! But what has it cost you – Estrién told us what happened.'

Anaïs shook her off, 'I'm fine, don't fuss. I did what needed doing, that's all.'

A worried Estrién arrived next, took her hand, 'I lost you, I thought I had failed you. What happened dear, where did you go?' He was as anxious as Amber, this was his new sister. They had only just found her when she disappeared again.

She explained to him. 'I knew what had to be done and where it would lead me, to *his* realm. It was the only way to repair the Circle. He started it, using me as the conduit. It had to be repaired between us.' She had beaten him temporarily, but was clearly exhausted. She trembled at the thought of what might have been.

Dane turned her to him, mage hands streaming light down upon her. 'Let me check you, goodness knows what this has this done to you?' He was worried about her, began his medical assessment, hoping she would let him in more than previously. He briefly examined her then stepped back, took her to one side, using the excuse of a more thorough medical examination.

'Anaïs, do you know …? he began.

'Of course… I already knew. I knew when you arrived at my tower, which is why I would not let you in to heal me.' She briefly went quiet before adding. 'It is *his* you know.' She turned a brightened, if care-worn face to him, glad to share her burden. 'You knew straight away, didn't you?'

He had wondered previously, but that had been weeks ago, too soon to tell properly. It also explained her aloofness.

He nodded, 'yes, I did wonder. It must be terrible for you.' He considered the situation. 'We can try and rid you of it, if you like ...' he suggested.

She shook her head vehemently. 'No brother, even such life as this might be, I cannot kill. It will take its course, however that may be.' She gave a slight smile, 'it's still half me, no matter what. I'm no incubator and of course, he wore a human body. No, I do not know the course of this, it is not given to me to see, but I do understand that to try to destroy it would still be his victory for I would have corrupted myself.' She touched his arm and spoke softly, 'I am not afraid brother, just concerned, but also know I will be in the right place for this.

I spoke to Lord Aldergard just before I left, dear Brother Elyan had also seen, he was after all, acting as my physician. We three discussed this and agreed upon the course of events. The priests will see to it, take care of it. If it is seen to be corrupted at birth, I will leave it in their hands to do as they think fit. If not, we will all watch over and guide it.

Lord Aldergard has assured me of this, so I am content.' She gave a slight smile. 'Lord Aldergard also assures me they will not tell the outside world, not the full truth anyway. This is something that must be kept secret for it could cause untold harm.'

Dane assured her he too understood.

Yet the thought of bringing that abomination into the world made him shudder. Sometimes women were too soft about these things, her loving heart might bring ruin upon them.

'Then may the Mother help us all,' he sighed.

They turned back to the waiting crowd. 'She's fine and healthy. No further damage.' He didn't rightly know if pregnancy was damage or not, probably the opposite.

Tamlyn stepped over and kissed her cheek. 'Hey little sister, you're staying this time aren't you? No more disappearing acts?' He grinned down at her, one hand ruffling her hair with filial affection.

She briefly smiled, she loved his gentle ways, his kindnesses. 'Well, I am going home now, back to Rosevale, but I assure you brother, I will be staying there. Come and visit us all when you can.'

The Brothers of the White Rose temple stood guard by her side, led her to their carriage.

'Waste no time, for he will follow me here when he sees the Circle is gone,' she shouted, possibly as a warning to both the assembled crowd and the temple Brothers. They quickly sped away.

'Take care of yourself, Anaïs,' shouted Dane. '...for *all* our sakes.'

Chapter 8

Across the barren waste, Manecaestr awaited. Dane inspected the waste ground, the scorches and burn marks, a complete circle around the city. He'd need several months and a full complement of mages to heal this. It wasn't just barren, it felt negative. He considered that whatever they did, there would always remain something wrong. Perhaps the Great Stag or the gentle Doe could heal it?

Perhaps it would just be better to cover it with a plethora of stones and rubble, make a highway all the way around the city, an arterial road? ...Maybe even new city walls? Dane stood shaking his head, leave it to the citizens, find out what they wanted.

It still needed cleansing though, a shaking off of its evil origins. He experimented a little with his oak staff, yes, it could be purified in time – a long time - there was hope.

He turned his head towards the city, hearing shouts, cries, even screams. The others were forming into battle lines, he could see Reave gathering a troop of her Rams together.

Estrién joined him. 'You coming with us Dane, or is your role out here with this?' pointing at the ground.

'With you of course, this can wait.' Dane looked across the field, sniffing the air. 'Bet they're glad of some fresh air in there, it smells like a bad rubbish heap. Right now I need to find Salli, we're going in together and I hope the whole White Shield will be by our sides. We've somewhere we need to go in there, the very centre. Merrie only knows what it will be like by now.'

Estrién understood. 'You lead, we'll follow.' He left to gather the rest of the team.

Cross-bolts were already beginning to fly from the crenellated city walls' turrets and towers, and the huge portcullises of Manecaestr were down and locked. Lord Black had sent siege engines and battering rams to enter the city, but it would mean high losses scaling the walls while the Hellboys were on the tops.

Reave ordered the Rams into battle order, a small square group similar to Grey's heavy eight square formation. Both Lord Black and King Duggan had offered her troops, the Rams were to be a portable team working for both kingdoms. They had been licked into shape over a mere few weeks, but were battle ready. First a row of six shield bearers with full length shields moving forwards. Then the shield bearers ducked down and allowed the next row to aim and shoot at the bowmen on the top of the walls, followed quickly by the third row, more crossbows. The tall shields came up again as the two rows reloaded, but then the fourth row of shield bearers ducked down and two rows behind shot line by line, before returning to the front again. The Rams shields bore a simple standard, jet black with two silver crossed bolts in the centre. It said everything.

She had three groups of these, plus another twenty ready behind overturned carts and moveable wooden mantlets, all shifted into place within minutes of the Time Circle's disappearance.

Reave's Rams slowly moved forwards towards the city walls, and treated the Hellboys to a barrage of deadly bolts.

Mages kept close by behind the mantlets, sending flame and electric at the archers and crossbowmen on the walls, some, like Dane, sent freezing ice to stop an attack before the archer could load; they became easy targets for the crossbows on the ground.

*

'We're under fucking attack! What the hell has been happening out there all this time?' shouted Colonel Rambolt to his orderly. 'Find Captain Barrett on the walls and give me an update ... Now!' The orderly ran off to seek information.

His friend and colleague, Lefwynn Hydeman, Master of the Saddlers and Leather-workers Guild heard the news with a degree of shock, before pouring out a large usquebae from the crystal decanter on the expensive walnut sideboard. Rambolt had arrived to discuss the results of the last council meeting, along with Eamonn Norland, Minister in Charge of Ordinance and Supply. All had just seen the blue sky that suddenly appeared over the city, and had stepped out onto the small wrought iron balcony of the plush third floor Saddler's Guild Office. It had a grand view of the city, one of the perks of Hydeman's position. They loitered a few moments breathing the newly-fresh air into somewhat muddied lungs before returning to the office.

Then they heard the shouts as the cry of *'attack!'* came through the city and a runner burst into the office exclaiming they were under assault. Rambolt needed information ... and fast!

Hydeman passed him the usquebae. 'Get that into you, you're going to need it before you leave.' He watched as Rambolt swigged it back before grabbing his cloak and sword from the small weapon's rack by the door. 'Personally, I'm going to barricade myself in up here, the flame only knows what will happen if they push through the gates.'

'Fuck that!' replied Rambolt. 'I'm more worried about what's going to happen inside the city itself. There's been sedition and rebellion for weeks now. I need every soldier on duty defending this city from both inside and out!'

He left to see to his defences.

Norland, the council officer, lifted a shrewd eyebrow and regarded his colleague. 'I think it is time for us to retire, is it not?' he quietly suggested, before gathering his cloak. He left to make arrangements at his equally plush office across the square.

Hydeman paused thoughtfully after they left. He walked over to the bookcase by the fire, pressed a hidden button. A small cupboard opened and Hydeman took out a heavy purse and a small sack from within before closing it again. He then went to the outer office of the suite he occupied, told the three staff there to go home, barricade themselves in tight; it was going to be a bumpy ride from now on. He then locked both the outer door of the office suite and his own door before pressing another button and pulling on what appeared to be a brass wall lamp. As it curved down towards him, the heavy sound of a stone wall shifting could be heard. An opening appeared in the wall, steps going down between the well built chambers of the Ancient and Honourable Saddler's Guild.

Unlike his predecessors however, Hydeman was neither Honourable nor Ancient. He picked up the cash deposits of the Guild – quite a hefty sum – and placed it into the large leather case he used for carrying important papers around the city. It had a chain he could lock around his wrist. He grabbed his cloak, somewhat flamboyant hat with a feather in it and his short sword before making his bid for freedom through the decidedly ancient and honourable tunnels. They led to more secret passageways and more underground tunnels. Manecaestr held probably as much of its life under ground as above, there were many such tunnels beneath the city, all created for clandestine purpose.

He hadn't exactly shone during the last months, he'd readily done the Adammite's bidding, and indeed some dirty work for them. His instincts told him it was over, at least here in Manecaestr and he wasn't going to be around when the shit hit the fan. With one last look around the pleasant offices he had occupied for years, he disappeared down the stairway.

*

Colonel Rambolt decided to waste no time. He spotted a fine horse tethered in front of the Saddler's and Leather Workers' Guild, commandeered it for his own use. The fact that he pulled off its owner who had just climbed on was irrelevant. The horse's owner picked himself up and dusted down his tunic, shaking his fist at Rambolt before realising who he was. He stood helpless as he watched his prized black stallion disappear down the street.

Rambolt caught up with his orderly. 'See me by the western gate, find out what you can,' before speeding down the main thoroughfare through the city.

The orderly, who was on foot, decided that his Colonel would get there long before him. Nevertheless he continued running towards the city walls. He never actually arrived however as three members of the W.A.R movement tripped him up and slit his throat long before he could make it to the city ramparts.

The W.A.R ladies were out in full force.

Up on the ramparts the young Captain was shouting for more Hellboys to move towards the western gates to defend them. Each gate held guard towers and there were small barracks close by for each of the four entrances. He was surprised to be joined by Colonel Mackenzie, once C in C of the forces at Draecastle, plus his small but lethal entourage.

'Came in through the North Gate, watched that temporal thing disappear. You've trouble ahead. King Duggan ...' he watched the Captain's eyes widen, '... yes, *King* Duggan, a fucking big troop of his own and the bloody White Shield brigade are here. Von Adamm and Kyneweth are dead; it's all over up there. Go inform that Commander of yours - Rambolt was it? Tell him I'll take over from here ... oh, and inform him Lord Black's sent troops also and they have their own band of crossbowmen ... it's a fucking mess.

I've sent for my boys but they're at Herringhold, could take a couple of days for them to arrive so we need to hold on. And you can also tell him that effing crossbow troop is led by a bloody woman!'

He turned angrily back to the battle going on at the West Gate. He wasn't going to be beaten by a *bloody woman!*

*

The female in question was currently in quiet discussion with Amber. 'Just point it up ....there,' Amber requested of her, 'good long rope and your crossbow bolt should do it easily.'

'Only when the time's right, Amber,' replied her friend, 'I'm not sending you to your death.'

Amber stood ready, like Reave, waiting for the appropriate moment.

Reave's Rams continued their hail of bolts, archers too joined in from further aside, and their defenders with the huge shields and mantlets slowly moved towards the West Gate of the city. Dane, Trevaine and Robson joined the mages sending flashfire and electrum up towards the battlements. It seemed that as fast as they took down the Hellboys, more arrived. It took time, but slowly an opening appeared.

'Keep that gap open on the top there,' shouted Reave, pointing to the area around the portcullis. 'Stop every Hellboy or archer from filling it; widen the gap as much as you can.'

Black had sent a large battering ram to have a go at the city gate, but each gate had been made from dwarvish steel, almost unbreakable. Nevertheless it would be useful in the city itself. Dane wondered if he could lift the chains of the portcullis, but they were set inside the heavy stone walls, his magic wouldn't budge it. One or two mages tried lifting the portcullis, too damn heavy.

Someone had to get inside and raise the portcullis manually using the gate controls.

Slowly however, a gap appeared just north of the gate and now the siege engines hurried in, long ladders on wheels, soldiers with ropes and hooks to clamber over.

'Now, Reave!' shouted Amber, 'while they're occupied.'

Reave took her cue and shot up at the tower next to the gate itself. The bolt disappeared through the small arched window; she pulled back, securing a dangling rope.

'If you see anyone in that window, shoot them, OK?' Amber shouted as she sped across the field, hotly pursued by Estrién ... no way was she doing this alone.

Amber stopped briefly to assess the climb ... pretty high to that tower window, but the gate controls, a huge wheel and a lever, could be seen close by. It was the only way to open the gates and let the attack force through. She leapt and grabbed the rope, swinging her legs against the wall for leverage.

Estrién, watching below, shook his head in disbelief as he saw his wife clamber nimbly upwards, how could she climb that fast? She suddenly disappeared through the narrow opening, a yelp was heard as someone must have entered the turret room. It wasn't Amber, he knew her yelp. Still, the rope was free now; he concentrated on climbing it too, somewhat more sedately than Amber.

'Come on,' she demanded as her bright head popped out of the window, 'we haven't all day!'

Estrién ducked as a bolt whizzed by his ear – Reave shooting at an archer above. Amber's head disappeared again, a sound of clashing of swords inside and *'fuck off, bastard!'* She sounded like she was enjoying it.

Estrién was not. Climbing ropes wasn't his forte. He slowly clambered up, puffing and panting by the time he reached the window. 'Bloody hell woman, how do you do it?' he gasped at her.

There it was again, she thought, the generic 'woman'. He always called her that when he was exasperated.

'Easy!' she replied, 'let's get this done, OK?'

He nodded agreement then briefly grabbed her hand and pulled her to him. He gave a quick look around to check there were no archers or Hellboys before kissing her on the lips, but Reave's Rams seemed to have cleared the ones on the ramparts by the gate.

'I love you,' he whispered.

'Love you too,' her eyes shining. 'Let's go.'

He took out White Star and led her through the door and down the steps towards the gate wheel. 'I'll keep them occupied, you make for the wheel, dear.'

She nodded, the gate guards below were already heading for them both. Estrién stood firm, swinging the blade in its deadly arc. Amber followed close behind, two shortswords waving menacingly, finding Adammite throats to slash. She also made for Adammite codpieces, get them in the you-know-what's, make them cry.

'Fucking little wankers,' Estrién heard her shout. 'Bloody little pricks. Were you just frightened of women?' She continued to lecture her victims even as she cut them down. 'I'll show you fear!' Then, 'put us in our place, huh? Well fuck you!' Daggers appeared from her waist belt, they were thrown with alacrity as more Adammite soldiers arrived on foot.

As Estrién cut through a dozen Adammites with White Star, he decided they made a pretty lethal team. He thought he'd ask Amber to tone down her rather colourful language though, it was a trifle unseemly.

But they were closing in on the gate controls now, he needed to concentrate, keep the guards off her, keep his wife safe.

Amber grabbed the ropes, they were turned around a pulley system and there was some sort of handle to push. She managed to unfasten the rope, but the pulley system was too heavy, she couldn't manage it alone. Estrién was busy keeping the guards from her, somehow she had to open the bloody thing. She pushed the handle again, no, couldn't budge it.

Shit, she would have to get help, go back up to the ramparts, see if anyone else was free up there. Although ... it looked like everyone was already occupied, fighting on the tops of the walls. She tried again, no, too bloody heavy.

Then another hand appeared, clad in brown leather, but clearly female. 'Just managed to sneak through, that guy of yours has one bloody marvellous sword.' The equally female voice belonged to a tall woman in snug fitting brown leather armour, a mask hiding her eyes. 'WAR movement at your service. Maybe one woman can't open this, but two surely can.'

She placed her hand on the bar and they pushed together. Slowly it gave way, slowly the gate creaked upwards, slowly the entry into Manecaestr became free.

As the gate opened, the Merrievian forces broke through, hurried into Manecaestr.

Estrién was swept away with the bulk of the forces, he and Duggan spearheading the campaign. Amber stepped back a moment, the two females hidden behind the gate posts. 'Thank you, much appreciated. I take it you've been busy during these dark days.' She clasped the woman's hand.

'Oh, yes, we have forces ready to attack now, to help with this. I'm Sister Louisa by the way, once of the Temple of Arboreal here. There is no longer a temple and only a few of us remain. I'm afraid ...' she hesitated, 'I'm afraid we are not so peaceful these days. Each of us learned to fight and to kill.'

'You had no choice,' replied Amber.

'We hide our identities, we'd have been murdered otherwise. We, among others who must be nameless, created this movement, Women's Army of Retribution, we think they deserve it.'

Amber nodded, 'let's take back this city.'

She hurried to catch up with Dane, Salli and Tamlyn who had been among the first to enter, swiftly followed by Robson and Trevaine. They would definitely be in the thick of it and Amber had some serious retribution of her own to deal out if she could.

She soon saw Dane, mad flashfire bursting ahead of him, Tamlyn and Salli by his side. 'Save some for me, guys,' she shouted. Tamlyn just grinned evilly, Amber wasn't the only one with scores to settle, too many elves had died or been enslaved here.

Estrién spotted them, came to join. 'Duggan's making for the Adammite Headquarters; he's got plenty of forces, including Lord Black's. Thought I'd be better joining you. Tell me where you want to go Dane, we'll get there, I promise you.'

They followed him through the city, Dane shouting orders as to direction. He knew exactly where he wanted to go. Salli, close by his side was occasionally heard to swear; between them, he and Amber turned the air blue around them. He was a mild-mannered man, had always been a calming influence on the group.

Now he was keyed up and angry, even his wand looked fierce; it held death today.

Many of the underground rebels joined the group, the fine women of the W.A.R. movement, the anti-Adammite human males, the hidden elves and mages. They crawled out of their concealed caches and crevices, secret hideouts and underground tunnels. There were more than the Adammites thought, they piled onto the streets and all felt blessed by the fresh, clean air now blowing through the city.

Not merely fresh air, but a wave of rationality, people of many kinds working together, people who had once been friends. The attacking forces brought hope, something none had dared for.

Estrién and Dane stood together at the front of their group, cutting a swathe through lines of determined Adammite supporters and troops. Dane's oak staff shot huge arcs of flames at the oncoming hosts, Estrién slashed and swiped. Many cried in pain, begged for mercy.

Dane merely shook his head, not this day, not after what he had witnessed. 'You gave no mercy to the helpless. Die the way you wished death on others!' as he sent fiery blasts upon them. Salli merely reached out and touched them, they screamed and dropped. He hoped he had enough mana to see him through the city.

Yet Dane rationed his mana, his magic, he wanted to be ready for those he believed deserved it most.

The rest followed them, every member of the White Shield blazing with anger. As they pushed and fought their way through the streets, Dane and Salli allowed themselves a degree of revenge. They were mages, it wasn't in their true nature to offer such, both were normally rational and fairly gentle beings, yet they were outraged at the sheer cruelty of the Adammites, it touched their souls.

Trevaine and Robson seemed to have attracted a following of mages, the group growing as they continued through the city.

They followed the White Shield to its centre, towards the slave market which had once been the beautiful Temple of Arboreal, desecrated beyond belief. They passed the squares that had once held piled up bodies thrown on to pyres, these had been nothing but ashes for some time. The Adammites could not afford to use fire under the dome of the Time Circle and had given up the practice. The new favoured method of punishment was slow torture followed by the chopping block, bodies needed to be buried quickly. The public squares of what had once been pleasant open markets and stores, meeting houses, cafes, inns, finance houses, the whole paraphernalia of a thriving mercantile city, had become nothing but open slaughterhouses.

Yes, the pyres were gone, but the streets and squares reeked of blood, the stains would never be removed. The chopping blocks with their woven baskets to collect the severed heads were still in place, as were whipping posts and racks, a cruel and horrible sight.

Now these squares were filled with Adammite soldiers gathering together to beat the upstarts who thought they could overturn their mighty machine.

They stood solidly in their formations and attacked from their well chosen standpoints. These weren't the Hellboys of the city walls; these were the shield and swordsmen, guards, bullies and activists, everyone fighting for his life. They had been trained for such an eventuality as this. They slowly moved forwards like the massive machine they were and cut down the attacking forces one by one.

Even the mages could not dispel them with fire and amberic lightning; true, it hit the shields and damaged the carriers, but it also bounced off the shields and hit the walls and buildings in the squares and streets, flashfire ominously flaring back upon the casters themselves.

They had to stop, change tactics in the confined spaces of the market squares, too many people and too many buildings around, people getting hurt from 'friendly' fire.

The Adammites stood squarely and continued the slaughter of their attackers with merciless precision. They were a machine, all parts moved at once, in time and in rhythm with the rest. Those around were scattered as they rushed through the smaller streets into the huge squares, beaten and swatted like flies.

It began to look like a massacre.

*

Reave and her Rams' troop wended their way slowly around the city walls after the gate was opened. Their role was to clear every Hellboy and archer from the walls before moving inwards, plus of course to take out any in the streets as they pushed through. They kept to their formations while the single arbalists used walls and buildings to hide behind.

It proved indeed a long drawn out fight, a circular tour of a large city, and they were not alone. They were followed by the dwarven Rovers, some of whom pushed enormous carts filled with crossbow bolts, replenishing the Rams as they ran out, collecting the used bolts from dead bodies. Others among them wielded deadly axes, tough ground troops against the ground forces of Adammites or Adammite loyalists.. They too had scores to settle and indeed, many a dwarven heart was satisfied that day as they took another Adammite head. 'You killed and maimed my brothers, now you pay!' they shouted.

Gourien's name was heard often, he had been special to many.

Garrett stayed by Reave's side; apart from his own trusty sword and bow he kept the two Morus hawks busy, sending information throughout the city and to King Duggan and Lady Violet. They had persuaded Lady Violet to remain on the outskirts with a few runners at her disposal – anything could happen in the close confines of the city and her duty was to oversee the whole operation, the hawks would keep her informed of the situation inside. She would then send troops or ordinance to the required spot, offer information and backup to each group.

Lady Violet was no fighter, but she was damn good at organisation. Besides, it was best to leave Lord Black's troops under the auspices of King Duggan, otherwise it would look like an invasion from Mercantia, something Lord Black wished to avoid. He knew the ethics and social principles of the folk of Manecaestr, they weren't too keen on all the cap doffing and forelock tugging that went on at Court.

The young King Duggan would also have to be careful, liberation was one thing, imposition of absolute rule another. The citizens liked to choose their leaders and spokespersons for their councils in Manecaestr, Adammite rule had been hard for many ... except for the elite. The old King Kyneweth had understood that as long as it was no threat to the throne and fairly paid its dues and taxes, a great and peaceful mercantile city should pretty much be left to govern itself.

Violet held a quiet talk with Duggan before he entered the city, explaining the more republican views of its people. 'If you wish to keep on their good side, do give them space, dear. As long as they are fair to all, allow them to make their own rules within the city. Don't come the heavy hand, OK?'

The young king nodded, he was learning rapidly, no choice. 'Understood, Ma'am. But there will be no quarter for Adammite traitors, none whatsoever. Can't let it fester, you see, it will only re-grow. Afterwards, we'll have to see, but I'll play it quietly.' He knew his troops would be greeted warmly but somewhat warily by the inmates of the city. They'd had enough of dictatorships to last them a lifetime. Nevertheless, he was their King, they must acknowledge that.

Meanwhile, Reave's mixed group of fighters, led as Rambolt complained, *by a bloody woman,* was on the other hand greeted with pleasure and admiration. They, like the White Shield group were received with gratitude. Reave was surprised when a small group of W.A.R ladies arrived complete with their own crossbows, purloined over the winter from raids on guardhouses and such.

'We'd love to join you, we've secretly been practising at night outside and in tunnels underground. Dying to use these weapons fully,' they told her.

'Well, don't *die* on me!' she replied archly. 'But you're more than welcome to join.' She quickly organised them among her ranks. She didn't have a large force, but it was lethal. The men of the Rams welcomed them with delight.

'Come on lass, come stand by me,' one shouted gleefully amidst the roar of battle, 'we'll show these buggers who's boss!' The WAR maiden took her place by his side as they proudly marched together around the city.

The cries of brave but foolhardy citizens in the city squares were terrible to hear. They came with swords and bows, axes or pickaxes, but there was no plan of battle, it was an outburst of sheer anger.

In other words... mayhem.

The city centre, like other cities before it, ran with blood.

In a dark corner of his other-world, *he* heard the crying souls and was pleased by the number of agonising deaths. *He* had dismissed the Adammites from his mind while he contemplated the news given to him by Anaïs. Nevertheless, they were his puppets, he ought to help.

...Probably, but only if necessary.

Nevertheless he made for Manecaestr, but he needed a body to enter. His essence alone could surely terrify an attacking horde, but it had the unfortunate side effect of also terrifying his own forces. A host was necessary, a 'between' state, less damaging on the whole. Not such an easy task, finding a suitable host was difficult, they often went insane or simply disintegrated. There had to be a degree of utter cruelty in the character of the host, yet pliable enough for manipulation. Soldiers were no good, too rigid and disciplined, simply entering a battlefield and picking up a dying corpse was a waste of time. Nor was entering their Commander, he had a role to play, besides they lost most of their memories when *he* entered them, not much good to be on the field without a clue as to who was doing what.

His shadow entered people's nightmares, he whispered secrets and lies, he could put fear into hearts and souls, but he had no way of truly feeling their pain, not in this realm. He needed a host to enjoy the anguish and the agony.

And once there, he would speak with duplicity and treachery, he had done it before. Whole kingdoms could fall. He knew the power of speech, rumour, half-truths and spurious accusations … or worst of all, false hope.

Therein lay his pleasure.

He looked deep into the city for some time before discovering a suitable host.

Lefwynn Hydeman had just stepped out of one of the city tunnels; he made it pretty close to the north gate when there came a strange flash of darkness and a feeling of giddiness, followed by the most intense pain he had ever experienced in his life. Whatever could be called a soul, spirit or simply personality was ripped to shreds as *he* entered him.

He inspected the new body, pleased it hadn't blacked out or collapsed, many did. Hmm… mature but not old, in good health, neither fat nor thin and wearing well-fitting and well made clothing. He checked his baggage; it seemed to be mostly gold coins and promissory notes of the banking system, plus a fair amount of jewels. The man was obviously escaping the mayhem then. He flicked off the over-elaborate hat the fool wore and promptly turned the body around back towards the city centre.

He didn't need a weapon, a flick of his fingers killed in an instant, or more slowly if he wished. Several people recognised him – as Hydeman that is - as he made for the centre, several tried to kill him. He left steaming, shrieking bodies in his wake.

The Adammites in the central squares stood firm and strong. As long as they maintained their solid battle formations they knew they were invincible. Estrién watched as people were mowed down by them, they slaughtered indiscriminately. He wondered how he could infiltrate their lines? If he could just break the formation there would be a chance.

Alas, unlike the plains by the bridge of Concorde or the hills near Pennyport, there was little space to manoeuvre. The streets leading to the main central square were filled with people, both the enemy and the innocent, he was unable to get by, nor could anyone else.

He looked up to some of the three and four storey buildings around the square, seeing archers in a few windows and on balconies, unsure as to whether they were Adammite followers or not. Arrows seemed to be flying haphazardly across the streets. It gave him an idea.

'Anders, can you get some of your mages and a few of our own archers up there into some of those buildings?' He pointed upwards at the random archers.

Dane understood, 'good idea!' He took Trevaine and young Robson with him, as well as Tamlyn, he had his bow with him, plus as many mages and archers as he could find. They made for the back streets around the central square. It wasn't easy, baulked in many ways either by hurriedly placed barricades or smaller groups of Adammites. *Too many ordinary people wanting to take part, to help, too often at the price of their own life.* Overturned carts, market stalls, hurriedly placed barriers with scared people behind, sometimes Adammite soldiers, people mixed up, running scared or fighting for their world … whatever their ideologies. They had to shout and explain or simply blast their way through, looking for weak points before using magic, careful not to let it bounce on walls, try not to hurt the local citizens.

Aim carefully, narrow the beam, hold in the mana, then … shoot!

Buildings too, they had to break down doors although some people gratefully let them in. Had to fight their way through angry Sons of the Blazing Sun cultists and Adammite devotees, many easily taken.

Dane finally made his way to the top floor of the Saddlers and Leather-workers Guild where he had seen a fine wrought iron balcony, perfectly positioned over the central square. Tamlyn followed him, knocking people out of the way, his sabre flashing. The door to the room was locked, yet another hindrance to be overcome, Dane did his fire, ice and electrum mage thing with the lock, it split open.

The room looked plush, the embers of a fire in the stately fireplace still warm. He had no time to admire the walnut desk and sideboard with the crystal decanters however, as he rushed to the balcony.

The other mages he had brought with him were beginning to move in place around the square. Mage hands and staves were lifted in readiness. Suddenly and unexpectedly, flashfire and lightning bolts streamed down upon the Adammite rows below. Trevaine could be heard shouting, 'now take *that*, bloody mage haters!'

They looked up in horror, screaming as retribution poured down, not from in front or behind them but from above, raising their shields to ward off the terrifying bolts of death. Long-held in anger burst out of the local mages, they too threw their wrath down upon the mage murderers. Tamlyn and the other archers, many elves like himself, aimed for the now upraised Adammite heads and throats.

The tightly-knit formations began to collapse.

Estrién waved up at Dane and Tamlyn, a quick nod of approval before running in, *now* was his opportunity. Nor was he alone, Amber was resolutely by his side, as was Salli. Streaming fire or flashing lightning wasn't his style, but his wand continued to bring death. He found, as Dane had said, that he was more intent on survival than anything. He had begun the day with anger in his heart, intent on retribution, but now he was cold, the wand merely a death tool to use ...

...as Estrién put the deadly blade White Star to the purpose it was created for.

The battle-maidens of the WAR movement joined in, as did the many secret groups of men and elves who had banded together to oppose and survive Adammite control. They waded into the fray while the mages and archers poured death down upon the central core of the solidly held formations.

Not so solid now ...

When they were satisfied they had caused enough damage from above, they too ran down to help in the streets.

Nor were they alone.

King Duggan also had an army at his disposal, they had earlier surrounded the main barracks and overpowered it. Most of the opposing forces were in the streets in any case, only a few, including cooks and orderlies loitered there. As

Reave had taken her small force on a grand tour of city walls, so Duggan took his through the various quarters of Manecaestr, clearing Adammites from their guardhouses and sentry posts, cleansing the areas as he moved. His troops took back the streets and moved ever closer and closer to the central squares where Estrién and the others of the White Shield were beginning to make inroads on the Adammite formations.

Duggan came in from the eastern end of the city, joined the fray, if nothing else it added to the general pandemonium. The young man was determined, like those of the Shield, to clear the city, take it back, free his people. Independently minded, proud people they may be, but they were still *his* people.

The squares now began to fall, Adammites breaking, often running. The way to the main Temple, currently the slave trading centre, became clear. Dane and Salli were in one mind, their goal to take the terrible slave market, destroy it. But it was where many of the Adammites had fallen back to, it having been a well guarded building. The troops dashed inside and hurriedly closed and locked the doors, hoping to have enough time to take hostages of the waiting slaves, use them against the Merrievian forces. Sons of the Blazing Sun cultists and acolytes followed them in to join the slave traders and the waiting slaves inside.

Dane stopped before the main doors of the building. Fighting was still going on around him but he could hear thuds and screams behind the large and heavy doors. It disturbed him, were they killing the slaves or just blockading the door? He didn't want to have come all this way to be baulked at the final moment.

They thought they were safe tucked inside the desecrated temple walls, they would make their demands using the slaves as blackmail.

For a moment Dane stopped, shaking his head, wondering, hoping he wasn't too late. He studied the huge locked and barricaded doors.

Then he simply laughed, *'been there before, mate!'* he shouted as he lifted his oak staff and aimed it at the hinges of the doors, just as he had once before in the dark and dismal Fae realm. He concentrated hard until a massive eruption shot through the staff and blasted first the hinge on the right – the door dangled slightly but still held. Then another blast to the left-hand hinge and the doors burst out of their hinges, falling in a heap and leaving a large gaping doorway for everyone to enter. He didn't have time to hear the gasps of amazement nor admire his own work as he too dashed into the building, pushing aside a few hurriedly placed chairs and benches..

He did see however the angry faces opposing him, most with weapons raised and ready to kill. Briefly he saw the scared faces of elves and humans in rags by the side, all waiting for an unknown and possibly terrible future.

The Adammites pointed their swords not at the intruders, but at the slaves, threatening to kill them.

He didn't care, nor did he give them time to either make demands or even use their swords. Up came the staff again, flame and damnation flew out, catching them off guard as the fire ripped through leather, and steel swords became too red hot to touch.

They would burn with the flames of their own Fire and Death cult.

'Go meet your Death God!' he shouted, 'Here are the flames you wish upon others!' Now he let loose his mana, now came the retribution he had longed for. He wasn't alone; all the mages who came with him and those hidden in the city had followed him.

Dane and his fellow mages now inflicted a fiery revenge upon the mage haters, the elf killers, the slave-traders alike. The city square and the Slave Market, once the gentle Temple of Arboreal, now blazed with fire and storm. The shouts and screams of frustration held in by those who had waited secretly in shadows for so long, rose to the very rafters of the old temple. The exalted cries of those now set free from bondage filled the air. Some too had been mages, they let loose with vengeance from behind the gathering troops, their cries too mingled with the mayhem in the temple.

But no one heard the screams of the Adammites, and no one gave a damn.

There was no pity given that day, nor the long night that followed - the backlash to overbearing oppression and cruelty can be overwhelming. Blood, as previously stated, will have blood.

Tamlyn saw most of this for the first time, he stared in horror at the elven slaves with their docked ears, bound by chains, dressed in cheap shifts or simply rags. Adammites always shocked him, but this city shook him beyond anything he had seen previously. He wondered what Elvinhaeme must be like now? They would go down soon, they had to help retake the realm.

Amber too, the loathsome contempt held by Adammite men for females hurt her depths; once more the twin dirks she carried came out in vengeance. There would be more bloodshed this day. The pair followed the blazing trio of Estrién, Dane and Salli, swords flashing and slashing, a lethal pair bringing the bloody bite of more hard steel to the conflict.

They cleared the desecrated temple and all of its buildings, its central hall, the priestesses quarters, the dining hall and kitchens, the school rooms, the meditation areas, all destroyed, too many had simply become holding cells for Adammite slaves.

Then they returned to the streets, blood heat and bloodlust burning for revenge. The battle carried on, it had a mind of its own; slaughter, or be slaughtered.

Yet somehow, as the day turned to evening and the squares and the temple darkened, as the frenzy of battle continued and people fought and screamed and ran, slipping in the blood of enemy or friend, merely desperate to live ... somehow everyone became separated. The streets were filled with smoke now, the smoke of mage fire and burning barricades, it became hard to see who was friend, who was enemy. Somehow they lost each other in their own private battles for survival through the streets of Manecaestr on that long and scream-filled night.

When they gathered together again in the cold light of morning, the smell of death and blood and stinking guts still contaminating their nostrils, exhausted, exhilarated and aching from the fight, they discovered Tamlyn was missing.

The Adammites were now fighting for survival, indeed, many a mind turned to the idea of escape. Earlier the previous afternoon, Colonel Rambolt had managed to gather his forces and they joined the groups all making for the central squares of the city where the main fight was taking place. He sent some via underground routes, they came up behind Estrién's forces, there would be no immediate let up in the fighting. Estrién's forces were surrounded.

Yet the Adammite army was battle fatigued now, they heard cries of victory upon the lips of the ordinary citizens of Manecaestr, it demoralised them, weakened them.

Estrién turned in blazing circles, White Star screaming; many ran from his terrifying blade, it proved as invincible as it had for Estrién's ancestors. Death came swiftly and in sweeping arcs through Adammite lines.

The Colonel wondered where to go, how to rally his troops, when a voice quietly spoke in his ear.

'Turn them around, Manecaestr is lost, we will get to the coast, sail back to Glasse where we can regroup.'

Colonel Rambolt peered into the face of the man he had once known as Lefwynn Hydeman, a good friend. But there was something far different about this person ... his eyes glowed and a power emanated from him like nothing he had ever encountered. It was, even for a hardened soldier, more than disturbing.

He took a step backwards away from the *being* ... this was not the Hydeman he knew – something had happened. He answered quickly according to the rules, the simple rules of battle that he understood and obeyed.

'Can't leave, it's not done ... anyway, had no word from Mackenzie, it would be mutiny, or at least damn cowardice leaving the field of battle like this.' Whatever his politics, the man kept to the principles by which he abided.

'Already spoken to him, he's trying to make his way back to the north gate – I've already seen to any problems, you'll find little opposition. We can sneak behind the lines, the Rams led by that woman have moved on. We can get out.'

The voice insinuated itself into his consciousness, yet he maintained the discipline instilled into him as a soldier. The Colonel was adamant, 'I'm not giving up Manecaestr, von Adamm would kill me!'

He was surprised to hear that Von Adamm had been dead for some months, that King Kyneweth was dead too, a new young King had taken his place and the towns all along the Long Ride from Manecaestr to Draecastle were all beaten.

'Impossible!' he cried.

Hydeman assured him otherwise. 'The White Shield are behind all this.' Yes, the Colonel had heard of them. 'We must regroup and make for the island safe bases,' the voice, that insidious voice continued. 'We retreat, regroup and retrain. Then we return for the White Shield, blast them out of existence.' He stood smugly. 'Once they are gone, we can retake this miserable world, make it our own again.'

The smile on Hydeman's face made Colonel Rambolt shudder, he'd never seen him in this mood before. He'd never felt anything like him either … what had happened to him?

He didn't really care, the Adammites were simply a tool, *he* just wanted the slaughter to continue. Besides, he needed a human army for his future son.

The Colonel nodded, understood, realised he had no choice but to obey this new Hydeman. He turned from the city centre and followed the strange figure of what had once been a good friend towards the North gate. He watched amazed as the figure flicked his fingers at attackers and they either screamed and ran off or dropped down dead. It was clear that whoever, or whatever Hydeman was now, he was not his old friend.

He wondered … if he had that kind of power, then why didn't he help in the city, get to the centre, re-take it?

But that would not have suited *his* purposes at all. He was enjoying the mayhem currently running through the city. The smell of fear and death were meat and drink to him. Let the puny little beings fight amongst themselves. *He* didn't give a damn who ultimately won, he cared nothing for their lives in a city he cared even less for. It was no longer on his radar.

Rambolt arrived safely, if it could be called so, at the northern city walls and saw his Colonel in Chief's troops defending the portcullis from the remaining assault forces. Hydeman scattered the last ones with a casual flick of fingers.

Mackenzie briefly spoke as they arrived. 'Come on, let's get out while we can. *Tactical retreat* hey, just a tactical retreat. Fight again another day, Rambolt, live and fight again another day,' he told him bumptiously. He done it before at Draecastle, would do it again if necessary.

The remaining forces of the Adammite army ran towards Herringhold to make for their base on the Isle of Glasse.

They also carried with them the unconscious and heavily bound body of Tamlyn. They would at least gain an important hostage out of this rout, a vague semblance of honour among a dishonourable set of thugs and murderers..

Chapter 9

The following morning.

There was panic among the companions of *Nim'randuel*, the Shield. An early spring mist only added to the confusion caused by smoke filled streets, the sharp smell of charcoal covering other, deathly odours. Perhaps nature intended it so, fewer horrors to see in the broad light of day.

They gathered together in the Temple Hall, dead bodies strewn everywhere. They were checking each and every body, looking for Tamlyn. He had last been seen just inside the doors of the Temple, not heard of since.

'We'll find him dear, don't worry,' Dane was heard to say to Amber as she wearily turned over another elven body. This one wore dark armour very similar to Tamlyn's, she knew it wasn't him, but she had become desperate.

'I sent word to Lady Violet, asked her, but no-one's seen him,' she replied anxiously. 'Where is he Dane, he would come here surely if he could? I'll carry on looking,' she continued, 'you help those poor buggers over there ...' pointing at once-bound slaves, many of whom looked half starved. None seemed to know where to go, shocked and dazed by the events.

He nodded, for now he would help, Salli was already wandering through the room with other healer mages. Once they had done here, there was a big city to heal. There was a hospital, a healing centre, but they needed to create makeshift field hospitals throughout the whole beleaguered city.

Still, as King Duggan went about the city himself, it was now also a liberated city, free of Adammite rule. He was pleasantly surprised at his welcome, he waved and smiled benignly at the citizens as he passed, heard shouts of *'hooray'* and *'bless you,'* and raised a victory fist in the air for a collective shout of triumph. Eventually he and his immediate forces ended up at the Council Chambers where Eamonn Norland, once Minister in Charge of Ordinance and Supply, was desperately trying to wriggle his miserable carcase out of the inevitability of death by beheading.

'I tell you, I only did what I was told,' he pleaded. 'I had no choice, they would have killed me.'

'You accepted everything they did and said, you made no effort to stop them.' Duggan surveyed the well appointed offices of the Council Chambers, they were very plush, just as many of the wealthy Guilds' offices were. Money enjoys luxury. He grabbed the man by the sleek lapels of his Council garments. 'You just continued enjoying *this,* didn't you? You didn't care!'

He sighed, sat down on the leather and oak chair by the desk. 'I suppose I did the same. I could not beat my father, King Kyneweth, nor could I dissuade him. I was too young and had no forces of my own to rely on. I would have left, but I was the eldest of five brothers, I needed to stay to look after them and to quietly oppose my father in as many ways as I could. Now tell me … prove to me you did the same, prove that you helped the ordinary people of Manecaestr, that you did not simply take on the role of the Adammite tyrant but actively opposed them.'

Eamonn Norland squirmed between the two guards who held him, desperately trying to think of excuses – there were none - when there was a knock on the door. A scout hurriedly rushed in, panting. He bent down on one knee before Duggan, then quickly rose.

'Sorry, your Majesty, been running all over the city, I have dire news sire.'

Duggan turned to the scout. 'I'm trying to interrogate one of the council traitors right now, it better be important, what is it?'

'The Elf, the member of the White Shield sire, Knight Captain Tamlyn Taenghelin, he's been missing all night.' The king looked shocked, he hadn't known. 'But, he's been spotted, the Adammites have him and they are all making their way back to the islands, to the Isle of Glasse, my liege. I've sent runners and scouts to follow them, and also to inform the Company of the Shield who are currently inside the old Temple of Arboreal.'

King Duggan stood and made for the door. 'Then there is no time to lose, we must follow and get this finished now! Send word to Lord Black and King Alexis, we need to invade while they are on the run – send out the Morus hawks.' He made to leave the room, but was delayed by one of his guards.

'What do we do with him, sire?' pointing at the miserable figure of Norland.

'Stick him in the deepest dungeon you can find ... and leave him there to rot,' came the somewhat ungracious reply.

Norland's figure drooped, he knew he should have escaped the city when his friend Hydeman left. Yet a miserable dungeon probably meant he was the better off of the two, he had no idea of the terrible fate that had awaited Hydeman.

*

King Alexis and the leader of the Freowulven, Jovan, stood numbly under the trees of Oakleigh forest. The king limped slightly although the mages had spent the last days healing his leg, frankly it seemed nothing in comparison with what lay around him.

'Why would anyone do this?' Alexis asked. He gazed with eyes that could not understand the mind that could authorise mass and indiscriminate murder on innocent lives.

'I don't think you have been truly aware – as I am – of the cruelty of the human male,' Jovan replied.

Alexis stared at his ally. 'No, I haven't. Only the last year of hell has opened my eyes. They took my Nerry, punished her, sliced the tips of her ears off, marked her in other ways too. Unfortunately I am now seeing daily the depths to which my own people can sink.' He placed his hand upon Jovan's arm. 'I give you my absolute assurance we are *not* all like this and we will find every one of them, bring them to justice one way or another.

You were offered the penalty of Outlawing rather than death, for your crimes. We always called it the 'Wolf's Head' judgement; indeed, you became the Freowulven, the Free Wolves. You accepted that punishment, banishment from society and death to any who contravened that rule.

However, we cannot banish these people, they will only return. There must be the most severe punishment for their followers, as well as some kind of restoration for the victims. Yet prisons cost a deal of money in upkeep, and there must be thousands of these Adammites. We can use them of course to repair and rebuild; prisoner chain-gangs or whatever.' He slowly shook his head, 'but it is almost as bad as slavery, an eye for an eye. I will have to think long and hard about their punishment.' He pushed back a stray golden lock over his ear, rubbed his chin where a short beard had formed over the last days.

'For the active soldiers and officers of the Adammite armies, those who willingly took part in the Adammite rebellion as well as the disgusting slave traders, they are traitors in every way, death is the only punishment.' His weary eyes met Jovan's. 'I'm sick of death, sick to my back teeth of it. I want my kingdom back as it once was.'

Jovan nodded sympathetically, he'd done his best to help. 'I gave you my word, sire that we would aid you. What happens to us now, my Freowulven group?'

The king laughed and clapped him on the back. 'You have been bloody marvellous. I told you, didn't I – a free and full pardon to every one of you who helped. You deserve this Jovan, and personally, I think you are now a different person to the Jovan who once roamed the Whitecap slopes. You have my gratitude.'

Jovan smiled, probably one of the first full smiles for years, he actually felt happy with himself. 'Come on, let's find out if anyone is left alive here.'

Mages and physicians followed the pair, scouts were sent throughout Oakleigh to see what was what, find either the living or the dead. Almost all the small animals were dead, but many elves still lived. They found them, mostly sick, in the centre under the huge winter umbrellas and in the haemewagons. The Elf Father came forward to greet them.

'You have come at last, we know what has been happening out on the plains.' He turned to Jovan. 'Do not worry, we do not place the blame for this on your shoulders, you did what you had to do and peace will come here finally. *This* ...' pointing generally to the ground, 'came through the streams and rivers, they poisoned our water supplies. Your bows and swords could not have stopped that. But we have mages and alchemists of our own, we are studying this and we boil all the water. Still it makes us sick but it is not as poisonous as it was. We still ask for all the help you can give us,' turning to the King.

One of the King's mages spoke up. 'I think it will clear as the spring rains cleanse the rivers and fresh water comes down from the mountains. We could try filtering it also before boiling and we will inspect the current supply to see if we can cleanse it further. Meanwhile,' he placed a kindly hand upon the Elf Father's shoulder, 'meanwhile we will see to your sick ... we will help your people to survive this.'

The Elf Father smiled, 'we need Dane here and that marvellous oak staff of his,' he chuckled, a sudden breath of relief, 'but you will do instead. We are grateful for all your help.'

King Alexis spoke loud. 'I have something to tell you, Elf Father. Jovan and his people worked hard for both you and my own forces. They offered their lives to help repel and destroy the Adammites up here in the north of Elvinhaeme as well as within my own kingdom. They are fully pardoned by me, they are no longer 'less than wolves' heads' sir. Please make this known.'

'I expected it might be so, nor have they committed any crimes while they were here. I will accept your ruling on this matter.' He looked Jovan fully in the eye. 'You are free among us, all of you.'

King Alexis continued speaking. 'We need to take the rest of Elvinhaeme now while there is mayhem in their ranks. I have already spoken to Commander Kielan Penlachl'en of the Dair Chev'al, they are all behind me. *Jovan* ...'staring him in the eye as the Elf Father had - he'd have to get used to that again, no free person had looked in his face for years - ' ... I'd like you to lead the attack against Belcast'el.

Penlachl'en will lead the mounted forces, but I want you to work with him and take us in. Will you do it?'

The Freowulven leader gave a half grin as he bowed formally to the king. 'With pleasure and with honour, your Majesty.'

They gathered their forces for the push against the city, assembling as the Adammites had, just to the north of Oakleigh, then began marching down through the stricken realm. They had almost reached the outskirts of Belcast'el when news arrived by Morus hawk about the liberation of Manecaestr. A great cheer rang through the rank and file as the King read the note aloud to them.

Later that day King Alexis received another note.

'*Adammites falling back to Isles of Glasse and Mere'garde. Must go after them - finish this. They've taken that young Tamlyn of the White Shield ... not good ... signed – Black Morus.*'

Alexis heaved a sigh, that was a blow. The news that they were leaving was a relief however. He sent a missive, '*We are taking back Elvinhaeme. It will take a little longer here, but we'll meet at Pennyport. Send forces down and you can have my ships... signed – Alexis de Lyon.*' He took out the small royal seal he carried, melted a little sealing wax over the closed note, pressed his seal over and cooled it before attaching it Lord Black's hawk. It would be weeks before Lord Black's troops would reach Pennyport though, but then it would take weeks for him to retake Elvinhaeme.

He watched it fly majestically through the air. *We're on the last lap*, he thought, *but Goddess only knows what awaits us on the Isle of Glasse.* A slight shudder ran through him.

Something evil was there and it was waiting for all of them.

*

The group heard the news with horror.

'They have Tamlyn?' Amber blanched, blinked her eyes to stop the tears, she must be strong for him. 'We must go after them.'

There was a general acceptance of this, no time to lose. King Duggan said he was happy to offer his forces, they could travel to Grimmpool, commandeer boats and he would send for his own ships from Claricotes near his fortress. They would go on to the Isle of Glasse, see what they could do.

'But now is your chance to take back Mere'garde,' Amber replied. 'They might already have gathered enough forces there to retake Draecastle.'

Duggan shook his head. 'Not a chance Amber, no one can take that by force. My father *gave* it away, remember? You lot sneaked in – and I am still unsure just how you did it - your group has some incredible skills – plus good old Gourien, but without my help, you were still in grave danger. No, it's quite safe, besides, Longshanks and my Chief of Staff keep me posted regularly, I know what's happening up there. But we must get to Glasse, Tamlyn is finished if we don't get there in time.' He liked Tamlyn, had struck up a good friendship with him, there was little difference in age and he liked his cheerful temperament.

'He's probably already finished,' came the pragmatic tones of Estrién.

'Estrién! You don't think that truly do you?' Amber was horrified.

'I don't wish to my dearest, but we have to prepare for the worst.' He looked sternly at her, 'even if they keep him alive as some sort of bargaining tool, Merrie only knows what state he'll be in, if or when we find him. Don't get your hopes up, that's all I'm saying.'

'For Merrie's sake, Estrién, can you hear yourself!' Dane cried. 'There's always hope!'

Estrién shook his head. 'I've been too close to death too many times to accept that. *Fate hangs by a thread and is easily snapped.* Remember what we said that night at Draecastle to each other? *In this life or the next.* We knew then this was no easy task.' He sighed deeply, 'we never thought we'd get through this, it's why you and I married, Amber, my love. It's why we bonded, legally bound ourselves to each other ... dammit, we expected it.

But, no, I'm not giving up, if that's what you think, we'll carry on to the end.' He stooped to kiss Amber on the lips, 'we'll find him, dearest if it's the last thing we do, whatever state he's in, and we'll bring him home, I promise you that.' He stood staunchly in front of her.

'He's alive, Estrién, I know it ...' Amber replied.

'You keep that thought, my love,' he advised, 'and you keep believing it!'

They went to collect their baggage, make their way to Grimmpool. Duggan called them later, he'd had news about Colonel Grey and the southern Adammite forces. 'King Alexis has repelled them, this Grey fellow is dead by his own hands. It seems he also had help from the Dair Chev'al and would you believe the Freowulven?' He seemed a little shocked.

Estrién smirked, "yes, I can easily believe it. Jovan their leader is a good friend of mine.'

Duggan appeared even more shocked. 'Oh ... *well then.*' It seemed the world was changing in many ways. 'The Adammites have retreated to Glasse where they've taken Knight Captain Tamlyn. Lord Black is sending forces down to Pennyport, looks like a full invasion is in preparation.'

'Then we can join forces, take on the Adammites on their home base.' Estrién sounded relieved, looked around at the others. 'We could go before them, get to Grimmpool now, take a ship if you could lend us some soldiers, your Majesty,' turning back to the king. 'We can take some mages with us too. Make this a rescue effort, perhaps cause a little mayhem before the main forces arrive.' He was already considering possibilities, glad to have something practical to take his mind off his worries about Tamlyn. This was positive news, could be used.

The others agreed, Dane went off to find if any mages could be spared. Suddenly he stopped, returned to the King. 'You could get one of your ships to call at Rosewater,' he suggested. 'I'm sure the Priests would like to help take back Mere'garde. Every one is a trained fighter, all handy with sword and staff. They say they will not attack, it is not their way, although they will defend their home. I suggest you tell them, now is the time to fight, Mere'garde was My Lady's home, it is up to them to defend it, take it back for her. You'll gain over a hundred skilled fighters if you do.'

The young king took this on board. 'I will send word. You are right; I should take Mere'garde while I can. You now have other forces at your disposal, I can concentrate on my own island. But.. Mere'garde is a small island, it should not take long … *hopefully*,' he grinned, 'then if I can, I will see you on the Isle of Glasse. Await me there, my friends, we are all in this together.' He left to carry out his own plans.

The group collected a party of mages and a company of Duggan's forces. They were marching towards the city walls when they were stopped by a familiar figure with a troop of arbalists behind her.

'Thought you were sneaking out without me?' Reave's Rams all stood stiffly saluting them, Garrett at her side. 'The Rovers are staying here temporarily to add a bit of necessary muscle to the city, but we are ready and waiting for your command.' She seemed a little unsure, hoped they still wanted her.

Amber threw her arms around her. 'Wonderful, Reave, you're just what we need. You are more than welcome.'

The group moved off to find a ship at Grimmpool to take them to Glasse, and to whatever awaited them.

*

The unfortunate Tamlyn couldn't remember much of the journey to the island, and he wasn't truly sure which island he was on. He didn't even remember being knocked unconscious, only that he had woken up a time or two to discover he was tied and bound in the back of a large haulage cart pulled by two horses galloping madly across the countryside. He wasn't alone; there were other captives, mixed elves and humans. Two guards watched closely and every time he woke he was brutally knocked out again. Then he found himself at the coast, dragged off the cart and was thrown into the hold of a cargo ship, along with the other captives, none of whom he knew. He hoped the others, his family and friends were alive, were still free. He wasn't even aware if Manecaestr had been fully liberated or not, although he thought the battles were going their way.

He had been given neither food nor water during the journey.

On arrival at … wherever … he was roughly manhandled off the ship and thrown inside a covered wagon. Again he was knocked unconscious, until he arrived here … wherever that was. A hood was popped over his head and he was marched down several flights of steps. He'd heard the clinking sound of a metal door or gate opening, his hood was ripped off and he was thrown down onto a hard wooden bed or board of some kind. Once more he was beaten into oblivion.

He awoke some hours later, his head in agony, to discover he lay in blackness on some stinking straw upon a flat wooden pallet. From the damp smell, mingled with the stink of urine and faeces, he considered it was likely to be a dungeon of some kind. Without his knowledge he had been stripped of everything but breeches; the straw prickled his naked back and he could feel the cold steel of manacles on his ankles. He lifted equally manacled hands from his bare chest, touched the wall to the side of the pallet, yes cold, slimy and reeking of mould.

'Definitely a dungeon,' he told himself.

His head and body ached from the constant beating, he felt bruised throughout and his mouth was parched. Suddenly there was a swell of nausea, vomit rising in his throat. He dashed up, shuffled across the cell away from the pallet, no point making his sleeping area even worse, and threw up in an even darker corner. He coughed and retched for some time, his head blazing. Then he bent down, shuffling for straw on the floor, managed to pick some up and cover the smelly mess, before turning around and fumbling his way back to the pallet. He could feel the chains attaching it to the wall, thankful he wasn't chained to the wall himself.

But manacled as he was, he felt helpless; he certainly wasn't going anywhere soon.

He wondered what they intended to do with him, clearly they had intentions of some kind? He considered that if he had been captured as some sort of bargaining point, he would probably still be wearing his clothes. The fact he was only wearing breeches did not bode well, at the minimum a disrespect, but beyond that? He didn't wish to dwell on that.

He'd readied himself for death many times over the last year, had actually expected it a few times, came damn close up at Draecastle. But that was a warrior's death, soon over with. Here, Merrie only knew, it could be prolonged and very painful. Besides, he didn't know if they wanted information from him, or merely wished punishment upon him as a member of the White Shield - or just for the fact he was an elf.

But he knew this, if they'd simply wanted him dead he would not now be lying here in this stinking dungeon. The more he thought about it, the worse his predicament appeared.

Think, therefore about escape instead. Keep the mind dwelling on that problem rather than dire possibilities. Besides, he knew his people would come for him when they found him missing. He knew it with absolute certainty.

They were One, they were bonded together, they cared. He could imagine how upset Amber must be, he wanted to reassure her he was alive, but naturally he could not do that. He hadn't even wished her farewell. But still he sent his love across the miles to her, hoping she could feel the warmth of his arms and the tenderness of his kisses.

Life had been good, so good between them. Somehow, for his family's sake, he had to hold on, stay alive. *Hold on to the belief in their love.*

He was disturbed from his reverie by the sound of a heavy door creaking open and the light of a wavering torch illuminating the cell. He quickly looked around taking note of his surroundings: it was a small cell, probably ten feet by six, three stone walls and a barred exit, stone flagged floor, straw scattered in places, *shit*, there had been a bucket in a corner, he could have puked up in that. Still, it would be useful later.

Two guards were coming down steps to the right, he craned his neck to see them, they were followed by a straight-backed and severe looking officer.

'Unlock the elf's cell,' he heard him order. 'He's needed for questioning.'

Uh-oh.

Tamlyn sat up and readied himself for whatever ordeal lay ahead of him.

*

The roads back through the towns of Loxely and Haregroves towards the coast were clear. Any Adammite had already crossed country and hurriedly made for the more southern fishing village of Herringhold. Duggan's soldiers could be seen guarding the main highway, even the torches in tall stone or metal urns by the sides were lit, the road cheery as night descended.

It felt almost normal ... until they remembered why they were making for the coast. Amber wore a permanent frown, Dane looked almost bereaved and Estrién merely appeared stern, his eyes set and determined.

'Wonder where he is on the island?' conjectured Amber.

'Headquarters, bound to be,' replied Estrién. That didn't help Amber at all.

They steered their borrowed horses towards the coast, although Estrién rode Elara, across the flat plain, the ever changing mage colours of Mad Max's Tower could be seen even as the rain drizzled.

'Grand sight ...' commented Dane, pointing across the plain. 'Bit like coming home, all those mages ...'

Amber just wished they *were* home, all together at Ravenscroft Hall. She couldn't imagine life without Tamlyn there, he was part of them. She saw his cheerful face in the air above her, his braids down, flaxen locks streaming in the wind. She longed to hear the laughter accompanying that image.

Captain O'Kelly greeted them as they boarded his ship. 'King Duggan sent word. All's ship shape for ye, we've put ballistae aboard should ye need 'em. There's a grand northerly, so if we cast off now, we'll make good time.'

Amber was amazed, she actually understood him. Everyone poured on board; places were found for Reave's group of arbalists. They crowded round the ballistae, anxious to try out the larger variety of their own weapons. Most of the time on board was spent practising with large harpoon type missiles attached to long ropes aiming at imaginary points in the sea.

With a brief 'dog down the hatches and anchors aweigh lads,' they set sail.

Several days later, the outline of the Isle of Glasse could be seen. It shimmered in the morning light, the famous haze over the island that gave it its name. It looked ethereal; a mystical glow lit the gentle green slopes of the Pen Bueno hills to the north of the island.

Dane stood near the prow of the boat watching his home come into view. His eyes misted over, his family lay here, murdered by those bastards. The dryad forest he knew was gone, the thought of all those gentle beings slaughtered by them was too much to bear.

But the thought of getting his revenge upon these people did nothing for him. No amount of counter-slaughter would bring back his home, his parents, his friends or the lovely little family of dryads who greeted them so warmly when his mother took him to visit her forest home. The sights, smells and sounds of his home were no more. To this day he could smell the aroma of his mother's freshly made bread, taste the thick creamy butter and her homemade rowanberry jelly, fragrant and sweet. He was sure he could smell it on the breeze.

'I'll make it right, mum,' he whispered to the wind. 'And Dad, I've tried to make you proud of me, I'll keep trying.' He thought of his new home near the Bollands hills, just inside the outcrops of Shirewood. 'I'll plant that oak, mum, and more fruit trees, and definitely a few rowans, we've got lots of room. I'll make a herb garden like you used to have, and learn how you used to make your delicious cordials. I'll keep it going, mum, you are not forgotten.'

It wasn't that he'd had a privileged life with lots of wealth, but they had never been poor and certainly never in want. It had been a good upbringing, kind and full of fun.

He saw his island shining in the morning sun and wept. Amber saw him, curled a loving arm around him, kissed him on the cheek.

'I know how you feel, Dane. We'll not let them die in vain. We'll keep their memories, they will live on through us. I ...' She stepped back a little. 'I've not spoken of this before, but my sister got me thinking,' her amber eyes gazed up and searched cornflower blue ones, she seemed to hesitate. 'When this is over, and we are back home, back at Ravenscroft, I think, if it's OK with you boys, well ... ' she hesitated again before continuing. 'I ... I think I'd like to start a family.'

Her gaze melted his heart; he was brought out of the past and into the future. 'My love, I can't think of anything better. Thank you ... and thank you for cheering me up. I reckon it's the best thing we could do.' Then he stopped, looked across the intervening sea to the island. *'If ....'* he stated.

'If what, dear?'

'If we live through this,' came the reply.

He could already see the large numbers of patrol boats around the island, he knew the main port to the south, Porth Gwythion would be heaving with their war ships. He wondered how they could get on to the island ... although, when he thought about it, they could take a few rowing boats. This wasn't an invasion - that would come later- but now, if they could just gain a foothold? He fished these waters as a youth, he and his friend had many happy days out on the water. That little cove they knew, where they used to go swimming, drink ale all afternoon? *Held a few good parties with wenches from the village there too ....*

Now that raised a brief smile.

It just might do, but it would have to be a night landing. He spoke to Captain O'Kelly.

'Nae problem, laddo, took King Alexis in on a night raid up Mere'garde. We canny go in by day anyways. Just pass the word when and where. But be careful, there be treachery around these waters, if the Adammites don't get ye, the rocks will. Davy Jones' locker awaits ye ...' And with those ominous warnings he left to splice the main brace, or some such.

Dane went to speak to the others about the landing.

*

He was pulled by the manacles around his wrists towards the steps He could only shuffle; the chains around his ankles didn't allow much leverage. The guards decided he didn't move quickly enough, they grabbed him under the shoulders, one on each side and dragged him. They followed the officer through a long, narrow, stone walled corridor.

He didn't resist, no point, it would only mean more beatings and he had no way of retaliating as yet. He took note of his surroundings however, watched closely the route they took just in case he could ever escape.

Escape ... he had to hold on to that.

The stone walls looked like he was in a fortress or castle, big heavy stone, ancient and strong. There were torches on the walls, basic, little more than a wooden club with kindling on the end. Not much, but a possible weapon, he considered. The room they dragged him into clearly had more weapons available, they were conveniently hung on walls. These were meant for use on their victims however: himself, and they didn't look too appealing.

Whips, cat-O-nine-tails, branding irons, nasty little knives of the very sharp and pointy variety, some strange-looking implements with serrated edges, cutters and beaters of every type.

A pair of large scissors, still bloodied, held pride of place. Tamlyn knew what they were meant for; he'd seen the results among his fellow elves.

It was warm in the room, very warm; a blazing fire in the corner might have looked cosy had it not been for the various pokers and other instruments heating to redness in the hearth.

There was a chair and a bed too, quite a comfortable room, except the chair was hard and had straps and strange wheels all over it. It looked jointed somehow, adjustable. A hollow curve in the top of the chair back obviously for an elven head to rest, was clearly for the convenience of the torturer. The bed was flat wooden, with more straps and a turning rack. It looked like it extended somewhat more than he would have cared for. The hooks on the ceiling with chains attached to them didn't look so good either.

None looked inviting and Tamlyn wondered which one he would be strapped to first?

He had no further time to consider as his manacles were hung over two hooks in the ceiling and he was raised a few inches from the floor. He saw the eyes of one of the guards as he was lifted … they looked feverish, excited at the prospect of what was to come.

…A sadistic little bastard then.

'When do you want it done, Captain?' the other guard asked the Officer in Charge who was watching Tamlyn closely.

'Not yet,' came the answer. 'I need him coherent for a while, at least until the Master sees him.' Tamlyn saw the guards visibly shudder, he wondered why?

He had no further time to wonder as he was brutally punched in his stomach, so fast he hadn't seen it coming. He stared wide eyed at the officer who took a step back.

'Good, I have your full attention. Now…' he strode purposely around the room as he spoke, 'we have a great deal to discuss and you may hang from there for an eternity if you choose. Or… you may sit more comfortably in the chair while you tell me about your friends, their intentions, the explanation of that horrible phenomena around Manecaestr – I was there so don't deny it - and why little dickheads like you have managed to fuck up so much of our plans?

Were you one of those who killed von Adamm?' He was curious; he knew little, stuck inside the time zone while big events were happening. This piece of elf-shit had answers he wanted. This little piece of elf-shit also needed showing who was boss.

Tamlyn couldn't help but smile. If the officer had needed to escape Manecaestr, his people had won, something for him to hold on to. He answered honestly. 'Yes, we took him out, although it was actually two of my friends who threw him over a balcony that night.' It was no good, he just couldn't help adding, 'you should have seen his smashed body on the floor the following morning, not merely smashed but a horse had trampled all over him. Not good, not good at all.'

He knew he shouldn't have said it, knew particularly when the first punch smashed into his face, followed by a knee to his testicles and another heavy slam to his stomach. He cried out, felt sick again, retched but had nothing to bring up. Eventually he spoke again. 'You asked … I answered, that's the rules, no?'

'You part of that White Shield scum?' The sneer on his face said everything.

Tamlyn wondered what to answer, would this seal his death or give him longer to live? Neither made any difference, he would not deny his family. 'Yes, *pure scum* …' he replied cheekily, wishing it wasn't in his nature to act with such stupid bravado.

He was rewarded by an uppercut to his chin, followed by a series of body blows. He closed his eyes tight as he swung backwards and forwards, the world around him nothing but sparks and vivid stars.

'What bloody magic brought about that effing circle around Manecaestr?' The Captain was curious, he'd only escaped by the skin of his teeth and it had been awful inside during the last months.

Tamlyn merely shook his head, it was beyond him. The little he knew would not suffice this man.

He was kicked and beaten again. It dawned on him, the guy didn't really need information, he wouldn't understand the esoteric properties of the Time Circle. No he merely wished to ascertain he had the right elf and wanted to punish him. He was getting his revenge for the loss of his leader and the discomfort of the time zone.

'I know little,' he gasped again, every muscle and sinew in agony, 'ask a mage. It was something to do with time and … and … something … *someone* terrible. There is … *someone* … outside us … *evil*. It was no normal magic.' He could barely speak, his tongue felt like rasping sandpaper.

The Captain stopped and stared. *Someone terrible?*

'What do you mean?' Now he was truly curious, this was close to home.

His voice was croaky, but he managed to answer. '*Him*, he who is behind all this. I cannot name him, but there is someone beyond us, someone or something of pure evil. I think…' Tamlyn concentrated deeply, trying to make sense of everything. 'I think he wants us all dead, he hates our world – *all* of us.' He took a breath and faced his interrogator in the eye. 'He cut off everyone in Manecaestr, Adammites and Merrievians alike. Now you tell me why?'

The Captain considered the words of the elf. He … *he knew who – or what – Tamlyn referred to.* But wasn't *he* on their side? *He* had done that, punished his own?

The Captain was a dutiful Son of the Sun, had worshipped the Flame as he had been told, and now, *now* their God walked among them. Von Adamm had said so, had explained the power of their God, and had even seen recently with his own eyes. He had felt invincible, strong in his manhood, true to the Flame, his Death cult.

But if what the elf said was true – and it seemed likely because that magic was beyond anything he had ever known - then his own God had done that? For a moment he lost his understanding, his faith, he was confused.

Only for a moment however, he felt *him* arrive. *Someone* stood in the doorway, a presence beyond life, filling it with shadow. It seemed to loom large, the torture room became infused with his essence. The cruel tools displayed on the walls were but a mockery of *him*, mere amateurs.

Red eyes stared contemptuously at Tamlyn. Now there came pain, greater than anything he had ever felt. There was no need of all these pathetic instruments, this being inflicted death as he chose, at will. Tamlyn's body shook from top to toe, his whole system on fire. He screamed out loud, but screams were lost on these people, on *him*.

And in the middle of the pain, Tamlyn simply wondered ... *why?*

He merely smiled and pointed. 'Strap him to the chair,' the calm tones of his voice understating the threat of violence to come.

Tamlyn was roughly pulled down from the hooks, thrown into the hard chair, strapped by legs and arms before his head was pulled back and his neck carefully strapped into the waiting hollow curve of the head rest. It could have been useful to a barber for trimming hair or shaving, but it was more than useful for cutting other, more essential organs.

'Now pass me the shears,' came the next order. Tamlyn could actually hear the smile in the cold voice.

Elves have very sensitive ears as Neria had tried to explain to Alexis, and before it was finished, Tamlyn, already in a very weakened and battered state, passed out.

*

They took the rowing boats towards the island, as once they had used them to enter Mere'garde. They came from the north-west, Dane thought there would be fewer ships that way, the only other ships would have been from Erin, making for Porth Gwythion on the southern side of the island with huge bundles of flax and barrels of ale. He pointed to a cove across the water, still in shadow in the dawning light.

'Careful, steer south more before going landward, some rocks close here,' He pointed the way he and Alvin his old friend had navigated these waters. His heart was thumping, he didn't really wish to land, too many memories.

Somehow they avoided the treacherous rocks.

As they stepped on to the familiar sandy beach, Dane hesitated for a moment. He sat down on a protruding rock and slipped off his boots, wriggling his feet In the sand. He took in great breaths of fresh, salty air redolent with the tang of seaweed, his youth and childhood. For a few minutes while the others were busy hiding the boats, he breathed deeply, filling his soul with home. Amber and Estrién watched him, waiting patiently. Eventually he dusted off the sand from his feet, replaced his boots and smiled across at them.

His home was no longer here, he knew that, it was with his loved ones in the comfortable Ravenscroft Hall in Shirewood. He'd moved on, left his childhood home behind. The memories would always be there, the good and the final bad one, but this pleasant island was no longer his.

'C'mon,' he told the others now returning to the beach. 'We've miles to go. I know where they will be, there is an old castle on the hill behind the main port, Porth Gwythion. The port is the largest town on the island and that old castle is perfect for a military base.'

'Who lived there?' asked Amber.

'Oh, no one, been empty for a century or more. Never had an overlord of any kind, at least none that I know of. We had a Council of Elders, like Manecaestr, used to sit in chambers in the port once a month, it's next to the castle. Dad was one, you didn't have to actually be that old, just either knowledgeable, or popular among the locals. We weren't exactly an unruly bunch, a quiet folk really.

To be truthful, no-one wanted to upset the dryads, they were the last of their line, important to us all. The island was beautiful and peaceful because of them. We … we just lived in harmony with nature here.' He stared into the dawn sky, his words seemed so little, yet they had meant everything in his life.

He set forth, wondering what they had now done to the island? The rest followed him onwards across the countryside towards the main port and the hold of the Adammites.

Chapter 10

King Duggan did as he had been advised, he sent word north to send several ships to Mere'garde and like Amber and the rest, commandeered ships from Grimmpool for himself and his forces. He left a good number of soldiers behind in Manecaestr to keep the peace and temporarily left several members of the WAR movement and leaders of the resistance in charge. They would create the next city Council and assume control.

Their first task there was to rebuild Merrie's temples. They emptied the coffers of the Adammites, put Adammite prisoners into chain gangs and made them work.

Duggan sailed northwards towards Rosewater. He had to use a row-boat to land there, the harbour wasn't large enough for the huge carrack he was sailing in. The priests welcomed him warmly, they already knew about Manecaestr. They met him in the warm reception hall of the temple, the rose window casting its beautiful shadow on the white wall. He was surprised to see a large group of them arriving in the hall as entered, all dressed in tough leather doublets overlaid by a hauberk of chain mail, heavy boots and carrying helmets. Some carried sword and shield, one or two bore a heavy longsword, some held long staves as weapons.

'We knew you would come,' Lord Ansell told the king. 'We will help, my Lady would expect this of us, it is our duty.

We are expert in the use of all these weapons, and we offer them in this cause.'

Duggan was relieved; he'd thought he would have to persuade them to come. They offered him a cheerful and welcoming meal before they left. 'One last meal together,' they explained, 'we do not know who will return. We have all signed wills and legal arrangements for any property we hold to be given over to the Red Rose Temple. We are prepared and ready.'

The Merrievian warrior priests then followed the King to the waiting vessel.

The ships all made for Meréport, the main port of the island. It was already buzzing and bustling when they arrived, several of his own naval vessels from Draecastle had but recently arrived. The port was mayhem.

The Adammite sailors were aiming their ballistae at Duggan's ships and huge trebuchets on land were catapulting large stones to scupper the king's vessels. Shouts and screams were everywhere, mostly orders hailed by the various commanders.

But the Adammites did not have so many ships here, only the few they escaped in from Draecastle. Duggan had commandeered their own ships from Claricotes before they left and they too had brought ballistae, were shooting huge bolts at the sailors. He watched one fly though the air, saw several sailors scattered, one pinned to the deck. He observed that his ships were already running alongside the moored vessels, sailors hastily throwing planks across or using ropes and hurriedly boarding the Adammite ships.

King Duggan jumped off his ship surrounded by his private guard. He watched the Red Rose priests file singly down the gangway; they were joining the troops he had brought.

He wished them well. His job was to rout the Adammites from their headquarters.

It looked like another long day ahead. The Red Rose warriors followed him into battle. Duggan was amazed by the ferocity of their attack, yet it was marked by a singular self-discipline. They seemed to fight as one, their thrusts, cuts and slices well timed, almost in unison. They looked out for each other too, taking care of flank attacks or deadly side swipes, their counterbalancing moves swift and graceful. It was almost like watching a dance, but a terrible, deadly one. When the king reached the headquarters building he watched the Warrior Priests smash open the windows with their staves, beat the heads of any inside before they climbed in. Lord Ansell opened the door for him.

'Come your Majesty, follow us through, we will open the way for you.'

The young king did so, then later followed them through the island with his own troops. He watched their strange balletic dance as they took out the remaining troops left on Mere'garde. These were Her warriors, the Lady Merrie's own graceful storm-troopers. Eventually he left them at Merrie's Tower, they were staring aghast at the remains of the gardens. There were no bodies however, the Adammites had picked up any corpses left behind by Estrién, had either burnt or given them burial. It hadn't been a massacre, many had been wounded or simply ran away in fear, but the Adammites had still lost too many lives that day. The gardens were a shambles and the priests shook their heads in dismay.

'We will leave priests here, this place must be restored. We will bring red roses and herbs from our gardens, ask the

White Rose order to send theirs also. We will bring this place to beauty again, have no fear.'

King Duggan thanked them, and left to root out the remaining Adammites on the island. There were few, almost all the rest had moved down to the Isle of Glasse.

He had been thrown into kingship, knew only what his father had taught him, plus of course the wise councils of Gourien. As the last of the Adammites either died or fled and the night drew in, he gazed across the darkening sea. Briefly he yawned, exhausted by the day's events, another day of fighting and slaughter.

'I've done my best, mother,' he said, although it is uncertain whether he referred to his own mother or the Lady Merrie. 'It's been a damn hard beginning to leadership though. I hope I can make my country peaceful again as you'd wish.' As a spring moon gently rose over the glimmering Sea of Silver, he gave a deep sigh, shook his head at the waste of it all and turned for his ships. He had promised Estrién and the White Shield, he would not fail them.

But all he truly wanted to do was return home.

*

In Elvinhaeme, Alexis, Jovan and Kielan had spent the previous week retrieving and retaking the smaller towns and villages of the countryside. Many of the Adammites had retreated to the villages, were using the elves as hostages. They were demoralised but desperate, on the run. They inflicted as much damage as they could before fleeing to the coast to make for the Isle of Glasse. Jovan felt he was causing even greater heartache to the local elves than before they were liberated.

Such is life.

They reached a point close to Belcast'el where King Alexis realised it was time for him to retreat, he had other work to do. It wasn't right for him to invade the elven capital city, not his role, the leader should be elven. He spoke to Jovan.

'I need to go now, *you* must take the city. I'll leave you with as many troops as you consider necessary and they are temporarily under your command. I have to get to the Isle of Glasse, get this war over with. Can you and Penlachl'en take it between you?'

Jovan laughed, took his hand and shook it. 'We've gathered plenty more forces as we've been going, people wish to help now there is hope. It is up to us, the elves. You have been wonderful and we thank you wholeheartedly, but it is now our turn. The ties between Elvinhaeme and Westerling have never been stronger. Go with Merrie's Blessings. *And...*' as the king turned to leave, 'your Majesty, I personally thank you for pardoning us all, the women too. We are and shall remain always grateful for that.' He bowed his head, right hand over his heart. The king acknowledged him and left.

He was about to make his way cross country to where his ships lay in Mab's Bay when he received another note from Lord Black.

'Knew you'd want my help, already on road, coming as back up for Glasse. Two days to Pennyport. I thank you for your ships. Meet me at Hollyporth instead?'

Hollyporth? He considered the idea. There would be resistance still there while all the Adammites fled, more so if the elves successfully took back Belcast'el, but if he arrived with his forces beforehand he could hopefully take the town, lie in wait for those trying to escape. There couldn't be too many ships there now, most were already sailing back to the Isle of Glasse, which was why he had needed to get to Pennyport to collect his own. With luck, he might even gain a few Adammite ships. So ... why not have a go?

He sent a missive back to Lord Black. *'Many thanks. Have issued orders to send some ships on to Hollyporth for my own use, the rest are for you. See you at Hollyporth.'*

He was winging it again, changing plans on the fly. 'It's what I do best,' he considered. He quickly sent word to Jovan and Knight Commander Kielan that he would try and make it to the coastal cities.

But he knew, no matter what, he didn't have anywhere near the number of ships the Adammites had. How he would get through their coastal defences around Glasse he had no idea? Like the rest of Mer'edrynn, they were still paying the price for allowing the fall of the Isle of Glasse in the first place.

'Never knew it would be so important,' he considered. 'Must take that on board in future; sometimes it's the smaller things that matter most.'

He stood straight and pulled back his shoulders. 'Come on men, time to get marching westwards, we've ports to take.'

His troops followed him to the coast.

*

Many young elves joined Jovan's forces as they battled for Elvinhaeme. They were surprised at the presence of the Freowulven leader, but quickly reassured by King Alexis that he and the Freowulven were free men and women. Tales of the Freowulven had rung in their ears, these were ruthless warriors.

They proved to be so as the towns and villages came and went, indeed many Adammites fled once they heard of the rout at the Bridge of Concorde. These men had swaggered and boasted as they took the homes and villages of defenceless, peace-loving elves, but it was quite another matter when those same elves became armed and dangerous.

They ran.

Belcast'el was another matter however. Commander Grey had not been so stupid as to leave the city defenceless. It was filled with guards and soldiers.

Jovan was happy to hear that the King would be making for Hollyporth, it was a weight off his mind but he knew he could not get by using elves alone. King Alexis accordingly left a company of soldiers with the new elven army. Jovan and Kielan worked side by side, their forces small but all expert archers and swordsmen, training the raw recruits as they went. They made quite a pair, the other elves joked that just the sight of their somewhat unprepossessing visages was enough to make anyone run. Yet each laughed at the other's ravaged face, telling tales of their unhappy encounters with bear and sabre cat.

It is difficult to say who outdid whom, their tales were somewhat embellished by alcohol, a few pipes of excellent leafroll and general bravado. Over several congenial discussions by the nightly campfire they developed a strong friendship.

They arrived at the city of Belcast'el on a warm spring day.

Spring... a time for sowing, tilling the land; a time of birth and renewal, not a time for death. Elvinhaeme reeked of death this spring.

The city gates, as at Manecaestr were closed, shut tight. They had been rebuilt by Commander Grey, were even more solid than previously. Hellboys were up on the city walls pointing down at the massing forces of elves. A few shot their bolts at the incomers, warning shots designed to scare.

Woodmoss had also travelled in with Jovan and Kielan, and the two mages who had protected him at Concorde were travelling by his side. Woodmoss enjoyed the more cerebral conversation of the mages and they were surprised to find he too had a deep and inquiring mind. They got on well. His elven friend from Oakleigh forest, Rowan Firethorne, joined them, brought with him more archers. Woodmoss discovered he was integral to the elven forces now and welcomed his new-found approval, even notoriety.

Jovan watched with admiration as the satyr carried his own version of a battering ram straight to the city gates. While the mages set up a protective barrier around him, and the archers shot at the Hellboys on the city walls, Woodmoss rammed the gates with an enormous tree trunk. After several heavy thuds and crashes, splinters flying, he took his equally enormous axe and hacked at the heavy bolts and locks until the gates shuddered open with a groan.

Freowulven and the mounted Dair Chev'al along with the company of Westerling forces led the way, followed by the large but greenhorn army of elves.

The Hellboys were the first problem, it is sad to note how many elves died as they bravely climbed the towers to the battlements of the city to overpower them. Mages helped of course, without them even more elves would have died that day.

The streets were still filled with guards, men with big mouths and large swords but little combat experience. Jovan's forces made short work of them, heard the cries of encouragement from the local people as they worked their way through.

By the time they reached the Palace grounds their numbers were swelled by locals, many of whom had not been idle over the winter months. It had been hard to fight back in a city overwhelmed by a fierce and terrifying army, difficult when so many had been in chains, or worse, captured and killed. Nevertheless they had collected together, formed their own resistance, hidden in the secret places that always exist within a large city.

Jovan saw the city squares had been used for public punishment and wholesale slaughter, as at Manecaestr. The remains of pyres could be seen, the rotting corpses of elves left hanging in rows along long-lined gallows, a warning to the rest. He couldn't understand, the elves had done nothing against humans. Why? What was the purpose of the Adammites, what had been the reasoning behind such slaughter? Was it hatred, or just to prove their supremacy? What put that into the minds of men?

Years ago, when Jovan had sought and killed those responsible for murdering his wife he had been in immense grief. Nothing could have stopped him; he knew he wasn't in his right mind. He escaped the hangman's noose by the skin of his teeth and was banished from society.

What drove these people to do the same to innocent lives?

He did not know the extent to which that *he* had controlled men's minds and hearts. *He,* who was outside life, held no love of life, his desire was to foment hatred and division. He had performed well, as had his minions.

Jovan knew nought of this, yet he had seen the results. Now he followed a fiercely determined Woodmoss through the streets to the palace gates, the grounds used as the Adammite headquarters and barracks. Here more Hellboys and troop formations awaited, these had been left especially to protect the palace should anyone wish to take advantage of Grey moving the majority of his troops northwards. They were ready and waiting for them.

Yet inside the palace the elves were already mobilising, galvanised by hope. Now that they saw a chance they took over the kitchens, handing out meat cleavers, sharpened knives, axes used for chopping wood, even the marble rolling pins and heavy brass candlesticks from the dining rooms. If it looked like it could be used as a weapon they took it. They attacked anyone inside the palace before rushing outside to join the fight against the main forces on what had been the beautiful palace lawns. These were nothing but mud and slush now. Carts and wagons that had cast great ruts in the grass were overturned as protection behind which stood ready the formations of Adammite storm-troopers. The elven slaves and servants made for the carts to pull them down, a fierce hatred in their hearts, their suffering had been too much at the hands of these people.

The Adammites who hated so much could not be surprised that they were hated in turn. The surprise was that they were hated by those who had held no hatred in their hearts before the invasion; trust in each other was lost, possibly forever.

Kielan swiftly ordered his forces to ride around the outer edges of the extensive grounds. The horses set off at a gallop, keeping close to the walls, still Hellboys raining down bolts upon them. They were too fast on horseback for many, reaching the rear of the gardens and quickly sending several volleys of arrows back up onto the battlements Another volley was sent across the heads of the Adammite force in the centre, raining from above., hitting them directly. Then they jumped off their horses to come in from the rear.

Jovan attacked from the front with his own Freowulven, the added Westerling forces and newly-armed followers.

At first the Adammite militia scoffed, killed many of the untrained elves, too many died that day in their bid for freedom. Yet the Adammites had nowhere left to go and no real commander to order them into position. As the fortifications were pulled down, or smashed to pieces by Woodmoss, their formations began to fall apart. Woodmoss now took advantage of every break in the lines. He watched for weaknesses, crashing into them with his axe, followed quickly by Jovan's Freowulven.

They were merciless and without fear, exactly as the elves had known they would be. Their reputation had come before them, and they lived up to the tales.

Slowly Jovan and Kielan made inroads through the groups until they both arrived in the centre. 'Well met, my friend,' shouted Kielan, his grim visage briefly brightened by a smile for his ally.

'Well met!' returned Jovan before they turned their backs on each other to resume the fight. Yet they found they fought side by side many times that day, each looking after the other, a helping hand at an appropriate moment.

By the time it was all over and they had reached the huge circular Hall of the palace, the fancy hall with all the marble and the ornate marble throne, they had both received many more cuts and slashes, their arms and faces bloodied, Kielan's leg had been ripped open again, he limped badly. There would be more scars from that day.

'By the Merrie, you get uglier by the moment,' exclaimed Jovan.

'Huh, seen yourself in a mirror recently?' returned Kielan, laughing. Their words seemed to echo in the large hall.

They both looked at the empty throne. 'There's no Dûc anymore,' Jovan told him. 'Who sits there now?'

'Well, I've no use for it, I'm Floriénne,' Kielan replied. 'It's certainly not my place to sit there, and King Alexis has no right to it.'

'Queen Neria was cousin to the Dûc though.'

'That may be so, but neither the king nor queen can be allowed to rule here, you know that. She'd have to leave him to claim the throne and that's certainly unlikely. There are no other contenders – they're either dead or they ran off, they certainly weren't here helping to retake it.' Kielan looked curiously at Jovan, then pointed to the throne and added archly, *'you* try it, you've just liberated most of Elvinhaeme haven't you?'

Jovan looked shocked as he studied the ornate affair. 'Well, I *could* try it for size,' he offered. 'I suppose it's my duty to keep the peace until the rightful Dûc or Dûchesse takes their place.'

He sat gingerly down upon the throne before jumping up and grabbing a velvet cover and a cushion or two from the various Ottomans and couches in the room.

'Damn cold on the rear,' was all he said as he sat down again.

He gazed around the circular domed hall, wondering at the fickleness of Fate? One moment he was an Outlaw, 'less than a wolf's head', but he had become the head of the wolves, *the Freowulven* ... the free wolves. Now he sat upon the throne of the Ducal Hall in Belcast'el, no doubt a temporary position.

He believed he had been given the chance to gain back his honour, yet somehow it meant little without the woman he had loved so much, the wife he had lost everything for.

Yes, he thought, Fate could truly be a fickle bitch.

He briefly gazed up at the vast domed glass ceiling above the throne, blue sky and fluffy clouds drifting across. For one moment he stared intently; curiously he could see his wife's features in the clouds above him.

She was smiling down at him, he knew that, felt her warmth in his heart.

Quietly he nodded, then put his fingers to his mouth and blew her a gentle kiss. 'I love you,' he whispered to the void. 'One day we will be together, my dearest. Until then, I hope I make you proud of me.'

Right now, there was work to be done.

*

It took Alexis longer to take the ports since many of the Adammites had fled to Hollyporth and Westlea. Hollyporth was in fact crowded and busy, ships coming and going, trying to rescue as many soldiers as they could, take them to safety on the Isle of Glasse.

The remaining forces fought fiercely as he entered the port city of Hollyporth, they no longer wanted it, but they needed time for everyone to escape. Their final orders had been to keep the port until the last moment, then make for the ships.

Alexis remembered coming here when he was younger, some royal visit with Neria for a spring festival. He loved how the city was filled with cherry blossom, indeed it was so beautiful that he had planted many back in Orlandium so that Nerry would feel at home.

There were no trees in sight, nor blossom of any kind. Every tree had been chopped for whatever the Adammites had needed it for and they didn't give a damn about flora. The white buildings still sparkled under the spring sun, but they looked dirty somehow, were in ill-repair. The

Adammites had used the city for their needs, they had not cared for it, neglect was seen everywhere.

Even the smell of the city was different. It was nothing but an overgrown army encampment and a tactical naval base. It stank, not of the sea or the foliage as it once had, but of glutinous pine pitch, liquid tar, linseed oil and grime.

Alexis' primed army waded into the enemy lines, he had no Woodmoss with him to batter down gateways or fortifications, he had little need in any case. This was a city without a leader, von Adamm had gone, Grey had gone and it was now full of fleeing soldiers, routed and demoralised by the very forces now storming through Hollyporth. Many ran for their lives, hurried to ships casting off before the King's troops could follow.

The elves of the city joined in, emboldened by the King's forces and the news about the battle at Concorde. Great cheers and cries rang out as the remaining Adammites fled.

He managed to capture a couple of their transport vessels, threw their Captains overboard and instilled his own. For a few days he settled in the old Adammite headquarters listening to and holding talks with traumatised citizens. News came that Belcast'el was free, the ports rang with shouts and cries of triumph. As for Jovan currently sitting on the throne in the capital, well, as Kielan had stated, it wasn't his place to do anything about it.

He'd been the only one brave enough to truly defend them. Alexis considered he deserved it.

He waited in Hollyporth until he saw the small fleet of his own ships arriving a few days later, followed by another half dozen flying Lord Black's colours. A black ensign with crossed swords between two death's heads looked ominous, but then, that was Black all over, outdoing even the Jolly Roger the pirates used. He watched Lord Black walk casually down the gangplank, full black armour and his bright longsword appropriately named Gutthrust hung purposely at his side. He greeted Alexis warmly.

'Well, young man, you've done well. Time I joined in this bloody affair. Let's get a move on.'

He was never one to waste words.

The two took a private meal together before each boarding their ships to set sail for the Isle of Glasse.

Chapter 11

Isle of Glasse, late Firstfire.

They decided to split up. Reave, her band of arbalists and King Duggan's small company of foot soldiers were to make for the main port, Porth Gwythion. The force was too large in one unit, too easily seen, open battle would only bring hordes of Adammite troops down upon them. Their orders were to stay hidden until either they received word that they were needed for some kind of distraction, as had happened at Draecastle, or to wait until the other ships arrived and come in from behind, a surprise attack.

Reave wanted to go with Amber and the rest, but Estrién pointed out that the Rams needed her now, their own job was mostly reconnaissance. Tamlyn was paramount and an attack could finish him should he still be alive.

'How do we get there? Reave asked.

'Keep the sea to your right and follow the contours of the forest when you reach it – it's at the other side of these hills,' replied Dane. 'I'd say go through, but it can be difficult, best not to get lost in there, it's massive. Once around it you'll see the port. We're not that big an island you know. It's about twenty miles from here, as the crow flies. I'd say a good day's march, but the hills can be steep and some of the countryside is rough moorland. Just stay out of sight, that's the important thing, so maybe two or even three days to the port. There are paths you can follow if the moon's up, a good time to cross without being seen.'

She nodded, she would meet them near the castle behind Porth Gwythion.

Amber watched her go. 'That's just six of us left, do you think we have enough?'

'More than enough,' declared Estrién. 'you, me, Dane, Salli, Trevaine and Robson. We're not taking on the might of the Adammites by ourselves, we just finding Tamlyn. Are we ready?' gazing purposefully at everyone. There was a general nod all round.

Dane led the way, the hills seemed empty so early in the morning, they hoped to cross as much as possible before too many Adammites were up and about. He'd told Reave to take the path around the old forest behind the hills, the dryad forest. Truth be known, he was glad all the other soldiers had gone. There were special paths through, mage paths; he would follow the paths his mother taught him and he hadn't wanted them watching him as he walked through weeping.

As they ascended the top of the next hill, Amber heard him shout out loud and watched him go down on his knees.

'Dear Goddess, no ...' he shouted, pointing across. 'You bastards!' It hadn't occurred to him where the Adammites had found the wood for their ships and war machines.

What had once been a beautiful forest, home of dryads, fauns, tree sprites and the rest, all the ancient, magickal but dying races, was no more. The valley ahead was nothing but tree stumps and burnt heather.

'The bloody parasites!' he exclaimed. 'They've used and abused this island, taken everything, given nothing.' He saw Reave's group ahead, they were keeping to the hills for cover. He stood up, his eyes blazing, quickly made up his mind. 'Come on, we might as well go this way, I need to know what, if anything is left.' His annoyance was palpable.

He needed to turn away from the ravaged forest, to check on something more personal. Who knew what these people were capable of doing? They had neither consideration nor respect.

They marched down the hill towards the sea, an hour later coming upon the blackened ruins of a house. The oak had gone, the gardens were rampant with dandelions, dock leaves and a host of nettles. He stepped through what had been a gate-way, even the gate had disappeared, ignoring the weeds and made for the stump of the oak.

'Thank Merrie!' he declared, bending down. 'This is untouched.' He frowned up at them. 'This is my parent's grave, at least they lie here in peace.' He stared at the burnt remains of the house, looted for anything useful. 'Bloody mess though ...'

Estrién placed a hand upon his shoulder. 'You are not alone, my brother, we're with you. I too understand, they did this to my childhood home. Yet,' he paused, turned to the others, 'we *will* prevail, we will not let this beat us. We have retaken much of our land, we shall finish this task.' He put his arm under Dane's shoulder, helped him up, 'come, let's be going, Tamlyn awaits.'

Amber turned him to her, gently stroked his hair, kissed him. There were no words to say, she had been there herself. She took his hand and led him out of the gateway.

They could see the patrols now on the main road across, the group kept out of sight, hid behind walls, ruins, hedges. They had no wish for either combat or discovery; eluding the patrols took them all day. Several small villages to the north-west were clearly military encampments now, and vast areas were given over to food crops and livestock; potato fields, barley and rye, farms with many outbuildings for storage, grain mills, chicken coops and fields of cows.

The grunt and squeal of pigs could be heard at what must be a slaughterhouse.

If nothing else, the Adammites cared about feeding their troops.

The island was busier than Dane had ever seen it. Further down across the valley, there was a large training camp. Several fields were filled with tents, closer to the centre were storage huts and barns, a massive mess tent and probably an ale tent from the looks of those staggering out laughing. Shouts and grunts and the clanging clash of swords came from a field where maybe two hundred or so men were training. There were no barricades, walls or fences. Who needed them here, when the only people on the island were themselves? Nevertheless, they looked as if they were on the alert.

Dane and the rest stayed hidden and crept carefully down the hillside taking advantage of every rise and ridge available.

A decrepit old barn sheltered them overnight and although they could not light fires for fear of being noticed, the mages heated up food and water for tea. Dane ladled calming herbs into the tea, and could be seen smoking his leafroll into the night. He slept little and could be heard swearing occasionally as night turned into day. The following early morning they made good time and reached the rear of the castle on the hill behind Porth Gwythion.

Once more Amber heard him swear. *'Bloody hell!.'* The ruined castle had been transformed into a mighty fortress. 'It was an old draughty castle, not too big, you know, a few towers and a main hall. Me and a few lads used to come and play in it, dared each other to reach the top of the old ruined tower to the north-west. Now it's bloody enormous.' He examined the large structure ahead of him. The front, sides and most of the rear were fortified, several times over, barricades and palisades everywhere. The officers of the Adammites clearly mistrusted their own men, kept themselves in safe seclusion. Clearly the old Council chambers had been enlarged, and used as part of the new Headquarters. Dane scrutinised the massive structure for a while before he suddenly gave a whoop.

'*Ha!* It's still there, they didn't bother rebuilding it. *I wonder* ...' He stood thoughtfully for a few moments. 'We need to check, but see, that ruined tower reaches into the hill behind, that's how we used to get in – the castle windows were too high and the door was a massive old oak one, even magic couldn't budge it. But we climbed up the hill – see how close the tower is – jumped across and snuck in through the back window, then .jumped down to the floor below. We spent our day trying to climb to the top – the tower steps have gone, it was a rare old challenge.'

Estrién stopped his flow of nostalgia. 'You think we can get in that way?'

'Possibly... worth a try, guys.'

Salli hesitated, 'don't know if I can jump so far, old bones might break.'

Amber just laughed, 'we've plenty of rope dear, no problem.'

Amber and Dane went off to reconnoitre, came back ten minutes later. 'We can do it, but not in daylight, the place is crowded. Looks like everyone's arriving here.'

'Then nightfall it is,' replied Estrién.

*

Tamlyn woke to consciousness once more, his near-naked body in agony and his ears burning fire. He discovered he was shaking; the blast from *him* seemed to have damaged his nervous system. Despite this, he felt completely calm inside, his mind only working overtime still on a method of escape. He looked across, there were torches lit just outside, filling his cell with an oily, tarry smell. Nevertheless there was dim light to see by. Bread and water were placed on a wooden tray on the floor by the cell door. He struggled his way off the pallet, every bone and muscle aching, realised he couldn't walk, either as a result of the mind-blast or simply sheer hunger. He crawled little by little to the tray, picked up the tankard with both hands, lifted it to his lips. It didn't taste so bad, it was cold and a little earthy, but it was blessed water. For a few moments he rested his back against the cell door, sipping the water, breathing deeply between sips. Then he carefully laid down the half empty tankard and with tentative hands picked up the bread. Yes, it was a little hard and stale, but that did not deter from the delightful taste as he put it in his mouth. It was dry, moistless, he would have given anything for a little butter or cheese, but it was food and therefore life. He ate with relish, occasionally sipping more water.

Eventually Tamlyn tried standing up. He grabbed the bars behind him, using them hand over hand to work his way into a standing position. He felt dizzy, yet not so light headed as before. He managed to walk slowly back to the pallet on the wall, sat down thankfully.

'Feels like I've aged fifty years,' he laughed to himself, discovering he could also do with using the bucket. He pushed himself up, shuffled to the bucket in the corner and relieved himself. 'At least I feel a little more comfortable,' he thought. 'Some soap and water would be good for a wash, but beggars can't be choosers as the saying goes.'

It was only then he remembered his ears, the last thing before he lost consciousness. He wondered why they burned so much, although he remembered why before he touched them. He lifted up his manacled hands, feeling first one mangled ear, then the other.

'Shit,' was all he said, seeing the dried blood on his hands, feeling ragged edges where elven points used to be. 'The Dûchesse will not like this,' referring to the Floriénne Court. 'Just not beautiful enough.'

Then he stiffened as the door to the dungeons was opened and he heard footsteps.

A guard unlocked the door, and once more he was dragged to the interrogation room for further questioning. Again he was hung up over the ceiling hooks. It felt like his arms were being pulled out of their sockets.

'Tell me,' said the Captain, nodding to one of his henchmen. 'Do you think your comrades will attempt a rescue?'

Tamlyn said nothing, what could he say? He could only swing from side to side as a cat-O-nine tails lashed mercilessly across his back.

'Surely you know, tell me how they are likely to do it. It appears they have some odd abilities. Tell me about them.'

Tamlyn laughed, where to start? He could talk forever about the strange things they did or attempted to do. But it seemed the Captain mistook his laughter for disdain. He was lashed again, back, sides, even his legs. Tamlyn danced a strange jig as the whip cut into him. Blood began pouring freely down his body. Despite the pain and the humiliation of being trussed up like a ham hanging from the ceiling, he suddenly became angry,

'*No!*' he shouted. 'Why don't *you* tell me about this God of yours, the one who doesn't care if you live or die!' He was rewarded with a fist in his stomach, then the Captain stepped back, spoke quietly.

'Is what you said true, about Manecaestr? That *he* did this to us?'

Tamlyn nodded. 'He didn't give a shit who lived or died, you were all punished by him.' He looked him in the eye. 'Your god created you in order to destroy Mer'edrynn. Then he waits to destroy *you*. He is not of us, not of our life cycle. He exists outside and hates all of us, you included. You were a means to an end, that is all.'

The Captain stared with troubled eyes. 'How do you know this?'

'Let me sit down, please?' Tamlyn looked him in the eye, for a few moments they stared at each other.

Then the Captain nodded, Tamlyn was taken down and allowed to sit unfettered in the hard chair. He breathed in deeply, exhausted. 'It's what we are, the White Shield you have heard of,' he explained. 'We have never wished harm upon other beings, unlike yourselves, but we have tried to counteract his evil.' Briefly he fingered his lip where blood was pouring, the cat had flicked over his face, lashed him across the mouth. He wiped away the blood. 'It's throughout the land, crops dying, filthy creatures spawning, we've fought them. Even the birds and animals fighting in huge packs against each other, is that normal? He loathes nature, most particularly *us*, all of us. We, who are, or were ... Merrievians.

He started all this, put these ideas into your heads, he has manipulated you to do his bidding. He simply wanted to destroy our society, by any means he could. We were never your enemy, nor are we the scum you imagine we are.' He saw the Captain nodding, a dawning understanding. 'When you have destroyed all the other races, he will let you die too. Perhaps create another war between yourselves, I don't know, perhaps bring famine and disease – he is attacking the land too – but you will eventually die out. Then he will have triumphed. I have seen all this as we have travelled Mer'edrynn, he has taken trust, friendship and hope from our world. He has made brother fight brother, divided whole families, brought nothing but death.' Again he repeated, eye to eye, 'we were never your enemy.'

For a few moments there was silence in the room, neither the Captain nor the guards spoke. Then he heard the Captain sigh.

'You speak truly, Knight Captain. I saw things in Manecaestr which I hope I will never see again. I ... I did things I am ashamed of, and will always be ashamed. I wondered why I did them, but if what you say is true, then it makes sense.' Briefly the Captain looked upwards as if trying to find a solution somewhere above him, perhaps trying to pierce the soot-flecked ceiling to the skies beyond. 'I forgot you, Lady Merrie, I forgot you, forgive me ...'

He took keys out of his pocket, chose one, bent down as if to undo Tamlyn's manacles.

He didn't complete the action. Tamlyn heard him scream, watched him fall as if in slow motion to the floor, staring eyes wide open in death agony. The two guards also fell screaming to the floor, were both dead before they hit the stone.

Tamlyn looked across from the uncomfortable chair. *He* stood in the doorway once more.

Red eyes blazed into his.

A finger beckoned him to follow. 'Come, we have guests.'

*

It was well after midnight when the group returned to the old ruined tower at the edge of the castle. Dane now understood why they hadn't bothered fortifying this area, massive hounds prowled and growled on their way around the fortress, They sniffed the ground, checking for unfamiliar smells, strangers.

'Wow, they're big,' commented Amber. One caught her scent, dashed across.

Estrién stepped in. He didn't take out White Star, they were growling and they would yelp as they died, alerting guards. Besides, he hated harming dumb animals. He stood firm, his thoughts calming them, his hands making their magickal signs.

They stopped, sat down on their haunches in front of him; he was no intruder, but a friend.

Salli quickly stepped forwards, touched them with his wand. 'They'll sleep peacefully for several hours,' he assured them.

Dane led them up the hill to the old tower, showed them the window. There was a gap between the hill and the tower, in the dark it was impossible to see how far down the gap went. 'We used to jump across,' he claimed, 'catch the bar in the middle of the window then pull ourselves through, but that was in daylight.'

Amber laughed, 'I see it's me again,' as she clambered across and into the window. She disappeared a moment. 'Just securing it a little,' she whispered, although they were alone up on the hill, 'come on over.' as she attached the rope to the central iron bar before throwing it across. Everyone hoped it would hold, the crumbling tower was centuries old.

Nevertheless, each arrived safely. There were a few steps, but most were missing, their small landing seemed very precarious, especially with the weight of six bodies upon it. Dane lit a torch he had brought, wavered it over the gap beneath them, not too far down to the floor. Amber let the secured rope down into the tower, they each slid down, eventually making it safely.

There was a door into the main hall, yet it had always been an empty gap, the old door in ruins. The Adammites had obviously made the tower more secure than previously. Naturally, it was locked.

Amber placed her hand upon Dane's as he made to unlock it. 'Dane... before we move in ... there's *something*... I can feel something bad, we need to be very careful here tonight,' she warned him. She had felt it for some time, a strange tension, a sour feeling in the pit of her stomach and on the edge of consciousness, even throughout the day. Now it was almost physical.

Dane nodded, touched her cheek gently with his fingers. 'I know dear, I feel it too, but there's no going back now.' He did his mage style lock-picking thing, it unlocked and they all walked through. He'd known it since they arrived on the island.

It looked odd; Dane had never seen the castle hall like this before.

The tall, wide room had no ceiling, it never had, the rafters had collapsed decades previously. The hall opened on to the black night sky. Yet the room itself was ablaze with light, flickering candles littered the edges of the floor, all shapes and sizes, some obviously the votive candles from the Temples.

Their eyes turned towards the northern end of the hall where a huge wooden throne had been placed, a soft velvet coverlet thrown upon it. The cover looked black in the candlelight, but was probably a deep purple in daylight. Tall elven candelabra stood on each side, candles flaring merrily, wavering in the slight breeze from above. In front of the throne was a small circular wooden table, rich and as dark in colour as the carafe of wine it held. A half-full silver goblet stood by its side.

Dane stared curiously, the huge trapdoor at the side of the hall was open. He and his young friends had tried for years to open it, to no avail, it had been nailed down. They had always been certain it led to dungeons, told each other gruesome tales about what was down there, but they had never succeeded in finding them. He saw steps going down, a wavering torchlight below. Then he looked back at the throne.

There was a collective gasp. Prostrated in front of the throne was the inert body of Tamlyn, arms and legs splayed open, a supplicant to an unknown god. He wore only breeches stained with blood, and cruel whiplash grooves covered his bloodied back and legs. The manacles were no longer there, but they could see raw skin where they had cut into him, he had clearly been bound.

Amber saw his ears, screamed out loud, '*no!*' and made to dash to him. Estrién held her back. 'Stay here, it's a trap!'

For a few moments they all stared at Tamlyn.

Then a door behind them opened and *he* came through. Each went for their weapons, none wielded them. With an arrogant flick of his wrists he scattered them all to the floor, each crying out in pain as they dropped. He locked the door behind him.

He looked down and sneered before walking slowly to his throne, the black cloak he wore now sweeping the floor as he stepped. Tamlyn was in the way, he kicked him aside. Amber heard his groan through her own pain as he rolled across just before she lost consciousness, her last thought, '*he's alive!*'

He sat down on the throne, took a sip of the ruby wine and inspected his captives. The prone bodies lay sprawled across the rough and dirty stone floor of the hall.

'*White Shield!*' he scoffed, '*You pathetic little upstarts.*'

He looked forward to the next few hours of slow torture before they died.

*

'Sire, I think you should come and see this,'

King Alexis sat up from the small cot in his cabin. The ship had rocked and swayed for the last few hours and he hadn't slept. 'What is it?' he asked the First Mate. He looked through the port hole, it seemed to be around dawn.

The first mate smiled, repeated himself, 'come and see,' beckoning the King.

Many were coming up on deck, all pointing to the south-west. Many were clapping their hands, laughing, shouting. Alexis wondered why?

The air was filled with the sound of whistling and clicking, he saw bodies splashing into the sea as they lifted above the water, bow-riding in graceful arcs. A huge school of dolphins, porpoises, even seals was swimming just behind them. Sharks led the group, their sharp fins pointing above the water line. It was an amazing sight, he stared, incredulous.

But it was the other sound Alexis heard that made him gasp, the whale song.

Two enormous white whales swam in the very centre of the group, their song entrancing, their movement the essence of grace. The twin kings of the ocean leapt forward in the dawning light. The rest of the school followed, obeyed.

They weren't alone.

Standing sure footedly on the backs of the two whales stood the Great Stag and the beautiful Doe.

King Alexis smiled, lifted a hand in greeting, the Great Stag nodded back at him. He saw Lord Black on a ship close by, standing on the bridge, watching in astonishment. Alexis laughed out loud, this was priceless.

'Forward lads, let's follow them, they know where they are going,' he shouted to the Captain, and frankly, anyone listening.

The day dawned brighter, the sea turning golden as they approached the shimmering Isle of Glasse.

'Goodness, it's beautiful,' thought Alexis. But there was no further time for admiration as the first of the Adammite boats spotted them, a three-masted caravel of the sort beloved by the Sevillain, used for patrol and exploration. It turned towards them, ballistae pointing at their flotilla. As the first huge bolt was let forth across the water, Alexis watched the school dive beneath the Adammite boat. Soon the small ship was rocking and heaving from side to side.

Laughter could be heard across the Merrievian fleet, as the boat eventually toppled into the water. Sailors were seen splashing and flailing in the water. The Merrievian ships ignored them. They were welcome to swim to their overturned boat, try and seek safety, but would receive no help.

They continued on towards the harbour where huge carracks were now pushing out to sea to challenge them. They never reached them, their ships were harried by an aquatic navy, sailors such as never before. The air was filled with splashes and calls, tail fins flicking as the creatures leapt, dived and pushed the fleet apart. Ships and boats wavered and sank, some simply turned upside down.

Alexis was devoutly thankful, he had little chance against their navy. Now the odds were different.

As they neared the port, the Stag and his mate jumped nimbly off the backs of the whales onto one of the large carracks. The two white whales saluted by blowing huge fountains of water into the air, before they too joined the rest of their marine forces.

The stag and his mate took no notice of sailors or deck hands trying to attack them, they simply used the ships as stepping stones, leaping from one ship to another, closer and closer to shore, making for the harbour. Sailors were kicked aside as they jumped and nimbly ran huge leaps and bounds across the intervening water between the carracks and caravels. The doe could be seen smiling, watching her husband, this was the dance of life she loved, the thrill of living. On they crossed, powerful legs jumping gracefully from one ship to another, all the way back to the waiting Isle. Eventually they reached a shallow cove, both made a final enormous leap into the air on to dry land before galloping across the sand towards the harbour wall.

It had been quiet down at the harbour, dawn just breaking, but it was soon filled by curious and terrified Adammites as the Stag stopped in his tracks, lifted his head and bellowed. The strange war-horn like sound, a force in itself, boomed loudly across the bay and the water.

The two whales sang their song and pitched into the battle, ships knocking against each other in the harbour, masts rocking, sailors running and screaming, jumping for their lives into the sea.

The sharks made sure the water ran red.

The dolphins, porpoises and seals continued their dives and leaps, harassing and knocking the ships until they crashed and overturned.

Eventually the sea seemed to be filled with sailors desperately trying to swim for shore. Both Alexis and Lord Black gave the order for archers. Between the archers and the sharks, few, if any reached the shoreline.

It seemed their aquatic friends weren't content with merely knocking over the Adammite navy. Gradually, led by the two enormous white whales, the massive school pushed the offending ships and boats out to sea, leaving a clear harbour for Alexis' boats to sail in.

He shook his head, never seen anything like it, nor would he ever again. He couldn't wait to tell Neria and little Anna'laeth. He wondered if anyone at court could paint what he had seen, keep it for posterity?

'Get ready men,' he shouted as he dashed down to his cabin, grabbed his sword and the rest of his kit. When he returned on deck, everyone, soldiers and mages alike, stood stiffly in their lines awaiting him. A few last words from him were probably in order, something to rally the troops, mark the seriousness of the day, their last stand against this Adammite foe.

He was never one for long fancy speeches, actions always counted more. Besides, he could see his troops were primed and battle ready, anxious to fight.

'It's our turn now lads,' he shouted, '... *and lasses,*' realising there were females among his ranks. *'Let's go kick ass ...!'* as the gangplank went down. There followed a great roar of approval.

He picked up the battered shield, waved his sword in the air and led the way down the gangplank onto the island. The huge edifice of the Adammite fortress loomed ahead of him. To starboard he could see a grim faced Black leading his own troops off the ships.

They met briefly in the harbour, Black was scratching the back of his head, sighing. 'Couldn't half do with a decent swig of Glenrite 'Ard right now,' he complained, gathering his troops.

Alexis just grinned. Adammites were pouring out of the fortress. 'I'll owe you one later,' nodding at the oncoming forces. 'See you there ...'

Black nodded, laughing back, 'keep you to that ... see you inside.' He made to move forward then stopped. 'Stay safe Alexis, take care, boy.'

Alexis smiled, he was getting used to this battle thing now. He raised his sword and ordered the charge.

Up in the hills, Reave's Rams and King Duggan's troops had watched them come in. They ran down the hill to join them. To the northeast, joining them, several ships appeared flying King Duggan's colours, he had kept his word.

From other hills, wild dogs, wolves and the few deer left upon the island ran to join in the cause as did the gulls and seabirds and other birds of the island. Their master had called, they would obey.

*

Some hours earlier.

Deep inside the fortress, in the roofless hall of the old castle, *he* sat smugly watching his group of enemies lying on the floor. It was still dark, the night had clouded over. Occasionally he would flick a finger, watch with satisfaction as one of the prone bodies twitched in pain.

Each felt him, not on the edges of their consciousness, but deep inside.

Each fought their own lonely battle.

Trevaine lay screaming silently, shaking his head from side to side as the pain hit him. He tried to block him out, it was impossible. He had never experienced pain like that in his life. Still, he concentrated, he had to make it stop, it would kill him if he didn't. He wasn't sure whether to fight it or just let it ride.

Robson too, curled up in agony, his stomach on fire, his loins screaming as if he'd been kicked over and over again. He raised his head and groaned with the pain.

Salli lay more quietly. He was used to taking pain into him on behalf of others; he clutched his wand, turning it slowly towards himself, trying to ease the pain that racked his limbs.

Dane shut his mind to the waves of agony, tried to imagine a wall of the strongest stone between him and *that* sitting on the bloody throne at the end of the hall. For a moment it worked, he shifted his body closer to Amber, his one thought to protect her, these might be their last moments. He carefully and agonisingly placed an arm over her.

Briefly she looked up, into his eyes, he could see, nay, feel her pain. 'I love you,' she told him, yet those words cost her dearly as more waves hit her in punishment. She waited until the pain died a little then managed to lift a hand. Estrién was lying next to her, she touched his shoulder. He shook as a wave shocked through him. The three bodies lay together in joint suffering. Their bodies twitched and jolted according to *his* whims.

Tamlyn woke, heard the shouting, the groans, knew they were there, his people, his family. Gathered his strength to cry out, 'I knew you would come. I'm sorry for this, so sorry,' before he too groaned with more pain.

The figure on the throne smiled to himself, flicked his fingers.

Seven bodies shuddered on the floor. He watched with pleasure as they wriggled and squirmed, arced their backs as pain ran through them.

Amber wondered how she could overcome this foe? He had been there too often in her life, always at the edge of her consciousness. Now he was here in physical form, or at least the borrowed form of an unfortunate human. She wondered how her sister had managed to keep sane, how she had met him in his own form, in his own realm, yet, she had prevailed. *Her inner strength must be enormous,* she thought to herself.

Then, through the pain, Amber heard a small voice inside her head. 'You can do it, sister ... the tapestry is not yet finished. A new scene begins, I love you Amber...' The voice faded away.

It renewed her, gave her hope. She took Dane's hand and held it tight, before finding Estrién's, ignored the searing pain inside her. Slowly she pushed herself up from the floor, first onto one knee. She whispered to them both, 'come, we can do this,' trying to stand upright, Dane and Estrién rising with her, 'Tamlyn needs us.' Their faces, like hers were a mask of pain but also grim determination.

Estrién silently screamed in agony as he took White Star from his back, still holding Amber's hand. He turned to her, nodding his head slowly. It was difficult to move. He said nothing but his eyes were filled with the rich light of love.

Slowly the three shuffled their way towards Tamlyn, every step a torment. Dane took a deep breath and managed to shoot magelight down at his prone body, he felt its blessed glow, before Dane offered him his hand, pulled him up. Tamlyn picked himself up, body shaking, racked in agony, but he joined his loved ones

The four stood together, eyes seeking each other, four hearts calling out to one another. Perhaps it is best to say they crouched together, for each was racked in pain, but all stared *him* in the eye.

Amber gazed upwards, 'look guys,' she said. Dawn's soft fingers were stealing across the sky, the blackness fading into violet and apricot. It looked so beautiful, a calming sight.

She gathered her energy together, stared *him* in the eye. 'You can strike us down, you can torture us until we die, but we die together. You will not break our bond. I have something you can never know nor ever feel, the love of these men.' She now stood proudly, before continuing. 'And these are good men, true to their purpose, fine and strong, loving and caring.' Her weak voice gained in strength. 'They are *her* men, sons of the Lady Merrie, true sons of Mer'edrynn. You can break our bodies, but you will not break our spirit. Whatever you do to my world, life will prevail, I assure you.'

'You are fools,' *he* snarled, 'your stupid sense of love and loyalty brought you here to die with your mate ... or *mates*,' he added with a salacious chuckle.

Estrién stood straight now, 'then we die together, and we go into *her* loving arms. We can face our ancestors with pride.'

A flick of the fingers sent agony throughout the four.

Tamlyn seemed to be beyond pain now, the last days had numbed him, and Dane's magic gave him relief. Now he spoke. 'My family came for me, I knew they would. I was sure from the moment I found I was captured.' He looked across the line of his loved ones. 'Best year I've ever had, worth dying for. *I love you.*'

Dane lifted his head, warmth spreading through him. 'Yes,' he agreed, 'been a wonderful year, best of my life. Can't think of a better way to go than by the side of you all.' He looked across to Estrién, was about to say more, then spotted something. He suddenly dropped to the floor, rolled behind Amber, grabbed his staff, came back. 'And if you think this is my last year with them, *then think again, mate!*'

Fierce electrum shot out of the staff straight into the face of the figure on the throne.

Now Estrién let go of Amber's hand, took the loudly-humming White Star in both and ran across the hall, the pain ignored.

Amber took out the two shortswords she carried in her knife belt, passed one to Tamlyn, grabbed a small dagger with her free hand and threw it straight into the eye of the momentarily blinded monstrosity across from her.

Salli got to his knees, he could barely move, but he pointed his wand at Robson and Trevaine, their pain temporarily gone. Both rose up, briefly they smiled at him, before fire and lightning shot from mage fingers at the throne ahead of them. Robson found his staff close by, he used it to shoot more fire. Salli staggered behind them, his wand shooting death.

Yet all knew, they could possibly break his host body, but the essence would continue. He might even use one of their own.

How do you destroy pure evil?

Outside the battle raged, led predominantly by Lord Black. Gutthrust obeyed his commands and did exactly what its name said. The sword cut deep into flesh and sinew, blood and guts followed his every step. Unlike Alexis he carried no shield, but two mages did their best to protect him as he slashed his way through the lines. He seemed to be enjoying himself.

Alexis did what he did best, rallying his troops, surrounded by his Corps de Lyons, making slow but sure headway through the Adammites.

Reave's Rams, along with Garrett and King Duggan's small company came in from the north-east. Crossbow bolts and arrows suddenly shot from behind the Adammite lines, not at the interlopers, but at the Adammites themselves. Lord Black waved across as Duggan and more troops jumped off their ships onto the harbour.

Gertie and Gracie took to the skies to join the gulls, ospreys and cormorants. Other hawks, red kites and kestrels from around the island joined them; they made for the Adammite army hurtling down from above.

All eventually reached the blockades of the fortress, they looked impregnable.

Not for long however, as these were swiftly kicked in by the Great Stag and the other stags who had joined him. The Great Stag and his Doe disappeared into the fortress.

The battle continued inside and outside, bloody cries, clash of swords and shields and the screams of men and women rang throughout Porth Gwythion.

In the ancient and decrepit hall of the old castle another battle played out. Now there appeared some kind of barrier around what had once been Lefwynn Hydeman, proud Master of the Saddlers and Leather-workers Guild. He, or whatever was his essence, no longer existed, but the body continued.

He stood up from the throne, he felt no pain no matter what they did, he could not. He considered it pathetic that these puny individuals thought they could beat him.

Still, they came, hacking at the wavering barrier he had created around him, not for his own sake but to preserve the body he wore. If anything he was amused. Now he lifted his hands again, snapped his fingers.

Things crawled out of the dirt and filth around the old ruins. Slime crept across the floor, bugs dropped from the sky, insects that bore no relation to any living species buzzed around the hall, biting and sucking blood from bare skin. ...His creatures, his abominations. Tamlyn particularly was targeted, his bare skin and freely flowing blood was the perfect temptation.

Now the mages concentrated on the wildlife, clearing the air and the floor around them. More came, yet more, the air filled with wavering wings and shimmering skittering bodies, all hell bent on bringing down the company, devouring their flesh.

Estrién stood in front of Amber, trying to shield her, waving his sword as he had with the doe when she called the wind in the tormented forest. He batted the creatures away. With one accord, the three males surrounded Amber, protecting her from the flying horde. The male instinct to protect the female was strong in them.

The air now seemed full of mage fire, as three elemental mages shot flame, the floor began to be littered with hundreds of tiny dead bodies. The figure by the throne merely laughed. He had pulled out the offending dagger from his eye, the socket wept red, and Estrién had sliced his arm before the barrier had been raised, but such meant nothing to him. He would pick another host later.

The buzzing army seemed to grow thicker, everyone surrounded by thick flying insects, leech-like beasts crawling up legs. Dane, Estrién and Tamlyn stepped closer still to Amber, shielding her. She smiled in their midst, she was quite capable of fighting too, but she understood - and loved - their concern. 'Thanks guys,' they heard her say.

They had always been a triangle of love around her. Perhaps ... perhaps it was as well they protected her now.

They heard a beating of hooves getting louder as they neared, then a massive hammering upon the old oak doors, the entry way from the main fortress.

They watched as the doors crashed open, they had been little used since the fortress had been built, no one cared about the old castle, it was merely symbolic. It looked a fine old building inside their strong new fortress, used for the occasional ceremony.

Two huge antlers tossed the heavy oak doors aside as if they were weightless. The great oak tree belonged to him, it would not obstruct him.

A tall figure walked through, upright, on two legs now, his majestic head held proud. His massive antlers were thrown back, a thick golden torc shone around his neck, a fine cloak of cloth-of-gold upon his broad shoulders. He wore hunter's boots and leather hose, but his massive chest was bare.

He raised his hands in the air, the hall turned silent. Then he stood to one side, turned and bowed to the figure following him.

A beautiful, shining figure entered the hall, golden, ethereal. Her rainbow cloak shimmered and wavered, bright as the morning sun now throwing its slanted beams across the hall onto the old stone walls. A new warmth radiated through, a touch of life; all felt it. She moved away from her husband, she simply wandered around the old castle hall. The flying, buzzing creatures disappeared, the crawling slime-filled leech-beasts crept back into the dirt, or to whatever filthy realm was their home. She cleansed the old castle hall of its filth.

That standing by the throne watched her with distaste, but did nothing.

Everyone breathed in the freshness of early morning air, clean and pure, sweet with the tang of spring. She briefly walked the hall, studied momentarily, then lifted her head and nodded. She stood to one side, her job over, for now.

Her husband acknowledged her, a brief thank you, before walking across the long Haul towards the throne and the shimmering barrier around *him*.

Once more he held out his arms. *Something*, something unseen but powerful beyond anything the group had ever felt, flew from his hands.

The barrier dropped, the Company of the White Shield suddenly felt their health renewed. They shook off their pains, stood straight and proud.

'Begone!' the proud voice boomed across the hall. 'Ye have no place in my world. Get ye hence from here.' The figure by the throne seemed momentarily to shrivel, before regaining his power and laughing.

'No, *you* are finished! Your time is over and my time is here and now,' he shouted back. 'your world is dying. I have power you cannot dream of.'

'No, thy forces are diminished, ye weaken with every moment. Canst thou not see that? Dost thou not feel it – ye have caused all those deaths, of both thine own and the innocent. Once thou may have been great, thou instilled terror. Thy very presence should send these people into madness, yet these people stand against thee, thy fear does not touch their hearts.' He stood firm, an uncanny light, sun-like and bright radiating from him. 'As these people - my shield, my Lady's Shield - have slowly taken back this land, have fought thine abominations, so *thou* hast diminished. Slowly thy power has waned.'

He merely scoffed, 'you cannot beat me Stag, you have been weakened too much. Once you were great, but that is long gone.'

'No, my power has been growing with every win against thee.' The stately figure seemed to grow, the sun shining upon his brow, the golden cloak radiant with light. 'Thou ar't finished,' he repeated firmly. His wife came to stand by his side. She too raised her arms. The Stag did the same; power flew from them both across the hall.

'Be gone, ye have no place here.' She spoke quietly and confidently. She too shimmered, a delicate radiance, yet she was as strong as her mate. It was simply that her type of strength differed to his. Once more the barrier dropped.

But the group saw the barrier begin to rise again as he regained his own strength, he would not be overcome. Even the combination of the two of them, the two spirits of nature, was not quite enough.

He would prevail and all life would die.

Amber looked at Estrién, turned to the other two, this could not be. They still had their part to play. *Now*, her eyes told them.

They smiled at each other, yes *now,* now was the time. It didn't matter what happened, they had to try. *To give their best*, as the Lady Merrie would say.

In this life or the next...

They went in as one, 'en quattro', as they had done before.

The four surrounded the figure of what was once the Guild Master, Dane shot forth amberic lightning, Amber and Tamlyn raised their shortswords, went for the chest, the heart, as Estrién raised White Star.

The sword whined pitilessly as it came down in a long and graceful arc, straight through the neck.

The mutilated figure slumped to the floor.

The Great Stag once more lifted his arms into the air, hands shooting magic that hailed from before time across the hall, his powers finally regained in full as the body fell. His booming voice could be heard throughout the fortress.

'*In the name of Merrie, thou art banished!*'

A horrible, infernal wail could be heard, screaming, screeching, a thousand cries of pain and hatred, echoing again and again, until finally fading into nothingness. The Stag stood straight, bold and strong, his wife by his side; both held their magic until the hall was silent.

There was a momentary silence, a brief pause of time before air pressure seemed to lift and *something* went. Then the ruined hall became normalised. There was a general intake of breath. They all realised that the sounds of battle outside the hall had stopped too.

Peace uncurled itself and tentatively wavered into existence.

He finally lowered his arms, sighed deeply and turned gratefully to the group. 'We thank thee wholly, we could not actually have done this without thee. I have regained my strength, but *he* was still powerful. It is thanks to thee and those like thee that my power returned, the strength of life, the joy of living. I and my kind are in thy debt.'

He walked over to Estrién, 'Thou hast been my Warrior just as I expected of thee. Thou will remain my warrior throughout thy life.' His profound gaze wandered the hall.

'Dane, Tamlyn, thou ar't true to Her, thou ar't Merrie's own. I thank thee, all of thee,' turning to Salli, Robson and Trevaine, 'We give thee thanks, brave spirits, kind souls. May life be good to all of ye, and may thee live long.'

He briefly nodded to them before returning to Estrién, pointing to his sword. 'Thou knowest there is more to Nim'estrien than mere steel dost thou not?'

Estrién nodded, 'I have always known so.'

The figure suddenly smiled mischievously, he knew Estrién wholly. ' … And thou knowest it takes a king to wield it?'

'I'm not being drawn into that,' Estrién laughingly replied, shaking his head. 'Besides, I've no crown,'

The tall and imposing being merely raised a mysterious eyebrow. He turned, bowed deeply and smiled kindly at Amber. 'Look after her,' he ordered the three males, gently taking her hand in his and kissing it. 'I told thee once before, *the future lies within.*'

The stately figure then bowed to all once more, a brief, 'come, my wife, it is time,' before returning to his stag form, his favoured form. The dazzling creature next to him turned likewise, they galloped from the hall.

'Always said you were a king,' muttered Tamlyn.

Estrién now turned to his own wife, kissed her on the lips. 'I love you', he said in a voice rich with admiration, 'you are just as strong as they are.'

For a short while nothing could be heard but kisses and sighs as the company hugged each other.

Tamlyn finally spoke amidst the kisses. 'Knew you'd come, I only wondered if I could hold out long enough.' He kissed Amber again, couldn't stop, 'I thought of you all the time, I remembered the good times.' He suddenly sat down on the hard stone, aching and exhausted. Salli gently touched him with his wand, taking pain away.

Dane watched his loved ones contentedly before looking up to the azure sky above, it was a grand morning. He held the oak staff high in the air and shot a mass of rainbow coloured petals from it. They showered down upon everyone.

Trevaine, Robson and Salli all stared at him. 'Thought you were an elementalist ... how did you do that?'

'It's what happens when there is a conjunction of an elemental mage and a dryad,' Dane laughed, repeating what he had once said to Amber. 'You get *me*! *Merrie's blessings, everyone!*'

More flowers and petals flew through the air as everyone clapped and cheered.

*

In a light and airy room, in the fair valley of Rosevale deep amidst the Windvale hills, a small, young/old figure bent over her loom. The tapestry looked beautiful; two dancing deer leapt over a sparkling brook curving its way through a forest of fine oak. Shafts of warm sunlight beamed through summer-green trees, small, shy creatures peeped out from behind bushes and a red fox nosed its way through the lush grass.

She sat back, it was completed. For a moment or so she stared thoughtfully, before picking up her needle once more.

Carefully she wove a figure into the corner, a young woman on the edge of motherhood. The new figure would probably alter the future, but the future was not yet born, nothing was set. Even she could not foretell.

Nevertheless, she gazed contentedly upon her work. 'What will be, will be,' she thought, feminine acquiescence tempered by womanly wisdom, unconsciously repeating the Great Stag's words, 'the future *always* lies within.'

* * *

The End.

Calendar

Month *Mer'edrynn* **Associated with:**

January *Endurance* first footing, feasting and friendship

February *Icefall* light in darkness, first love, preparation of the land

March *Shroving* Spring equinox, Mother, sowing and impregnation. To shrive - to make or impose a penance

April *Oestra* Quickening, fertility rites

May *Firstfire* Beltane, hawking, courtly love, romance

June *Helios* Lumentide, Midsummer's Day, summertime, weddings, joy

July *Shearing* Heat of the sun, sheep shearing, Male magic, manhood

August *Herneset* Lammas, hunting and the Glorious 12th, hay making, wheat, fulfilment.

September *Harvesthaeme* Autumn Equinox, Michaelmas 29th Carrots & horses! Game, harvests vines, fruition

October *Goldleaf* Halloween or Samhain, ploughing, healing. Female magic

November *Firings* All souls Day, Bonfire, fireworks, burning leaves. Dying, endings, purification

December *Nightturn* Yule 21st, shortest day - the Long Night. Winter. Beginning/endings.

*23rd December the traditional '**Year and a Day**' Feasting, boxing day, puzzles and games*

Appendix

Elvhen – the speech of the elves of Mer'edrynn (mostly spoken in Floriénne)

Ar'amé: of love
Ar'essa: loved one - feminine.
Ar'esson: loved one masculine
Bastedo: Bastard, swear word, of uncertain parentage.
Beainne: Fine and healthy
Bel: lovely
Belcaste: beautiful
bel sil'està: Beautiful to behold, beautiful features. Bonny.
Calice: a chalice or cup.
Cast'el: castle
daêth: meaningful, deep
the Dair Chev'al the Oaken Knights of Floriénne
Dairhalle, or hall of oak. The oak is the wood elves' sacred tree
Decorum: Correct, straight, of honour
Draconae of dragons
Dûc / Dûchesse Duke and Duchess, pronounced doochessa
Dulci'aré that which is sweet or soft.
Dulcior: gentle
Dulc'esta mea - term of endearance, 'my sweetness'.
Eormynn Human.
Elaine; A young woman **elain'ae** a tender soul, a gentle person.
'elvian – pertaining to or belonging to one elf.
Elvién: of elves.
En *el'andis*,: in all the world.

En quattro:: Four square, relates to an elven dance, but also four working together as one.
Ent and
Es is
Esil he is
Esel she is.
Estaran the king
Estarian: of the stars, the heavens
Feu: fire or fiery
Foraes dair oaken forest. Shirewood.
Freowulven: (literally) Free Wolves.
Gilsylien: light of the heavens, a holy light.
Haemewagon A small wooden hut on wheels, usually with carvings.
Illucidae: understanding, to make clear.
Illuminae: to bring light.
in perpetuis - forever
Lauralae The laurel tree, a tree of heroes and champions.
Liefl'en: dearest, dear one.
Lumen: Bright,
Lumien: To shine, radiate light.
Lumeneum - (that which is) bright
Mia: my or of mine
Maliaté: wrong, bad
Maliatus: dreadful
méchan - competent
Menaedai: wood spirits, similar to dryads.
Mûcheld slang derogatory and vulgar elven term for someone. Excrement.
Nim: white, reflecting or of reflective nature,
NimEstrién White Star
nix virandem elven phrase, loosely translated as 'sex, or virility, isn't everything.'
Paradais Paradise, also literal - along the lines of the oaks.

Qu'ell That which is ....
Qu'elle: that which is — feminine
Quattro; group of four
Ran'duel: a shield.
Rosea: of roses. Also, pink, blushed, a ring.
Rugosa or rugosae: ruddy, red faced.
Salixae: The willow tree, a tree of sadness *weeping willow*. Also a painkilling balm.
Sanguinae: of blood
Sentus: To feel, **Sentaé** (I feel)
Sel malia! That hurts!
Si'aré : of my heart 'Qu'elle ben si'are' - an elven statement of love - 'you hold my heart'.
Soleus: The sun or anything associated with the sun, can mean heat or light.
Sol'eteum: touched by the sun.
Sulis : of the sun, solar
Sylvanii: generic term, the tree people, people of the woods
Tué: You, feminine
Tui: You, masculine.
Triumvantis : of great triumph, wonder, a feeling of great pleasure.
Venienté: travel or voyage
'Vint'ii, Vest'ii, vit'ii!' : Wine, feasting and life! An elven toast from Floriénne. (pronounced *ventee, vestee,veetay*)

Bel sil'està lumeneum   Bright and bonny

Est ben Elvién: It is good (beautiful/fine) to be elven.

'Nim'randuel - Soleus D'rendiél - Gilsylien - Estaran'elvian' He who is the White Shield and wields the

Sword of Light which shines like the Heavens, is the true King of the Elves

Sulis estrién nim lumien - runes - several meanings: essentially, *'of the sun and the star is the white luminescence.'*

Printed in Poland
by Amazon Fulfillment
Poland Sp. z o.o., Wrocław